# "Cease!"

Brother Sotura held up his hands suddenly and walked to a position in front of the class. The silence was perfect.

"I see that some of you still believe that you can gain an advantage by using bone and muscle. Perhaps you secretly wish to be kick boxers?

"To move within the form is not enough. You must become insubstantial. No one can kick the wind. No one can push water. It is of no value to make even the most perfect soft-fist if, at the moment of impact, you tighten the muscles. Chi is the source of all of your strength—direct it into your hand as it is needed. Remember that you hold a caterpillar in your curled fist. Its hairs tickle your palm." The monk paused as a tiny, blue butterfly drifted by and settled on Shuyun's shoulder. The instructor smiled. "I will demonstrate."

He took a step forward and reached out to Shuyun, gently removing the butterfly from his shoulder. Closing his hand over the insect, the instructor moved to the wooden gate that led into a walled garden. Pausing for a split second to take a stance, the monk suddenly drove his hand through one of the gate's thick planks, which splintered and broke with a loud *crack*. Pivoting gracefully, Brother Sotura held his hand out to the class—a perfect soft-fist—and then released the butterfly, unharmed, into the air. All of the class knelt and touched their heads to the stones.

# THE INITIATE BROTHER

## BOOK ONE

### SEAN RUSSELL

# DAW BOOKS, INC.

## DONALD A. WOLLHEIM, FOUNDER

375 Hudson Street, New York, NY 10014

### ELIZABETH R. WOLLHEIM
### SHEILA E. GILBERT
### PUBLISHERS

First Printing, April 1991

5  6  7  8  9

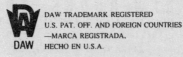

DAW TRADEMARK REGISTERED
U.S. PAT. OFF. AND FOREIGN COUNTRIES
—MARCA REGISTRADA.
HECHO EN U.S.A.

PRINTED IN THE U.S.A.

## DEDICATION

This book is dedicated to my grandfather, Stan Russell, in his ninety-fourth year, and to the memory of my father who loved books.

## ACKNOWLEDGMENTS

I would like to thank my family and friends who supported my efforts tirelessly and more selflessly than anyone could have a right to expect.

NORTHERN WASTES

RHOJO-MA

SEH

River Chousa

DENJI GORGE

ITSA

SHONTO FIEF

Fuga River

CHIBA

IKA CHO

Bay of Mists

Grand Canal

Mountain of
the Pure Spirit

CHOU

DENTOU

TSUYII

CAPITAL

Inner Sea

YANKURA

Lake of the
Lost Dragon

ŌE

ISLANDS OF KONOJII

CAPE
UJII

NITASHI

SUMMER
PALACE

Bay of the
Blue Whales

N

EMPIRE OF WA
during the Reign of Akantsu II

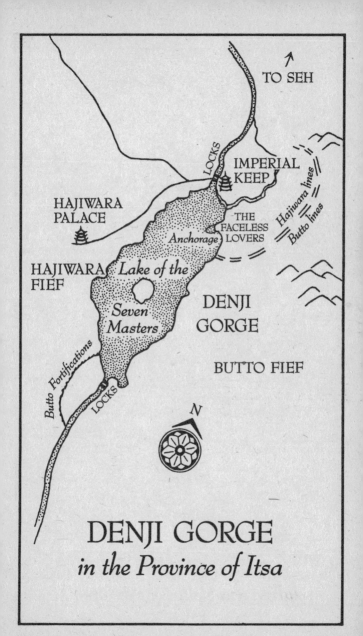

TO SEH

LOCKS

IMPERIAL
KEEP

HAJIWARA
PALACE

THE
FACELESS
LOVERS

*Anchorage*

*Hajiwara lines*

*Butto lines*

HAJIWARA
FIEF

*Lake of the*

DENJI
GORGE

*Seven
Masters*

*Butto Fortifications*

LOCKS

BUTTO FIEF

N

# DENJI GORGE
*in the Province of Itsa*

As one reads the history of our Empire, it becomes apparent that we have always had a preoccupation with our past. For two thousand years we have written the chronicles of our dynasties, histories that reach back into the distances of time to the Kingdoms of the Seven Princes. It is interesting to note that we are taught to value all of these works equally. Yet, as we read back through them, each successive chronicle seems less factual and more storylike. When one has studied the writings of antiquity, it can be seen that history and fantasy become indistinguishable.

*The Spring Analects;*
*Hakata.*

# One

The practice of condemning messengers, the Supreme Master thought, had not developed without reason. The old man looked down at the scroll he had received from the Floating City that very morning and he shook his head. A lifetime of dedication and effort and still he received messages like this. It seemed a great injustice.

Brother Hutto, the Primate of the Floating City, wrote that Botahist Brothers were being accosted on their travels by criminals and ruffians: accosted by the people of the Empire!

The Supreme Master slowly began to roll the mulberry paper scroll. The attacks were not the true problem—one would have to search a lifetime to find someone more able to defend himself than a Brother of the Faith—it was what these attacks said about the situation in the Empire and the attitude of the new Emperor. This was the Supreme Master's real concern.

He set the scroll on the corner of his writing table. Brother Hutto had written that several of these robbers had been injured recently, but this did not seem to be a deterrent. If anything, the attacks were increasing. The old monk reached for the scroll as if to read it again, but stopped himself. There could be no doubt of what it said.

If only the Emperor would turn his attention to the roads! That would be an indication that this new dynasty was capable of something more than ambition.

The Supreme Master took a deep calming breath. Emperors, he reminded himself, come and go; the Faith is eternal. It was important to keep the proper perspective.

Of course, Brother Hutto had recommended that a *display* might be appropriate. It was an old solution but one that had not been employed for many years. The Supreme Master lifted the scroll again and hefted it as though it were Brother Hutto's suggestion he weighed. Perhaps a Brother of the Faith *should* enter the Emperor's kick boxing tournament during the River Festival.

Yes, the Supreme Master thought, he would allow a monk to enter, but not a senior Brother; no, that would not have the desired affect. He would allow a junior Initiate to compete—the smallest, youngest looking Initiate that could be found. That would be a message neither Emperor nor subjects could mistake, a message to spread down all the roads of the Empire!

Fortunately, it appeared that finding the boy would not be difficult. The Supreme Master felt satisfied with this idea. Not only would it fit his purpose, but there was historical precedent for such an act. The Lord Botahara himself had first been a warrior and, in his time, had entered the Emperor's tournament—though the other fighters would not compete against him.

Lord Botahara had crossed the cobbled courtyard to the fighting ring and the cobbles had *broken* under his feet. The story was no longer believed by the population at large, such was their lack of faith, but the old monk knew it to be true. The Supreme Master himself could. . . . Well, it was wrong to be proud of one's accomplishments—after all, what were they compared to the Enlightened One's and he had overcome pride altogether.

Addressing the problem in Brother Hutto's letter had been the first difficulty of the day. Difficulty two had just disembarked at the monastery's wharf. Sister Morima; Botahist nun, acquaintance of forty years (could it be that many?), would grace him with her presence as soon as she finished her bath. Days like this were sent to try him! The Supreme Master had always hated surprise visits. That was one of the many beauties of the monastery on the island. There were almost no visitors at all, let alone any coming unannounced.

His mind drifted back to the report from Brother Hutto. What was that ass of an "Emperor" up to now? The old fool had lived on past all predictions. It happened sometimes, and not always to everyone's advantage. The only benefit of this Emperor's long life was that he did not leave a mere child to follow him, which invariably meant succession struggles. But then, the heir was no prize either, and not friendly to the Botahist Order. Well, the Brotherhood had plans and plans could be adapted to changing situations, just as one adapted one's strategy at the gii board. Botahara taught patience as a principal virtue and the Supreme Master adhered to the principal virtues whenever possible.

The old monk let his eyes drift over the design set into the opposite wall in polished woods. Such a perfect pattern—abstracted from the blossom of the Septfoil, one of the ninety-four healing herbs. Seven petals within a septilateral, within a circle, the design intersected by the seven lines of power. So simple. So complete. The work of Botahara was a constant source of joy to him.

I am a fortunate man, he thought, and then realized that someone was approaching down the hallway. Sister Morima.

There came a tap on the frame of the shoji.

"Please enter," the Master said, his voice the model of quiet dignity.

The shoji slid aside, revealing the great bulk of the Botahist nun. She was dressed in a long, unpatterned kimono, in a most unbecoming shade of yellow, gathered at the waist with the purple sash of the Botahist Orders. Her hair was cut short like a boy's, offering no softness to relieve the square line of her jaw. She was, the Supreme Master noted, tanned like a peasant.

"Sister Morima. We are honored that you would come so far out of your way to visit us." He rose from his cushion and bowed formally. The nun returned the bow, though only equally.

"The honor is mine, Brother Nodaku. To visit the mon-

astery of your *sect* is a privilege granted to so few . . ."
she stopped, as if at a loss for words.

As he had planned earlier, the Supreme Master moved
his writing table aside, but the nun did not apologize for
interrupting. He offered her his cushion and took a second one from a wall closet.

"I bring you greetings and wishes of long health from
Sister Saeja," Sister Morima said as the Supreme Master
seated himself opposite her.

"And how is Sister Saeja? Well, no doubt?" Brother
Hutto's report had mentioned that the head of the nun's
Order had recently returned from her annual pilgrimage
to Monarta, the place of Lord Botahara's birth, and the
old nun was slowing down noticeably."

"She is as constant as the river and as supple as the
willow wand, Brother Nodaku, a continual inspiration to
us all."

He always found this ploy of hers—using his common
name—disconcerting, as though the Initiate Nodaku had
suddenly been caught impersonating the head of the
Order.

"That is good news, Sister. Do you have other news
you can share? We are so isolated here!"

She flashed an amused smile. "I've just returned from
the island of the barbarian, Brother. I'm sure your news
is more recent than mine." The Supreme Master
remained silent, but the nun offered nothing more.

Lifting an ivory hammer that sat before a polished
bronze gong, the monk asked, "Cha?"

"Thank you, yes, Brother, and some food, if it is not
too much of an imposition." She bit off the last words.

The Supreme Master almost laughed as he tapped the
gong. He knew the nun's weakness. *Brother Nodaku*,
indeed! Footsteps sounded in the hall and then, as a
knock was heard on the screen, a second set of footsteps
joined them.

"Please enter," the Supreme Master said with under-
stated authority. The face of Shuyun, the senior Neophyte who was causing all the fuss, appeared and before
the Supreme Master realized what was happening, the

face of the Neophyte servant came into view also. The two boys were startled by the unexpected presence of the Botahist nun. For an instant they stood in awkward silence and then they both bowed, bumping each other in the half opened doorway.

"Do you need me to serve you, Supreme Master?" the second Neophyte asked.

"That is why I sound this gong," the old monk said evenly. "Please, bring cha for Sister Morima and me. And some food. The Sister has not yet eaten due to an unforgivable lapse in our manners!"

"Immediately, Supreme Master." The boy bowed and hurried off.

"Shuyun-sum?"

"Excuse me for interrupting, Supreme Master. I was told to come here at this time to discuss my Seclusion."

The Supreme Master had forgotten.

"Have you completed your term, Initiate?" Sister Morima asked suddenly.

Shuyun bowed to the nun, while watching his master out of the corner of his eye. He decided it would be impolite not to answer.

"I'm only a senior Neophyte, honored Sister, but yes, I have just finished my Seclusion."

"Good for you, senior Neophyte. Did you stop the sand?" she smiled as she asked this question.

"No, honored Sister," the boy said, his tone serious, "I failed to stop the hour glass from measuring time. I can count the grains and name each one as it falls, but that is all."

The Botahist nun was unable to hide her surprise.

By the Lord Botahara, the Supreme Master thought, what karma has arranged for the Sister to be here now!

"Shuyun-sum, Sister Morima has graced us with her presence, so our interview must be postponed. I will call for you at another time."

Shuyun knelt, touching his head to the floor, and backed out of the room. "Thank you, Supreme Master." Then, suddenly emboldened, he asked, "May I join the junior Initiates in chi quan? They're about to begin."

The Supreme Master nodded his assent and made mental note to speak with the boy about addressing him after being dismissed.

As soon as Shuyun was out of hearing, the woman asked, "Is this true?"

"Yes, Sister, the junior Initiates train in chi quan every day at this time."

"You know what I mean, Brother!" She allowed impatience into her voice. "Is his chi ten ability so far developed?"

The Supreme Master shrugged. "I have only spoken to him just now."

The nun adjusted her posture, sitting more erect, forcing herself into a studied calm. "I believe he was telling the truth." She drew a deep breath and then almost whispered, "By the Lord Botahara!"

The sounds of the chi quan class drifted in from the courtyard and filled the silence in the study.

"And what do you plan to do with such a one, Brother?"

"If he learns to walk the Seven Paths, he shall serve Lord Botahara, as do all of our Order."

"Which is to say, you will indenture one with such abilities to some power-hungry lord, and draw him into the intrigues of the Empire for your own gains."

The Supreme Master was surprised by Sister Morima's sudden attack, but forced himself to remain calm; his voice, as always, was controlled. "We should not forget that the Lord Botahara was a peer of the Empire, born a 'power-hungry lord,' as you say. The political intentions of our order, such as they are, have always been aimed at maintaining a climate in which the following of Lord Botahara can grow. We have no other purpose. *Your* Order benefits as much from our "intrigues"— which amount to nothing more than giving sound advice—as does my own, Sister Morima."

"I am not a Neophyte in need of instruction, Brother Nodaku. I choose my words with great care. So, you will take this boy and thrust him into a society of decadence where even the best training may not save him? Three

of your Order died of the Great Plague—don't deny it!
Botahist monks *died* of disease! Could you really be willing to risk one with such talent? What if he could learn
to stop the sand?"

The Supreme Master fought to maintain his outward
calm. How did she know about the plague deaths?
Everything possible had been done to keep them secret.
What a world! Spies everywhere! "To serve a peer of
the Empire is a great test, Sister. If a member of our
Order cannot pass it . . ." the old monk shrugged, "that
is his karma. Stopping the sand is much more difficult
than serving among the peers."

"Who was this one in his former life?" Sister Morima
asked, pushing what she sensed was an advantage.

The Supreme Master shook his head, "We do not
know."

"But he was a monk or perhaps," the nun touched her
tongue to her lip, "perhaps a Sister?"

"That seems probable, Sister Morima."

"He chose from among the objects offered?"

"Yes, of course."

"And you say it is *probable* that he was a monk?"

"Wouldn't you agree?"

"Huh."

The Supreme Master realized he was revealing more
than he intended. The truth was that he had no idea who
the boy had been in his former life. As a child, when
Shuyun had come to the Order he had been tested in
many ways. One of these tests was to choose, from
among a random array of objects, those commonly used
by members of the Order. Shuyun had chosen all the
correct objects—a feat almost unheard of—but subse-
quent tests to discern who the boy had been were unsuccessful. This had never before happened. Perhaps
Shuyun *had* been a Sister! The Supreme Master found
this thought unsettling.

"When will you give up this meddling in the affairs of
the world, Brother, and concern yourself with the perfection of the spirit, as my own Order does?"

"I assure you, Sister Morima, that we are as concerned with the spirit and its perfection, as you are."

"But you are more concerned with perfecting the spirits of the wealthy, yeh?"

"Our temples and retreats deal with the less fortunate also, Sister, or have you forgotten? It was our Order that found the cure for the Great Plague, saving peasants, merchants, and peers alike."

Footsteps sounded in the hall and then came a tap on the shoji.

"Please enter."

Two Neophytes bowed and came into the room carrying trays.

"I will serve the cha," the Supreme Master said.

A small wooden table was moved to the center of the room. The servers moved with studied precision, anxious not to bring shame to the Supreme Master or the monastery.

The Supreme Master prepared the tea according to the practices of a thousand years, while the servers laid small platters of rice and vegetables on the table.

"Please, serve our guest first," the ancient monk instructed, and then, with fascination, he watched the nun select from each dish offered, her pupils wide with pleasure. Such a foolish weakness, the Supreme Master thought. If she were a Brother of our faith, she would be required to live on water and air three days out of seven for the rest of her life to show mastery of her desire. He dismissed the servers and poured the steaming cha, offering the first cup to his guest.

"I am not deserving, Brother. Please take this cup yourself."

"Your presence honors me; please, I insist." He proffered the cup again and this time she received it with a bow which he returned. Outside, on the small, private porch, a cricket began to chirp. The chi quan training continued in the courtyard. The Supreme Master poured his own cha and tasted it. Perfect! The cha leaves were grown in the monastery's own garden and overseeing the cultivation of the cha plant was one of his continuing pleasures. He ate a small portion of rice, to be polite, and watched the nun as she tried to hide her gluttony . . . and failed.

The Supreme Master knew that, when the food was gone, Sister Morima would reveal the true reason for her visit—and he wouldn't need to guess what that reason was. He sipped his cha.

He could hear the swallows building a nest under the roof of his balcony. They would make a terrible mess, but he loved to watch them and make friends with them. Such beautiful fliers!

Looking at the running time glass on its stand, the Supreme Master began to exercise chi ten, stretching his time sense until the sand appeared to slow as it fell. He looked down at the steam rising from his cha in languid swirls, like impossibly fine curtains moving in a breeze. He smiled inwardly.

What if this young one *could* stop the sand, as the nun had asked? What if he could do more? Since Lord Botahara, no one had stopped the sand—not in a thousand years! Why did they all fall short of the Perfect Master? The old monk's own teacher had had more highly developed chi ten abilities than any of his students and he had claimed to have fallen short of *his* Master.

The Supreme Master felt the warmth of the cha bowl in his hands. Such a simple pleasure! He pondered the secret that, for so long, only he had known, and wondered who else might have this knowledge now. The sand, the sand. He turned his gaze to watch the grains as they fell.

Lord Botahara, the Perfect Master, through the discipline of chi ten, had learned to control his subjective sense of time until the world slowed around him. All Botahist monks could do this to greater or lesser degree. But the Enlightened One had gone far beyond this. It was written that Lord Botahara would meditate upon the running sand until it not only stopped but, to His eye, it ran backward. The mere idea awed the Supreme Master. It was said that Lord Botahara could *move through time like a swimmer through water*. The monk had meditated upon this every day for as long as he could remember, but still, the meaning of it eluded him. He knew that it had been wise to make this part of the *secret knowledge* to be passed from one Supreme Master to the next. How was he to explain what even he could not understand? There was no answer.

Sister Morima had finished eating, and he noted how well she hid her sense of shame. The Supreme Master lifted the lid of a porcelain bowl and offered her a steaming, white cloth. She took one to clean her mouth and hands.

"More cha, Sister?"

"Please, Brother Nodaku. The food, by the way, was delicious."

He poured, holding back the sleeve of the long kimono worn by all Botahist monks. Loose fitting pants that came to mid-calf, sandals, and the purple sash of the Botahist Order completed their clothing.

Sister Morima took a sip of her cha, replaced the cup on the table, and composed herself. The moment had come.

"Sister Saeja has again instructed me to ask you, in all humility, if members of our Order may come to study the scrolls written by Lord Botahara."

The Supreme Master stared into his cha, turning the cup slowly on the table. "Sister Morima, I have assured you that the scrolls you study are the same as those studied by my own Order. The last time we spoke I offered you my personal scrolls and I offer them to you again. The words you have are the words of Botahara as transcribed by the most well versed monks of any age. They are, I assure you, the most perfect copies possible."

"We don't doubt, even for a moment, the abilities of the scholars who have transcribed Lord Botahara's words, Brother. For us, this is a matter of spiritual interest only. You have come to be the guardians of this treasure, yet it is the legacy of all of Lord Botahara's followers. We wish only to look upon the words of the Enlightened One, as you have. We don't wish to remove them from your excellent care, Brother, but only to send a delegation—perhaps two or three of our most learned Sisters—to examine the scrolls—under your supervision, of course. There is no reason for you to protect the scrolls from us. We revere these treasures as do you."

"Sister, the scrolls, as you know, are very old. They are handled but once in a decade, when we unseal them to inspect for the slightest signs of degeneration. They are resealed almost immediately. All of us make do with our transcribed copies. *All* of us. I can say nothing more. I have an oath and a sacred trust which I will not violate. Please do not ask me to waver in this area of duty, Sister Morima."

"I would never ask that you break your trust, Brother, but you . . . you are *Supreme Master*. You may alter decisions that were made when the world was not as it is now. This is wisdom. Botahara taught that change was inevitable and to resist it, folly.

"Perhaps two or three of my sisters could be present at the time of one of your examinations? We would not hinder you in your duty, I assure you. Certainly it is allowed for the followers of the *Word* to attend this ceremony?"

Cunning old cow! How, the Supreme Master wondered, was he to get around this? "Let me consider your words and take counsel with the seniors of my Order. To do as you suggest would be to break the practices of a thousand years, Sister Morima. You must realize that such a decision cannot be made quickly. I will say no more and, please, understand that I can promise nothing."

"Ah, Brother Nodaku, your reputation for wisdom is indeed well deserved. I thank you, a thousand times over! You honor me to listen to me for so long." She bowed to him. "If you were to decide to allow us to be present at a time of examination—and I realize you have not promised this—but if; when would this be?"

The Supreme Master looked up for a second as though he needed to calculate when such a momentous day would come.

"It will be nearly nine years from now, Sister Morima."

"A short time, Brother, the days shall fly!" she clapped her hands together like an excited child. "How close to nine years, Supreme Master?"

He paused again, "Eight years from now on the seventh moon."

She drained her cha and then said with emotion, "May you attain perfection in this lifetime!"

And may you attain perfection *tonight* that I might be done with you, the Supreme Master thought.

"The ship did not have a large cargo to unload here, Brother, I'm sure they must be waiting for me. May I ask one more thing before I leave? When might we expect a decision on this matter?"

"I cannot say, Sister."

"Perhaps you could give me some estimation, that I might allow my Sisters a time to which they may look forward?"

"I cannot say, Sister Morima," the monk repeated, a hint of annoyance in his voice.

She bowed. "As you say, Brother, it was not my intention to impose upon you." She rose from her cushion with surprising grace and bowed again, the old monk rose with her and bowed simultaneously.

"I have kept you too long, Brother. You have honored me with this interview. I am in your debt."

"It is I who am honored, as your visit has graced our monastery. There can be no debt in such a matter."

The nun bowed a last time and backed out of the room. At the door she stopped for a second, catching the Supreme Master's eye. "What if this young one develops a perfect ear for truth?"

The Supreme Master ignored what was implied in this question, answering without hesitation, "Then he shall see not only the truth of Botahara's words but also the truth of our sacred work."

A senior Neophyte came down the hall to escort the Sister through the maze of Jinjoh Monastery. She nodded as though acknowledging the wisdom of Brother Nodaku's answer, turned on her heel, and was gone.

The Supreme Master stood for a moment, staring at

the closed shoji, and then slid aside the screen that opened onto his private porch. A swallow flitted off the almost completed nest, protesting the intrusion in a high voice. The Supreme Master did not step out onto the wooden deck but instead hung back in the shadow provided by the roof. In the courtyard below he could see the junior Initiates practicing the Form. He took a half step forward, bringing more of the courtyard into view, until he could see all of the students, each standing in his own Septima—the geometric design identical to the one set into the Supreme Master's wall.

The instructor moved slowly and with perfect grace before the rows of pupils. They had come to the end of the sixth closure now and most of the students were faltering, though an untrained eye would never have been aware of this. Shuyun was in the second row, conspicuous for his small size and for his confidence. The boy's movements were precise and flowing, executed without hesitation.

Sotura-sum had not exaggerated. The senior Neophyte's form made the more advanced students look clumsy; indeed, he rivaled the instructor in his control. The Supreme Master watched, fascinated by the spectacle.

"Never before have I seen such a sight," he whispered. "Who could this child have been?"

Beyond the courtyard wall, of white plaster and wood, he could see Sister Morima being escorted down to the waiting ship. She moved with a light step for one so large of frame. The woman was far more clever than he had given her credit for. He would have to be more careful in the future—far more careful.

He had no intention of letting her, or anyone else, see the scrolls. Not now, not in a hundred years. The matter was no longer within his control. He felt his body slump, ever so slightly, and he fought this sign of resignation. How could this have happened? he wondered for the ten thousandth time. Every precaution had been taken. Every precaution! But it didn't matter now. Nothing mattered. The scrolls were gone. Stolen from under the sleepless eye of the Sacred Guard of Jinjoh Monastery.

The twenty junior Initiates, including one senior Neophyte, came to the end of the seventh closure and stopped, absolutely motionless, in the ready position. The senior chi quan instructor stood looking at the students before him, all of them barefoot and stripped to the waist. When none of them wavered in their stance, he nodded, satisfied.

"Take a partner," he said quietly. "We will spar."

The boys broke into pairs and resumed the ready position.

"Shuyun-sum," the instructor beckoned. "You have never sparred?"

"No, Brother Sotura, senior Neophytes only push-hands."

The instructor seemed to consider for a moment. "You will learn soon enough. Today we will both watch. Begin!"

Sotura walked among the combatants, stopping to watch each pair. The sparring started slowly, following the stylized movements of the form and then gained momentum until all movements became a blur, as each student sought a point of resistance against which he could push or to which he could deliver a blow.

Shuyun began to stretch his time sense, practicing chi ten to allow him to analyze the sparring as it increased in speed. The motions of the combatants became fluid and endless, each movement leading into the next without hesitation.

Brother Sotura held up his hands suddenly. "Cease!" he ordered, and walked to a position in front of the class. The silence was perfect.

"I see that some of you still believe that you can gain an advantage by using bone and muscle. Perhaps you secretly wish to be kick boxers?

"To move within the form is not enough. You must become insubstantial. No one can kick the wind. No one can push water. It is of no value to make even the most perfect soft-fist if, at the moment of impact, you tighten the muscles. Chi is the source of all of your strength—direct it into your hand as it is needed. Remember that you hold a caterpillar in your curled fist. Its hairs tickle your palm." The monk paused as a tiny, blue butterfly drifted by and settled on Shuyun's shoulder. The instructor smiled. "I will demonstrate."

He took a step forward and reached out to Shuyun, gently removing the butterfly from his shoulder. Closing his hand over the insect, the instructor moved to the wooden gate that led into a walled garden. Pausing for a split second to take a stance, the monk suddenly drove his hand through one of the gate's thick planks, which splintered and broke with a loud *crack*. Pivoting gracefully, Brother Sotura held his hand out to the class—a perfect soft-fist—and then released the butterfly, unharmed, into the air. All of the class knelt and touched their heads to the stones.

"That will be enough for now. Go and meditate upon chi. Try to become a breeze so soft that even a butterfly would be unable to perch on your will."

Shuyun opened the gate with its broken board and went into the large garden beyond, a garden known for its many paths and private bowers overlooking the island and the sea. He found a nook formed by flowering rhododendrons and settled cross-legged onto a flat stone. For a moment he contemplated the display of his chi quan instructor—basking in the perfection of it.

The boy, Shuyun, had emerged from his Seclusion that morning and felt both a vast sense of freedom and at the same time a loss of freedom like none other he had known. Perhaps at no other time in his life would Shuyun have the opportunity to spend so much time totally alone. The Supreme Master had been right; six months could be a lifetime. A lifetime alone to meditate upon the Word of the Perfect Master.

The routine of his Seclusion had been relentless. Rise with the sun and practice chi quan on the pattern set into the floor of his one-room house. At midday he took his only meal and was allowed to meditate or compose

poetry in the enclosed garden. Then came an afternoon
of chi ten. Sitting within the Septima, concentrating all
his being upon the Fifth Concurrence where the sand
glass sat. Then, again in the afternoon, chi quan practiced before his wall-shadow until dark, followed by meditation on the Seven Paths. He was allowed three hours'
sleep before sunrise.

Each afternoon Shuyun had sat, as he was sitting now,
on the pattern and practiced the discipline of chi ten.
Controlling his breathing, feeling chi drop to his *Ooma,*
the center of being, he had reached *out* with his chi,
sending it into the lines of power in the Pattern. And
each day the sand ran more slowly in the glass as Shuyun
learned to alter his subjective time.

The ability to alter one's perception of time was not
unknown beyond the walls of Jinjoh Monastery. The kick
boxers could do it, to a degree, and some of the best
tumblers and dancers spoke of it. Shuyun wondered if
perhaps everyone experienced the stretching of time in
brief moments of complete concentration. But only the
Botahist Orders had discovered the keys to its mastery:
chi quan and chi ten, the disciplines of movement and
meditation represented in the pattern of the Septima,
the Form which taught perfection of motion and total
concentration.

"Entering the mind through the body," Lord Botahara
had called this. Shuyun was beginning to understand. It
was as though he had finally begun to do that which he
had only understood before in words.

Sitting on the rock overlooking the sea, Shuyun felt
chi drop and he began to push it out from his body,
imagining that it rushed out into the infinite space around
him to slow all motion.

A leaf fell from a ginkyo tree and spiraled endlessly
downward. Anxiety touched the young monk and he felt
his focus waver, but the leaf kept falling ever so slowly
and Shuyun's confidence returned. He was able to concentrate on the play of sunlight on the planes of the leaf's
surface as it fell against the background depths of a blue
sky. Finally it touched the surface of a small pond and

sent ripples out in perfect circles. Shuyun counted the tiny waves and named each one after a flower as it died at the pond's edge. A poem came to him:

*The spring has blossomed*
*Yet a ginkyo leaf*
*Falls endlessly*
*Into the lily pond.*

Shuyun released a long breath. Relief swept through him and it felt like an endless, powerful wave. Twice during his Seclusion he had lost control, or so he thought. Twice his altered time sense had seemed to distort and he had found himself somewhere . . . somewhere he could not describe. And when he had returned to the usual perception of time, it was with a crash which he knew indicated loss of all control. His teacher had never warned him of this and the young monk felt a strong fear that he was failing to learn what he must learn to become a senior of his Order.

He had intended to speak of this with senior Brother Sotura but did not, deciding it would be better to wait. And he felt now that he was gaining control. There had been no reoccurrence of this strange experience in several months.

A memory of the time before his Seclusion came to him: kneeling before his teacher, listening.

"You must always move within the pattern, you must even breathe within the pattern. Chi will strengthen in you, but you must never try to become its master. Offer it no resistance, only allow its flow. Chi can never be controlled. You can only make your will synonymous with it."

If his master had not said this, Shuyun would not have believed it possible. But now that his Seclusion was complete, he began to understand. He also began to see the wisdom of his teachers.

I must meditate upon chi. Shuyun thought. I must become a breeze so soft that even a butterfly cannot push against me.

After a timeless time a bell rang and Shuyun brought himself out of his meditation. He rose and walked calmly through the garden. It was time to bathe in the hot spring and then partake of the evening meal.

He paused at the gate to look again at the splintered board and his earlier joy at his teacher's demonstration became complete. The shattered board had been replaced and into the new board a monk had carefully cut a hole the shape and size of a butterfly. From his position, Shuyun could see the blue sky through this hole. With a last look, the young Neophyte hurried off. All the senior Neophytes would want to hear about the butterfly-punch which he alone among them had seen.

Brother Sotura, chi quan Master of Jinjoh Monstery, mounted a stairway which ended in a hall leading to the Supreme Master's rooms. He had bathed and changed into clean clothes, taking time to compose himself before meeting with the head of his Order. The instructor knew of the nun's visit and was concerned.

He tapped lightly on the shoji of the Supreme Master's study and waited.

"Please enter," came the warm voice Brother Sotura was expecting. He slid the screen aside, knelt, and touched his forehead to the grass mats. The Supreme Master sat at his writing table, brush in hand. He nodded, as his rank required, and then began to clean his brush.

"Come in, my old friend, and sit with me. I have need of your counsel."

"You honor me, Supreme Master, but I fear that in the matters you consider, my counsel will be of little value."

"Take a cushion and dispense with this fear. I need you. That is that. Do you desire food?"

"Thank you, but I have eaten."

"Cha, then?" He reached for the ivory hammer.

"Please, cha would be most welcome."

The gong sounded and immediately there were footsteps in the hall.

"Please open," the Supreme Master said before the knock came. "Cha for Sotura-sum and me. And please, see that we are not disturbed." The boy bowed and slid the screen closed without a sound.

"Well, Sotura-sum, I had a most interesting visit this afternoon with the old cow." He paused and smiled, then shook his head. "She very nearly extracted a promise from me that certain members of her Order would be allowed to be present at our next examination of the scrolls."

The chi quan master remained silent.

"Very nearly but not quite. I told her I must confer with the senior members of my Order, which is what I am doing now."

Brother Sotura shifted uncomfortably. "It seems they will plague us until they have seen the hand of Botahara. I hesitate to suggest this, Supreme Master, but under the circumstances it may be wise to satisfy this curiosity. We have in our possession very ancient scrolls, perfect copies in fact. There are none living but perhaps four members of our own Order who could possibly know they are not real. I realize this is hardly an honorable path, but . . ." He shrugged.

"Honor is a luxury we may not be able to afford at this time, Brother." The Supreme Master looked down at his hands, examining them as though they were mysteriously changed. "We dare not raise suspicions about the scrolls . . . not now. I will consider your counsel, Brother, I thank you."

The server approached, though he had barely had time to go to the small kitchen and return. The Supreme Master cocked an eyebrow at the other monk.

"They have begun to anticipate me. Have I become old and predictable? That would be a danger. Do not answer, I shall meditate upon this."

The cha was served, its bitter-sweet aroma filling the room.

"Do you still think it is possible that the Sisters have the scrolls, or did your visit with Morima-sum do away with that path?"

"I can't say. Sister Morima may not be party to such knowledge. But if she is, and came here only to blow smoke in our eyes, she did admirably. I believe that she did indeed come to try again to gain access to the scrolls—but of course, one can never be sure. Sister Morima is an accomplished actress and no fool."

"So, we have not eliminated a single possibility?"

The Supreme Master nodded and sipped his cha.

"Did Brother Hutto's report offer anything?"

The old monk shook his head. "Robbers have begun to accost members of our order on the highways of Wa. He recommends a *display* to curb this. Another Initiate has disappeared—Brother Hutto suggests that he is a victim of robbers. I can't believe it! The new Emperor has consolidated his power almost entirely, with one curious lapse—he has allowed the old Shonto and his family to live."

"How is this?" Brother Sotura rocked back on his cushion. "He cuts his own throat! What deal could those two possibly make? Shonto is absolutely loyal to the old Imperial line."

"Yes, but the Hanama line is no more. It is true that there are others with a claim to the Throne at least equal to Lord Yamaku's, but they failed to join against the Yamaku until it was too late. There is no help for them now. The old Shonto was betrayed and captured during a battle he may well have won. Lord Yamaku, or should I say Akantsu the First, Emperor of Wa, allowed him an honorable death—the two old foxes had fought side by side in the past. Lord Shonto composed his death poem, and when the Emperor heard it he relented and lifted his sentence on Shonto and his family!"

"The old fox has taken leave of his senses! Next he will set the *wolf* on the throne beside him. What was this poem, did our Brother say?"

The Supreme Master reached for the scroll and unrolled it.

*After a lifetime of battle*
*And duty,*

*At last!*
*A moment to write poetry.*


The chi quan instructor laughed with pleasure. "I commend them both for their wisdom. Only a fool could destroy one so clever."

"There is more," the Supreme Master said. "A week after the stay of execution, Lord Shonto's heir, Motoru, announced that he had married Lord Fanisan's widow and adopted her daughter. The two women emerged from hiding under the roof of the family the Emperor had just spared."

"The Shonto have always been bold. My concern for their Spiritual Advisor, Brother Satake, has been misplaced. Again the Shonto survive the jaws of the dragon. Had Lord Fanisan already fallen to the Emperor?"

"He fell to the plague first, poor man, leaving the Emperor in the awkward position of not being able to do away with the Fanisan women openly. Lord Shonto's son has saved them from an assassin, I'm sure. At least for now."

"So, young Shonto will marry off this adopted daughter to the Emperor's son, legitimizing the Yamaku claim and tying the Shonto to the new dynasty. The entire family has genius!" The instructor's voice was full of admiration. "And what of the plague, Supreme Master, have there been recent outbreaks?"

"We seem to have been successful. There has not been a single case reported in three months. But all the damage has been done. When the plague fell upon the Imperial family, Lord Yamaku mobilized. It was a great risk, but the confusion in the Empire gave him the only chance he would ever have. And now we have a bloodsucker on the Dragon Throne."

Neither man spoke for a moment. The room darkened as the sun set. The Supreme Master lit an exquisite porcelain lamp.

"The Emperor still does not require the services of a Spiritual Advisor?"

"No, Sotura-sum, he still fears our influence. We must

watch this one carefully as he is very dangerous to us.
His son will be no better. These will be difficult times
for our Order. We must all flow like water and wind or
we will be damaged—not destroyed—but years of work
hang in the balance."

The Supreme Master poured more cha. "Senior Neophyte Shuyun was sent to me today and arrived during
the sister's visit—a terrible mistake. He was indiscreet."

"How so, Supreme Master?"

"She knows of his chi ten ability."

"Unfortunate, but she cannot begin to suspect his true
potential. I feel I'm only beginning to realize it myself.
Shuyun joined the junior Initiates at chi quan, today.
They were clumsy beside him!" He looked up at the
older monk. "What will we do with him?"

"He will, no doubt, become a Spiritual Advisor to a
peer of the Empire and spread the teachings of
Botahara."

"Shuyun would make a perfect advisor to an Emperor,
Supreme Master."

"A very remote possibility. Other things seem more
likely and almost as useful. We must intensify Shuyun's
training without making him appear too special. I want
to know his potential. He has never sparred, has he?"

Brother Sotura shook his head.

"How long would it take to bring him up to a level
where he could win the Emperor's kick boxing
tournament?"

"He could win it today, I'm sure, but I think he should
train more specifically for such a test. Not long—perhaps
two months."

"Begin his training tomorrow. I have a feeling that
you and he will make a journey to the River Festival in
the autumn." The old monk stood and moved to the
open balcony screen. He stared out into the open courtyard for a moment. It was lit only by starlight and the
shadows played tricks on the eyes.

"You have doubled our security?"

"Yes, and I check the guards personally every night."

"You are indispensable, Sotura-sum." The Supreme

Master finally asked the question that each of them carried with him day and night. "If the Sisters do not have the scrolls, who else would want them?"

Brother Sotura was quiet for a moment as he considered his answer. "Their value is inestimable, for that reason alone anyone might want them. But no thief could effect their sale and remain unknown—word would surely get out. The greater possibility is that someone has stolen them for political reasons. Anyone who would benefit from a secure hold over the Botahist Brotherhood is suspect."

"The Emperor?"

"He would earn my first suspicion. He does not love us. There are no monks in his household to keep such a secret from and he is one of the few who could accomplish the theft."

"Who else?"

"Lord Shonto, Lord Bakima, Lord Fujiki, Lord Omawara, perhaps half a dozen others, and the magic cults, though I don't believe it was them."

"And we still don't know when they were stolen?"

"Sometime in the last ten years."

The Supreme Master shook his head. "All of the guardians of the Urn have been questioned now?"

"All but two, Supreme Master."

"And they?"

"They died of the plague."

"Huh."

The lamp flickered in a draft from the open screen.

"If the scrolls have been taken to blackmail us, why haven't they approached us with their demands?"

"Perhaps the time is not yet right for their purpose, whatever it might be."

"There is another possibility, Sotura-sum. What if the scrolls have been destroyed?"

"I refuse to believe anyone could perform such sacrilege!"

"The followers of Tomsoma?"

"They are bunglers and fools! They could never have accomplished the theft."

"I'm sure you are right, Sotura-sum. We have spies in their midst?"

"Yes, Supreme Master, and we have contacted them. They report nothing out of the ordinary."

"You are thorough, Brother Sotura."

The Supreme Master stood for a moment more and then turned from the open doorway. "Thank you, my friend, you have been most helpful."

The chi quan master rose and bowed before backing out of the room.

"Sotura-sum," the Supreme Master said, stopping the monk at the door. "I saw your instruction of the junior Initiates today." The Supreme Master bowed deeply to the chi quan instructor. Words were unnecessary. From the Supreme Master, there was no greater honor.

# Two

From where he stood by the steps to the quarter deck, Kogami Norimasa could see the Botahist monk silhouetted against the stars as he leaned by the rigging that supported the main mast. Kogami had been watching the young Brother ever since he had boarded the ship, though the sight of the monastery where the Perfect Master had begun writing his great works had begged his attention.

Very few had seen Jinjoh Monastery and Kogami counted himself fortunate to be among the few in yet another way. For too long he had been among the many—just another in the legion of faceless bureaucrats who served the Dragon Throne. And a very remote throne that had seemed!

As an Imperial Functionary of the Fifth Rank, Kogami had not caught even a glimpse of the present Emperor. Yet, whether the Son of Heaven knew it or not, Kogami had been of immense benefit to him, though of course the Functionaries of the Fourth and Third Ranks had received the credit.

But this injustice was about to be rectified. Kogami Norimasa's abilities had finally been recognized, and by no less a figure than Jaku Katta, the Emperor's Prime Advisor and Commander of the Imperial Guard. Such incredible luck! Such amazing good fortune! Kogami's wife had burned incense at the family shrine every day since then, despite the cost.

After so many years of laboring to make the Emperor richer, Kogami Norimasa would now see the rise of his own fortunes—Jaku Katta had promised him this.

Kogami Norimasa, Imperial Functionary of the Third Rank.

Not since the fall of the Hanama had Kogami dared to even dream of rising to such a position. And that was not all! Jaku Katta had granted him an Imperial Writ which would allow him to participate personally in trade outside of the Imperium—in a limited way, of course—but still, it was a privilege granted so few outside of the aristocracy. Kogami Norimasa was exceedingly clever with money and now he would have a chance to prove it beyond a doubt, on behalf of both himself and the Emperor.

This would help compensate for the shame he felt at not having become a soldier as his father had wished. But he wasn't made for military life; that had been apparent from his early youth, to his father's lasting disappointment. His father had been a major in the army of the last Hanama Emperor and had died resisting the Yamaku entry into what was at that point an almost empty capital. That was the cause of Kogami Norimasa's stalled career.

If the plague had not decimated the Imperial Capital and, with it, the bureaucracy that made the vast Empire run, Kogami knew that he would never have been allowed to keep his head, let alone swear allegiance to the new Emperor. But now, after eight dark years in which he had risen only from the Sixth to the Fifth Rank, he was moving again! The papers had been delivered to him by Jaku Katta's own brother, papers that bore the stamp of power; the Dragon Seal of the Emperor of Wa. It was as if the gods had decided to once again grant Kogami a future.

The ship was only two days out of Yankura now, perhaps less. He prayed the winds would remain fair. Two more days of watching this young monk and then he would be back in Wa and his new life would begin.

Kogami looked again at the Brother who stood motionless on the rolling deck. He had been there for hours, dressed lightly but not seeming to feel the night's chill. They were all like that, Kogami thought. The monks who had been his teachers when he was a child had felt neither the heat nor the cold—or anger or fear for that matter. They remained enigmas, always. Even after seven years in their charge Kogami knew so little of them. But the Brothers had left their mark on him, and he knew he would never erase it.

Despite his feelings about the Brotherhood, Kogami did not object to his wife keeping a secret shrine to Botahara—though it was really against his better judgment to allow it in their house. This was not something that was disallowed; in fact, many families he knew did the same, but, like Kogami Norimasa, they wisely kept their beliefs within their own walls. The Emperor had turned his back on the Botahist faith and any who expected to rise in His service did the same, at least outwardly. Of course, this went against the teachings of Botahara, Kogami realized, but his wife was doubly pious for his sake. The monks themselves did not follow the teachings of the Perfect Master, as Kogami understood them, for the Brotherhood meddled in politics and acquired property and wealth. Kogami sighed. What a complicated world. Time would take care of it all, though, and the Faith would still exist when Emperors and monks had passed. It had always been so.

Outside the Imperial Service, people worshiped as they pleased and, despite the Emperor's hatred of the Botahist faith, he had not made the mistake of openly offending the Brotherhood. The Botahists held a great deal of power in the Empire and the Son of Heaven was too aware of this.

Kogami shifted his position to try to gain more shelter from the wind. The dark form of the monk remained unmoving at the gunnel. Perhaps he meditates upon the full moon, Kogami thought, and felt a twinge of guilt as he looked up at the pure, white disk of the autumn moon.

I have done nothing wrong, he told himself. To watch is not a crime. That was undeniably true, but there was a slim possibility that he might be required to do more.

The words of Jaku Katta came back to him again and he analyzed them for the thousandth time.

"You will assist Ashigaru, if he requires it, though this is unlikely, otherwise you are just to observe. Get to know this monk. Buy your way into his favor if you must, but find out everything you can about him."

Assist Ashigaru? Assist in what? Kogami had not asked. Somehow he knew that to ask that question was to put his new future in danger. Kogami Norimasa, Functionary of the Third Rank, had pushed these thoughts from his mind.

So far, the man Jaku spoke of had not required Kogami's assistance—he prayed it would remain so. The priest, Ashigaru, was below decks with Kogami's wife and his daughter who was suffering from a sickness of the sea. Kogami had disliked the priest from the moment the man had boarded the ship from the island of the barbarian.

A large man with wiry hair and beard, Ashigaru had the look of the religious fanatic—as though he'd been out in the sun far too long. He had the habit of repeatedly tugging the lapels of his robes as he talked, pulling the material closer around him, protecting himself from a cold that no one else perceived.

For the first few days of the voyage, Kogami had spoken to the priest only in passing, just as Jaku Katta had instructed. But since his daughter had fallen ill, he'd exchanged words with Ashigaru often. This, of course, was entirely natural and should raise no suspicion; still, Kogami was most concerned about such matters, for his entire future depended on how well he performed his duty on this voyage.

He marveled again at his good fortune. Of course he had been a perfect choice for this matter. He had traveled several times to the island of the barbarian on business for the Emperor, always posing as a vassal-merchant for some minor lord. The Son of Heaven would never have it known that he participated in trade like a common merchant! So Kogami had become a trader and traveler and, except for the time away from his family, he had come to find pleasure in this life. But on this journey Jaku Katta had asked him to take his family with him. It was not an uncommon thing for a vassal-merchant to do, especially one who was adding to his personal income on the side, as more and more seemed to be doing. Jaku had thought the family would add to Kogami's appearance of innocence, so his wife, daughter and maidservant had accompanied him—at the Emperor's expense, of course.

Kogami had found much amusement in watching the reactions of his family to the absurd customs of the barbarians. They had laughed about it in private. What fun they had mimicking the things they'd seen! But now his daughter had fallen ill and Kogami had asked the priest, Ashigaru, to see her, as the members of religions were all more or less skilled in the practice of healing.

A gong sounded and sailors began to emerge from below for the change of watch. Silently the crewmen went about their routine of examining all critical parts of the ship's running gear. The rigging was checked briefly, but expertly, except for the shrouds where the silent Brother stood. The captain of the watch motioned toward these, shaking his head; and the sailors passed them by, leaving the monk to his meditations. The Botahist Brothers were invariably given such respect, even by those who did not love them.

For his part, the silent Brother stood by the rail, thinking about a woman he had never met. Her name was Lady Nishima Fanisan Shonto and she was the adopted daughter of Lord Shonto Motoru—the man Shuyun journeyed to serve. Shonto's previous Spiritual Advisor had left a most complete report detailing everything his successor would need to know about the House of Shonto and though Shuyun had only needed to read it once to be able to recall every word, he had read the section dealing with the Lady Nishima twice, as if to reassure himself that it was true. The words of Brother Satake, Shuyun's predecessor, revealed the man's great affection and admiration for the young woman. Shuyun felt that, in this matter, the old monk had come very close to losing the Botahist Brother's eternal objectivity. This made the woman even more intriguing.

Satake-sum was not a man to be easily impressed, indeed he had been one of the most renowned Botahist Brothers of the century, a man who surely could have become Supreme Master if he had so desired. Satake-sum's talents had been legendary, for he had attained levels of accomplishment in several endeavors that usually required the single-minded dedication and study of a lifetime. And, in many ways, this young aristocrat had been his protégée.

Lady Nishima Fanisan Shonto—Shuyun liked even the sound of her name. Already she had gained fame for herself as a painter, a harpist, a composer of music, a poetess—and these, if Brother Satake's report could be believed, were merely the most visible facets of a personality of even greater cultivation. It was no wonder she was so sought after. A woman of such unusual talent, the only remaining heir of the powerful Fanisan House. What other woman of the Empire was so entirely blessed?

Shuyun contemplated the perfection of the moon as he thought of this matter and a poem came to him:

> *I am drawn always toward you,*
> *Your delicate and distant light,*
> *Face which I have never seen.*

The poem seemed to release him from thoughts of Lady Nishima, at least momentarily, and he was left with memories of his earlier trip to Wa. That had been a truly exciting journey. Shuyun had lived in Jinjoh Monastery from such an early age that he had formed no clear memories of the Empire, just as he had no recollection of his parents. On that first voyage, the River Festival had been his destination and Brother Sotura, the chi quan master, had been his companion. The newly initiated monk had struggled to contain his excitement and maintain an appearance of decorum, lest he bring embarrassment to the Botahist Order.

Though eight years had passed since that journey, Shuyun could still recall the trip in vivid detail.

They had been like wanderers from a far land, cast up on an unfamiliar shore. And there, before them, lay all of Wa, compressed into a space that could be walked in a day. The River Festival, lit by ten thousand lanterns, attended by uncounted people; an endless ebb and flow of humanity along the banks of the moving waters.

To have come to this from Jinjoh Monastery. . . . It was as if Shuyun had completed his meditation in a barren, silent room, opened the screen to leave, and there, where a tranquil garden should have been, twenty thousand people milled and laughed and danced and sang. To the boy from the island, it seemed that unreal.

Shuyun had followed his teacher through the crowds. Lanterns of all colors hung from the trees, and where there was no lantern light, moonlight seemed to find its way. Shuyun had seen ladies of high birth carried through the crowds on sedan chairs, smelled their perfume as they passed, laughing and hiding their faces coyly behind fans. And the next moment he had stepped over wine victims lying in their own disgorge. Fascination had caused him to pause beside the tumblers and jugglers, forcing Brother Sotura to return and find him raptly watching every movement, every trick, lost in the slow-time of chi ten.

Shuyun and Brother Sotura had passed a tent with beautiful young women beckoning at its door, and though the women had made signs to Botahara as the monks passed, the youngest of them had tried to flirt with Shuyun and had laughed when he looked away.

Brother Sotura had led him over a footbridge into a park, and Shuyun felt as though he had entered another kingdom. The riotous noise quieted, and the pungent smoke of cook-fires was replaced by the delicate aromas of cut flowers and rare perfumes. Drinking and laughter continued, but those drinking and laughing were dressed in elaborate silks and brocades, unlike any the young monk had never seen. Shuyun was certain Sotura had sought this place out, yet he did not know why.

They had passed by a group of people whispering and gossiping at the edge of a circle of willows, and had come upon a stage lit by lanterns. A woman sat on cushions at the edge of the stage and read from a scroll to a silently attentive audience. Her voice was as clear as winter air, yet the words she spoke were weighty and formal. Shuyun had realized that an ancient play was being performed, and had recognized the language of antiquity, understandable, but charged with vowels that rolled oddly off the tongue.

Sotura had settled down on a grass mat, motioning for his student to do likewise.

*"Gatherer of Clouds,"* the master had whispered, and Shuyun had recognized the title from his studies.

As the play unfolded, Shuyun had become entranced by the portrayal of a central character who was an eccentric Botahist monk, a hermit unconcerned with the day to day lives of the other characters but deeply committed to the esoteric, the intangible. It was the first time Shuyun had seen a monk depicted by someone outside his Order and he found this a fascinating if not a reassuring experience.

It was hours before Shuyun emerged from the world of the stage and he found himself deeply moved by his first encounter with theater.

Two days later the kick boxing began. The official who registered Shuyun for the tournament could barely hide his amusement when he realized that it was not the chi quan master but the boy who accompanied him who would compete. The politely disguised smiles quickly disappeared as Shuyun won his first contests with an ease that surprised everyone but Brother Sotura. Of course, his first opponents were not highly skilled by the standards of kick boxing, so the small monk, though he gained some respect, was still not thought to present a threat.

It was on this journey to the Empire that Shuyun first

encountered violence. Though he had trained in chi quan for many years, the young Initiate had never seen a man consciously try to cause another damage. Among the kick boxers were those who had forsaken honor for cunning and brutality.

But Shuyun did not lose his focus. And Sotura showed a careful confidence in him.

As the two monks observed other bouts, it became apparent that two men fought outstandingly and were favored to win: an Imperial Guardsman named Jaku Katta, and a lieutenant of the Shonto family guard. Shuyun saw the Imperial Guardsman fight, though briefly, and it was easily apparent why he had earned the name "Black Tiger." Jaku Katta was not only strong and fierce, but he was exceedingly clever and possessed a sense of balance which was almost uncanny. He was almost twice Shuyun's size.

As Shuyun faced opponent after opponent, he began to feel chi flow through him with a strength and power he had never known before. He came to realize that the violence of his adversaries enabled him to draw from an unknown reservoir of power—a well which could be tapped only when he faced true danger. Boxer after boxer was forced from the ring. Crowds began to follow Shuyun's progress.

As they prepared for the bout with the Shonto lieutenant, Shuyun noticed his teacher glancing at the gathered crowd. Following his instructor's gaze, Shuyun saw a group of guards in blue livery surrounding a man, a girl, and an old Botahist monk.

"Beware of this one," he said as Shuyun stepped into the ring, "it is impossible to know what training he has had."

Shuyun obeyed the instructions of his teacher and approached the match with extra caution, but Sotura's concerns proved unfounded. The man was as good if not better than any the young monk had yet faced, but he was still a traditional boxer and knew only the path of resistance.

There was only one more contest after that, the one

in which Shuyun faced the Imperial Guardsman. Shuyun knew that the man was physically impressive, he towered over the diminutive monk like a giant, but as Shuyun entered the ring he momentarily lost focus. For, like the tiger he was named for, Jaku Katta had gray eyes. The young monk had never before seen a man whose eyes were not brown.

It soon became apparent that Jaku would have bested the Shonto guard. He was faster than all the previous fighters Shuyun had faced, much faster. And he thought as quickly, changing an attack in mid-strike—moving with the perfect balance of a cat. Still, Shuyun turned all blows aside, all kicks. And Jaku kept his distance, dancing away after each onslaught. He had obviously studied Shuyun in the ring and purposely drew the contest out, hoping the monk would make a mistake. No one should test his patience against that of a Botahist monk.

Jaku was the one to err in the end, suddenly finding himself in a corner. But he would not surrender and wildly fought to gain an advantage, desperately using every bit of skill and strategy known to him. In the midst of a complex series of punches and kicks, Shuyun deflected a blow, and even as he did, he knew that *something* had happened, something unique. There had been no feeling, no touch. It was almost as though he had deflected the punch with chi alone!

And Jaku faltered. Only one with an altered time sense could have perceived it, so quickly did it pass, but Shuyun did not fail to mark it. The Black Tiger had *faltered!*

Surprise paralyzed Shuyun for a split second, and in that time his opponent recovered. The contest did not last long after that. Jaku's motivation seemed to have abandoned him.

Shuyun knew he had won a victory for his Order and hoped that it would restore respect for the monks of his faith as it was intended to do. He felt no personal pride in this, as was only proper. But his training could not stop him from feeling terrible doubts. What had happened in the ring with Jaku Katta?

It was not till several days later that Shuyun brought up the subject with Sotura. "Is it possible to deflect a blow with chi alone—without making contact with the body?"

The chi quan instructor had considered for a moment, as though the question was only of theoretical interest. "I do not know if it is possible. No such incident has been recorded, not even by the Perfect Master. This would seem to make it unlikely, Shuyun-sum. It is a good question for meditation, however."

Shuyun realized his perceptions must have been colored by the intensity of the moment. His teacher would certainly have noticed anything unusual.

Yet after this journey, Shuyun noticed that Sotura's attitude toward him had changed. He was still a junior Initiate, but he was treated differently somehow, as though he had earned greater respect. Shuyun found this both gratifying and, at the same time, unsettling.


A flock of water birds skittered away from the ship's bow, their sleep interrupted by the passing behemoth. Shuyun turned his mind from his memories, which he found endangered his sense of humility, and watched the clouds pass in front of the moon.

He voyaged again toward the Empire, this time to serve the man that Brother Satake had described as ". . . endlessly complex, as full of possibilities as the third move of the game of gii." The description would have applied to any number of Shonto lords back into antiquity when the House had first emerged as the *Sashei-no Hontto*. But by the time the Mibuki Dynasty had united the Seven Kingdoms the Sashei-no Hontto had become the Shonto, and they had begun what would become one of their consistent practices—they had married their first daughter to the heir of the Mibuki Emperor.

Hakata the Wise had been an advisor to the fourth heir of the Shonto House and had dedicated his great work, *The Analects,* to his Shonto liege-lord. The history of the Shonto continued in the same vein through all the years. Other Houses appeared, flowered and then wilted, often within a single season, but the Shonto endured. Certainly they had times when they seemed to be in disfavor with the gods, but these were short-lived and the House invariably emerged, stronger and richer than before. Of the Great Houses of Wa, very few exhibited such resilience.

The words of the Mori poetess, Nikko, came to him:

*The dew becomes frost*
*On frightened leaves,*
*And the seasons turn*
*Like a scroll*
*In the hands of the Shonto.*

Lord Shonto Motoru was presently without a wife, though he did maintain consorts, but by and large, the Lady Nishima had taken over the duties her mother had once so ably fulfilled. The Shonto household continued to run smoothly and their social events were still noted for their elegance and imagination.

A cloud obscured the moon from Shuyun's view and the wind seemed to ease a little. The island of Konojii was not far off and fear of the pirates that infested the coastline would begin the next morning and would not abate until the ship rounded Cape Ujii and entered the Coastal Sea.

From below, a woman emerged, her steps silent on the wooden deck. She was dressed in the manner of the women of the middle rank, yet she had a dignity and bearing that often comes to those who have suffered great loss or hardship and survived. Given a change of dress and a smile that appeared more easily, she could have been the wife of a minor lord. But her smile had been forgotten and she had been the spouse of Kogami Norimasa for seventeen years.

The match had been made when his future had looked very bright indeed. He, the scholar who had just passed the Imperial Examination, and she, the daughter of a minor general—that gentleman, at least, had seen the rightness of Kogami's career even if his own father could not. They had all had futures then, when the Hanama ruled, when the Interim Wars and the Great Plague were just muddled riddles that, only later, the soothsayers would claim were clear omens.

"Nori-sum?" she said as she approached her husband in the moonlight.

"How is she, Shikibu-sum? Has the priest eased her pain?"

"He has given her a potion that has made her drowsy." She reached out and found her husband's hand in the dark. Her voice quavered. "I wish we had asked the monk to see her. She is very ill. I have seen this before. I don't believe this is her spirit out of balance with her body. This pain and swelling on the side of her abdomen, it is poison collecting, I'm sure. I'm afraid for our daughter."

Kogami felt a growing sense of alarm. Ashigaru had assured him it was only a sickness of the sea and Kogami had believed that—he had needed to believe it. But what if the priest was wrong? What if this *was* poison collecting, as his wife said, and his daughter needed more help than this Tomsoian priest could give?

Ashigaru was the Emperor's man, as was Kogami Norimasa. And the monk, if not the Emperor's enemy, was at least perceived as a threat—though in some way that Kogami did not understand. There was no love between the followers of Botahara and the followers of Tomso. Kogami knew that the priest would be more than insulted if he suddenly were to ask him to step aside so that the monk could practice what the followers of Tomso called "heretical medicine."

"We must give the priest a little time, my faithful one," Kogami whispered. "If there is no improvement, we will ask the monk to see her."

"But . . ." Kogami held up his hand and his wife choked back a sob. "I apologize for this lack of control. I am not worthy of your respect. I will remove myself from your sight and sit with our daughter."

She turned to go, but he stopped her, his voice soft. "If she grows worse . . . send the servant to inform me."

He was alone again in the moonlight. The sea had eased its motion since the wind had abated, but Kogami did not notice—inside of him a storm grew.

The moon emerged from behind an almost perfectly oval cloud and took its place among the stars. The constellation called the Two-Headed Dragon appeared on the horizon, first one eye and then the other, peering out above the waves. A sail began to luff and two crewman hurried to tend it. Men went aloft to set a tri-sail as the wind fell off and a reef was let out of the main. The ship began to make way at renewed speed.

Around the iron tub that contained the charcoal fire, men gathered to brew cha. When they spoke at all, it was in whispers, the formality of cha drinking reduced, of necessity, to mere nods and half-bows aboard ship. In a most deferential manner, a sailor went to offer a steaming cup to the Botahist monk, but the young Initiate shook his head. If he spoke at all, Kogami could not hear him.

Kogami had approached the monk himself, earlier in the voyage, and had met with a similar rebuff. Having known the ways of the Botahist Brothers since his earliest days, Kogami had sought out the monk at a time when they could not be overheard and offered to make a "contribution" of fine cloth to the Brotherhood in return for a blessing. There was nothing uncommon in this and if the offer was made with tact (one did not go with the gift in one's hands), a refusal was unusual. Yet when he had finished his carefully worded speech, the monk had turned away, leaving Kogami in a most humiliating situation. Then without even looking at him, this boy-monk had said, "Give your fine cloth to someone who has need of it, then you will be blessed."

Kogami could not believe he had been witness to such a display of bad manners! He had been forced to walk away, his parting bow unreturned. What if that had been observed! He had never known such anger and shame. Even now he felt the humiliation as he recalled the event. The Botahist Brothers were capable of such hypocrisy, Kogami thought.

Botahara had taught that humility was the first step on the path to enlightenment, yet the monks who professed to walk this path displayed an arrogance that would shame a Mori prince. It was clear that this young monk needed some education, away from the confines of Jinjoh Monastery, for he did not yet understand the practices of his own Order.

Kogami tried to calm himself. Anger, he knew, would affect his ability to perform his duty to the Emperor, and he could not let this occur.

Kogami's anger was soon dissolved and not entirely as a result of his own efforts. His childhood teachings, learned at the feet of the Botahist Brothers, could never be entirely forgotten and a single phrase surfaced from his memory though he had tried to suppress it: "Give to those who have need and you will be blessed." So Botahara had answered a great prince who had come offering a gift in exchange for a blessing—a gift of cloth spun of gold.

Ashigaru appeared in the hatchway, his breathing loud as he labored up the steps from below. The smell of sanja "spirit flower" preceded him, its sickly-sweet aroma causing a chill of fear to course through Kogami. The dried petals of the sanja were scattered over the dead or those thought to be near death, to drive away evil spirits.

Kogami Norimasa's mouth went dry and his hands shook.

"Is she . . . is," his voice failed him and suddenly he found it hard to breathe. Reaching out for the rail, he steadied himself.

Ashigaru looked solemn but not at all hesitant. "She is in the hands of the gods. Whether they choose to take her now or return her to this plane is their matter. I have scattered the blossom of the sanctified flower around her. No evil spirits can possess her no matter what occurs."

"But *you* said it was only a sickness of the sea! You said it was *nothing*." Kogami spoke too loudly.

The priest drew himself up. "Don't tell me what I said or did not say! Do you not know your place? I have protected your daughter from spirits that would torment her for all eternity. Could you save her from this fate?" The priest tugged at his robe and glared off into the darkness. Yet he did not walk away as Kogami expected. Instead, he stepped closer. "Listen, Norimasa-sum," the priest said in a lowered voice, "we must not argue. We do *his* work, yeh?" And Kogami knew the priest was referring to the Emperor, not to the Father of Immortals. It was the first time either of them had acknowledged their true reason for being aboard.

"He can be generous . . ." Footsteps sounded on the stairs and the priest fell silent.

Kogami's wife stepped into the broken moonlight that fell between the rigging and the sails. Across the distance that divided them, Kogami tried desperately to read his wife's face but could not. She looked at the two men—and she hung her head. Then a sound, which neither man could hear, came to her from below and she raised her head, meeting their eyes.

Her face was beautiful in the moonlight, Kogami thought, beautiful and strong. She turned on her heel and strode across the deck to where the Botahist monk stood at the rail. Kogami Norimasa made no move to stop her, even though he felt his future slipping away like daylight over the horizon.

She cannot understand what this act will mean, Kogami thought. Even so, I bless her.

"What is she doing?" Ashigaru demanded.

"She is asking the Botahist monk to attend to our daughter." Kogami was gratified that his voice sounded calm. The Fates have decreed this, he thought, it is karma. One cannot fight the Two-Headed Dragon.

The Initiate monk, Shuyun, heard the woman's footsteps behind him and turned slightly. He had been expecting her to come—or her husband, the trader in cloth. It depended on how ill the daughter was. He had overheard the crew talking of the young woman's sickness and knew the Tomsoian priest had been asked to see her. So Shuyun had waited, knowing that if the girl were truly ill the parents would put their religious scruples aside and come to him, the only Botahist monk on board, the only person who understood the secrets of the body.

"Pardon my lack of manners," the woman said, an obvious forced calm in her voice. "I apologize for interrupting your meditations, honored Brother, but it is not for my sake that I do so." She bowed, formally. "I am Shikibu Kogami, wife of the merchant Kogami Norimasa-sum."

Shuyun nodded. "I am honored." He did not give his name as it was assumed that everyone aboard would know it.

"My daughter is very ill. She suffers from the gathering of poisons. The right side of her abdomen is afire with the signs of this. She is unable to move from her bed. Honored Brother, could you see her?"

"Is she not in the care of the Tomsoian priest, Shikibu-sum?"

"He has scattered the petals of the spirit flower over her and commended her into the care of the Immortals." She looked down at the deck. "He can do nothing for her. I am a follower of the True Path, Brother Shuyun, and say my devotions daily. She is my only daughter. I . . ." The woman's voice broke, but there were no tears.

"I will come," the monk said, looking into the woman's careworn face.

Descending into the dull lamplight of the aft cabins, Shuyun was confronted with the overpowering scent of the spirit flower. The Botahists always took this smell as a bad omen.

On deck a mere zephyr touched Kogami's neck and somehow that reinforced the tranquillity that had come over him when he saw his wife walk across the deck toward the Botahist Brother.

"The currents of Life cannot be refused. They are the only course possible. The most powerful Emperor may choose at what hour of the morning he will rise, but whether his spirit will slip away before the dawn, this he cannot order." So the teachings of Botahara read. Kogami felt every muscle in his body relax.

The priest grabbed his shoulder roughly, "You must stop her!" he hissed as the monk disappeared below.

"I cannot," Kogami said quietly, not even struggling to free himself. "You have given my daughter into the hands of the Immortal Ones. She is no longer your charge."

"Nor is she that monk's! You damn her for eternity. Do you not understand that? They defile the sanctified human form. Her spirit will be cursed and condemned to darkness!"

"But I can do nothing, Ashigaru-sum. The monk has been asked to attend her. I will not humiliate my wife by ordering him away."

"You will not humble yourself, you mean. You fear the boy: How could Jaku Katta-sum have chosen a coward for this matter?"

"And what of you, Ashigaru-sum? Will you defy the young Brother? Or has Jaku Katta chosen two cowards?" Kogami snorted, unable to contain his contempt for the priest any longer. He realized that the crew was watching, wondering what would happen, but it no longer mattered.

I cannot sacrifice my daughter to the Emperor's intrigues, he thought.

Unseen by the priest and the bureaucrat, a sailor slipped below to the captain's quarters.

The priest pulled himself up to his full height, staring down at the small man dressed like a successful trader. He gathered his robe about him and walked away with exaggerated dignity to the aft companionway.

Kogami Norimasa made no move to follow. The currents swirled about him, he would not struggle.

In the woman's cabin, the Botahist monk knelt in the lamplight beside the bed of the stricken girl. She lay, obviously drugged, yet still in considerable pain, and though she made no sound her eyes screamed with the effort. The maidservant had opened the girl's robe, shaking off the petals of the sanja flower. Shuyun could see the swelling—red, and radiating heat. The mother had understood, even if the fool of a priest had not.

"You must be still," Shuyun said, his voice strong and assured like one much older. "I will not hurt you. You need not worry."

She managed half a smile that dissolved into a shudder of pain.

The monk took a small crystal from a gold chain around his neck and held the cylinder lengthwise between his thumb and forefinger. A pale, green light seemed to come from within the polished stone, though it may have been only refracted moonlight. Moving the stone above the girl's skin, Shuyun slowly followed the lines of her life-force radiating out from the afflicted area, the stone amplifying his chi sense like a water-finder's rod.

The monk did not flinch when the door banged open, revealing the half-lit form of the Tomsoian priest. The women gasped and the girl flinched in fear, causing a new spasm of agony to course through her.

*"You damn your daughter to eternal darkness!"* the priest accused thickly, ignoring the monk who had risen fluidly from his knees and half-turned toward the door.

Shuyun spoke quietly to the two women so the girl would not hear. "I must have the ebony chest from my room *immediately*. There is little time."

"He will desecrate the sacred body. There is no forgiveness for this," the priest said, his voice rising.

No one moved. Shuyun glanced down at the girl who was bathed in sweat and shaking uncontrollably. It was almost too late for her. But there were edicts within his own Order forbidding any monk to do violence to a member of another church except in self-defense.

A sailor's face appeared in the dim passage behind the priest and Shuyun addressed him, ignoring all formality, "I must have the ebony chest from my quarters, immediately."

The man gave a quick bow and was gone. The priest and the monk stood facing each other across a space of two arm's lengths. One man's eyes burned with the fires of fanaticism and fear—the other's watched and measured. There was no fear.

The sailor appeared, carrying the dark wooden box, but the priest stood his ground and would not let him pass.

"I must have my trunk. Stand aside," Shuyun said, his voice still quiet, emotionless.

"You do not order *me!*"

From the hallway the captain's voice was added to the confrontation. "Ashigaru-sum, please, do as the Brother asks. I do not wish to have you removed."

The priest glanced over his shoulder, "To threaten me is to threaten my church. We bask in the light of the Son of Heaven. Already you have earned his disfavor, as has this *heretic,* this defiler of the spirit's vessel."

The captain did not respond. At sea his word was law, but he was no fool and knew that it was never wise to earn the Emperor's disfavor—not *this* Emperor.

The situation was in danger of losing all motion, and Shuyun knew he couldn't allow that, couldn't wait for the captain to weigh the situation. He took a step forward, his eyes never leaving the large man blocking the door. The priest's eyes flared and his hand moved imperceptibly toward his left wrist, a subtle motion, almost impossible to see in the dim light.

Yes, Shuyun thought, that is where the knife is. He changed the position of his hands to counter this threat and sank lower on his leading leg. They were an arm's length apart now and Shuyun altered his time sense, slowing the world around him.

But the priest suddenly froze in his place, like a man who has seen a sand-cobra rise before him, and the monk stopped in mid-stride.

"Stand aside. I must have my chest."

"You dare not," the priest hissed, the air rasping out of constricted lungs. There was sweat on the man's brow, though the night was turning cool.

"Now," Shuyun said, his voice calm in the room charged with tension.

The older man felt his pulse begin to race out of control.

"I have the Emperor's protection!" he almost pleaded.

In the dim light, the monk's movements were barely seen. There was a sound of cloth tearing and then he stood with the priest's knife in his own hand. Through the scent of sanja flower, he could smell the poison on the blade's tip. The priest had lost his balance as he stepped back, now totally overcome by fear. Hands caught him, taking his arms. He gasped but could not find air. He did not notice when a second knife disappeared from his sash. He was half-carried, half-dragged onto the deck. For an instant his eyes met Kogami Norimasa's. The trader did not look away to spare the priest from embarassment. Kogami Norimasa smiled openly.

He gloats, the priest thought, unable in his state to feel anger. Two sailors held him as he leaned over the rail and was violently ill, completing his public humiliation. Ashigaru sank to the deck in a heap, his beard and clothing soiled. His mind whirled. The monk must die, screamed his thoughts. The trader must pay! May this ship and all aboard her be swallowed by the ocean!

For a moment he fell into utter darkness, and when he returned to his senses he was sure that the monk had opened him with his own knife, releasing his spirit which had then appeared in a hall before the seated form of Botahara. The Enlightened One had barely looked at him before pronouncing him unfit to return to Life as a human. Botahara had turned over a sand glass on a stand and the grains had fallen like feathers through the air—so slowly. Ashigaru's new life would be thus—interminable, without event.

The priest shook his head to clear it. The deck hurt his back and his leg lay twisted under him where he had fallen like a drunk in his own vomit. The sky spun overhead when he moved, so he lay still watching the masts sway among the stars. The air was cool and the moon stared at him openly, unmoved by his fall. Soon the anger would return, the hatred.

\*    \*    \*

More lamps had been brought to the cabin and the mother asked to leave. Shuyun raised the empty cup that sat beside the bed. He smelled it.

"Was this the only thing the priest gave her?"

The maid servant nodded. Shuyun set the cup back in its rack. For a change, one of the priests had not done his charge irreparable harm. Loda root, the sleeping draught. The girl would survive the potion's after-effects, which were considerable.

Several wide sashes had been used to restrain the patient, but they did not stop her from shaking or reduce the pain. Shuyun held her head gently and opened one eye to the light. He nodded. The maidservant knelt to one side, ready to assist him without question. She was a good choice, the monk realized. She had all the signs of one who had seen many births and had nursed countless of her charges through their childhood illnesses. She also had utter faith in the Botahist trained.

From a silk case, Shuyun removed needles of silver and gold, sterilizing each one before carefully inserting the point into the girl's skin. The chi flow of her body was interrupted, and suddenly there was no pain. The girl's face softened, and her breathing became regular, almost normal.

The edge of the tiny knife was unimaginably sharp. When Shuyun drew it across the girl's skin, she felt nothing. The monk was not a second too soon.

The priest Ashigaru mounted the steps leading from below. He ignored Shikibu Kogami seated on a cushion outside her cabin door. Ashigaru had washed and changed, and though he still felt weakened and unwell his anger carried him onto the deck. Ignoring the staring eyes, he crossed immediately to Kogami Norimasa who still held his position by the rail. All caution was abandoned now. The priest didn't care who saw them talking. He had decided on his course of action.

He grabbed Kogami's sleeve, roughly, and spun the smaller man around. "Now, Kogami Norimasa, you will earn your rewards." The man's voice was a hoarse whisper.

"Everyone watches," Kogami protested.

"Let them watch and damn them for it!"

"Ashigaru-sum, please!" The trader was alarmed by the man's manner and by the frenzy in his voice.

"Listen to me, Kogami," the priest spat out the man's name, "Jaku Katta will hear of your treachery. You have my word that if you do not follow my instructions now, you will not pass beyond the docks with your head on your shoulders. Katta-sum has no patience with failure and I do not intend to try *that one's* patience."

"But I . . . I was only ordered to observe, to report. I . . ."

"You lie, Kogami Norimasa. You were ordered to assist me and assist me you will. That, or you will lose more than your recent promotions. Do you understand?"

The smaller man nodded, unable to answer. The hand that held him shook with anger, and the priest's eyes were wilder than ever.

Looking around him for the first time, the priest caught the stares of the crewmen, even as they turned away to avoid his eyes.

"Take this," Ashigaru said, slipping a small packet into Kogami's hand and closing the unwilling fingers around it. "When the young Brother has finished damning your daughter to the Netherworld you must take him some cha. No doubt he will be grateful. Make sure the cha is strong and that the contents of the packet which I have given you is stirred into it.

"Your head hangs in the balance, Kogami Norimasa, *Functionary of the Second Rank*. The monk need only drink the cha. No one will know it was poisoned. You will not be held accountable by the Imperial Courts, I guarantee it. After all, the monk has saved your daughter. How could you wish him harm?

"Remember Jaku Katta of the flashing sword and let the memory of such a worthy general bring you strength."

The priest bowed formally to Kogami Norimasa who returned the gesture as if in a dream.

He felt himself being swept along on the outgoing tide, beyond safety, beyond hope. He gripped the wooden rail with both hands and stared down into the rushing water. A glowing path of phosphorescence stretched out along the ship's wake. He felt the tiny package in his sleeve pocket as it brushed against him. I am going to take the life of a Botahist Brother, he thought. What karma will I acquire! It will not matter that I am not blamed. He tried to work some saliva into his mouth but couldn't.

I have no stomach for murder, he thought, no stomach at all. How could my life have come to this?

"Pride," a small voice said from within. "Pride has brought you to this. Your life was good and yet you walked around as if under a dark cloud. Always wanting more. Humility, Botahara taught, humility."

*I will not face Jaku Katta,* his mind screamed! He could see the point of Jaku's famous sword arcing toward him.

And so he stood at the rail in the moonlight, a soft zephyr caressing him, Kogami Norimasa, the Emperor's servant, the Brotherhood's student—a man entirely at sea. Before him the Two-Headed Dragon had risen and stretched its wings across the southern sky. I am doomed, Kogami thought, and knew it to be true.

The monk emerged from below and spotted Kogami Norimasa leaning against the rail. He crossed the deck to where the man stood, and the trader jumped when the monk cleared his throat.

"May your harmony return within the hour, Norimasa-sum. I believe your daughter will recover entirely, though she will be very weak and should not be moved any distance for several days after we have docked. You may look in on her, but do not wake her."

Kogami Norimasa put his hand to his face and seemed close to breaking down but took a series of deep breaths and regained a semblance of control.

"I do not know a way to express my gratitude for what you have done, Brother Shuyun. Nothing one such as myself can do would begin to repay the debt I owe to you."

"I am a student of the Great Knowledge. How could I have done otherwise?"

Kogami Norimasa bowed deeply. "It moves me, Brother, to find one who follows the Way so completely. To meet you is a great honor." Kogami, the bureaucrat, was shocked·by the sincerity of his own words.

Shuyun bowed slightly in return. He realized now that the trader had at one time been a student of the Botaharist Brothers. The signs were all there, the inflection and the careful choice of words. The posture, the mixture of fear, awe, and suppressed resentment that so many students developed. Yet the man wore no prayer beads or icon to Botahara and he associated freely with the Tomsoian priest. *A lost one*, Shuyun concluded.

"If you wish to see your daughter now, you may," Shuyun repeated thinking the man had not understood.

"First, allow me to bring you some cha," and before Shuyun could answer, the trader-in-cloth was on his way to the charcoal fire amidship.

Shuyun watched the man go, but his attention was diverted by the sight of the priest who was seated, almost hidden, in the shadow of the foresail on the ship's bow. That priest bears watching, Shuyun thought. A man who feels he has been humiliated is a dangerous man. But he was confident that the priest was a physical coward. Ashigaru would never confront him again. Even so, Shuyun regretted the incident. If the girl's life had not been in danger, he would not have allowed the confrontation to develop. There was enough tension between the two faiths as it was, and though everyone believed that the Emperor's interest in the Magic Cults was for purely political reasons this still gave the Tomsoian priests an advantage. The Emperor was unpredictable and could use an incident between the faiths as an excuse to try to suppress the Botahists. For this reason, the Botahists restricted their activities and waited. It was only a matter of time. The followers of Tomso were without discipline or patience and their use to the Emperor was limited.

Shuyun could see Kogami's back as the man bent over his cha preparation. He was taking unusual care, it seemed. Gratitude, Shuyun thought.

Finally the trader rose and started across the deck, which now barely rocked on the quiet seas, yet Kogami stared intently at the two cups he carried as though spilling a drop would mean the loss of all his family honor. The moon was obscured again by clouds and Shuyun had trouble making out the trader's face as he approached, but Shuyun sensed *wrongness* in the man's carriage. All his years of training came suddenly to focus on the man before him. Shuyun knew the feeling well and had been taught to trust it completely. He controlled his breathing and took the first step into chi ten—time slowed and suddenly the trader seemed to float toward him, each step stretched to many seconds.

It is there, Shuyun thought, in the voice of his body, the wrongness. The monk waited now, waited for the knowledge that would come from his focus. He made himself an empty vessel, easier for the understanding to fill him.

And so it arrived, not like a flash, but like a long-familiar memory, one that had no surprise attached to it—and no doubts. It was there, in the merchant's right hand, the wrongness, like a knife concealed in a sash. Yet it was only a cup of cha. Shuyun could smell the herb in the air.

The merchant came floating to a stop like a man in a dream, while everything about him screamed fear and guilt and sorrow.

Is it possible that anyone could not see this, Shuyun asked himself? Can people be that blind? The man's fear was more obvious than the look of a lover for his beloved. Shuyun could smell the fear in the man—a pungent tang coloring his sweat. But it was not the monk that the merchant feared—at least not entirely—Shuyun was sure of that. But what was it?

"My daughter has been . . ." the merchant started, words coming with great difficulty, "the greatest source of joy in all of my life, though I have not always known it. I can only offer you this small token, for there is no way that I may express the gratitude which I feel." The merchant bowed and proffered a cup to Shuyun, but it was from his *left* hand!

Shuyun did not return the bow but nodded at the cha Kogami still held. "Why have you chosen this?" The smell came to the monk now—faint, so faint—the poison.

The merchant fought to maintain his control. Without answering, he began to raise the cha to his mouth, but the monk's hand was there, stopping him. The fingers rested so lightly that Kogami could barely feel them, yet he could not raise his arm. His hand trembled with the effort.

"Why have you chosen this?" Shuyun asked again.

"Please," the man whispered, his dignity beginning to dissolve, "do not interfere, Brother."

But still Shuyun restrained the man, seemingly without effort. "But that cup was to be mine."

The merchant's eyes widened and he shook his head choking back a sob. "Not now, not now. . . ." He stared down into the steaming cup. "Karma," he whispered. Then he looked up to meet Shuyun's eyes. "It is not the place of a follower of the Way to interfere in a matter of . . . continuance. It is the law of your Order."

The monk gave a slight nod and his hand was gone from Kogami's arm.

The merchant released a long sigh that rattled in his throat. "Listen, Brother, here is my . . . death poem," he said, forcing the words out.

> *"Though long veiled by clouds*
> *And light,*
> *Always it has awaited me,*
> *The Two-Headed Dragon.*

Beware of the priest, Brother. Beware of his master."
The man drank off the poisoned cha and dropped the cup over the side. The desperation in his eyes was replaced now by utter and total defeat.

"May you attain perfection in your next lifetime," the monk whispered, and bowed formally.

Kogami Norimasa crossed the deck and seated himself in a position of meditation in the shadows. He composed his mind, hoping that, in his last moments, the poison would not rob him of all dignity. He tried to fill his mind with the presence of his wife and daughter, and when the end came, these were his final thoughts.

# Three

Lord Shonto Motoru was in a state of extreme harmony with both himself, which was usual, and with the world, which was less common. He rode in a sampan sculled by four of his best boatmen and guarded by nine of his select guards. Ahead of him were two identical boats and behind three more. All had a large man and an elegantly kimonoed young woman seated inside, only partly visible through side curtains.

The canal they moved along was lined by high walls of plaster and stone, broken only by the arched entrances onto the waterway. Each entrance had solid gates extending to the water from which point metal grillwork descended to an underwater wall. Behind these well guarded facades stood the residences of the hereditary aristocracy of the Empire of Wa. Out of the walled gardens drifted occasional strains of music, laughter, the acrid odor of burning charcoal, perhaps a hint of perfume.

"I thought you said you were feeling secure, Uncle?" the young woman said. She was, in fact, his legally adopted daughter but had called him uncle from the day she could form the word and still persisted in its use, sometimes even in public.

"I am feeling secure, Nishi-sum, which is to say that tonight I'm not concerned about what the Emperor may be plotting. He needs me, for the moment. As to any others who may wish me short life—I'm a little more cautious. Thus the decoys, if that is why you ask. Security, as you can see, is a relative term." He laughed.

"I think you are only happy when you are going off

to war," Nishima said. Pulling the curtain aside slightly, she peered out to assess their progress, and there, riding the surface of the canal, was her reflection, wavering like a flame. My eyes are too large, she thought and closed them slightly, but it then looked as though she were squinting so she gave it up. Her long, black hair, worn up in a formal style, was held in place by simple, wooden combs, inlaid with a motif of fine silver. She took one last look at herself, sighed, and jerked the curtain closed. The Lady Nishima Fanisan Shonto did not agree with the general assessment that she was a great beauty. To her eye, the bones of her face were too strong, her eyes the wrong shape, and, worst of all, she was too tall. She did not consider the mirror her friend.

"How long will this campaign against the northern barbarians take?"

"Not more than half a year, though I will stretch it out to the tenth moon. It is always dangerous to be too successful in battle. The Emperor is not too secure himself, yeh? But for now he needs me and we both know it."

"It would be good if your Spiritual Advisor would arrive in time to accompany us. That would be a great help, yeh?"

"Ah, I have not told you? He came to Yankura this morning. I received word from Tanaka. He calls our new Brother 'a fine young colt in need of breaking.' "

"The monk has been sent to the right liege-lord then, Uncle. Do you know anything about him?"

"I have a full report. He seems to be somewhat special, even for a Botahist Initiate, very skilled as a doctor, very learned. I have a letter from him—the brush work is superb! I must show it to you." He paused to pull a curtain aside a fraction of an inch to check their progress.

"Tell me, Nishi-sum, do you remember going to the River Festival in the year I married your mother?"

"Oh, yes, I could never forget that festival, Uncle, we had been in hiding for so many long months and then suddenly we were secure. What a beautiful autumn that was."

"I seem to remember that as being the year the young Botahist Neophyte bested some of the strongest fighters I have ever seen, including one of my own lieutenants on whom I had bet heavily."

"Yes, I remember. I wanted you to bet on the monk because he was so small and showed no fear, but as usual you ignored my excellent advice."

"You were precocious even then. Well, I may be wrong, but I believe that boy is our new advisor. *Brother Shuyun,* does that sound familiar?"

"Shuyun . . . yes, that could be. If it is the same monk, you will have to rebuke him for causing his liege-lord such a great loss of money." They both laughed, and then fell silent, lost in their memories.

When Nishima resumed the conversation, it was on a more subdued note. What of Lord Shidaku, Uncle, now that he has failed to contain the barbarians?"

"Lord Shidaku is a great administrator and a terrible general. The Emperor sent him to Seh to deal with the problems left by the old bureaucracy, before the raids began. He was never meant to be a military leader. The Emperor acknowledges this and has transferred Lord Shidaku to his personal council. Lord Shidaku has thus been honored and his failure to contain the barbarians . . . overlooked. The Emperor is seldom so wise—good administrators are rarer than good generals, if the truth be known."

The sampans turned into another canal, and the wall of the Emperor's palace grounds appeared on the left. Guards on regularly spaced towers saluted as the water-borne entourage passed.

"Ah, you're a governor now, Sire, see how they honor you."

Shonto grunted, refusing to look.

"So, Nishi-sum, how will the Emperor entertain his guests tonight?"

"Dancers, certainly. They are his favorites, for obvious reasons. Perhaps a short play. The finest foods, of course. Music. Maybe a poetry contest, which you will not be allowed to enter because of your esteemed father's reputation."

"Good. Unlike my father, I could not win the Emperor's poetry contest if my life depended on it. But you, my only daughter, are the one who should not be allowed to enter! I will bet on you if there is a contest." He checked their progress again.

"Which of the Emperor's sons will pay court to you tonight, Nishi-sum?"

"You tease, Uncle. The sons of the Emperor will not notice such a plain-face as me. Nor would I want them to. Boors! All three of them!"

"But Nishi-sum, I have it on good authority that Prince Wakaro holds you in high esteem."

"Oh, Uncle, you must be teasing. You know I aspire to the life of a painter, or perhaps a poet. I would be miserable married to an insensitive oaf!"

"Oh, you are too great an artist to marry an Emperor's son?"

Nishima colored. "Certainly not now, but who can tell what the future will bring. Women produce all the finest art in the Empire, no one can deny it. Don't laugh! I challenge you to name seven great male artists."

"Haromitsa, Nokiyama, Basko . . . Minitsu made some fine paintings . . ."

"Already you are grasping at shoots. You see, it could be a crime against our culture to make me a wife!"

Shonto laughed derisively. "I am your *father* and your *liege-lord*. If I decide that it is in your best interest to marry someone as *unworthy* as an Emperor's son—someone who could himself be Emperor one day—then you will do so!"

Lady Nishima lowered her head. "Yes, Sire. Please excuse my bad manners. I have acted in a manner unworthy of your respect."

"I will consider this apology."

They sat in silence until the sampan turned into the palace gate and then Nishima spoke. "Satsam, Rhiyama, and Doksa the print maker."

"I was getting to them."

"Yes, Sire." Nishima tried to hide her smile.

The sampans docked at a stone stairway and the boatmen scrambled off to hold the craft steady. An aide to the Emperor hurried down the steps. Lord Shonto held the curtain aside so the guards could see that no one was hidden inside.

The aide bowed as Lord Shonto and his daughter stepped ashore. They were escorted up the steps by the black-clad Palace Guard to a large open house with a massive, winglike tile roof set on carved, wooden posts. Shonto removed his sword and handed it to one of his own guard, for no one went armed into the Emperor's presence except select members of the Imperial Guard. Assassination had too long been a tool of aspiring sons and ambitious peers for those who sat on the Dragon Throne not to have learned caution.

The sound of flutes and harps came from one of the gardens and kites of every shape and color decorated the wind.

"The Emperor is receiving his guests in the Garden of the Rising Moon beside the Seahorse Pond. Would you like an escort, Lord Shonto?"

"I know my way, thank you."

The aide bowed and Shonto nodded in return. They walked under a long portico built in the same style as the gate house. To their right, a glimmering pool descended in three falls—the Pool of the Sun—full of flashing sunfish. Beyond this stood the most intricate hedge-maze in the Empire, planted by the ruler Shunkara VII nearly four hundred years earlier.

The Island Palace was the Emperor's primary residence and it was impressive not only for its size but for the astonishing beauty so many centuries of royalty had created. Originally built at the beginning of the Mori dynasty the Island Palace had been razed by fire and rebuilt three times in six hundred years. The buildings were from five distinct periods yet placed in such a manner that harmony was never broken. The finest artisans, in a culture rich in artisans, had wrought and painted and carved and sculpted in an attempt to create perfection on earth.

At the end of the portico was a terrace of colored stone which looked southeast into the Garden of the Rising Moon. The Seahorse Pond bordered the garden's farthest edge. A wooden stage had been erected on the pond's shore and within viewing distance in front of it stood a raised dais under an ornate silken canopy. A line of guests moved past the dais beneath which the Emperor sat, now hidden from Shonto's view.

Perhaps two hundred Imperial Guards surrounded the Emperor on three sides, kneeling in rows that radiated out from the jade-colored canopy. A dragon design was woven into this semicircle by the clever placement of guards in crimson to form the spread Dragon Fan of the Imperial family.

His Imperial Highness, the Most Revered Son of Heaven, Exalted Emperor of the Nine Provinces of Wa and the Island of Konojii, Lord of all the World's Oceans, Akantsu II was a small, dark man of fifty-two years.

His father, Akantsu I, had founded the Imperial line of the Yamaku when he had ascended the throne during the chaos of the Great Plague that had decimated the population a decade and a half earlier. The former Imperial family, the Hanama, had fallen victim to the disease as it swept through the capital and there had been no hesitation by any number of pretenders, both legitimate and not so, to take the fallen family's place.

The struggle for the Dragon Throne had been short and brutal, and the outcome as much a matter of chance as martial skill. In the end, the faction that lost the fewest men to plague emerged victorious. The civil war lasted little more than three years, yet it was long enough to shake the Empire to its ancient foundations. Minor families rose to the status of Great House overnight, because of their role in a single key battle. Foot-soldiers became generals and generals peers, as the rigid social structure of the Empire crumbled.

After two hundred and fifty years of relative peace

and economic prosperity under the Hanama dynasty, the line had ended in disease and flame. A third of the population had died before the Botahist Brotherhood found the key to both immunization and cure. The social fabric of Wa had been torn beyond restoration and, under the Yamaku, order wasn't a priority. The roads beyond the inner provinces were unsafe to all but the largest parties; pirates infested the coastline and private wars abounded—and the Emperor obviously believed this state of affairs was to his advantage.

In constant fear of being deposed, the Emperor had devised a number of methods to keep the aristocracy resident in the capital where the Imperial troops were supreme. By dividing the year into four "Social Seasons" the ruler could then "invite" the lords he most feared to attend whichever seasons he chose, being careful to separate any potential alliances by keeping some members isolated in the provinces. Refusing the Emperor's invitation was an open act of treason, and staying in the capital when your presence had not been requested led to immediate suspicion on the part of the Emperor's guard.

To further his control, Akantsu II had disallowed the use of any harbor but Yankura, the Floating City, for the importation of trade goods and made death the penalty for smuggling. All trade could then be easily taxed by the Imperial customs officials as well as monitored by the ever present Imperial Guard. This way, other harbors—traditionally under the control of a single powerful lord—could not be used as an excuse to create large armed forces for "security" reasons. The Emperor was thorough in his bid to hold all the reins of power.

Despite his lavish parties and his love of the social life, Akantsu II remained an enigma, even to those closest to him. His unpredictability did not win him friends, as he was known to ignore acts of loyalty as often as he rewarded them. The physical life was what drew him—hunting, hawking, dance. He sponsored kick boxing tournaments often and was known to be a fine swordsman and without fear. He had once dispatched an assassin, unaided, and then personally beheaded all the guards on duty for their failure to protect him. Like his father, Akantsu II was a formidable man.

As Lord Shonto and Lady Nishima descended the stairs, they could see the Emperor seated on a cushion, talking with his guests. His kimono was Imperial crimson belted with a gold sash, and he held the sword of his office across his lap in a jeweled scabbard. The Empress was conspicuously absent, and though she was said to be ill it was well known that she was out of favor. A young and exquisitely beautiful Sonsa dancer was the Emperor's current mistress—that is, she was preferred among a half-dozen.

"There is your cousin, Kitsu-sum," Lord Shonto said as they crossed the garden.

"Oh, good. I must talk with her."

"She is your competition for the Emperor's sons, I think."

"Thank you for pointing that out, Sire."

"That is, unless I marry her first. She's not very pretty, but I have great affection for her."

"She's the most beautiful woman either of us know, and you dote on her." Nishima chided.

"Huh! I'm far too old to indulge such weaknesses."

The Lady Kitsura Omawara saw them coming across the garden and favored them with her famous smile. Numerous hearts began to flutter. She walked toward her cousin and Shonto. Her kimono, a print of butterflies in flight, hung perfectly, the long sleeves swaying as she moved. Silver combs with jade inlay held up her dark hair and her eyes were highlighted by the most subtle use of makeup. She was a woman used to the sound of flattery.

"Kitsura-sum, you are the reincarnation of all the Empire's great beauties!" Nishima said, taking her cousin's hands.

"Lord Shonto," Kitsura said, bowing. "Cousin, how lovely you look. And, Lord Shonto, I believe you grow younger by the day."

Shonto bowed lower than his position required. "I was just telling Nishima-sum that your kimono is ill-fitting, you're skinny for your age and you walk like a boy, but because I am so fond of you, I will offer to take you from your father's house."

Both women laughed. Kitsura bowed deeply. "You do me too much honor, Sire. I think you try to turn my head with flattery. Truly you are your father's son. But I am too naive and inexperienced for a man like you. I would not allow my father to take advantage of your kind nature."

"It is a small thing. My house is full of stray cats already. Look at Nishi-sum. Ungrateful daughter that she is, I have affection for her all the same. Charity toward the undeserving must be a weakness of mine."

"You see what I must live with, Kitsura-sum? I think the Emperor would reward us if we pushed his new governor into the Seahorse Pond. Otherwise he will bankrupt the province of Seh by filling the Governor's Palace with 'stray cats.' "

"We will have to ask the Emperor's permission in this matter." She turned to look at the dais, but then became more solemn. "I think the Emperor will request that you play for his guests, Nishi-sum. I have already been asked, and could not refuse. I hope you won't be angry, but I suggested you might consider a duet with me?"

"Oh, no! I have not practiced. What will we play?"

"Play the 'Song of the Enchanted Gardener' " Lord Shonto offered.

"You and your *Enchanted Gardener*, Uncle. Don't you ever tire of hearing it?"

"Can one tire of perfection?"

Nishima rolled her eyes. "Now we will receive a lecture in the philosophy of aesthetics. Run, Kitsura-sum, I will try to hold him!"

They laughed as they crossed the garden toward the receiving line. A gong sounded, announcing the hour of the cat. It was near dusk and servants began lighting colored lanterns.

Lord Shonto and Lady Nishima stopped several times to greet guests and exchange news.

At one point Nishima touched her uncle's arm and whispered to him, "There is Lady Okara, the painter."

The woman stood among a throng who seemed to be her personal court. It was obvious that they hung on her every word.

"She is almost never seen at social gatherings. I must try to work up my nerve to meet her."

"I will introduce you, Nishima-sum, she is an old friend."

"Don't tease me, Uncle, this is a serious matter. She is the most accomplished painter of the century! I have admired her work for years."

"I do not tease. Come, flutter your eyelashes at the Emperor and then I will introduce you to your goddess."

The line moved along very slowly, the guests trying to hold the Emperor's attention as long as they could, thus signifying to what degree they had the ruler's favor. In their turn, they knelt before the dais on a grass mat and touched their heads to the ground. The Emperor never rose or bowed to his subjects but nodded slightly to recognize their presence. Lord Shonto and Lady Nishima were announced by an aide and bowed low, remaining in the kneeling position.

"Lord Shonto, Lady Nishima, I am honored that you have come."

"The honor, Sire, is ours entirely," Lord Shonto answered for both of them, as his position required.

The Emperor turned his attention to Nishima as if there was a matter of great importance that demanded immediate attention. "Lady Nishima, I wish to ask you a great favor."

"Name it, Sire, and I shall comply."

"We have already asked Lady Kitsura if she would play for our guests and she has honored me by agreeing. Would you accompany her?"

"I am hardly a musician of sufficient skill to perform for such an esteemed audience, but as the Emperor asks, it would be my honor to do so.

"I must apologize though, Sire, for I failed to anticipate this request and did not bring an instrument."

"One shall be found for you, then, one that I'm sure will be to your liking. What will you play, Lady?"

"Certainly we would allow the Emperor to make that decision if the selection is within our skills."

"Wonderful! Do you know the 'Song of the Enchanted Gardener'?"

"Yes, Sire. A lovely melody and a fine choice."

"Good, good!" He broke into a toothy grin which disappeared just as quickly.

Turning to Lord Shonto, the Emperor changed his tone of address and immediately had the attention of all those around him.

"Lord Shonto Motoru, Imperial Governor of the Province of Seh, as I have invested you, when do you leave to protect our northern border?"

"Within the week, Sire. My household and my forces prepare."

"You are efficient as well as courageous. How long will it take to teach the barbarian rabble proper respect for the Emperor of Wa?"

"I have sent my son ahead to assess the situation and have not yet received his report but, even so, I hope the campaign will be short."

"The barbarians are poor students, but I send them my best teacher. A year, then?"

"A year should be adequate. Lessons learned too quickly are most easily forgotten."

Rising to his full sitting height, the Emperor said, "Do you hear? The new Governor of Seh will cleanse our northern border of the barbarians in one year!" He bowed slightly to Shonto and said, his voice surprisingly cold, "I salute you, Lord Shonto."

The assembled guests followed the Emperor's example and also bowed to the kneeling lord. The gathering became unnaturally quiet, and Lord Shonto felt a sudden chill.

Nishima became aware that she was being stared at and noticed out of the corner of her eye that Prince Wakaro, the Emperor's middle son, was kneeling at one side of the dais. She was careful not to meet his eyes.

The Emperor raised his hand to an aide. He did not bother to look at him, and the man hurried forward carrying a silken pillow across which lay a sword in a very old scabbard. The Emperor took the weapon, unsheathing it and examining it with an expert's care. Shonto felt the skin of his scalp tighten.

"Do you know this blade, Lord Shonto?"

"No, Sire," Shonto said, his voice perfectly calm. Conversation flared suddenly, then quieted at the sight of the weapon.

Looking up from the sword, apparently satisfied, the Son of Heaven smiled, but his eyes were hard. "This sword belonged to the famous ancestor for whom you were named, Lord Shonto Motoru, who gave it as a gift to the Emperor Jirri II, his close friend. The Emperor and Shonto Motoru later fought and conquered the northern barbarians in the time of their greatest power, as you no doubt know. Sadly, Lord Shonto was killed by an arrow in the final battle." The Emperor tested the sword's edge with his thumbnail. "This is a gift to you, Lord Governor." The Emperor's expression was unreadable.

The aide came forward again, taking the sword from his master and placing it on the mat before Shonto.

"This is a great honor, Sire. I will always endeavor to be worthy of it." The ritual words seemed strangely hollow to Lord Shonto.

"See that you do. Put it in your sash, Motoru-sum. You may wear a sword in my presence."

Shonto bowed his head to the mat before taking up the weapon. "I will wear it always for the Emperor's protection, Sire."

"We must speak again later." Around them the sound of conversation resumed. "Lady Nishima, we look forward to your recital."

Lord Shonto and Nishima bowed once more, rose, and backed away. A young man dressed in the black kimono with the Dragon Fan of the Emperor's staff stepped forward.

"Lady Nishima, I have an instrument for you, and the Lady Kitsura awaits. May I escort you?"

Nishima touched her uncle's arm. "Remember, you promised me an introduction." There was much unsaid between them as she turned to join her cousin.

Shonto watched his daughter as she disappeared into the crowd, her long sleeves dancing as she moved. She is precious to me, he thought, and this is a dangerous time for such feelings.

He turned toward a table laden with food, his hand resting on the unfamiliar hilt of the ancient sword of his namesake. Lady Okara appeared among the river of passing faces. She bowed to Shonto, who returned the formality with equal courtesy. Without any discussion they began to walk toward the edge of the garden, away from the press of people.

Large, flat stones had been arranged along the pond's shore in a pattern of studied randomness, asymmetry being one of the laws of Waian art. Stepping out onto these islands of granite the two old friends were alone.

"So Mito-sum, I have just watched as you were honored and threatened at the same time," Lady Okara said. She was a tall woman with immense dignity and presence and Shonto admired her greatly.

"It was quite a performance." Shonto seemed to consider for a moment and his body visibly relaxed. "No matter. Tell me, Lady Okara, how has the Emperor tempted you to one of these—what is the term you use?—social dog fights?"

"He used the greatest of all coercions—he appealed to my vanity. The Lady Okara is here to be honored, and one does not refuse to be honored by one's Emperor.

"He has had my *Twenty-one Views of the Grand Canal* set to dance. I admit to being curious as to how this has been done. I might add that I'm more than a little suspicious. Art is not something that the Yamaku have ever shown an interest in." She reached out and the hand which squeezed Lord Shonto's was cold. "What possible use can he have for me, Mito-sum?"

"I can't imagine, so perhaps the compliment is real. You richly deserve it, you know."

"Even you have become a flatterer!"

"I see your lovely daughter is with you, Mito-sum. You've waited a long time to find her a husband, yeh?"

Shonto shrugged.

"Perhaps the Emperor will choose his heir soon and that will help you with your decision?"

"That doesn't seem likely," Lord Shonto sighed and looked over his shoulder. "He doesn't think that anyone is fit to replace him on the Dragon Throne, including his sons. This makes all of them somewhat less suitable as husbands."

"But if one of these sons had a good advisor, he might last long enough to pass the Throne to *his* son, making the mother very important."

"The Shonto family have never had designs on the Throne, Okara-sum, everyone knows that. I don't think my grandson will carry the Sword of Imperial office, and that does not concern me.

"Finding Nishi-sum a suitable husband, without insulting the Imperial family—*that* is my real problem."

"She carries too much of the old Imperial blood for her own good. If you marry her to the Yamaku, you strengthen their claim, and if you marry her elsewhere her sons will always be a danger to the Emperor. I don't know anyone who has enough power to risk having her as a bride."

"You're right, Okara-sum, there's no one—not now."

"Poor girl." The woman's voice was sad. "She is a soldier on a vast gii board."

"She is the *Empress*, but refuses to recognize it. Nishima-sum would like nothing better than to marry a poet and spend the rest of her life pursuing art—but this is not possible."

"A life in art is not as easy as it sounds, Mito-sum. I know."

They turned away from the Seahorse Pond after allowing themselves one last moment to enjoy its reflecting beauty. Their conversation turned to less private matters as they rejoined the other guests.

"I must introduce you to Nishima-sum. She idolizes you."

"Best she meet me, then, and learn that I am human— I would be happy to receive her."

Servants were spreading straw mats and cushions on the lawn before the stage and the guests had already begun to seat themselves in anticipation of the night's entertainment. Shonto and Lady Okara chose a position off to one side nearer the back. Better places were available for people of their rank, but Shonto wanted to be able to watch both the stage and the Emperor. He had not survived as long as he had by missing opportunities to scrutinize those in power.

Cushions were arranged on the stage and a harp of carved ivory set before them. When everyone was seated, a man of the Imperial court, a scholar of some note, appeared on the stage and bowed twice—once kneeling, for the Emperor, and once very low but standing, to the audience. The first full moon of autumn showed its copper rim on cue.

"Honored guests of the Emperor of Wa," the scholar began, "the Emperor has asked the Lady Nishima Fanisan Shonto and the Lady Kitsura Omawara to honor his assembled guests with a recital of the 'Song of the Enchanted Gardener.'" The man bowed to the curtain from behind which the Ladies Kitsura and Nishima emerged. They bowed twice and took up their places before the attentive audience.

In her hand Kitsura held a silver flute almost half her height in its length and Nishima sat poised behind the harp. They began.

The flute and harp followed each other in delicate measure, through the three movements without hesitation or error. It was clear the cousins had played this piece together many times. Out of the corner of his eye Shonto watched the Emperor. He could see the middle son sitting to one side of the dais watching the performance raptly. Yes, Shonto thought, I have a problem. He looked back at the Emperor and realized that the father was equally captivated. I hope it is Kitsura that he desires, Shonto thought. He gazed up at the young flutist and felt a stirring himself. And to whom, he wondered, will Lord Omawara marry his daughter? He put the question aside for further consideration.

With a moving crescendo in intricate counterpart, the "Enchanted Gardener" drew to a close and the music was over. The applause was more than polite.

The courtier returned to the stage. "It is the Emperor's wish that these instruments, which once belonged to the courtesan Ranyo, be presented to Lady Nishima and Lady Kitsura in gratitude for their performance."

The members of the audience bowed as the players left the stage.

"She plays very well, Mito-sum," Lady Okara said. "Who was her teacher?"

"My formal Spiritual Advisor, Brother Satake. He was a man of many talents. I miss him."

"They are a charming breed, the advisor monks. Do you think they are educated to be that way?"

Shonto shrugged. No, Oka-sum, he thought, what they are taught is *focus*. It is the source of all their abilities—and what I wouldn't give for that one skill!

Nishima was making her way through the crowd toward her uncle and Lady Okara, her progress slowed by the need to stop and acknowledge each compliment. She stopped and bowed at almost every step.

"Nishima-sum," Shonto said as she slipped off her sandals before stepping onto the mat, "The 'Enchanted Gardener' has seldom known such enchantment." He bowed deferentially to his daughter. "I must say that the Emperor's musical tastes . . ."

"Are exactly the same as yours, Uncle," she leaned toward him to whisper, "and nothing to be smug about, let me assure you."

Shonto turned to his friend. "Lady Okara, may I introduce you to my impertinent only daughter, Nishima-sum."

"I am honored, Lady Okara. I have long been an

admirer of yours, and if my secretive uncle had told me before this evening that you were friends, I would have asked him to introduce us long ago."

"After listening to your performance, I must say the honor is mine. How lovely you play, my dear. If you paint as well as your father assures me you do, then your talent is prodigious indeed. You must come and visit me in my studio one day."

Nishima broke into a smile, "I would be glad to, Lady Okara. Thank you."

The moon had now risen sufficiently to cast light into the garden where it made a path across the Seahorse Pond, and mixed with the colored light from the lanterns.

The courtier came out onto the stage again and bowed twice before speaking. "Tonight the Emperor asks that we pay honor to Lady Okara Haroshu whose series of woodblock prints, *Twenty-one Views of the Grand Canal*, has, at the Emperor's request, been set to dance by the Sonsa Troupe of the Imperial City."

He turned and bowed toward the curtain from behind which the first dancers would emerge. Unseen attendants shaded the lamps and cast the stage into comparative darkness. Dew glistened on the lawns and a warm breeze came in off the nearby lake.

Wooden drums began a low, syncopated rhythm and a single lantern was unveiled to reveal a group of dancers, dressed as peasants, stooped under invisible burdens in the predawn. A flute began to mingle with the drumming, the notes fluttering like a butterfly on a breeze. The half-dozen dancers, wearing the loose fitting clothes and the flattened, conical hats of field workers, began to drop their burdens and dance along the tow path. More lanterns were unveiled illuminating the backdrops, which were painted in a style similar to Lady Okara's, though greatly simplified. The dancers began a series of pantomimes of courtship and revelry, the suppleness that came from long years of Sonsa training captivating the crowd. A young woman stepped forward to dance a solo and Nishima touched her uncle's arm.

The Emperor's new lover, Shonto thought. Of course

Nishima had never seen her before, but he was sure she was right. And yes, the woman was beautiful. Even in her peasant costume the perfection of her dancer's body was obvious.

Dance your best, Shonto thought. The Emperor is not always kind to those he discards. Your only strength then will be your talent, because no one will dare to take you to wife.

But she could dance! She was not just some flower the Emperor had plucked and set in the sunlight. She was a talent. Perhaps this would protect her. With some effort he turned his eyes away to study the Emperor. The ruler's admiration for his Sonsa was absurdly blatant—no more subtle than the emotions of a child. She is in no danger from him tonight, anyway, Shonto thought, unless his lust is to be feared.

The drumming returned to its original cadence, then stopped abruptly, the dancers frozen in the poses of the peasants in Lady Okara's print, *On the Tow Path at Dawn.* On top of the curving bridge the Emperor's lover balanced, her arms thrown out gracefully and one foot in the air as if she had just jumped for joy. The lanterns were shaded as the applause began. The guests near Lady Okara bowed to her and paid her compliments.

Six more of the *Twenty-One Views* that made up the Grand Canal sequence were performed, each as clever as the first, four featuring the talents of the Emperor's lovely Sonsa.

How he flaunts her, everyone thought, but what will become of her, poor child? She was not of a good family, as everyone knew, a vassal-merchant's daughter, and therefore not entirely without education, but still. . . . There was no denying her talent, though. Breeding or no, she would have been a marvel during any dynasty.

The dancing came to an end and received prolonged and enthusiastic applause. Lady Okara was surrounded by bowing guests, all of them wishing to be seen with anyone so honored by the Emperor.

Lady Okara rejoined Shonto and Nishima as her admirers wandered off to eat and laugh and court and gossip.

"Oh, Mito-sum, this isn't good for a person, all of this," she waved her hand to encompass the garden in general, at a loss for words. "I must pay my respects to the Emperor before I leave."

"Okara-sum, don't be in such a rush to go. The worst is over. You have survived! Let me get you some wine so that you may begin to enjoy the rest of the evening." Shonto smiled at her, his voice full of affection. He was touched by his friend's discomfiture.

"Well, one cup and then I must go," Lady Okara conceded.

Shonto left his friend in his daughter's care and set off to find a servant. One came to his aid before he had gone far.

"Lord Shonto," an unfamiliar voice called. A young man who looked vaguely familiar strode toward Shonto across the lawn. The lord sent a servant hurrying off to look after Lady Okara and turned to speak to the young man.

"Excuse my bad manners, Lord Shonto," He bowed. "I am Komawara Samyamu."

Ah, yes, Lord Shonto thought, the same slim build and the long thin nose. If this youth is anything like his father, his apparent lack of muscle is deceptive. The old Komawara had been a strong swordsman and lightning fast.

"I am pleased to meet you, Lord Komawara." Shonto returned the man's bow. "I met your father several times when I was young. He was an impressive man."

"Yes, a great loss to us all, I'm afraid. I honor his memory." He caught Shonto's eye and hesitated briefly before he went on. "I understand that you will come to Seh as our new governor. It is about time that the Emperor sent us a soldier! I mean no disrespect to Lord Shidako—he has admirably resolved the problems left by the corrupt Hanama bureaucracy." He let the statement hang in the air, but Shonto didn't take the offered opportunity to either criticize the Hanama or to praise the Yamaku.

The young lord was obviously unnerved by Lord Shonto's lack of response, and his resolve seemed to flounder momentarily. "Your daughter plays very well, Sire. The Shonto continue to produce artists, to the good fortune of the rest of us. I have recently read your father's memoirs—what a delightful approach he took to his life!"

Shonto nodded, letting the man ramble on, wondering what this young lord's purpose was.

Lord Komawara's eyes hardened and he regained his determination.

"Will you come to Seh soon, Sire?"

"Yes, very soon."

"That is good. Perhaps you will get to the bottom of these mysterious raids."

"I didn't realize that they were thought in any way mysterious, Lord Komawara." Politics, Shonto thought, everyone must have a theory.

"It seems, Sire, that only I find them unusual. May we speak privately, Lord Shonto?"

"Certainly, I am most interested." Shonto pointed off to their left where they could talk without being overheard. He had liked the old Komawara immensely, though he'd been a man doomed by his refusal to change with the times.

"As a native of our northern province, Sire, I have had first-hand experience of the ways of the barbarian tribes all of my life," the young man began, the tones of his father's voice occasionally echoing among the words. "I have traded with them when we were at peace, and fought with them the rest of the time. I have to say that in both areas they are formidable and have no code of honor whatsoever!

"Through all the years that we've warred with them, though, two things in their behavior have remained consistent. They are always bold. Bold beyond anything *these* people would imagine," he waved a hand at the assembled guests with a slight disdain, "and, whenever it is possible, they take our women. This never fails! It is more than just the fair skin. One of our servant girls is valued above the daughters of their most powerful chief! A woman of Wa is the greatest prize a barbarian can have. Of course this has always been their undoing. The men of Seh cannot live with this dishonor, so we cross the border and burn their villages, driving them back into the barrens—for a time.

"This game of raiding our villages and estates always has the same end, yeh? But recently, Lord Shonto, the behavior of the barbarians has changed.

"It has always been their practice—for hundreds of years—to press their attacks with total commitment and when our reinforcements arrive, to either stand and fight or, if they are vastly outnumbered, to wait until the last possible second before they retreat. This is the kind of bravura I expect from them. They despise cowards more than anything. But in these new raids they don't risk a single man! They are always gone before our reinforcements arrive and they seldom even break through our stockades. I know them, sire, I have watched them all my life. This is not proper barbarian behavior!

"This is why I consider it to be a mystery. These attacks make no sense. Even in barbarian terms they are without purpose. They have taken very little plunder and no women though they have had opportunities. Yet I seem to be the only one who thinks the barbarians are acting in an unusual manner. It is said, though not to my face, that my odd ideas are the result of my youth. So you see, you may have wasted your time listening to the babblings of a child." Komawara laughed nervously.

"And what do those who are not hampered by youth say?"

"They say the barbarians become weaker and more cowardly every year and that soon they will be afraid to even cross our borders. "The men of Seh believe that their prowess as warriors have the barbarians cowering in fear."

"Ah. And from your position of relative inexperience, what do you recommend?"

"So far we have not taken a single captive. The barbarians are too cautious. I recommend a quick sortie into their lands with the express purpose of taking prisoners. I have often found that when two men speak from their hearts, much can be learned. But no doubt this is an immature view that I will soon grow out of."

"I, for one, value the opinions of the young. They are not informed by long experience, but they are also not the result of mere habit. I shall consider your words with great care, Lord Komawara, I thank you."

"It is my duty, Lord Governor. I am honored that you have listened."

"Now tell me, what is it that brings you to the capital when Seh is in such danger?"

"Unlike most of my neighbors, my lands are well guarded and fortified. My father believed in spending more on defense than on trade, yeh? In this way he was a bit old-fashioned. The result of his belief is that, though the Komawara are not poor, we have not the position we once had. To my everlasting shame, my father sold part of the family fief before he died. It is my hope to buy this land back and to restore the good name the Komawara once had."

"Everyone knows the name of Komawara to be ancient and respected. I'm sure you will have even greater honors under the new dynasty."

"I hope you are correct, Lord Shonto."

So, Shonto thought, this is what the young one desires—a return to former power. It was an old story and Shonto had heard it many times before. Most of the secondary Houses in the Empire had the same dream, though in many cases the former power was mythical. But not so with the Komawara. They had once been the true rulers of the north—and long before the Imperial Governors had been created. At times the Komawara had even rivaled the Imperial family in military strength. More than one Komawara daughter had been a bride to an Emperor—but that had been long ago; their power and influence had waned in the early days of the Hanama.

During the two hundred years that sea trade had developed, the House of Komawara had slowly declined as had all the clans that clung to the past. The old Komawara had seen the error of his ways, and before his death had sold some of his fief to raise capital for his heir to start trade. This had been a great sacrifice on the part of the old lord, one which had saved his son from the stigma of having sold family lands.

Virtually all the old noble families had made the transformation to merchant families, yet they still clung to the fiefs as they always had because to lose them was to become merely merchants. The past was gone, but the habits remained—the merchants were traditionally disdained. This, of course, didn't stop most peers from having their own vassal-merchants whose positions and rewards went far beyond those of other servants. Occasionally vassal-merchants gained real power in Houses with weak rulers—some even began trading for themselves or bought their freedom from their lords. The latter was a new development that had been illegal in the past and some thought it should be illegal again.

"Lord Komawara, tomorrow my vassal-merchant Tanaka will arrive with my new Spiritual Advisor. My merchant is a man of some skill in the world of trade, perhaps our Houses could enter into a venture that would be of mutual benefit. I would be pleased if you could share a midday meal with us tomorrow, if that would be convenient."

"The honor would be mine, Lord Shonto." The young man's face betrayed his surprise and pleasure.

He will learn, Lord Shonto thought. "Good. Come along and meet Lady Okara and my daughter, Lady Nishima."

In the colorless moonlight they found the two women with Kitsura, drinking wine and giggling. Kitsura fanned herself furiously as the men approached, as if that would take the blush off her face.

"Allow me to introduce my friend from Seh, Lord Komawara," said Shonto, giving the youth much more importance than his age and status deserved.

"We wondered where you had disappeared to, Uncle. The speculation, in fact, has completely occupied us," Nishima said, sipping her wine casually. Kitsura covered her mouth with her fan.

"Yes, I can see how it would," Shonto said. "Lord Komawara has been advising me as to the present situation in Seh, and we have been discussing other business."

Kitsura composed herself and fixed the young lord with a cool eye. "Lord Shonto is shrewd beyond compare in affairs of state. You must be wise beyond your years, Lord Komawara, to offer him advice." She smiled her disarming smile.

Be nimble, Shonto thought. She will not hesitate to find you wanting. A woman in her position does not need to reserve judgment.

Komawara shrugged. "One does not go to the gii Master expecting to equal him, Lady Kitsura, it is enough to simply learn. I have only presumed to provide Lord Shonto with some small measure of information that I believe to be accurate. The conclusions that Lord Shonto draws will, undoubtedly, be very instructive."

Lady Kitsura raised her fine eyebrows, the look of the skeptic.

"What brings you to the capital?" Lady Okara asked pleasantly, turning the conversation abruptly—a comment on Lady Kitsura's behavior.

Lord Shonto smiled. Thank you, Oka-sum, he thought. I don't wish to offend Lord Komawara. I must have all the allies in Seh that I can. Even this boy may prove to be important. Who can tell? Only a fool discards an ally unnecessarily, no matter how insignificant.

More wine was served and the conversation returned to its earlier gaiety. Lord Komawara proved able to hold his own in conversation, both in knowledge and wit, giving Nishima hope that the court in Seh would not be of as little interest as she had imagined. She had never traveled to the outer provinces and, like most residents of the capital, felt that even the wealthiest peers of the outer regions must be dreadfully parochial.

For their part, the peoples of the outer provinces, especially in the north with their history of barbarian wars, felt that the residents of the inner provinces were decadent and soft. To their lasting satisfaction there seemed to be some evidence in history to support this thesis. Virtually all of the long-reigning Imperial dynasties were founded by families from the outer provinces. The Hanama were a case in point, coming from Chou, in the far west, where they had long been influential.

Shonto's fief lay on the edge of the "civilized" inner provinces along the central sea coast, so he was claimed by both southerners and northerners alike—a state of affairs he did much to promote. His was a good fief of moderate size in the Empire's temperate belt. The land was exceptionally fertile and, because it was bounded by mountains and the Fuga River, easily protected. The Shonto House had long prospered in these lands and their capital was known as a center of culture and learning.

An aide from the Emperor's staff interrupted their conversation, bowing low to Lord Shonto. "The Emperor wishes to know if he may have the honor of your company—all of you."

"Of course," Lord Shonto answered. "When should we attend him?"

"Now would be convenient, Sire."

"Certainly. Please tell the Emperor that we are honored by his request."

The aide made his way through the crowd, Lord Shonto and his party in tow.

He needs me, Shonto thought, he knows that. Putting a hand on the unfamiliar sword hilt, Shonto tugged to see how tightly it sat in the scabbard. It slid with ease.

They joined the throng surrounding the Emperor's dais while the Son of Heaven spoke pleasantly to a man and woman kneeling before him. The courtiers followed the conversation closely, laughing politely at the appropriate times or nodding their heads in silent agreement, their sensitivity to their master's requirements sharpened by a lifetime of study. The Emperor gestured to the audience mat before him, and nodded to Shonto and his companions. All of them knelt and touched their heads to the mat.

"I am pleased you accepted my invitation so quickly," the Emperor said, and then before anyone could respond he gestured to the dais. "Lord Shonto, Lady Okara,

please join me. We must make room for these fine young
players and their companion."

There was more bowing and polite exchange, for to
be seated on the same level as the Emperor was almost
unheard of. Servants hurried forward with fine silk cushions for the Emperor's guests.

"I hope, Lady Okara, that you felt tonight's performance was an acceptable translation of your work?"

"Far more than acceptable, Sire, inspired I would say.
I do not feel worthy of such praise."

"Ah, but it is never for an artist to judge her own
worth, that is for those of us of lesser talent. Is that not
so, Lord Shonto?"

"Talent comes in a myriad of forms, Sire. To be able
to recognize great art is a talent all its own, I think."

"You see, Lady Okara, it is the role of the Shonto
family to teach the Yamaku appreciation of art. Do not
protest, Lord Shonto! Your father once taught mine a
most unforgettable lesson in poetics and now his son
offers me instruction in the appreciation of art. I bow to
you, Lord Shonto. You are right that a talent is needed
to recognize great art. Perhaps I should create an office
of Aesthetic Judgment to which I would appoint Lord
Shonto, for the betterment of the Empire." There was
general laughter and nodding of heads. Shonto tried to
maintain an outward calm, not sure where this was leading.

The Emperor seemed to remain genial. "It is fortunate
that in my Empire there are many people with this talent
Lord Shonto mentions, for everyone recognizes the
beauty of your art, Lady Okara. So you see when Lord
Shonto corrected me a moment ago, he also complimented me and everyone in the Empire simultaneously.
What am I to do with one so clever?"

The courtiers nodded agreement, apparently vastly
amused by the Emperor's logic.

"I will have to give this great thought," the Emperor
said, contemplating Shonto. He turned again to Lady
Okara. "For too long now the Yamaku have been
neglecting their responsibilities to the artists in our

Empire. A culture is only as great as its existing arts, don't you agree, Lady Okara?"

"Wholeheartedly, Sire."

"This very night I intend to begin to rectify my family's neglect of our responsibilities toward the artists of Wa. Those of us who can should support the cause. Don't you agree, Lord Shonto?"

"Absolutely, Sire," he answered, reserve obvious in his voice. What is this about, Shonto asked himself? He had a growing fear that whatever the Emperor planned, the entire evening had been staged for this one purpose. But where did Oka-sum fit into this? It was out of the question that she would conspire with the Emperor against him. Or was it? His mind raced. Every faculty was in full operation trying to provide him with a single clue that would allow him to sidestep the Emperor's thrust when it came.

"Lady Okara, perhaps with your assistance I will be able to help the worthy artists of our land. I propose an Imperial Patronage, a generous patronage, I might add. I want to encourage our best artists to take on a talented young apprentice. Lady Okara, I would be honored if you would be the first to accept." He smiled warmly.

The artist tried to hide her shock. "The honor, Sire . . . is mine. It . . . I accept, certainly, but I don't feel worthy! I feel there are others more deserving."

"Ah, Lady Okara. As our friend, Lord Shonto, has said, perhaps I have a talent for recognizing great art. Let me be the judge in this matter. Do you accept?"

"I do, Sire. I thank you." She bowed low. Applause broke out at Lady Okara's acceptance.

"Now we must find you a worthy apprentice—one of whom you approve, of course." The Emperor paused as if deep in thought. Too late, Shonto realized what lay ahead.

"Lady Nishima," the Emperor said, addressing Shonto's startled daughter, "if it is mutually acceptable to both you and Lady Okara, I name you to be the first apprentice of the Imperial Patronage." The Emperor smiled broadly, pleased with himself. The courtiers masked their shock at the Emperor's bad manners.

It was unheard of to put anyone in a position where they must accept or reject another in public. All such arrangements were traditionally done in private, through a third party, so that no one would lose face in the event of a refusal or rejection. All eyes were turned to the two women to see how they would resolve such a dilemma.

Lady Nishima, despite her youth, had the benefit of a lifetime of Shonto's training. She responded at once. "Sire, this is a dream come true. I will immediately gather together some of my work and send it to Lady Okara so that she may make a decision in this matter. And to be fair, Sire, perhaps other artists should be given the same opportunity? An artist of Lady Okara's importance should not expend her efforts for any but the most deserving. I'm sure all would agree." The entire speech was delivered in a most humble tone, the Lady Nishima's gaze cast down.

The Emperor's face contorted in annoyance—he was not used to having his wishes thwarted. He regained control almost immediately.

"Lady Nishima, your fairness is a credit to you, but you must allow me to be the judge. It is my talent to recognize art and artists, yeh? Lady Okara, I ask you to accept Lady Nishima as your apprentice. Her talent, I must tell you, is beyond question."

Shonto watched with a sense of helplessness—the struggle was entirely in the hands of his daughter and Lady Okara and he could only pray to Botahara for assistance.

Nishima was to be a hostage. That was what the Emperor desired, to keep her in the capital, isolated from Shonto and his army. She was a prize. The Fanisan blood and the Shonto name and power. Which son did he want her for? Would it be the heir? Yes, Shonto thought, that would make the most sense, but there were also reasons to wed her to the least powerful son—an attempt to nullify Shonto. Which son would be heir?

Lady Okara swallowed in a dry throat, visibly shaken

at suddenly finding herself cast into the center of the Emperor's designs. Court intrigue was the one thing she had avoided all her life.

"I trust your judgment totally, Sire. I would be honored to give Lady Nishima the benefit of my limited expertise, *whenever* it would be convenient to her." This was her only card and she cast it out, desperately hoping Nishima would pick it up.

"It was my intention," the Emperor said, "to invest the patronage on an annual basis, starting immediately. I trust that will be convenient."

"Excuse me, Sire. I don't wish to sound ungrateful," Lady Nishima said in her quiet way, "but I am now torn between my duty and this dream you have offered me. My father and liege-lord is about to undertake a serious campaign on the Emperor's behalf. It is my duty to Lord Shonto—and to you, my Emperor—to give the head of my House every assistance possible. As my father has no wife to run his household, I am more necessary than a daughter would normally be. She looked up suddenly, meeting the Emperor's gaze. "I have always been taught that duty takes precedence, it is our way. I do not know how to resolve this problem."

The Emperor was unable to hide his frustration. He looked around, struggling with his rage, looking for someone to vent his considerable temper on. He was being outmaneuvered by a mere girl. He hadn't expected her to hesitate for even a second—he had been assured that the bait was perfect.

"Lord Shonto, certainly there are members of your personal staff who can carry out Lady Nishima's duties for you. Not as well, no doubt," he hurried to add, "but can't you live without her for awhile?"

"No sacrifice is too great, Sire." Shonto answered without a second's hesitation, much to his daughter's dismay. "A warrior can live without everything but weapons, if need be. I can certainly survive if my household is less efficient than I am used to it being."

The Emperor smiled broadly. "It is settled, then. The

arts shall flourish again as they did in the time of the Mori!"

There was loud applause. Several of the wealthiest lords present, inspired by the Emperor's example, offered to invest patronages of their own. If there had been any aspiring artists in attendance they would, no doubt, have found themselves suddenly able to live in a manner they had never dreamed possible.

Having accomplished his immediate purpose, the Emperor turned his attention to Lady Kitsura with whom he spoke in a most flirtatious manner, forgetting himself completely. This was the Emperor at his social best, entirely engaging, and Lady Kitsura was equally charming and many times more attractive. Lord Shonto watched the play between them with great interest. Twice he politely tried to draw Lord Komawara into the conversation, but the Emperor brushed these attempts aside as if he hadn't noticed. Shonto noted the young lord's neck becoming increasingly red, though his face remained calm, a slight smile crossing his face now and then at a remark or quick response.

The autumn moon had moved far into the western sky by the time the party began to break up. The Dance of Five Hundred Couples had been performed on the lawn, the long-sleeved kimonos creating the illusion of water flowing in the moonlight. Poems had been composed and recited. Assignations arranged, plots hatched, betrayals conceived, and large quantities of food and wine consumed. For those not singled out by the Emperor, it had been a most satisfying event.

Lady Nishima, though, was truly desolate. Even her harp, which had once been used by the legendary courtesan Ranyo to pacify the Mad Emperor, gave her little solace.

"I have failed you, Sire," she said once the sampan was out the palace gate. "I stepped into the Emperor's trap like an uneducated serving girl. All of your trust in me has been misplaced."

Shonto grunted, it was not his place to make excuses for the failings of either his children or his vassals, so he let Nishima continue, barely listening to her as he pursued a tiny thread in the evening's conversation. His fine memory led him back through every turn of the conversation that his intuition told him held the key to his problem. Finally he laughed loudly and slapped his daughter on the knee, making her jump.

"I don't see how there can be humor in this, Uncle! I am to be hostage within the city while you are at the other end of the Empire!" She was close to tears.

"Nishi-sum, I will tell you this only once, because if you do not understand it now, you never will. All plans have flaws—without exception! The trick is to find the flaw before the trap closes. In this case the trap is not yet closed, and I have found the flaw." He laughed again, immensely pleased with himself. Shonto, like his father, loved to lecture. He continued. "This is why I always beat you at gii, I don't wail and tear my hair when things go against me. You must always remember when setting a trap that it is not enough to know your opponent's weaknesses, you must also have made a careful study of his strengths. Half-wisdom is the most dangerous foolishness.

"Console yourself, Nishima-sum. You did the best that could have been done under the circumstances."

Nishima brightened a little. "Tell me, Uncle, what is the flaw? I cannot see it."

Shonto pulled the curtain aside to check the boatmen's progress, grunted and refused to say more, leaving his daughter to ponder the problem perhaps in the view that it might be instructive to her. There were many things to occupy his mind, preparations to make, his Spiritual Advisor to train, information to gain, and false information to spread. But something that should not matter at all kept returning to his mind.

The Emperor's lovely Sonsa had brought Lady Okara flowers, thanking her for the inspiration that had shaped the evening's dance. The exchange had been polite in the extreme, though the young dancer's very real shyness and infectious laugh soon won over Shonto and his companions. She had surprised Shonto by asking him to be her partner in the Dance of the Five Hundred Couples.

He had been thrilled by her Sonsa skills as she moved through the measures of the ancient dance. As the music ended and the applause began, she had leaned close to him and whispered, "Good fortune in Seh, Lord Governor. Sleep lightly, there are always greater dangers than the barbarians." Then she was gone, leaving Shonto with only the lingering scent of her perfume.

Why, he wondered, had the Emperor instructed her to say that? Surely he did not think he could throw Shonto off balance with a few simple feints?

"Strange, yeh?" he said aloud.

"Pardon, Sire?"

"Strange young man, Komawara, yeh?"

"He seemed quite normal to me, Sire, and not very experienced. You should advise him to return to the outer provinces as soon as possible. He is a lamb among wolves here in the capital."

"Nishi-sum, have I ever told you that you place too much value on those qualities that are the most superficial?"

"It is my evening to fall short of your expectations, Sire. I apologize most humbly."

"Social bearing and wit, it is true, are not as highly developed in the outer provinces as they are here but, contrary to what most people think, that is because the residents of the outer provinces have better manners."

"Oh, Uncle, you romanticize the country folk like a bad poet," Nishima objected.

Shonto snorted. "What I've said is true! The *veiled barb* has never become the *art form* it is in the capital, for the simple reason that, in the outer provinces, insults are answered with swords. I always find my dealings with the people of the north most refreshing. A man only needs to keep his sword arm free and his tongue in check to enjoy the social life of a place like Seh. I much prefer that to the insignificant concerns of the Imperial courtiers!"

Yes, Shonto thought, a stay in the provinces would do Nishima good.

# Four

Shonto's private garden was small but entirely exqui-site. The designer, Shonto's former Spiritual Advisor, had joined all of the garden's elements into a delicately balanced whole that expressed both unity and diversity without losing the composition's harmonious sense. Shonto thought of the garden as a fine piece of music wherein all of the elements complimented each other, while the underlying structure was one of tension. The garden was widely thought of as a work of high-art and was much copied throughout the Empire. The present gardener's major problem was to maintain the essence of the original design while allowing the garden to grow, for it was, after all, a living thing and to stultify it would be to initiate a slow death.

Shonto knelt next to the babbling stream that fed the small pond, and pulled his sleeve back before plunging a hand into the cool water. He groped around in the shallows until he found the large stone he searched for and then raised it, dripping, into the sunlight. After a moment's contemplation, he replaced the rock farther upstream, so that it now rested half exposed in the minia-ture rapids. The lord listened intently for a few moments and then adjusted the rock slightly, listened again, and nodded, satisfied.

He rose and walked back toward the house, stopping every few paces to listen to the results of his efforts. Stepping out of his sandals, he seated himself on a cush-ion on the low veranda and listened to the sound of the breeze through the bamboo stands, the buzzing of insects, and the rippling rush of his stream.

"Better," he muttered, nodding.

Recently the stream had lost its clarity and for several days, Shonto had spent some time each morning trying to regain it, though not always to the delight of his gardener, who felt that such matters should be left to those properly trained.

The day was new, the sun not yet over the wall, and Shonto had slept only a few hours after the Emperor's party, but he felt relaxed and refreshed. The events of the previous night were still strong in his mind.

Almost soundlessly, servants appeared from the inner apartment and set a low table before Shonto. A square covered bowl, which held steaming cloths, and two other bowls, one of peeled and sliced fruit and one containing a hot grain mash, were arranged on the table. A light mead was poured into a cup and offered to the lord, who received it with a distracted nod. He listened to his garden. A single servant remained, kneeling behind him in utter stillness.

An almost imperceptible tap sounded on the shoji and the servant opened it a crack, to listen to a whispered voice.

"Your pardon, Lord Shonto," the servant said quietly, "it is Kamu-sum. He feels it is important that he speak to you immediately." Shonto waved his hand to have the man allowed in. Kamu, Shonto was well aware, never interrupted him without real purpose. The man was Shonto's steward and had served his father before him. He was old now, gray-haired and wrinkled like the face of a storm cloud, but his knowledge of the affairs of the Empire was invaluable and he was conscientious—one might even say meticulous—in the extreme. He still appeared vigorous and strong and he had long since learned to compensate for the right arm he had lost in battle.

The steward came in and knelt easily, bowed his head to the mat, and remained kneeling without a sign of impatience.

After a moment Shonto spoke. "I have adjusted the

Speaking-stream, Kamu. Does it seem more focused now—sharper perhaps?"

Kamu bowed his head slightly and closed his eyes. After a few seconds he nodded. "The clarity is improved, Sire. To my ear it sounds sharper."

"Too sharp, do you think?"

Kamu bowed his head again. "Perhaps, Sire, but it may be that the water flows too rapidly."

"Hmm. I have wondered that myself. Perhaps if the bamboo were thinned, then the sharpness of the water would not be so obvious.

"The bamboo is a little heavy, but in the fall winds the leaf-sound will be higher."

"Huh," Shonto said, still concentrating on the garden music. "Tomorrow I will slow the water somewhat and see.

"Now, Kamu, what is it that could not wait?"

"Jaku Katta is here, Sire. He arrived unannounced and requests an audience on the Emperor's behalf."

*"Unannounced."* Shonto made a long face. "Unusual, yeh?"

"Most, Sire."

"I will see him here. Station guards out of sight. He must come alone. That is all."

The old warrior bowed and rose. He was not surprised that Shonto had chosen to meet Jaku in the garden. Staging was very important in these matters. To receive Jaku in the garden would make it very clear that Jaku had interrupted the lord at his morning meal, which would put the visitor at a disadvantage. It would also make a young upstart like Jaku aware of just how much a lord of Shonto's stature could afford to indulge himself—the garden would make that point perfectly.

Shonto heard the sound of men moving into position around him and then the garden was peaceful again. He turned his attention to the problem of Jaku Katta, the Emperor's prime advisor and Commander of the Imperial Guard. Jaku was the Emperor's eyes and ears throughout all of Wa and controlled the vast spy network that the Son of Heaven felt was necessary to maintain his rule. At the age of thirty-five, Jaku Katta was known to be one of the most powerful men in the Empire, and one of the most ambitious. The son of a small land holder, Jaku had first come to the Emperor's attention as a kick boxer, champion of all of Wa for almost a decade before his duties to the Emperor took precedence.

Shonto searched his mind, dredging up odd facts and stories about the man who was about to join him. Jaku Katta was not married and was an almost legendary womanizer. His memory was apparently prodigious and his mind supple and cunning. He was, in fact, the kind of man Shonto would have trained himself—had he discovered him first—but then there was the issue of Jaku's ambition. Shonto wondered how great the man's loyalty was to any but Jaku Katta—and perhaps the two brothers, who were his immediate lieutenants.

Jaku, Jaku, Shonto thought, now I will have my chance to measure you.

Reaching behind him Shonto moved his sword, which stood upright on its stand, to within easy reach. He ordered the servant to bring more mead and a second cup. He smiled broadly. It was going to be a long, full day and Shonto relished the thought of it. So much to do, so much to prepare for! He joined his hands, back to back, over his head and stretched his upper body like a young sapling growing toward the sun. Jaku, Jaku, Shonto thought, what fun we shall have!

Without any noticeable signal, the servant moved to open the shoji. Inside the opening, Kamu bowed low.

"General Jaku Katta, Lord Shonto."

Shonto nodded and Jaku stepped through the doorway dressed in the black uniform of the Imperial Guard, on his right breast, the Dragon Fan of the Imperial House, surmounted by the six small crimson dragons denoting a general of the First Rank. Under his right arm Jaku carried a finely crafted dress-helmet, reminding Shonto that the general was left-handed.

The general knelt and bowed surprisingly low to

Shonto and remained kneeling, refusing the cushion that the servant offered.

"This surprise visit honors my House, General," Shonto said, bowing slightly. "Please, join me in some mead."

"It is my honor to be received, Lord Shonto," Jaku answered, without apology. His gaze was drawn out from the veranda into Shonto's garden. "It is as everyone says, Lord Shonto. This garden is the pattern of which all others are but imitations."

Shonto gave a half nod, "It was designed to be neither too elaborate, nor too ostentatious—as I prefer all things—so the essence is not masked in any way but only enhanced."

Neither man spoke for a moment as they contemplated the garden. The servant leaned forward unobtrusively and filled porcelain cups.

"I have been trying to bring the water sound back into harmony with the rest of the garden, Katta-sum. Tell me, does it seem too sharp to you?"

Jaku Katta closed his eyes and listened, without moving. Shonto studied the man's face, which was strong featured, especially the jaw and the high forehead. The eyelids were heavy, almost sleepy, under dark brows. Jaku's thin lips and wide mouth were not quite hidden by a magnificent, drooping mustache. Just above average height and perfectly proportioned, Jaku knelt across from Shonto with an easy, relaxed poise which was also present in his movements, and the lord remembered that the other kick boxers had named him the Black Tiger, after the steely-eyed cat.

Jaku's eyes were aberrant in color—a light, icy gray rather than the almost universal brown. Both his brothers were green-eyed, which was also unusual, though somewhat more common. The eyes were just another factor in Jaku's mystique—"the entirely uncommon man."

"I feel the stream is perfectly in balance with the whole. I would not touch a pebble of its bed," Jaku said opening his tiger-eyes.

"You do not think the bamboo should be thinned?"

Jaku listened again. "No, Lord Shonto, I think that it's perfect. I have never in my life heard nor seen such a beautiful garden."

Shonto nodded, "I thank you for your opinion, Katta-sum. So, General, tell me. What is it that brings you here so early?"

Jaku set his cup carefully on the fine wooden table and composed himself before speaking. He met Shonto's eyes and the lord was startled by their intensity.

A mark for you, Jaku, Shonto thought, you understand the power of this gift.

"The Emperor has asked me to express his concern for your safety, Lord Shonto."

"Ah. I am touched by his concern, but the Shonto have long since learned to take precautions and, of course, I will take more now that I represent the Throne in Seh."

Jaku continued to hold Shonto's eye. "Your new Spiritual Advisor arrives today?"

Shonto almost laughed. You cannot throw me off so easily, my friend. We *both* have been keeping track of his progress.

"I have been expecting him for the last few days. Why?"

"The Emperor has reason to believe that this monk is a threat to you, Sire."

"I see. And is this so, General Jaku?"

Jaku looked down at his strong hands at rest on his thighs and then he met Shonto's eyes again. This tactic, Shonto realized, would soon lose its impact.

"We have reports on this young monk that we find . . . disturbing, Lord Shonto."

"Can you elaborate, Katta-sum? Nothing about the young man seems at all out of order to me."

Jaku cleared his throat quietly like the bearer of some bad news, news that it would pain him to reveal. "We have received reports that this monk—this Initiate Brother Shuyun—has been given a great deal of special training, the nature of which is not entirely known to us. During his year in Wa as senior Initiate he was apprenticed to the most accomplished Botahist Brothers who treated him almost with deference. The entire time he was in Wa the Botahist Sisters spied on him and even tried to maneuver a young Acolyte nun—in disguise, of course—into his company. They were, by the way, unsuccessful.

"It seems that this boy-monk possesses powers that are unusual even for the Silent Ones," Jaku spoke the term with distaste. "And he has been chosen for you, Lord Shonto, the Emperor's most trusted governor.

"We fear that there is a plot against you or against the Emperor or both. The Botahist Brotherhood can never be trusted. They have strayed far from the teachings of Lord Botahara and have meddled in the affairs of the Empire far too often. I cannot believe they have changed in this regard, despite the platitudes of their current leader." Jaku fell to silence and Shonto could see that he was controlling his anger in the manner of the kick boxers—his breathing became even and his face almost serene. The fighters always looked so before a contest.

Shonto listened again to the sound of his garden and wondered if Jaku, with his boxer's sense, was aware of the guards nearby. He would, no doubt, realize that they must be there—being trained to stillness could not prevent that.

"It seems to me, Katta-sum, that the Brotherhood has been most obliging, in fact unusually so, to our Emperor. Did they not make a present of the land that the Emperor wished to purchase from them not more than a year ago? Have they not blessed the Son of Heaven and his line, thereby assuring the support of all the followers of Botahara? No small thing!

"There are rumors that they have offered the Emperor greater services than this and he has refused."

"They offer nothing without its price! They are merchants of the human soul, trading their so-called enlightenment for power and gold. They are hypocrites, without loyalty to anything but their own aspirations."

Ah, Shonto thought, did not Botahara say that we hate

in others those things which are the least admirable in ourselves?

"So, Katta-sum, I don't understand what it is the Emperor wishes of me. I can hardly turn away my Spiritual Advisor now. That would be out of the question! I have made an agreement. Besides, I have paid very handsomely for this monk's service—gold in exchange for the knowledge of the soul, as you have said. Perhaps you have come merely to warn me of the Emperor's suspicions in this matter?"

"The Emperor thinks you would be well advised to send this monk back to his teachers, Lord Governor."

"General Jaku," Shonto said in his most patronizing tone, "I cannot do that on the scant information you have given me. Our family has employed Spiritual Advisors continuously for *over five hundred years*. It is a Shonto belief that we have profited from these arrangements. I can hardly believe that the Botahist Brothers would send a monk who was a threat to the Emperor into the Shonto House. It would make no more sense than sending such a one to Jaku Katta!" Shonto laughed and motioned to have their cups refilled.

"It is as the Emperor said: you will oppose him in this matter," Jaku said coldly, ignoring the laughter.

"Kattu-sum, the Emperor is an intelligent and reasonable man. He cannot expect me to turn away my Spiritual Advisor and insult the Botahist Brotherhood on so little evidence. If you have more information, enough to convince me, well, that would be different. Can you tell me why the Sisterhood was following this young monk? This is very unusual, yeh?"

"In truth, Lord Governor, we don't know."

"Huh. So I have been warned. I will watch this monk with great care. There is little else I can do, yeh?"

"There is *one* thing." Jaku turned his eyes on Shonto again, but the effect was gone. "The Emperor has suggested that a servant be assigned to this monk. A servant who is trained to watch and report. I have such a servant. If there were any danger to you, Sire, he would see it."

"He would report to Jaku Katta, yeh?" Shonto could not help but smirk.

"All of his reports would go through you first, Sire."

"I see." Shonto swirled the contents of his cup. "The Emperor does me great honor with his concern, but it is unecessary. I am Shonto and do not need to have a *boy* sent to look after me. I will deal with this monk in my own way. If there is cause for concern, I will send word to the Emperor himself." Oh, Jaku, Shonto thought, you must truly believe that you have leverage or you would never suggest a plan so transparent. But Nishima will be safe, he told himself, as he had so many times since yesterday evening, I will see to that.

Jaku turned his gaze back to the garden. "As you wish, Lord Governor," he said, but his voice did not ring with resignation.

Yes, Shonto thought, this is a man always to be wary of. The Black Tiger—someone who could explode out of darkness without warning.

"The Emperor has given your daughter great honor, yeh?" Jaku asked suddenly.

"He has honored my entire household with his concern and generosity." Shonto said almost by rote.

"This is so. It is good to be in the Emperor's favor, yeh?" Shonto didn't answer, so Jaku went on. "I have been instructed to tell you that the Emperor will see to your daughter's safety while you are in Seh. He is very fond of her, and who could not be? She is lovely, talented, and possessed of great charm—such a rare combination."

"The Son of Heaven need not trouble himself. Lady Nishima will be well guarded."

"To guard Lady Nishima is not *trouble,* Sire, it is an *honor*. I would perform this duty to our Emperor personally, if I could." Jaku turned to Shonto and lowered his voice. "But as it is, my reach has grown long. Many blows can be warded off by *anticipation*—this is an essential skill of the kick boxer. It is the skill that makes me valuable to the Emperor."

Shonto listened to this performance, fascinated. He almost forgot to respond.

"And what danger do you anticipate for my daughter, Katta-sum?"

"At the moment, none, but I rule out nothing. I want you to know, Lord Shonto, that I think your daughter a person of far too much importance to be under threat by anyone—*anyone* at all."

Ah, Jaku, it is as I suspected, your loyalty is the servant of your ambition. And now you aspire to too much! This long reach of yours may yet leave you with empty hands. But what a fine animal you are, Jaku! Such amazing *hunger!* Yet you think this hunger is your strength, when it is your weakness. You must learn to control your desires. Ah, I lecture, but of course you cannot hear.

"You know, Katta-sum," Shonto said turning and looking out into his garden. "Sometimes I think that there are forces outside these walls that are causing an almost imperceptible but continuous change in my garden. Like a man's spirit, yeh? If he allows the outside world to breach his inner walls, his clarity will be lost. One must always guard against this, don't you think, or we may lose our tranquillity?"

"I'm sure you are right, Lord Governor," Jaku answered, but his voice suddenly seemed far away.

Shonto watched while Jaku again relaxed his muscles as the kick boxers did—a settling of the body, as though it had just made contact anew with the earth. He seemed to have turned his attention elsewhere, toward the garden, and he had achieved perfect stillness, eyes closed, his hand at rest on his sword hilt. Shonto said nothing, fascinated by the great cat before him as it sank into total concentration.

Yes, even the sound of my garden is that beautiful, Shonto thought, just as the shoji to Jaku's right exploded toward them. One of Shonto's personal guard swept the remains of the screen aside as he came through, face impassive, his sword beginning a tight arc toward Jaku Katta. *Chaos* erupted all around them!

Magically, Jaku Katta seemed to be in the air from his

kneeling position, his sword in hand, even as Shonto reached for his own blade. The shoji to the inner house jerked back at the same instant that Jaku's right foot caught his assailant's forearm, spoiling the blow aimed at Jaku's torso. Two guards burst through the bamboo stand as Jaku's sword flashed. The assailant smashed the low table as he fell, dead, and Jaku landed on his feet beyond the veranda's edge, his sword at the ready, his stance strong.

"No one moves!" Shonto yelled from his position, standing, his back against a post, sword out. The young servant stood, unarmed, between his lord and the shattered wall, prepared to intercept anything that might come. The sounds of men running and shouting came from every direction.

Kamu appeared, pushing between the guards at the door, but stopped, stricken by the sight of the dead guard in Shonto livery. Behind him stood Jaku's lieutenant whose eyes darted everywhere as he assessed the danger.

Shonto dipped the point of his blade toward the corpse, "Who is this, Kamu?"

The steward turned to a lieutenant who stood in the frame of the shattered shoji.

"Tokago Yama, Sergeant of the Guard, Sire." He bowed to Lord Shonto but kept his eyes fixed on Jaku Katta.

"He attempted to assassinate his leige-lord," Jaku's voice sounded strongly, imposing itself over the confusion, "but fortunately Jaku Katta was in his way. I saved Lord Shonto from having to clean this one's blood off the Emperor's gift."

"Kamu," Shonto turned a cold eye on the steward, "all of the guards in this garden are now foot-porters. You will break their swords personally. A guest in the house of Shonto has been endangered. This is unacceptable!" Shonto paused, regaining control of his anger. "Where is the captain of my guard?"

"He comes now, Sire."

"Good. Send for my worthless gardener and assure Lady Nishima that all is under control."

Shonto turned his back on the scene and stepped off the veranda. He nodded to Jaku who followed the lord into the garden. Both men kept their swords in hand.

"Katta-sum, I can never apologize for this occurrence. *Never* has such a thing happened while I have been head of this House. I owe you a great debt."

"I did what any man would have done in my place, Sire. I ask for nothing in return except that you consider the danger around you. To bring one of these treacherous monks into your household now, I'm sure, is a mistake. I beg you again to reconsider."

"Your concern honors me, General. Certainly I will consider your words."

The captain of Shonto's guard and the chief gardener arrived at the same moment. Both knelt and touched their heads to the ground, showing none of the fear they felt.

Shonto motioned the gardener to follow but ignored the captain. Crossing to the far wall the lord stopped before an exquisite chako bush. The shrub had been shaped by an artist of some accomplishment and was beautiful even to the most uninformed eye.

"This is a present to you, Katta-sum. It is a piece of my inner harmony, yeh? A token of gratitude for today. Shall I send my gardener to choose a place for it in your garden? I believe he is the best in all of Wa."

"That would be a great honor, Lord Shonto. But my humble garden is not worthy of such beauty. Now it is I who am in your debt."

Shonto turned to his gardener, "You will accompany General Jaku to his home and consult with him and his gardener in this matter. You will prepare this chako immediately." Shonto turned back toward the porch.

"Every man must have the best garden he possibly can, Katta-sum. It is essential to the human spirit. When a man has as much to do as you and I, he needs a sanctuary, yeh? A place which nourishes the soul. Don't you agree?"

"I do, Sire."

They passed the kneeling captain again and proceeded

to the veranda. Servants were just in the process of replacing the ruined shoji and already the grass mats had been changed and a new table set with cups.

Shonto handed his sword to his servant who sheathed it and returned it to its stand.

Both men sat on the veranda edge while servants washed their feet, for they had gone into the garden barefoot.

"Again I thank you, Katta-sum. I will consider what you have said with great care."

Jaku nodded. Your chako will be the centerpiece of my garden." Jaku came to his feet on the veranda and paused. "I thank you for your time, Sire. To have seen your garden has been a great lesson. Unfortunately, the Emperor's business calls."

A servant brought Jaku his helmet. Shonto and his guest exchanged parting bows and Jaku was gone, escorted by Shonto guards. The shoji closed and Shonto was alone with his servant and the Captain of the Guard who still knelt in the garden's center. Except for the trampled bamboo, there was no sign of the attempted assassination. The garden was again tranquil.

Shonto tapped the table impatiently, "Where is my fruit?" he demanded. The servant bowed quickly and turned to crack the shoji. Shonto gestured to have the cups filled and the boy leaned forward to pour.

"Fill them both," Shonto instructed. Raising a cup, the lord turned to face his servant. "A toast," he said. The boy was confused but looked attentive all the same.

"You cannot toast without a drink," Shonto nodded at the second cup. The servant still hesitated and then realized what honor his lord offered him. He reached for the second vessel.

"To your new position—junior assistant to Kamu. You have studied arms?" The boy nodded as if in a dream. "Good. You will begin tomorrow. What is your name?"

"Toko, Sire."

"So, Toko, you were brave today and quick. These are important qualities. You may do very well if you pay attention and learn quickly. Drink." Shonto looked at the boy as if seeing him for the first time. How long had he been one of Shonto's personal servants? The lord did not know. The boy was no more than sixteen, so he could not have served long. Certain qualities were looked for in servants; physical competence, a softness of voice, attractiveness, and an inner stillness that made them totally unobtrusive. Toko exhibited all of these.

The boy touched his head to the mat, "This is too great an honor, Sire."

"We will see. But today you are still a servant and I am waiting for my fruit."

The boy turned to the shoji, opening it a fraction, and then placed a bowl on the table.

"Kamu-sum is here, Sire," the servant said softly.

The lord nodded and turned back to the garden and began popping segments of a peeled orange into his mouth. The old man was there, bowing, waiting in silence. Shonto finished his orange, savoring each segment, having so recently been reminded of how easily it could be his last.

"So, Kamu, a morning of surprises, yeh?"

"I feel nothing but shame, Sire. This lapse in security is my responsibility entirely. An assassin among your own guard. . . ." He shook his head in disbelief. "I . . . I grow old and forgetful, Sire. I am no longer worthy to serve you."

"I will decide that. Has our young Brother arrived?"

"Not yet, Sire."

"So," Shonto nodded toward the Captain of the Guard, "I will talk with this one now."

Kamu rose and went to the single step off the veranda where he cleared his throat. The captain raised his eyes for the first time since entering the garden. Kamu nodded, commanding without words in the manner of those accustomed to power.

The steward turned to leave, but Shonto raised his hand and Kamu returned to his place and his silence.

The Captain of the Shonto House Guard walked toward the two men sitting on the veranda. He had no doubt about who was to blame for the morning's incident and he had no doubt of what the result of it would be—and that, the captain believed, was justice. For this reason he remained entirely composed and Shonto had a second of admiration for the man's unruffled dignity. It would not sway him in his judgment, however.

Rohku Saicha had been the Captain of the Guard for a decade. He was forty-seven years old. During the time of Shonto's father, the captain had been a reknowned soldier and had risen through the ranks during the Interim Wars that led to the establishment of the Yamaku Dynasty. It was said that when it came to intrigue Rohku could uncover a plot before it had been spoken. This had made him the perfect choice for Captain of the Guard—until today.

Rohku Saicha stopped before Shonto and took the sheathed sword from his sash, laying it carefully on the gravel border before the veranda. He bowed his head to the ground and spoke without looking up.

"I return this gift to you, Lord Shonto. I am no longer worthy of it."

Shonto nodded. The immediate responsibility for any breach in security belonged to the Captain of the Guard and though he was of lesser rank than Kamu, the captain's will prevailed in matters of security. Below the lord himself, the ultimate responsibility for anything occurring within the Shonto domain rested with the steward and he could therefore be held to blame, though this would not be usual—at least not in Shonto's House. He was not known for the irrational purges of his staff that other lords indulged in.

"So, I ask you both. How is it that this assassin, this Tokago Yama, came to be in my personal guard?"

The Guard Captain spoke. "Tokago Yama is the son of Tokago Hideisa who was a captain in your father's Fourth Army. Hideisa-sum was killed in the battle in which your father was betrayed, I honor his memory. The Takago have served the House loyally for seven generations, though Yama-su . . . Yama has brought them eternal shame.

"He was assigned to your personal guard recently,

Sire. I did this at his request because he said," Rohku stopped and spoke slowly, recalling the words with care, "that guarding his lord required utter concentration and took his mind away from his grief. I was swayed by this, Sire. His wife and son were drowned not long ago aboard a boat proceeding from the Floating City.

"Yama was always an exemplary soldier, Sire. I misjudged him entirely." The man's shoulders sagged, but his voice remained calm and respectful.

So, Shonto thought, no one knows but me. How strange. They let their sense of failure cloud their thinking.

"There was no indication of Yama's change of loyalty?"

"Since the loss of his family, Yama has been withdrawn—as one would expect. Of late, he has gone off by himself whenever he could, but in his duties he has always been most conscientious. I valued him, Sire, and I believed he revered you."

"I remember the accident," Shonto said, "a river junk, yeh? Was it ever found?"

Kamu spoke, quietly. "No, Sire, it disappeared beyond Yul-ho. Strange, because the river there is shallow and easily navigable. It never reached the light-boat at Yulnan, disappearing with all hands and a valuable cargo."

"We did not consider piracy?"

"On the river, Sire?"

Shonto shrugged and went on, "So, how is it that a man who, I'm told, revered me became an assassin, Kamu?"

"His grief, Sire. It must have driven him mad."

Shonto grunted. I'm surrounded by romantics, he thought, *Botahara save me!*

"So. A perfectly good soldier, from a long line of Shonto retainers, is driven mad by grief at the loss of his family and attempts to assassinate his liege-lord during a meeting with a representative of the Emperor—a man who just happens to be one of the most formidable fighters in Wa?"

The two men before Shonto made no sound, as indeed they would have made no sound if he had whipped them.

"Has it not occurred to you that Yama could have chosen a better time? He had great opportunity, yeh? One of my personal guards?"

"Excuse me, Sire, but that is why madness makes sense. Why else would he choose to assassinate you at . . ."

Shonto slammed his fist on the table, his patience at an end. "He was *not* trying to assassinate *me!*"

The wind played in the bamboo, the stream burbled. There was no other noise.

"I was not here at the time, Sire," Kamu said in a small voice, "but I was informed that Yama had attacked you and that Jaku Katta stopped him."

"Yes, Kamu, and who told you that?"

"A lieutenant of the guard, I believe."

I'm sorry, Kamu, but you deserve this. "Toko," Shonto said over his shoulder, surprising Kamu by knowing the servant's name. "Can you remember who gave Kamu this information?"

"Jaku Katta," the boy answered quickly, embarrassed that he was being used to shame Kamu.

"I do not understand, Sire," Kamu said, all traces of his normal ease of manner gone.

Well, I won't shame you further by having the servant explain things, Shonto thought.

"Tokago Yama was trying to kill Jaku Katta." Shonto said, and he was sure the boy behind him nodded. "Jaku blew smoke in your eyes, Kamu."

"But why? Why would Yama try to kill Jaku here, in your house? And what would make Jaku say the attack was aimed at you?"

"I can think of a hundred reasons. They could all be wrong."

"Perhaps," the captain paused to gather his thoughts, "perhaps Yama believed his wife and child to be still alive. Taking hostages would explain why the ship was not found. Stranger things have happened." The Guard Captain seemed relieved to learn that his lord's life had not been in danger. Of course, this made no difference to his failure of duty. "It becomes a question of who would want Jaku killed in the House of Shonto at the hand of the Shonto guard. The Emperor would have no choice but to respond. Two birds with one stone, yeh?"

"Jaku has many enemies," Kamu said.

Yes, and Shonto has enemies, the lord noted.

The servant moved to answer a tap at the shoji, and then whispered to Kamu who moved to the opening. There was more hushed conversation, which Shonto ignored.

"Excuse me, Sire," Kamu said. "Guards have just found Yama's brother, Shinkaru. He has fallen on his sword in the back courtyard."

The Captain of the Guard shook his head sadly, "Shame," he whispered without meaning to.

"Huh," Shonto grunted and then addressed the sky. "Does no one in my House know his place? I would have talked with this brother before he *indulged* himself!" The lord drank off the rest of his mead in a single swallow and immediately the servant replenished the cup.

"Did we question the keeper of the light-boat at Yulnan?" Shonto asked suddenly.

"He was questioned by the Imperial Guard as soon as we reported the boat missing.

"But we did nothing?"

"The Imperial Guard administer the waterway, Sire."

Shonto stared into his garden for a long while, then he spoke, his manner suddenly light. "We need to find out why Yama tried to kill Jaku Katta and we need to know immediately. We will spare no energy in this matter. If the wife and child didn't drown, we must know. We will talk to everyone who would have had reason to be on the river that night. Perhaps the Imperial Guard will learn of our inquiries and lead us to someone with knowledge.

"The second thing I want is *Jaku Katta's soul!* I want to know everything about him—everything! He must be watched always. When he sleeps, I want to know his dreams. And his immediate lieutenants—these green-eyed brothers—watch them also. Have we anyone in the general's house?"

Kamu shook his head.

"Then get someone. If Jaku can infiltrate my house, then I can infiltrate his." Shonto's mind was racing now, each thought seeming to lead to a dozen others. "All care must be taken. No one else—I mean no one!—must learn what Jaku's true intention was. The Black Tiger must never know that we have seen through his charade—if he even suspects that this is so, our advantage will be lost. He has saved Lord Shonto from an assassin. No one inside or outside of this garden should hear otherwise. We do not know who else Jaku may have in this house." Shonto cast his eye on each man in turn. "Is this understood?" All nodded. "Good." Shonto looked out into the garden, thinking.

"The Emperor's Sonsa—find out what you can about her also. There is much to do. The Shonto have been inactive too long. It is a mistake to believe that because we threaten no one, no one is threatened by us."

"Captain." Shonto surprised the guard by using his rank. "You are in charge of these matters I have just spoken of. Also, you will be responsible for Lady Nishima's safety while I am in Seh—we will discuss this later. If you perform these duties successfully, you will have redeemed yourself. You may go."

"But Sire . . ." the captain stammered, "they will say you have grown soft!" He was obviously shocked at how lightly he was being treated.

"Good! Let Jaku Katta think that I am soft. The truth is I need all of you. I can afford no more indulgences among my retainers. Go."

The man bowed and rose, crossing the garden on unsteady legs. He left by a concealed gate, his mind in turmoil. He could not overcome the shame he felt at being allowed to live.

Shonto reached into the fruit bowl distractedly.

"Are you sure, Lord Shonto?" Kamu said, hesitation in his voice. Only his age and position gave him the privilege of asking such a question. "The captain is right, the entire Empire will hear of this."

Shonto glared at the old man. He was tempted to dismiss him, the question ignored. "No, Kamu, it is not wise, it is an impulse. A message for Jaku Katta to ponder. What is done is done. We are in a much better position now than we were an hour ago. Jaku Katta has revealed that which he meant to hide. For this knowledge I could forgive Rohku almost anything."

Kamu shook his head forlornly, and spoke to no one in particular. "It is perhaps time for me to retire. I no longer see the things that my position requires me to see. I am adrift in all of this."

"You were not here during the attack, so you could not have seen what I saw. The Black Tiger was *prepared* for the assault! He knew it was coming. Only after Yama was certainly dead, did Jaku claim this was an attack on me.

"I am amazed by this, Kamu. Two possibilities seem clear to me: someone wanted Jaku dead in my house by the hand of a Shonto guard—someone who was both an enemy of Jaku and mine—but Jaku got wind of the plot and decided to use it to his own advantage. It appears that he has saved my life, yeh?"

"The second possibility is that Jaku planned the whole thing to unsettle me, to make me believe that Jaku is an honorable man or a thousand other reasons. Until we know more, it would be foolish to say."

"Should we not ask ourselves if Yama had his own reasons for wanting Jaku dead?"

"This does not seem likely. A Shonto House Guard and the advisor to the Emperor? If Yama did have private reasons for wanting to destroy Jaku, then it would seem unlikely that the general would know about them or that Yama would do it here, where the Emperor would certainly hold me responsible. Everyone who knew Yama must be questioned, perhaps that will give us a clue."

Shonto sipped his mead and stared into the void. "There is something else I need to know, Kamu. Quite recently, within the last two years, the old Komawara of Seh sold a piece of his fief. I need to know how much was paid for this land and I need to know today, before the midday meal. I will have Lord Komawara as a guest and we will share our fare with Tanaka and perhaps the young Brother. We will see. Have they arrived yet?"

"They are expected within the hour."

"Good. I will meet with them as soon as they have bathed and refreshed themselves. Open the upper reception hall to the sun. That will be formal enough. You may go."

The old warrior bowed and rose, backing out through the shoji the servant opened behind him.

"Oh, Kamu." The steward stopped. "You will take Toko here as an assistant. Train him, and if you feel he is of any value then see what he can do, yeh? That is all."

Shonto was alone, his mind racing to try to make sense of all the information the morning had provided. His thoughts settled on Jaku Katta.

That man, thought Shonto, is cunning beyond belief and willing to take great risks. But he is rash! Oh, he is rash! He believes this display will win me to his side. Jaku the brave, Jaku the prescient, yeh? Who could not want such a formidable man for his ally—or for a son-in-law? Shonto truly believed that Jaku was capable of precipitating a crisis in Wa in the belief that one as nimble as the Black Tiger could only gain by it. So he thinks that he can hold the Emperor in the palm of one hand and Shonto in the other, but he holds a *scorpion* and a *wasp*. Shonto smiled broadly. What fun we had today, Jaku! Don't make too many mistakes too soon; we can have more fun yet. Shonto laughed aloud and banged the table with the flat of his hand, completely unaware of the servant kneeling behind him.

So, Shonto thought, I go to Seh and the Emperor believes this fits his plans, while Jaku thinks my journey is to his benefit. The game begins in earnest now. The board must be turned around so that only Shonto will benefit from Shonto's moves.

There was one last piece of information that Shonto had that he was sure Rohka's inquiries would not reveal. Jaku Katta had only once lost the kick boxing championship of Wa and that had been eight years earlier. If Shonto was right, the Black Tiger had been defeated by a young Botahist Neophyte. Shonto rubbed his hands together. What, he wondered, were the Botahist Brothers sending him?

The lord's attention was drawn back to the garden. Cocking his head to one side he listened, then suddenly he laughed long and loud. The trampled patch of bamboo now whispered with an entirely different voice. The garden had regained its harmony.

# Five

Only the Emperor's most trusted advisors were received in the private Audience Hall off the Imperial apartments. Only the most trusted advisors and spies.

The man who bowed his head to the floor before the Most Revered Son of Heaven had at one time served as a spy but had risen to the rank of general and Commander of the Imperial Guard.

"Be at your ease, Katta-sum," the Emperor said, gesturing for the general to raise himself and kneel in comfort.

"Thank you, Sire."

Kneeling before the dais in his black uniform, the Commander of the Imperial Guard seemed entirely relaxed, and that could be said of few who came before the Emperor.

"The autumn trade winds seem to have taken a deep breath, Katta-sum. It will be good if they carry with them all that we need to fill the treasury."

"I'm sure they will, Sire. All the reports indicate that this will be an exceptional year."

The Emperor nodded, waving the Dragon Fan in a gesture of salute. Voluminous robes of gold bearing the Imperial Dragon seemed to increase the Emperor's size three-fold, making his sword of office, which stood to one side on a stand, seem insignificant.

"So tell me, General," the Emperor said, snapping his fan closed, signifying an end to the polite formalities, "how was your visit to the esteemed Lord Shonto?"

"It was as you said, Sire." Jaku shook his head slowly. "This young monk has some special significance attached to him. Shonto was unmoved when I told him of your displeasure at his decision to employ a Spiritual Advisor. A hint that his daughter could be vulnerable while he was in Seh was ignored, and when I informed him that you, Sire, were considering halting all sea traffic out of Yankura, to 'starve the pirates,' he merely shrugged as though it wouldn't cost him triple to transport his goods in and out of his fief by land. There was no moving him, Sire."

The Emperor's smile disappeared to be replaced by a scowl. "These treacherous Brothers are up to no good, Katta-sum. They plot with the cunning Shonto, I know it. This stir over a young monk it is most uncommon." The Son of Heaven shook his head. "What can be so unusual about a young Initiate? Something is very wrong here, I feel it."

"I fear you are right, Sire. But soon we shall know more. The ship bringing Shonto his monk has docked. A messenger is coming, even now."

"That fool Ashigaru? What can you expect from that fanatic?"

"Nothing directly, Sire. He will certainly fail, but the attempt will have been made by a Tomsoian priest. That will throw the Brotherhood into an uproar. And the one I sent to watch is most observant. I chose him personally. We will know the details of Ashigaru's failure and that will give us a measure of Shonto's monk."

The Emperor snorted. "It were better if the ship and all aboard her went to the bottom. Then we would be rid of this Botahist thorn forever."

"If the ship *could* be sunk, Sire. There's an excellent captain in charge of a fast ship. A Shonto man, undoubtedly. He will not come by the usual sea lanes, and once he rounds Cape Ujii we dare not touch him. The traffic is too great and the act would be known.

"'I think this way is best. We send Shonto and his Botahist servant north together. We keep the Lady Nishima here in the capital, and Shonto's son will be sent to administer the family fief. The family will be spread throughout the Empire. Shonto will get no warm reception in the north, this being the slap in the face we intend. The northern lords are proud and will not take kindly to the suggestion that they cannot guard their own border against the degenerate barbarians. Shonto's time in the north will not be pleasant, I assure you, Sire."

The Emperor laughed. He nodded. "I am too impatient, Katta-sum. You do me good. Your foresight is most appreciated."

Jaku bowed his head. "You do me too much honor, Sire. I am not worthy."

The Emperor raised his eyebrows at this. "So what is this story of an assassin in Shonto's garden?"

If Jaku was surprised, he showed no sign of it. "I was about to tell you, Sire."

"Of course."

"It was really a bungled attempt on Shonto by one of his own guards. He would not have fallen to it, he is too quick. It seemed appropriate that I dispatch the assassin, thereby curbing any suspicion that the Throne was behind the attempt. It was an embarrassing situation, Sire, Shonto threatened by one of his elite guards and the murderer stopped by your servant. The whole Empire will know of it by week's end. Shonto will look the fool—and we send such a one north to save the men of Seh!" Jaku smirked.

"Don't be so smug, General. It would take more than that to damage the reputation of Shonto Motoru. He is a shrewd man and you would do well not to underestimate him."

"Of course, you are right, Sire. I apologize for my lack of humility." Jaku touched his head to the mat.

"Shonto must be kept off balance and must never know what is afoot, Kattu-sum. He is too masterful a player and we cannot afford a single error."

"Everything goes as planned, Sire. In three days Lord Shonto will depart for the north, leaving Lady Nishima here in the capital. Everything we had hoped for has been arranged in Seh—everything and more."

"We still have concerns, Katta-sum. Promising the governorship to two different parties is a great risk."

"But neither of them can speak of it openly, Sire. If Shonto were to hear even a rumor that someone was preparing to take his place with your approval—there would be no hope for the man. Shonto has never hesitated to eliminate a rival, nor has he ever failed. We must have at least two parties working against Shonto, Sire, and two will be just sufficient.

"In the off chance that Lord Shonto does find out about the plot . . ." the general shrugged, "we know nothing of it."

"It is still a great risk! If our hand is seen in this, Shonto's suspicion may turn to us entirely. That would be disastrous!"

"Shonto suspects everyone, Sire—everyone at all times. And after today he even has his own staff to fear." Jaku smiled coldly. "We cannot fail, Sire, I am sure of it."

"We hope you are right, Katta-sum. Others have thought they held the Shonto in their hands and have been cruelly surprised. Such surprises are not appreciated." The Son of Heaven banged the heels of his hands together with force. "*Damn* my fool of a father! If he had done as I advised, he would have done away with the old Shonto when he had the opportunity!"

"But then the son would have sought revenge, Sire," Jaku reminded him.

"Yes, and we would have fought him then as we fight him now! I see no difference. We cannot sit securely on the Throne while the Shonto live. They have too much power, too much ambition, and this Fanisan daughter— she is the eye of the storm that threatens to overwhelm us. If Shonto gives her to a great House, then there will be war. There will be no choice. And oh, how he bides his time! Whom will he pick as ally? Whom?

"*Damn* that superstitious fool! *Damn him!*" the Son of Heaven banged his fist on his armrest and cursed his Imperial father with passion.

"Perhaps your father did you a favor, Sire," Jaku said tentatively. "Now you fight Shonto Motoru on your terms and not on his. And this time there is no soothsayer secretly in Shonto's pay to strike fear into our hearts if we move against the Shonto clan. Things are very different."

"Yes, Katta-sum, you are right. I know you are." The Emperor's fit of anger passed as though it had never been. "We must talk again tomorrow. I wish to be kept informed on this matter at all times. And I'm still expecting a written report on the situation in Seh, Katta-sum, you haven't forgotten?"

"It can be in your hand within the hour, Sire."

"Good. Tomorrow, then."

Jaku Katta touched his head to the mat, palms flat on the floor, then rose and backed out, leaving the Emperor alone in the heavily guarded Audience Hall.

The Emperor stroked his mustache and smiled, the heavy lines in his face disappearing. He laughed.

The Son of Heaven ordered food and ate, attended by several servants, his mood improving by the moment.

You are almost in my hands, Shonto Motoru, I can feel it! And I keep my hands very strong in anticipation.

He laughed several times during the meal for no apparent reason, which startled the servants who were unused to gaiety in their master. It unsettled them considerably.

After he had eaten and finished a lingering cup of cha, a retainer knocked and announced Lieutenant Jaku Tadamoto, younger brother of the esteemed general.

"Ah, my report," the Emperor said, waving the servants out. The lieutenant entered—a tall, slim version of his famous brother. But Jaku Tadamoto had none of the physical presence of the champion kick boxer and could be as inconspicuous as a servant—until he spoke. Not that his voice was unusual; it wasn't that, it was his use of words that commanded one's attention, for he used them, not in the offhand manner almost universally heard even among the educated, but like an artist used a fine tipped brush—with infinite discretion and precision.

Jaku Tadamoto was also a scholar of some accomplishment and possessed a fine critical mind. His interest in the past gave him a much broader view than his older brother who, though brilliant in his own way, tended to concentrate on the immediate at cost to the future.

The Emperor had only come to realize this through a spy he had placed in Jaku's midst—a master spy to watch the spy-master! So despite Katta-sum's attempt to keep his younger brothers in the background, the Son of Heaven had skillfully arranged to meet the young men by demanding that messages passed between the general and the Emperor never be delivered by a lackey, no matter how trusted. So the two brothers became messengers and the Emperor came to know them. He realized immediately that one was of no consequence, a common, unexceptional soldier, while the other, Tadamoto, was brilliant.

Jaku Tadamoto prostrated himself before the Emperor.

"Be at your ease, Lieutenant," the Emperor said, with warmth.

"Thank you, Sire. I am honored that . . ." He went through the formalities the situation required and the Emperor let him do so, not yet ready to allow the familiarity that he granted Jaku Katta.

Finally the Emperor gestured with his fan. "Have you something for me from your esteemed brother?"

"I do, Sire, the report he promised you this morning."

"Excellent. Please leave it here." The Emperor pointed with his fan to the edge of the dais. As he had ordered all the servants out for the sake of privacy, there was no one to carry the scroll and it was out of the question that the Emperor would receive it himself.

"May we enquire into the well-being of your family?" the Emperor asked.

"I am honored that you would ask, Sire. My wife and son are healthy and dutiful and ever grateful for the honor the Emperor has given our name. My brothers . . ." he broke into a smile. "Excuse me, Sire, but how can they be anything but blissful at their good fortune in being allowed to serve our revered Emperor?"

"Ah. And what of your brother's concerns? Is he still

troubled by the unfortunate woman and child he had taken under his roof?"

"They trouble him no more, Sire."

The Emperor waited.

"They have departed this plane for the time being."

"How sad. An accident?"

"The woman took her own life and that of her son, Sire."

"So tragic, yeh? After all your brother had done for them?"

"Most certainly, Sire."

"And you still don't know who she was, this woman?"

The brother of Jaku Katta shifted uncomfortably and the Emperor fixed him with an intense stare.

"It seems possible, Sire, that this woman had been at one time a very minor lady-in-waiting to the Lady Nishima Fanisan Shonto. Though it seems more likely that she was a favored servant."

The Emperor moved, placing an elbow on his arm rest and leaning his chin on his fist. He showed no other reaction.

"How kind of your brother to take in a woman who had fallen from such a position. Few would have such compassion. And to tell no one! Modesty, no doubt. Very noble of him. Of course, we will say nothing of this to him. It shall be his secret, but we must admit that this act of kindness has affected us greatly."

There was silence while the Emperor digested this new information.

"So, the Lady Nishima. Hmm. I wonder if this unfortunate woman would have provided Katta-sum with any information about the great lady?" His eyebrows rose, punctuating the sentence.

"It seems possible, Sire. Information about the Shonto is crucial to the Imperial purpose at this time."

"Ah, yes, the *Imperial purpose*."

"My brother would never bother the Emperor with mere speculation, Sire. I'm sure if he can verify any information he may have received, then he would report it."

"I don't doubt it for an instant, Lieutenant, so say nothing about this conversation. I would never have a man as proud as your brother think that I doubt him. Not for a moment."

"As you wish, Sire. You can count on my discretion."

The Emperor nodded his thanks. "The Lady Nishima is a desirable woman, yeh?"

"I agree, Sire."

"Unfortunate that Katta-sum does not have the rank to merit such a woman. Most unfortunate."

Jaku Tadamoto said nothing.

"And what of my lovely Sonsa, Tadamoto-sum? Have you done as I asked? I wish to be reassured that she is in no danger."

"I assure you that she is not, Sire. And her devotion to you seems unquestionable. She lives only for dance and for her Emperor."

"Huh. I am truly fond of her, Tadamoto-sum, but," the Emperor paused as though searching for words, "I am an Emperor, after all, and she . . ." He let his open hand drop. "But I would like to see her happy and settled."

Ah, I have your attention now, young Jaku, the Emperor thought. "I must consider this. An Emperor must always be fair, yeh? Just as he must reward loyalty. I will consider this."

Jaku Tadamoto nodded agreement.

"Yes," the Emperor said distractedly, then he turned his attention back to the man sitting in front of him as though seeing him for the first time. The Son of Heaven smiled broadly.

"I thank you for discussing these things with me, Tadamoto-sum. I worry about your brother. He is so dedicated in his duties and takes so little time for himself, yeh? We must talk again. There are other matters we wish to discuss with you. We value your counsel, and your loyalty has not gone unnoticed. We will talk soon."

Jaku Tadamoto backed out of the Audience Hall, his heart soaring.

A look of confusion came over the Emperor's face as

the doors closed. He shook his head. How could such an intelligent man allow his desires to set his course, the Emperor wondered? Strange. Well, perhaps he *would* give Tadamoto-sum the girl at some future date. No one else would dare to court her. The Emperor smiled at the thought of the previous night. Tadamoto-sum had not earned her yet.

Such strange brothers. So Jaku Katta desires Lady Nishima. The Emperor snorted. Had the general taken leave of his senses? The entire family will bring ruin upon themselves over women! Lady Nishima! Jaku must realize how impossible that is. The Black Tiger plots—but what? A secret alliance with Shonto? To deliver me into Shonto hands? Perhaps he plots with one of my useless sons. Is it possible that Jaku could be truly smitten with Shonto's daughter—endangering himself like a lovesick fool?

The Emperor reached behind him and took the ancient sword of his office from its stand, drawing it half out of its scabbard, without thinking.

And what of this woman and her son, he wondered? A maid of Lady Nishima, huh. I'm willing to wager a province that she was connected with the attempt on Shonto's life. If that is indeed what it was! Oh, Katta-sum, what a disapointment you are to me. This throne infects everyone around it with the desire to possess it. Worse than any woman, yeh? He laughed bitterly. The difference between us, Katta-sum, is that I possess this most desirable of women, the Throne, while you never shall.

There came a knock on the screen to his right and a servant opened the private door revealing his Sonsa mistress, a questioning smile on her face, her head cocked to one side showing the fine curve of her neck.

"Ah, Osha-sum!" He broke into a toothy grin as she came toward him, seeming to float as all the Sonsa did. The shoji closed behind her as she crossed the room, without a bow, directly into his arms in one lithe motion, seeming to curl all of herself against him at once. His face flushed and his pupils went wide with pleasure.

"How good to touch you, Sire. My body misses you."

"Since this morning?" he teased.

"Oh, yes. Certainly. It missed you as soon as we parted and gave me no peace all through my training. I danced so badly, completely unable to concentrate as a Sonsa should."

He kissed her neck and she arched it with pleasure. The fine silk of her kimono seemed almost as soft as her skin as he touched her. The bow of her sash came undone easily as soon as he pulled it and the Emperor realized it had been tied in a "lover's knot." He laughed at this discovery.

"Oh, hoh! The servants will have noticed," he teased.

"Oh, no. It isn't possible, I can tie the knot perfectly. No one can tell the difference. I have practiced for you."

"You have so many talents that are never seen on the stage. Are all the Sonsa so talented?"

Her outer robe of sky blue fell open to reveal her three inner kimonos and these he opened slowly, kissing her shoulders, thrilled by the softness of her skin. Her breasts were tiny; he had never known a woman so small.

"The light in my chamber is beautiful this time of day," he whispered to her, his breathing already heavy. She took his face between her hands and kissed him passionately.

A shoji behind the dais opened into a hall that led to his sleeping chambers. Sunlight poured into the room through paper screens set high in the walls, a beautifully filtered light like the sun falling through forest leaves. A massive, low bed lay bathed in this light, its coverlets of flower patterns resembling the forest floor. They sank into this softness.

She did not find him unusual as a lover, this man who commanded so huge an Empire. In fact he would have been quite ordinary but for the passion he had for her which seemed boundless. And he was *strong*, stronger than she would have guessed and the Sonsa were usually unerring judges of the human body. The Son of Heaven knelt slowly, lifting her with him, supporting her with little effort.

When they finished, he was like a man who had fought a battle. He lay on top of her completely spent, his breathing deep and languorous. At that moment she always felt amazing abandon, and her mind wandered in the most surprising manner, leading her to wonder about other men, many of them, like the tiger-eyed Jaku Katta whom she had seen earlier as he came from his audience with the Emperor. And Lord Shonto, with whom she had danced the night before. She laughed at herself for these fantasies, calling herself "the secret Yellow Empress" after the Empress Jenna, who, it was said, had known a thousand men while she controlled her son on the Dragon Throne. It was even rumored that she had known her *own* son. Amazing!

Yes, she thought, that is me, the secret Yellow Empress, desiring every man who catches my eye. She laughed inwardly, desiring them but making love to them only when she danced, and making them want her in return.

Osha thought of Shonto as she lay warm and still aroused. She had brushed against him as they had danced the Dance of the Five Hundred Couples. A certain amount of flirtation was expected in these dances, but she had been *shameless* and had learned that he was hard-bodied, like a much younger man, and fluid in his movements for one with no training. The famous Lord Shonto, the man her Emperor hated. Osha had been so curious to know who this man was when the rumors were stripped away. But of course there had been no time for them to speak, not there. All she had learned was that he was quick of wit, which she had expected, and that he seemed to enjoy the company of younger people, surrounded as he was by his daughter's friends.

Why did the Emperor hate this man? Most curious. But he would never discuss Shonto with her, never Shonto. So very odd.

She drifted off into a soft dream, the *Yellow Empress* inside her given full reign. Osha smiled as she slept.

# Six

Lord Shonto sat on a low dais in the upper Audience Hall leaning on his arm rest, chin in hand. He gazed out at the long, empty room and watched the dust particles turning slowly in the sunlight that streamed through the open wall. On the straw-matted floor a pattern of large rectangles glowed golden in the light that fell between the posts. The autumn day was warm, the air rich with the smells of the season.

Shonto consciously controlled his breathing and tried to empty his mind of all its noise. He needed time to think after the visit of Jaku Katta. The lord sensed danger. Things were happening too quickly, becoming a rising wave of events that he neither controlled nor understood.

No one realized how much hope Shonto placed on the coming of his Spiritual Advisor, and now that the hour of their meeting had arrived he felt sudden, and unexpected, doubt. This was not Brother Satake returning; this was a very young man, a stranger of questionable loyalty with a lifetime of Botahist dogma behind him . . . and little experience of the real world—the very unspiritual world of Wa. Over the years Shonto had grown used to the quiet opinions of his former advisor, and relied heavily on the old monk's penetrating insight—and that was what bothered Shonto. Satake-sum had had long years of experience that the lord, his junior by several decades, had been able to draw upon. But his new advisor was almost as many years his junior as Satake-sum had been his senior.

Shonto drummed his fingers on the arm rest. The

attack in the garden had affected him more than he liked to admit. How could such a thing have happened in his house? Oh, Jaku, my sixth sense tells me that you were behind this "assassination attempt." If so, I will soon know. Even a Black Tiger can place a foot wrongly. Even a Black Tiger can be hunted.

A tap on the shoji brought Shonto back to himself. The face of a guard appeared in the doorway.

"Tanaka is here, Sire," the guard said quietly—not "Tanaka-sum," just "Tanaka," the merchant, technically a servant.

Shonto nodded and the guard pushed the door aside, allowing a corpulent man in a dark robe of the merchant class to enter. Shonto did not smile, though Tanaka's "disguise" always amused him. In Yankura, the Floating City, where the merchant oversaw Shonto's vast trading interests, he was known for the quality of his clothing and his penchant for hats in the latest fashion. But here, before his liege-lord, he was somber and dressed in a far from new, traditional robe of his class.

The merchant bowed his head to the floor in the most humble manner and then sat back, saying nothing. The shoji closed behind him.

"Come forward," Shonto said, gesturing to a place before the dais.

Tanaka walked forward on his knees, stopping several paces away from his lord. Shonto regarded the merchant, a man who had served his father. A loyal man. Tanaka's intelligent face stared back at him and Shonto realized that the merchant was making his own assessment of his liege-lord. Shonto smiled.

"It is good to see you, old friend," the lord said, paying the older man greater respect than the use of the honorific "sum" could ever convey.

Tanaka bowed. "I am honored that you receive me, Sire. May I say that it is good to see you looking so well. I was most concerned when I heard of the events of this morning."

Shonto nodded, not surprised that the news had reached Tanaka. The merchant had his own sources in

Shonto's staff, all well meaning, and impossible to purge for that very reason.

Except for the Lady Nishima, Tanaka was the closest thing to a friend Shonto had, and, in a way, their difference in rank was what allowed their friendship to exist—in Wa equals too often had conflicting interests. But the difference between Shonto and his merchant could never be bridged—master and servant always—and so the understanding between them, out of necessity, never seemed to breach the conventions of the society. But it was an association that both men valued and protected with all of their considerable powers.

"And how are things in the Floating City?"

"The Floating City seems to be floating these days on rumor and intrigue and an army of Imperial Guards dressed as anything but Imperial Guards."

"This is unusual?"

"Not perhaps unusual, Sire, but 'escalated.' This young Brother seems to have the servants of the Emperor most concerned."

"The actions of the servants of our Emperor can never be explained. Does your work go well?"

"Very well, Sire. This should be the most productive year ever. May I ask if you have heard the rumor that his Imperial Highness, in his wisdom, is considering outlawing coastal traffic in an effort to 'combat the pirates'?"

"I have heard this, though Jaku Katta-sum was here this morning and said nothing of it. Do you think it's true?"

"I hope not, Sire. It would have a great effect upon you and your allies. I believe that the Province of Seh would also feel the effects of such a law. Strange that this single action could be so entirely selective in whom it affects, yeh? Of course, we could survive it for a year, but even that would begin to tax us, and your allies—they would either be ruined or no longer allies. Personally, I believe we should consider other methods of dealing with this situation, if it arises."

"Other methods? Please continue, Tanaka-sum."

The merchant looked steadily at his lord for a second before speaking. "I make it my business to watch out for merchants who represent . . . powerful factions in Wa. If your interests are affected, I personally believe it would only be karma if these merchants I refer to were to be affected equally.

"If the pirates are deprived of coastal traffic to prey upon, they will no doubt be forced to turn to sea traffic. More difficult for them but not impossible, especially if they were to have certain intelligence, yeh? And there are ways of importing goods other than those sanctioned by the Son of Heaven."

"But those are outlawed and the penalty is death. Dangerous, yeh?"

"If you or your representative were to do so, Sire, certainly that would be dangerous, but others have their own business, their own karma."

"And how soon could these other methods be employed?"

"Tomorrow, Sire."

"Ah! So you have been anticipating this change in Imperial policy, old friend."

"It is my duty to guard your interests to the best of my ability, Sire. To that end, I make sure I hear rumors at their origin."

Shonto laughed and clapped his hands once, loudly. A screen opened to his right. "Bring cha for my guest and me.

"You are a most valuable man Tanaka-sum, I think you should have a large estate on my fief to retire to when you are ready to rest. And your young son, the one with all the curiosity, if you approve, he shall go into my officer corps."

The merchant bowed formally, overwhelmed by the suddenness of these gifts. "Agree? Of course! How could I refuse these honors. I accept on my son's behalf. He shall make a fine officer, Sire, I'm sure of it. Thank you."

Shonto shrugged. Cha arrived in steaming pots and separate tables were set for the two men, a servant kneeling by each, but Shonto waved them away. "We will pour for ourselves."

When the shoji closed, Shonto leaned toward his guest, "So tell me about our young Brother."

"Ah," Tanaka lifted the lid of his tea pot to smell the steeping herb. "He is indeed something special, something out of the ordinary. You received my report of his sea crossing?"

"I read it while you bathed."

The vassal-merchant shook his head. "Strange, the man committing suicide like that—the Emperor's man. He had nothing to lose offering the poison to Shuyun-sum, yet he chose not to." The merchant looked up, catching the lord's eye. "He is a magnetic young man, Sire. He has that quiet strength all the Brothers have . . . but to a greater extent. He has . . ." Tanaka groped for words.

*"Tranquillity of purpose."*

The merchant stopped short. *"Tranquillity of purpose*; yes, Sire.

"He met with Brother Hutto when he arrived in Yankura. I had no instructions, so I allowed him to do so."

"You acted correctly. How was the old monk?"

"I didn't go myself but sent guards as escort. They reported that Brother Hutto treated Shuyun-sum with great respect—almost as an equal."

"They exaggerate, surely! I would be surprised to hear that Brother Hutto thought the Emperor his equal."

"I was not there, Sire, but I believe the reports to be accurate."

"Huh. Did the two of you talk?"

"Some, Sire. He is like most Botahists, difficult to draw out, but even so I managed to find out a number of things."

"Such as?"

"He is well informed, Sire. The Brothers appear to have excellent sources of intelligence and obviously they have been preparing your advisor with care. His knowledge of the powers-that-be within Wa is good; his view of the political situation, broad; and, I must admit, he even has a working understanding of our economy, which I believe I have added to."

"No doubt. Did you talk of Seh?"

"Yes, and again he knew who the strongest lords were and what the history of their alliances has been. He knew who had married into which family and who could be considered as a possible ally. He views the entire endeavor with suspicion, though he said you were undoubtedly the finest general in Wa and the logical choice to send to Seh.

"Shuyun-sum also said something else, Sire, something I had not considered. He seems to think that there is a historical pattern in the barbarian wars, and that pattern, he believes, has now been broken." Tanaka paused as if gauging his lord's reaction, but Shonto said nothing so the merchant went on. "Shuyun-sum thinks that there is a twenty-five year cycle in which the last seven years see an escalation which may or may not then lead to major war depending on the situation of the barbarian tribes. Our young Brother thinks that certain factors are critical at this point—the economy of the tribes, the strength of their leaders, the quality of the resistance they experience in Seh, and also the effects of the climate on what *they* call *agriculture*. All of these things affect their ability and their desire to mount a major campaign against the Empire. Shuyun-sum has pointed out that it has been over thirty years since the last Barbarian War."

"Interesting. Do you think this is his own observation?"

Tanaka stroked his beard, his gaze far away. "A good point, Sire, I don't know."

*A message*, Shonto wondered, is this a message from the monks? He poured his cha and Tanaka did likewise. The lord began his habit of turning the cup in his hand as he stared into its depths, looking for answers, for questions.

"Did you ask him how he will resolve the conflict between his service to the Shonto and his alliegance to the Brotherhood?"

"I did, Sire. He said the interests of the Brotherhood and your interests were not in conflict."

"I see. And?"

"He seems to believe it, Sire. He is young despite his abilities—only time can erase naivete."

"His answer is not good enough, though it will do for now. Even the Botahist trained are not beyond influence , we shall see."

A swallow swooped through the open wall and out again, landing on the porch rail where it sat regarding the two men. Shonto watched the bird for a few seconds then said, his voice betraying a trace of weariness, "I heard a nightingale three evenings past, singing in the moonlight . . . it would be good to have peace again, yeh?"

"It would, Lord Shonto."

The two men sipped their cha and looked into the garden.

"Have you heard the most recent pronouncement of the Botahists' Supreme Master, Sire?"

Shonto turned his gaze from the swallow, "What now?"

"The Botahist Brothers have decided that though it's true women cannot attain enlightenment because they are too attached to the cycles of the earth, they can attain much greater spiritual knowledge than was formerly believed. Apparently they still think that women must finally be reborn as men before they can attain enlightenment. That point, they have not given up."

Shonto shook his head, "So, the celibate Brothers have finally realized that women have souls." The lord snorted. "How can such intelligent men suffer under so many delusions? If Brother Satake had become Supreme Master, he would have united the Sisterhood and Brotherhood and done away with this squabbling."

"That is one of the many reasons Satake-sum could not have become Supreme Master, Sire."

"True, my friend, true."

"The activities of the Botahist Brotherhood in the past

years have begun to intrigue me, Sire. Their policies seem suddenly out of character, inconsistent."

Shonto's interest rose immediately, "I have thought the same thing, Tanaka-sum. The Brotherhood has never been known to ingratiate itself with anyone in the past, but now they recognize the Yamaku dynasty of their own volition, receiving nothing in return but the Emperor's scorn; they gift the Son of Heaven valuable land, again receiving nothing in compensation; and now this sop to the Botahist Sisters. I believe that even I have been treated unusually. Kamu-sum arranged a most reasonable price for the services of our young Brother. He was full of suspicion afterward."

Tanaka shook his head, causing a golden drop of cha to fall from his mustache onto his dark robe. "The Empire is in the grip of some strange magic, Sire. I would have said that the Botahists would never lose their arrogance, their nerve, yet look at this! I do not understand. They must know that, despite his own convictions, the Emperor could never touch the Brotherhood without bringing about his own downfall. His own soldiers would take his head if the Guardians of Botahara's Word were ever threatened. I am less and less sure of what transpires in the Empire. Excuse me, Sire, I don't mean to sound pessimistic."

"Good, there is enough pessimism among my retainers over this appointment to Seh, and then this omen, this 'assassination attempt.' Huh!"

"It is only concern for their liege-lord, Sire. There is more to this appointment to Seh than meets the eye. Everyone feels that. We all fear treachery from this family that calls itself Imperial. We all fear the Yamaku trap."

Shonto's nostrils flared, "I've been in and out of a dozen traps in my time and have only wisdom to show for it. Have my own retainers come to doubt me?"

"Never, Sire! Their faith in you in unshakable, but they are concerned nonetheless, because they honor you, and the Shonto House."

Shonto sat for a moment staring into his cha. A knock

at the entryway seemed loud in the silence. The screen slid open and a guard's face appeared.

"Excuse me, Sire. Kamu-sum has sent the message you requested."

"Ah. Enter."

The servant, Toko, who had earlier in the day become an assistant to Kamu, knelt in the doorway and bowed. Shonto motioned him forward and he moved, kneeling, with the grace of one who has performed this act countless times. Removing a scroll from his sleeve and setting it within Shonto's reach on the dais, he bowed again and retreated the appropriate distance.

Shonto checked the seal on the scroll and then broke it, finding Kamu's spidery brushwork inside. "You may go," he said to the boy. When the shoji slid closed behind the servant, Shonto turned to his merchant. "After I have met with Shuyun-sum, you will join me in a meal with the young Lord Komawara. You remember his father?"

Tanaka nodded.

"The old Komawara sold a piece of his fief before his death, undoubtedly to allow the son to begin trade; so the new Lord of the Komawara is here to begin this endeavor. He will need guidance." Shonto consulted the scroll again and quoted a substantial sum in Imperial ril. "I wouldn't think he has the entire amount available, but we will assume he has a good portion of it. Do you have some venture he could invest in that would prove profitable?"

"For a knowledgeable man this is a time of great opportunities. I'm sure we can get the young lord started, but truly he should have his own vassal-merchant, Sire."

"But finding or training such a man takes time and I want him in Seh, not here."

"In that case I believe I can accommodate him until a suitable vassal-merchant can be found. I may be able to locate an acceptable person myself, if this would serve your purpose, Lord Shonto. But, Sire, surely you should assess him some part of his profit otherwise he will feel it is charity—a proud man would not allow that."

"As always, your advice is sound, Tanaka-sum. What would be appropriate in such a case?"

Tanaka caught the corner of his mustache between his teeth and worried it for a second, making his lord smile.

"Eight parts per hundred would be too generous, Sire . . . twelve parts would be fair."

Shonto smiled again. "Ten, then. I will suggest it over the meal. I want this young man treated with respect, old friend. He is not powerful in Seh, but he seems knowledgeable and that will be just as important."

"And he is the son of your father's friend," Tanaka said.

"Yes. He is the son of my father's friend," Shonto repeated.

Tanaka nodded and filed the figures away in his fine memory. Even as he did so, the merchant found himself observing his lord carefully. He had watched Shonto all the nobleman's impressive life—had watched the precocious child grow into the strong-willed young man, the young man become the head of one of the most powerful Houses in Wa. It had been an inspiring process to witness. Tanaka, though fourteen years older, had had his own education to concern him in those days, but still he had come to know Shonto Motoru—had come to admire him. The man Tanaka saw before him now looked like the gii Master that indeed he was—a man who surveyed the board in all of its complexity without thought of losing. A man who came alive to challenge.

Tanaka had often played gii with Shonto when they were young; the lord had learned the game too quickly and left the merchant-to-be far behind, but still he remembered the Shonto style forming—bold and subtle in turns. Equally strong on defense or offense. Shonto would understand the traps Tanaka laid better than the merchant understood them himself, sometimes stepping into them with impunity and turning them against their surprised designer. Yet the peaceful life of the gii Master was not possible for the bearer of the Shonto name and the lord had indulged his passion for the game for only a short time. In the end he had made gii subservient to his larger needs—using his skill at the board to make a point to any of his generals who questioned his decisions too often. The military men prided themselves on their ability at the gii board, yet few in all of Wa had the skill to sit across the board from the Lord of the Shonto as an equal.

"It seems a long time since the days when we played gii, Sire."

Shonto smiled warmly, "We still play gii, my friend, but the board has become larger than we ever imagined and now we share the pieces of the same side. Individually we are strong, together we are formidable. Don't ever think I'm unaware of this. The world has changed, Tanaka-sum; for better or for worse doesn't matter, it has changed irrevocably and therefore so must we. A strong arm and a sharp sword are not what they once were. We play a different game now, and in the next exchanges you will be a general in your own right. The Shonto interests must be protected at all costs. They are the basis of our future strength. Never forget that."

The merchant nodded and then, emboldened by his lord's confidence, spoke quietly, asking the question that weighed on him, "Why are you going to Seh, Lord Shonto?"

Without pause Shonto answered, "Because my Emperor commands it and therefore it is my duty."

Tanaka's eyes flicked to Shonto's sword in its stand and back to the Lord. "I heard of the Emperor's empty threat at his party. He cannot possibly believe you will fail?"

"No, I'm sure he doesn't. The barbarians are already beaten." Shonto paused and tapped his arm rest with his fingers. "And who else could he send to Seh that has my battle experience? Jaku Katta? No. He likes to keep the Black Tiger close to him, and not just for his protection. Lord Omawara is dying, I'm sad to say. There are a few others who have the fighting skills but would not command the respect of the men of Seh. The plague and the Interim Wars have destroyed a generation of worthy generals, Tanaka-sum. I am his only choice and yet . . .

he thinks I am his greatest threat. So, until the barbarians are put down, I believe I am safe from whatever the Emperor plots. I have a year—an entire year—that must be long enough."

The two men were silent then. Lord Shonto poured more cha, but it was overly strong so he let it sit and did not call for more.

"I am ready to meet my Spiritual Advisor now. Perhaps my spirit has need of this, yeh?" He clapped his hands twice and servants scurried in to remove the tables and the cha bowls. The guard opened the shoji at the far end of the hall. "Please bring in Brother Shuyun and the honored Brother."

Shonto felt his fists clenching involuntarily and he forced them to open, assuming a posture of studied ease. In the back of his mind he heard his own voice saying that Brother Satake would not have been fooled by this act. Satake-sum had missed nothing—not the tiniest detail.

Guards opened the screens at the end of the hall to their full width and a young monk, accompanied by a senior Botahist Brother, stepped inside. Yes, Shonto thought, he is the one, and visions of a kick boxing tournament years before flashed before his eyes.

The two men bowed in the manner of their Order, a quick double bow, low but not touching the floor, a gesture reserved only for the seniors of their faith or the Emperor.

Shonto stared at the small monk, ignoring his companion. Young, the lord thought, so young. Yet he seemed calm under this scrutiny. But was it real, Shonto wondered, was it that same inner stillness that his predecessor had possessed? Brother Satake had been a man who had not been in a perpetual state of reaction—constantly vibrating with the motion around him. With Satake-sum, there had been only stillness and silence—what the old monk had called "tranquillity of purpose," something Shonto had been able to achieve only to the smallest degree. "I offer no resistance," Satake-sum had answered when Shonto had questioned him, and that was all the explanation the lord had ever received.

Now Shonto found himself staring at this young man and trying to detect this same quality in the first seconds of their meeting.

He nodded and then spoke formally, "Come forward, honored Brothers, I welcome you to my House."

The two monks stopped within a respectful distance of the dais, Shuyun kneeling so that the shadow of a post fell in a dark diagonal across his chest, leaving his hands and his face in golden sunlight.

"Brothers, I am honored by your presence as is my House."

The older monk spoke in a soft voice that rasped deep in his throat. "The honor, Lord Shonto, is ours. I am Brother Notua, Master of the Botahist Faith, and this is Brother Shuyun."

Shonto nodded toward his Spiritual Advisor, noting the fine structure of his cleanly shaven face, the perfect posture without trace of stiffness. But the eyes unsettled him—the eyes did not seem to belong to the face. They were neither young nor old, but somehow ageless, as though they viewed time differently, and remained unaffected by it. Shonto realized that everyone was politely waiting for him to speak.

"Your journey has not been uneventful, I am told."

The young monk nodded, "There was a sad occurrence on board ship, Lord Shonto, but it found resolution."

"And the young girl?"

"She was well at the time she was taken from the boat, but understandably unhappy."

"I am curious about this incident, this merchant Kogami. He was a servant of the Emperor?"

"It would appear so, Sire."

"Did you realize that, Brother?"

The older monk observed this exchange carefully, he was surprised that Shonto had gone into this incident so soon, almost before it was polite to do so. Of course what was polite for a Botahist Brother and what was considered so for the Lord of the Shonto were different things."

"I thought it was so. The priest invoked the Emperor's protection during our confrontation . . . and then there was the poison. Such treachery is the way of the priests."

Shonto was silent for a moment. "And the priest, what happened to him?"

"He was met in the Floating City by Imperial Guards dressed as followers of Tomso." He said this with assurance and the lord did not doubt it was the truth.

"Huh. In the future you will not go beyond the walls of a Shonto residence without guards. The Empire is yet unstable and dangerous even to the disciples of the Perfect Master." Shonto looked around suddenly as if something were missing, "May I offer you mead, Brothers?"

Servants appeared at Shonto's call, and tables, laid with cups and flasks of fine mead, were set before the guests. Polite inquiries into the health of one's family would normally have followed, but Shonto turned again to the young monk. "Brother Shuyun, you should know that you replace a man I esteemed above all but my own father. You take up a difficult position."

"Brother Satake was an exceptional man and as honored in our Order as he was in your House, Sire. I'm sure he was irreplaceable. It is my hope that I may be of equal value to you in my own way."

Shonto nodded, seeming to find this answer acceptable. He hesitated a moment and then said, "Brother Satake, in an uncharacteristic moment, once demonstrated what he called 'Inner Force' by breaking a rather stout oar that had been placed across the gunnels of a sampan. He accomplished this by merely pressing down upon it with his hand without being able to bring the weight of his body to bear, for he was sitting at the time. None of the oarsmen could do this, and they were as strong as any of their profession, nor could I, and I was a younger man then. Do you know how this feat is performed, Brother?"

Shuyun shrugged slightly, "I am Botahist trained," he

answered simply, and Shonto saw the young man's eyes dart to the table before him.

Shonto clapped and servants slid aside the shoji. "Remove these things from Brother Shuyun's table."

After doing their master's bidding, the servants bowed and backed toward the exit.

"No, stay," Shonto said on impulse. I will have all the servants know of this, he thought. Then, committed to this course of action, Shonto clapped his hands twice and ordered the guard to enter and observe.

Brother Notua cleared his throat and then spoke in his soft voice, the rasp more pronounced than before, "Excuse me, Lord Shonto, but this is most ... unexpected."

Shonto drew himself up and answered, enunciating each word with care, "Is it not the custom that I should test the monk who is to be in my service *for a lifetime?*"

"It is, Lord Shonto. Excuse me if I appeared to criticize." The old monk smiled sweetly. "It just seemed to me ... Shuyun-sum has so many talents," the monk looked up at the fire in the lord's eyes. "Of course, this matter is for you to decide, excuse me for interupting, I ... please excuse me." He fell silent.

Shonto turned to Shuyun, "Do you have objections to this test, Shuyun-sum?"

"I am ready to begin, Sire, if that is your wish."

Shonto paused, deciding. "Begin," he said. He watched as the young monk entered a meditative state, slowing his breathing, his eyes focused on something unseen. Glancing at the older monk, Shonto realized that he, too, had begun to meditate. Strange, Shonto thought, but his attention was taken up by the younger monk.

Shuyun focused his being on the table in front of him. Time slowed and he followed the pattern of his breathing, a pattern as familiar to him as the halls of Jinjoh Monastery.

The table before him was beautifully made of iroko wood, a wood so dense that it would sink in water; "Iron Tree" it was called by the peasants who cut it. The top was twice the thickness of a man's hand, two hand lengths across, and stood at a convenient height for a person kneeling. Shuyun knew the table's joinery would be flawless and each plank selected for its strength and beauty—there could be no weakness in the structure, so there could be no weakness in his will.

In the sunlight streaming into the room, the monk's face appeared as peaceful as the face on a bronze statue of Botahara. Very slowly he drew his hand in a low arc and placed it, palm down, on the center of the table. The tight grain of the wood felt warm against his skin. Sunlight illuminated the fine hairs on the back of his hand and forearm. *He pushed.*

There was no visible change in the young monk's body, no sign of strain. And the table stood as solid as if it were carved from stone.

Botahara forgive me, Shonto thought, I have set him a task at which he must fail. Memories of an oar shattering came to him. Shonto cursed himself for this ill-considered act. Hadn't the old Brother tried to warn him?

Suddenly there was a sharp *crack*, and slivers of dark wood flew in all directions, spinning in the sunlight. The old monk drew back like one who has been brutally awakened by a slap, and on his face, clear for all to see, was a look of fear. The table had not buckled, it had exploded.

Guards and servants stood in the hall like statues of stone. The table lay smashed in the center like an animal broken under its load. Shonto slowly picked a sliver of iroko wood off his robe and turned it in his hand as though it were entirely alien material. No one else moved, no one spoke, preserving the moment as long as possible. Then Shonto bowed low to his Spiritual Advisor and everyone in the room followed his example.

Shuyun watched through his altered time sense as Lord Shonto bowed, watched the ripple of muscle that showed even through the man's robe.

Slowly Shonto returned to a kneeling position, his awe apparent, even to those not Botahist trained. But there was more than awe, there was wonder—wonder at what he had seen in the old monk's face.

Shuyun bowed in response as deeply as the shattered table would allow. He began the return to real-time; the sound of the birds changed tone, he watched Lord Shonto blink and the movement took only a fraction of a second.

Shonto nodded to the guard and the servants, dismissing them. "Shuyun-sum, my steward Kamu will take you on a tour of the grounds and give you the passwords. Please join us for the midday meal with Lord Komawara. Thank you." Shonto nodded to the monk, again with deference. "Brother Notua, please leave your papers with my secretary. It has been an honor."

The two monks bowed again and Shonto was sure that the older monk faltered almost imperceptibly as he rose but caught himself and backed from the room with dignity, leaving the lord in a state of confusion.

Shonto and Tanaka were alone again, but neither of them spoke. Before them the table lay broken, and Shonto noticed for the first time that the legs were pressed through the thick floor mats. He turned to Tanaka who was plucking a spear of iroko wood from his beard. Like his lord, he examined it carefully, as though it had a secret to reveal.

"How much weight would that table bear?" Shonto asked.

Tanaka shook his head and shrugged, "The weight of five large men?"

"Easily," Shonto shook his head. "Impossible, yeh?"

"According to my understanding of the principles of nature, yes, Sire. Even if it were possible for him to bring his entire weight to bear from a sitting position, he should have merely pushed himself away from the table." He shook his head and turned the sliver in his hands again. "I'm glad I saw this with my own eyes, otherwise I would not have believed it."

Shonto said nothing for several long moments. He considered asking Tanaka if he had seen the old Brother's reaction but something stopped him. Finally his eyes came back into focus and his face brightened. He smiled broadly. "A most interesting morning, Tanaka-sum! I wish to refresh myself before Lord Komawara arrives. Please join us later, in the summerhouse in the main garden."

He clapped his hands twice and spoke to the guard and servants who appeared. "See that no one disturbs this." He gestured to the broken table. Rising, the lord turned to leave by his private entrance, a servant rushing to take up his sword and follow.

Tanaka bowed but did not move until Lord Shonto was gone, then he went closer to the table, full of curiosity. The guard, who had positioned himself inside the door, cleared his throat. The merchant looked up, "Amazing, yeh?"

The guard nodded but continued to stare at Tanaka.

Suddenly the merchant realized that he still held the shard of iroko wood. He raised it. "What shall I do with this?"

"Lord Shonto ordered that nothing was to be disturbed."

"Ah, I see." Tanaka looked suddenly puzzled. "But as this clung to my beard, and I don't think Lord Shonto wished me to remain here until he has made a decision on what he will do with this table, I am puzzled."

The guard realized that Tanaka was having fun with him and despite the fact that Tanaka was a servant and the guard was an officer, there was no doubt in the man's mind that Tanaka was far more important to Lord Shonto than any legion of soldiers. "I think it should stay in the room, Tanaka-sum," the guard said, using the honorific.

"But anywhere I put it will not be its natural place and, therefore things will be disturbed, yeh?"

The guard felt his temperature begin to rise, but he remained outwardly calm. If the merchant forced him to go to Shonto to clarify what should be done about a sliver of wood, the lord would be furious. The guard shifted uncomfortably.

"Perhaps," Tanaka offered, "I could place it near where I sat and that will be the best we can do, yeh?"

The guard broke into a grateful smile, "Yes, I agree. That would be best. Thank you, Tanaka-sum.

The merchant returned the smile and set the piece of iroko wood on the floor in the agreed position and then swept out of the room with as much grace and confidence of manner as a lord.

Neither guard nor merchant was aware that a servant watched all of this through a crack between shojis, and that when he repeated the incident to Kamu, who had him repeat it to Shonto, the lord laughed and banged his fist on his arm rest with pleasure. The servant was greatly surprised by this reaction. Humor was sadly lacking among Shonto's retainers.

# Seven

*The canal beyond my garden*
*Is like a dark vein,*
*And yet I cannot*
*Take my eyes from it.*
*Where has he gone this long night?*
*And why does the canal*
*Flow so loudly?*

*Origin unknown but attributed to*
*the poetess, Lady Nikko,*
*or one of her students*

Lord Komawara Samyamu, the ninth Komawara Lord to be so named, watched the bustle on the canal's edge as his boatmen deftly guided his sampan among the throng of craft that filled the waterway. He had chosen to pass through a commercial area where cargo from the Floating City arrived, not because this was the most scenic or the quickest route to the House of Lord Shonto Motoru, but because Komawara wanted to see the variety and volume of trade—to see the commerce of the capital with his own eyes.

Soon, he thought, soon Komawara goods will arrive at these very quays and then there will be a change in the Komawara fortunes.

The young lord's sampan was preceded by only a single boat, in which rode his guard, and neither craft was of the ornate variety commonly seen in the capital. Komawara's steward had pressed him to hire more boats of better quality so the young lord would not arrive at the

Shonto estate looking like a country pauper, but Komawara had decided against this. Shonto, he knew, was too clever a man to be impressed by appearances and it was also likely he would have made himself familiar with Komawara's exact situation. Shonto would be able to acquire such information with ease, and would do so, out of course, with a new associate.

Yes, Komawara thought, and it is likely that no one, not even the Emperor, knows the scope of Shonto's holdings. I would look the fool to arrive in hired sampans, to wear a lie.

I am of an ancient House, he reminded himself, as ancient as the Emperor's. I have fought twenty skirmishes with the barbarians, a handful of duels, and I taught those cattle thieves, the Tomari, that the boundaries of my fief cannot be encroached upon. Shonto is a general of great reknown; he will judge me by what is important, I need have no doubt.

Yet the Lord of the Komawara did have doubts. He was on his way to meet the Lord of the Shonto, and who knew who else, for a meal. The Shonto! A family with a history unlike any other's. To think that Hakata the Wise, upon whose teachings were based all the principles of the Empire's government and law, had been a retainer of Shonto's ancestors. Generations ago a Shonto lord had sat with Hakata himself and discussed justice and moral philosophy as today people discussed the thoughts of the Wise One at their own tables. It was a Shonto lord who had the writings of Hakata inscribed upon the One Hundred and Three Great Stones that lined the Walk of Wisdom in the Shonto garden. The One Hundred and Three Great Stones at the Emperor's Palace and at the Imperial Academy were but copies of the Shonto originals.

Yet the man Komawara had met at the Emperor's party had not seemed at all impressed with his own greatness. In fact, he had seemed very direct, a man who had no time for vanity and who spoke from the heart. Komawara had liked him immensely.

And the daughter, Komawara thought, a smile appearing involuntarily. But then he shook his head and the smile disapeared. She is to be an Imperial Princess, perhaps an Empress, and I—I am the poor Komawara from Seh. My family is ancient enough, but my holdings are nothing. He sighed.

And the cousin!—she is even more beautiful. But she is also more dangerous. Even the cold-fish Emperor becomes a boy in front of her. With a wife like that I would be lost. I would abandon all the pastimes of true men and do nothing but write love poems and court. What a fool I would become! Ah, well, there is little danger that I will wed Kitsura Omawara, so I need not lose sleep in worry.

Komawara gazed at the scene around him. Ships of all sizes, though of common design, lined the quay—the shallow draft river junk with its high stern and blunt prow. The bargemen, many bare from the waist up even on this cool autumn day, worked quickly, swinging cargo ashore with booms and tackle. The smaller junks of the river people swept past in every direction, without course or thought to safety, whole families sculling with all their strength and yelling at every boat within range as they moved goods out to the inns and the myriad shops and private homes of the Imperial Capital. Komawara reached out and trailed his hand in the cool water.

He marveled at how clean the canals were. The Imperial Edicts governing the waterways forbade the dumping of refuse, dunnage, or human waste into the canals. The penalties for doing so were severe in the extreme. Yet, Komawara thought, perhaps they need not be so. Human waste was used to fertilize the rice fields of the great plain and the capital provided the majority of that most essential material—he had seen the dung barges early that very morning. Beyond that, the people of Wa were never wasteful and always fastidious by nature. But, the lord thought, the waterways of Wa are the veins and arteries of the Empire and we would die without them. Their preservation cannot be left to chance.

They passed out of the main canal and down a byway lined with prosperous inns and tea houses. Traffic on the waterway thinned. Along the stone quays lining the canal walked merchants and minor peers, landholders, and not a few soldiers—among them Komawara thought he saw the blue of Shonto livery.

Areas such as this attracted him, they were perfect places to gather gossip. He had spent a good deal of time on this trip sitting in tea houses and frequenting inns, listening to conversations, asking questions, enjoying the role of the naive young lord from the outer provinces. He had learned a great deal. For instance, that very morning he had overheard two Imperial Guards whispering about a failed attempt on Shonto's life!

He also knew, as did most of the population, that Shonto had paid the Botahist Brothers for the services of a Spiritual Advisor. The Emperor, Komawara thought, will not be pleased. Yet it might be worth the displeasure of the Son of Heaven to have one of the Botahist trained in your service. But what a price it must be, he thought. How many could afford the cost of such an advisor? No, it wasn't the money that made the Botahists' services prohibitive—it was the greater cost— the displeasure of Akantsu II, Emperor of Wa. Very few could pay that price, very few indeed.

They turned again, into an area of residences this time—not the residences of the great, they were further toward the outskirts. Komawara himself might afford a home in this area one day soon. He admired the houses set in their small gardens, half hidden by walls, and imagined himself as prospective buyer, choosing among the better locations, imagining which garden received the afternoon light. He laughed at this fantasy, and turned back to his thoughts.

So Shonto will come to Seh. When he sees the truth of my situation there, will his interest in me disappear? He had no sure answer to this question. All he could be certain of was that Shonto was known for his loyalty, and their fathers had shared a mutual respect. My fortunes can't help but rise with the good will of the Shonto . . . as long as the Son of Heaven does not become too disaffected by Shonto's independence. Perhaps I should

advise the lord against taking on this monk? Komawara
rejected the thought immediately. Shonto, he knew, had
advisors of great reknown—he must be careful not to
presume too much.

It is not my place to advise Shonto Motoru, he
thought, not yet. Though when he comes to the north,
Shonto will need all the support he can arrange. The
men of Seh do not take kindly to the suggestion that
they cannot deal with the barbarians themselves.

He pondered again the behavior of the savage people
and found it, as usual, unexplainable.

Ah, well, Komawara thought, if all goes as I hope, I
will have a powerful ally, an ally who will soon be the
Governor of Seh. So few days in the capital and already
my fortunes have begun to rise! But perhaps I should be
careful not to alienate the Son of Heaven entirely. It has
been nine generations since a Komawara resided in the
Governor's Palace in Seh. That, he thought, is too long.

Beyond the garden of Shonto Motoru were arranged
the other gardens of the estate. Some, like Shonto's,
were small, enclosed and private, while others were
open, with large areas of lawn for outdoor entertainment. Pathways bordering ponds wove in and out of the
stands of exotic trees, then ascended to the next terrace
into a garden with a different theme, another purpose.

Streams meandered, seemingly without design, among
arbors, under the arches of bridges, and through stands
of cherry and willow and pine.

Lord Komawara could not help but compare these gardens with his own in Seh—the comparison was humbling.
And this, the lord realized, was Shonto's secondary
residence!

He followed Shonto's steward down a long, tiled portico. The steward, Kamu, had met him at the gate and
despite the young lord's lack of entourage, had greeted
Komawara like an old and honored friend of the Shonto
family. Komawara knew of the one-armed old man by
reputation. In fact, his own father had spoken of him
often, for Kamu had been a great swordsman in his

day—a man around whom legends had grown. In Seh such a man would have been made a minor peer, but it was known that Kamu felt it a greater honor to serve the House of Shonto than to be a lord in the outer provinces. There were many who would make the same choice.

Turning a corner, they came at last to a gate, which Kamu opened before standing aside to allow Komawara to step through. The old man bowed as he passed, "Lord Shonto awaits you, Lord Komawara. May your stay with us be pleasant."

Komawara Samyamu bowed and went through the gate. A set of steps, made of stones set into the bank, led the lord up into a stand of pines. The aromatic scent was strong on the breeze and reminded Komawara of the forests of Seh. The path branched, and on the walkway which turned left, a fist-sized stone tied with a thong of softened bamboo marked the way he should take.

Intentionally, Lord Komawara slowed his pace and began to observe the details of his surroundings. It was possible that the path left unmarked was the more direct route to the place where he would meet Shonto, but this way had been chosen for him, perhaps for a certain autumn flower that bloomed there, or because there was a view Lord Shonto wished his guest to see. There could even be a message on this pathway, and if that were so, he must not miss it. Lord Komawara opened his senses and breathed as if in meditation.

The path rolled down a low hill, the large flat walking stones, like footprints disappearing among the pines. Rocks, forming a grotto, grew up around him, and then, a few paces on, he was again in a pine arbor. Moss carpeted the floor, thick and green in the sunlight that filtered through the branches. The path forked once more and again the walkway to his left was marked. This footpath also wove its way down, giving him the illusion that he descended into a valley.

The notes of a flute carried to him on the breeze and he paused to listen. The tune was unfamiliar, melancholy, haunting. Komawara thought for moment of the beautiful Lady Nishima and wondered if this hidden musician could be her.

He went on, not wishing to keep Lord Shonto waiting, while still taking the time appropriate to the enjoyment of the walk his host had planned for him. He came to a small arched bridge crossing a stream where the water babbled among sounding-stones, and then the path turned to follow the water course a few paces through lime trees. The branches parted to reveal a pond—a pond carpeted in yellow water lilies, the favorite flower of his father.

Lord Komawara sat on a boulder of coarse granite and gazed out upon the lily pond. "I knew your father," the message said, "he was an esteemed friend. Here we may honor his memory, in this place he would have loved." Komawara Samyamu looked down at his sandaled feet and there, beside the boulder grew the flower of his House, the pale mist-lily. And there, the blossoms appeared at the bowl of a weeping birch, a tree which symbolized purity of purpose; close by, the shinta blossom, symbol of the Shonto House, was planted between carefully arranged stones—the symbol for both hardship and loyalty.

Lord Komawara's hand fumbled for the familiar feel of his sword hilt, but it was not to be found, for it had been left in the care of Kamu. He rose, not quite sure where he was going. Inside him he felt his spirit swelling, the memory of his father seemed to inhabit him and he felt strangely at peace with himself, with his surroundings.

Setting his feet before him, he turned back to the path though his body moved as if it were without weight. The way rose up again among birch trees whose leaves had begun to yellow with the autumn. Up, until the pond of lilies lay in a pattern below, like embroidery on a woman's kimono. Rising behind the pond, he could see the borrowed scenery, blue mountains, far off, maned white like the ghosts of lions.

Here on this rise he found a tiny summerhouse of rustic design and the plainest material. Through the round "window of the moon" that overlooked the pond, Komawara could see the silhouette of a sitting man. Lord Shonto Motoru.

As he came around to the open side of the structure, Komawara saw that Shonto sat before a table studying a large map. The young lord bowed formally. Shonto looked up, and he smiled and nodded in return.

"Lord Komawara. Please join me." He gestured to a cushion to his right and Lord Komawara stepped out of his sandals and entered the summerhouse.

Through the window of the moon, the lily pond and the rest of the grounds spread out below with the mountains behind providing both balance and contrast. The view from the adjoining open side was of the hills northeast of the city with the Hill of Divine Inspiration, and its several large temples, off in the distance.

On a small, round stand, below the window of the moon, a plain vase held an arrangement of pine boughs and branch-maple, the leaves red with the passing season while the pine symbolized constancy of life. It was a simple arrangement, elegant and carefully executed.

The map before Lord Shonto covered the areas from north of the capital to the northern steppes, the point where Seh ended and the lands of the barbarians began. Komawara glanced down upon it expectantly, but Shonto acted as though the map were not there.

"Would you care for mead or rice wine? Cha, perhaps?"

"Thank you, wine would be perfect."

"You enjoyed your evening at the palace?" Shonto asked as he raised his hand, turning it slightly in signal to an unseen servant.

"Yes, it was most enjoyable. I must say that your daughter plays beautifully."

"Lady Nishima will be pleased to hear you've said that. Perhaps she will join us later," Shonto said and saw Lord Komawara's pupils go wide with pleasure. "It is unfortunate that on such short notice I could not have invited Lady Kitsura also. She is such pleasant company, don't you think?"

Komawara laughed. "Yes, most certainly. But if you surround the table with such beauty, I would be unable to concentrate on anything else. Even now, this view and your perfect garden call for my attention. But of course, you are a more disciplined man than I, Lord Shonto. I see that you can concentrate on the task at hand," Komawara gestured to the map, "without falling prey to distractions."

Shonto smiled. A servant arrived and poured wine in silence.

"Do not confuse lack of choice with discipline. I am forced by circumstances to contemplate the details of my pending journey to Seh." Shonto sipped the cool wine and looked down at the map before him. "Did you encounter any difficulties on your journey south?"

Komawara followed the lord's gaze, tracing the route he had taken from Seh—seven hundred rih along the Grand Canal. "I traveled with a moderately large force, my own guard and a group of other travelers. We saw no sign of bandits, though we heard many stories of others who were not so fortunate. Here," Komawara placed a finger on the map about halfway to Seh, "I was delayed by the Butto-Hajiwara feud, but we were eventually allowed to pass when it became apparent that we were no threat to either side. I paid no bribe myself—I refused!—but others paid rather than wait. That is their business. The Hajiwara delay everyone, hoping to see profit from those whose time is of value. They are just short of levying a tax for passage, but I believe that would finally stir the Emperor to some action."

"Huh, an unfortunate situation, this feud."

"Yes and it should not be allowed to continue. A war that disrupts traffic on an Imperial waterway is unacceptable! The Butto and the Hajiwara are virtually demanding tribute from those foolish enough to pay. And the Emperor allows this!" The young lord took a drink of his wine, embarrassed by his outburst.

"I am concerned about this situation myself. I do not wish to be delayed on my way to Seh. Do you recall the manner in which the battle lines were drawn when you passed?"

Lord Komawara set his cup down and began to study the map, placing an elbow on the table as he bent over the intricate cartography. He began to massage his brow in a manner Shonto realized was reminiscent of his father.

The area that had become the center of the dispute between the Butto and the Hajiwara was a gorge on the Grand Canal, surrounded by high granite cliffs. On the map the gorge appeared as a swelling in the canal, with a small, almost round, island in its center, making the gorge look like an eye with an island pupil—the eye of the storm that raged around it. At either end of the gorge, locks were situated and these were held by the opposing armies, which possessed fiefs on either side of the river. Only at the captured locks did either family have a foothold on the other's land.

Komawara Samyamu, as a warrior and native to Seh, the only province in the Empire forced to defend its borders, had taken an immediate interest in the war, and it was this perspective that Shonto valued.

The young lord placed his finger on the map. "The southern locks are held by the Butto and all along their flank they have established earthworks on the Hajiwara lands. These fortifications were not built overnight and have been planned with skill using the natural terrain to its best possible advantage." Komawara ran his hand in an arc along the west bank of the river. "The outer fortifications, which consist of earthen and reinforced siege walls and trenches, run from the cliffs above the river, here, to an outcropping of granite that I would place here." The long finger tapped the paper. "The inner fortifications are strongly built of wood and are protected from behind by the cliffs. A bridge across the canal has stone palisades guarding either end but on the eastern shore, the Butto side, there are no fortifications, though the guard towers placed along the canal bank are only a stone's throw apart.

"The Hajiwara have not had to prepare in quite the

same way, as they took the Imperial guard tower situated beside the northern locks. This tower sits on an outcropping, which forms a large natural, and quite unassailable, fortress. Whether the Son of Heaven was involved in this is a point that many still debate, though I myself doubt this theory. I believe the Hajiwara took the castle through the simplest tactic of all: bribery. It is their way. From the tower they have managed to push their front out across the plain as far as these low hills. Here the Butto have contained them and the battle lines remain static."

"What is your opinion of these palisades? Could they be breached?" Shonto asked.

Komawara looked at Lord Shonto, wondering if the great general was patronizing him but decided this was not so—the Lord of the Shonto had no need to do that. Komawara also realized that Shonto would already have thorough intelligence on this situation—so he must be testing the younger man, finding out what he knew, how he thought. Komawara forced a calm over his mind, realizing that much of his future would depend on his answer.

"The fortifications have no apparent weakness that I know of and both have a very great advantage in that their backs are protected by cliffs and, across bridges, the opposite shores are entirely in their control for many rih.

"To overcome either stronghold, it would be necessary to cut the bridges and isolate them. A massive frontal attack and sustained siege would no doubt be effective in time, but this would take months. The bridges could possibly be rebuilt during that time, and this would almost certainly save them." Komawara realized he was speaking his thoughts, wondering aloud, but no inspired answer came.

"Stealth," he said finally. "Stealth and surprise. I know no other way. The bridge would have to be taken or another way found to enter either fortress. It would be difficult, perhaps not even possible, but it is the only way." Komawara stopped again, his mind racing, realiz-

ing that he had no solution, nor any way of finding one
so far from the fortresses that guarded the canal. I have
failed the test, he thought, and tried not to show this
feeling of failure.

Shonto nodded, not taking his eyes from the map. "My
generals all say the same, but as of yet we have no solution to the problem. Perhaps we will not need one. I
thank you for your counsel." Shonto nodded, as though
satisfied, and began to slowly roll the map.

The next signal Shonto gave was so subtle that Lord
Komawara did not see it, but Shonto turned to him suddenly and asked, "I would be honored if you would take
a moment to meet my vassal-merchant; you may find
what he has to say of interest."

Shonto said all of this in a tone which indicated how
trivial a matter this was to lords of their stature, but they
should indulge this man whose concern was money, as
one would indulge a very old relative.

"I would be honored, Lord Shonto. I would not think
it an interruption at all." Komawara answered, copying
Lord Shonto's manner of amusement and politeness.

And at this, the merchant Tanaka appeared, coming
up the rise. He was dressed in clothes identical to those
he had worn earlier and he walked in the manner of a
servant, eyes down, his face serious, all of his motions
subdued. After the story he had been told about Tanaka's interchange with the guard, Shonto almost laughed
to see the merchant looking so subservient. I hope he
doesn't overplay this, the lord thought, feeling sudden
misgivings.

Tanaka came up to the summerhouse and knelt in the
fine gravel before it. He bowed, careful to keep his eyes
cast down.

Shonto stared at his merchant and suddenly a weariness came over him. There is enough intrigue around
me, he thought, enough falseness.

"Tanaka-sum," Shonto said surprising the merchant by
using the honorific before a stranger. "Come, we have
no time for this charade. Lord Komawara understands
the importance of your position. Join us." Shonto ges-

tured for the servants to bring another table. There, he thought, this young one should know the truth of the times. I was right this morning, I have no time to indulge children.

If Komawara was affronted by this, he managed to hide it.

"Lord Komawara, it is my honor to introduce you to Tanaka-sum, my valued counselor. Tanaka-sum, you have the honor of meeting the son of an old friend and ally of the Shonto, Lord Komawara Samyamu."

The two men bowed, Tanaka purposely deeper than the lord, and then he rose and joined Shonto and his guest in the small house. A table arrived for him and mead was poured into his cup.

"We have just been discussing the journey to Seh. Lord Komawara has recently traveled south along the canal."

Tanaka set his glass down, "Ah, and will you return north with Lord Shonto?"

"I had not considered this. I do have to return to Seh soon. The situation there is so unsettled. I don't wish to be away any longer than I have to be."

"You would be most welcome to journey to Seh with us, Lord Komawara," Shonto said, "though I intend to leave within a few days and will have little time for leisure. Perhaps this wouldn't allow you time to complete your business in the capital?"

"This is a generous offer, Lord Shonto. I will certainly see if it is possible."

"Please do, your company would be most welcome." Shonto signaled again and a servant appeared to refill the cups. "Tanaka-sum, tell us about this venture you mentioned to me, I think it would interest my guest."

Tanaka set his cup down, and cleared his throat quietly. "At Lord Shonto's request I contracted to puchase all of the corrapepper of a grower who has his fields on the southernmost of the islands of the barbarian. Due to the disfavor of the gods, the other islands were struck by an evil storm which ruined the corrapepper harvest.

This terrible misfortune has left us in control of virtually all the surviving corrapepper crop.

"Due to the unfortunate circumstances I have described, there will certainly be inflated prices for corra-pepper this year—of course, we shall have to pay more to protect our crop from theft by the unscrupulous barbarians, but still, if Botahara wills it, our profit should be great."

Tanaka glanced at Lord Shonto, and then continued. "The investment in this venture has been large, so on the advice of Lord Shonto, I sought partners to share the risk . . . and the profits. Due to family matters, one honored friend has been unable to continue in our venture. It could not be helped," Tanaka hastened to add, "and we feel his conduct has been beyond reproach, but his withdrawal has left us with an opening for a new partner or partners, as you can see."

"I don't know your plans, Lord Komawara," Shonto said, "but this would seem a good opportunity for you and we would welcome your involvement. You could invest whatever you wished to risk, up to . . ." He looked at Tanaka.

"Perhaps 200,000 ril."

Lord Komawara shook his head. "But certainly this is too generous, Lord Shonto," he protested. He meant to go on but could not marshal his thoughts.

"Of course," Tanaka hastened to add, "you would be assessed some part of your profit, Lord Komawara." He pulled awkwardly at a ring on his little finger. "Let us say twelve parts . . . no, ten parts per hundred."

The young lord paused to contemplate. "It must be twelve, then, if I am to agree."

"Certainly ten would be customary, Lord Komawara," Shonto said, eyeing his merchant, but Tanaka would not meet his gaze.

"I am honored by your offer, Lord Shonto, but I think you can understand that I cannot accept it unless I am sure it is not charity." Why, Komawara thought, why would someone in Shonto's position do this for someone of as little concern as I? Did he really hold my father in such high esteem?

Shonto seemed to consider Komawara's words for a moment, but it was the young lord's assessment of the barbarian attacks that kept coming to mind. Yes, Shonto thought, what he said about the barbarians rang with truth. None of my generals saw mystery in the attacks.

"Lord Komawara, it is not my intention to offer you charity, which obviously you do not require, but only to offer you this small service in return for something I need. Something I need now. I require your counsel—I realized that when we first spoke. I also value Komawara loyalty—it is a trait that your family is known for and it is beyond price. If you wish to begin trade in the name of Komawara, I give you that opportunity. In return, I hope you will journey with me to Seh to give me the benefit of your knowledge of the north."

Komawara said nothing. He appeared to be weighing Shonto's words as though they were made of nothing but insubstantial air. But he could find no trace of deceit in them. I bind myself to the Shonto and Shonto destiny with this, he thought, and he found the idea somewhat disturbing. Reaching out, he took a drink of his wine, and then, setting his glass down, he said, "I accept this offer, Lord Shonto, Tanaka-sum. I am honored by your words. I only hope my counsel will prove worthy of your investment." There, Komawara thought, it is done.

"I don't doubt it for a moment." Shonto signaled for more wine. "We must eat—it is our most common form of celebration, is it not? Tanaka, will you join us?"

The merchant seemed to struggle within himself for a moment. "I am honored by your invitation, Sire, but there are so many things to attend to before your departure. . . ."

Shonto turned to Komawara. "I cannot even tempt my retainers from their duties. Is this a common problem, do you think?"

"It is a problem most lords wish they suffered from, Sire."

"Tanaka-sum, I bow to your sense of duty. Another time."

Tanaka bowed to the two lords and took his leave, walking away with the quiet dignity Shonto admired.

"So, Lord Komawara, I'm sure the two of us can enjoy our food as much as three?"

Komawara nodded. Servants brought the midday meal—simple but delectable fare, elegantly served in the summerhouse overlooking the pond of yellow water lilies. Under the influence of the food, the fine wine and Shonto's conversation, Komawara achieved an almost euphoric state. Being a Shonto ally looked less daunting than it had seemed earlier.

"The food, Lord Shonto, was of a quality that would satisfy an Emperor."

Shonto bowed slightly. "You are kind to say so. Cha?"

"Thank you, that would be perfect."

The rustle of silk was heard from the path below and then Lady Nishima appeared, on cue, followed by two of her ladies-in-waiting and a young maid. If Komawara had found her enchanting in the moonlight, he realized that the sunlight brought out her true beauty, as it did the flower of the morning-vine.

Dressed in a robe of spring green embroidered with a pattern of falling ginkyo leaves, the Lady Nishima Fanisan Shonto seemed to shine among her companions, as though the sunlight did not bless them with its warmth. She stopped and bent down to examine a bush by the edge of the walk, and the gold of her inner kimonos appeared at the nape of her fine neck. Lord Komawara felt both thrilled and terribly nervous.

At the sight of her uncle, Nishima smiled with unconcealed affection. She handed her parasol to the maid and stepped out of her sandals before entering the summerhouse. The two lords returned her formal bow.

"Nishima-sum, how kind of you to join us."

"The kindness was yours in inviting me, Uncle." She took a fan, shaped like a large ginkyo leaf, from her sleeve pocket and waved it open in an easy gesture.

"Lord Komawara, how pleasant to see you again so soon. Did you enjoy the Emperor's party?"

"Entirely. I have had the sounds of your music with me ever since and it has made my day most pleasant."

"You are too kind." she said, but she was not displeased by the praise.

"Have you met our new Spiritual Advisor?" Shonto asked.

Nishima turned her attention to her uncle now. She examined his face, looking for signs of the attempt on his life, but she saw no concern or anxiety. Indeed, he seemed entirely relaxed—she glanced at his companion out of the corner of her eye.

"I have not, Sire, though I understand he is to join us."

Shonto nodded toward the pathway and Nishima saw a young monk of the Botahist Order walking toward them.

*Yes,* Nishima thought, *that is him,* I remember. And the diminutive monk in the kick boxing ring became clear in her memory. The other fighters had appeared so massive and the boy-monk had seemed so small . . . yet completely calm. The same calm was somehow still apparent in this Brother, and as she watched him approach she was overcome with an unexpected emotion. Suddenly, the Lady Nishima wanted to hide. She looked around almost in a panic, then her years of training took charge and she regained her composure. But she was disturbed by this sudden surge of emotion, left shaken by it.

The monk, Shuyun, stopped at the entry to the summerhouse and bowed to his liege-lord and his guests.

"Brother Shuyun, please join us." Shonto said and gestured to the servants. A table large enough for four was exchanged for the individual tables and this gesture surprised Lady Nishima, for such an arrangement was usually reserved for immediate family only.

Brother Shuyun was formally introduced to Lady Nishima and Lord Komawara, neither of whom betrayed a trace of the intense curiosity they felt for this young Initiate. Lady Nishima was especially intrigued after the

report she had received of the monk's display that
morning.

The utensils for the making of cha came and Lady
Nishima, as one of the most famed hostesses in the capital, took charge of the preparation. At the same time
she guided the conversation deftly and with great charm,
impressing Lord Komawara, who was intimidated by the
urbanity of the women he met in the capital.

The drinking of cha, like every activity of the aristocracy, was formalized and governed by its own particular
aesthetic, though among the aristocrats, it had not taken
on the aspects of ritual that it had among certain sects
within Wa. In its existing state of formality, Lady Nishima was able to bring her considerable imagination to
bear upon the social aspects of drinking cha. Today she
had it in mind to do something different, something that
she knew no one present would associate with cha. How
to introduce it in a manner that seemed natural, that was
her problem.

"Will you come to Seh with Lord Shonto, Brother
Shuyun?" Komawara asked. He has having trouble not
staring at Lady Nishima, though his warrior's discipline
was just barely winning.

"It is for Lord Shonto to decide," the monk said, and
offered no more.

Lady Nishima felt sudden resentment toward the
Botahist monk and his cold manner. It is their way, she
thought. But still it annoyed her. Looking at the monk
kneeling across the table from her, she searched for the
man behind the mask. This had been an obsession for
her with Brother Satake, their former Spiritual Advisor.
With Satake-sum she would stoop to almost any ploy to
see him laugh or grow impatient—anything that seemed
a human emotion. It had been a frustrating campaign,
for she had seldom been successful.

When the tea had been poured and offered in its
proper way, Lady Nishima began to ask Lord Komawara
questions about Seh and about the barbarians and their
motives.

Lord Komawara answered her, being careful not to let

the conversation stray too far from the approved tone for such occasions. "Their motives are not the same as ours, Lady Nishima. You cannot understand them in our terms. As to what will happen, who can say? I cannot tell the future, and for this I apologize." He bowed with mock sincerity.

"Lord Komawara, there is no need to apologize to me for not being able to predict the future. I am quite capable of doing *that* myself."

Knowing his daughter's humor, Shonto took the bait quickly, "Nishi-sum, how is it that I have not been aware of this talent? Or was it simply lost among your myriad of other gifts?"

"Not at all, Sire, it is as you say. You are far too perceptive not to have noticed such an ability in your favorite daughter. The reason that you have not, until now, been aware of this skill is that I myself became aware of it only this morning. In fact it was just after sunrise. I sat combing my hair when suddenly I was overcome by . . ." her eyes went wide, "Deep Insight! Yes, and I thought immediately, I must tell all of those around me of their futures. They will find it most useful."

"Ah," Shonto said, keeping a straight face, "Deep Insight! Do the Botahist Brothers have experience of this phenomenon, Shuyun-sum?"

"Certainly, Lord Shonto, and it is well known that it is most often experienced while combing one's hair. That is the reason Neophyte monks must shave their heads—so they don't experience Deep Insight before they are prepared for such a momentous occurrence." As he finished saying this he smiled, causing a thrill to course through the Lady Nishima.

The man behind the mask! she thought, but then the smile was gone and across the table sat one of the Silent Ones, unmoving, without apparent emotions.

"Well, Lady Fortune Teller, I, for one, would be interested in seeing what can result from Deep Insight, if you would so honor us." Shonto said.

"Gladly, Sire, but I must warn each of you . . . I can

take no responsibility for what you may learn of your futures, either good or bad."

"Agreed," Komawara said, "only the gods will be held responsible." And then remembering the Botahist monk, "Botahara willing," he added.

The assembled guests acted as though they had not heard the reference to the gods, the mythological beings that the Botahist religion had replaced, but Shonto found himself thinking, Well, it is true, he *is* from the provinces.

From her sleeve pocket Nishima took an ornate canister of black leather decorated with a pattern of white wisteria. She shook it and the jangle of coins caused everyone to laugh for they all knew the sound—the coins of Kowan-sing.

Kowan-sing was one of the inumerable methods of divination popular in Wa. Almost every possible object had been used at one time in an attempt to foretell the future: bones, the lines of the face, stones, crystals, entrails, cards, even the gii board. Kowan-sing, though, had history to lend it credibility, for it was thought to have been practiced by the indigenous people. The people who had been displaced by the Five Princes so long ago that the histories could not agree on a time.

"Who shall be first?" Lady Nishima asked, rattling coins again.

"Lord Komawara must have that honor," Lord Shonto insisted.

Cups were moved aside so the coins could be cast.

"Are you ready to know your future, Lord Komawara?" Nishima asked.

Lord Komawara nodded, and in one fluid motion Nishima spread the seven silver coins across the table.

All heads bent forward to examine the arrangement of the coins.

"It is clear that the pattern here is *The Boat*, Lord Komawara, symbol of both travel and prosperity." Nishima said, not raising her eyes from the table.

"With the slight movement of two coins it could easily be *The Cloud*, could it not?" Lord Shonto asked.

*The Cloud* was the symbol for romance, as all knew, and Lord Shonto's comment caused Komawara some discomfort.

But Lady Nishima did not seem embarrassed by what Lord Shonto implied. "As you say, Uncle, but *The Boat* is too clear for *The Cloud* to be influential here, excuse me for saying so."

"I bow to your superior source of knowledge," Shonto said, nodding to his daughter.

"Here, Lord Komawara, it can be seen that one coin spoils the line of the keel." She touched the coin with a long finger, careful not to change its position. "It indicates a danger to you, something you should beware of, perhaps, as *The Boat* indicates, on your return journey north. But also, prosperity may hold some danger for you. And again here, the coins that make the mast show that it is falling, indicating that there is danger in your immediate future. Only you could know what this might be." She touched another coin, the only one that did not bear the outline of the *Mountain of Divine Inspiration.* "Here, the Prime Kowan is temptation; the open fan. Only time will tell what is hidden by the fan. All that can be said with certainty is that temptation will figure in your future, possibly related to prosperity, I cannot be sure. But temptation can be dangerous." Nishima looked up and the serious faces of her companions reminded her that she had meant this to be fun.

"You seem to attract danger, Lord Komawara," she said in a whisper. "Perhaps it is unwise for us to sit so close to you." She looked about with wide eyes, as though something terrible was about to fall on them from the sky. Everyone laughed in appreciation. And then, in the voice of an old crone, "you must keep your sword sharp, young Sire. The great world is full of . . . danger! You must watch behind you . . . and in front of you, not forgetting either side. Danger, danger, danger . . ." Her voice trailed off and her companions broke into applause.

Water arrived, and Lady Nishima took a moment to prepare more cha.

"Now, Uncle, I believe you must be next."

"I am honored."

Lady Nishima collected the coins and shook them again in their leather canister. Twice she removed the top and was about to cast them when she stopped, as though inspiration had fled. But then she looked up, a mishievous grin on her face.

"You do enjoy tormenting me, don't you," Shonto said.

And his daughter laughed and cast the coins of Kowansing, her long sleeve streaming behind the graceful sweep of her arm.

Shonto put his elbow on the table so that it hid the coins from the young woman's view. "Ah, Nishi-sum! This is most interesting, most unusual!"

Laughing with the others, she snatched his arm out of the way. "Ah, Uncle, this *is* interesting. Who would think that your pattern would be *The Dragon*? It is not as clear a pattern as Lord Komawara's, but the eyes are certain, and here," she pointed, "is a curving tail. *The Dragon* symbolizes both power and mystery."

Nishima paused then, examining the coins with complete concentration. In the distance, a flock of cranes passed south over the plain, unnoticed by the occupants of the summerhouse.

"Mystery and power are the keys to your future, perhaps there is a power that will affect you and your endeavors, yet the source of this power will be unknown. The body of *The Dragon* itself seems to be twisted in an unusual manner, as though the power will appear in an unexpected form. Here," she touched a coin, which this time had landed with the fan down, exposing the other side: the *Sheathed Sword*, "the Prime Kowan is the hidden threat. It cannot be known if the sword is sharp or dull, but it is always a danger and must never be ignored. The sheathed sword also indicates treachery—danger from an ally perhaps."

"Can it not also indicate peace?" Shonto asked.

"It can, Sire. But in combination with *The Dragon*,

this does not seem the most likely interpretation. Excuse me for saying so."

Shonto shrugged. "It is you who speak from Deep Insight."

"Perhaps, Sire, you should seclude yourself for the remainder of the year in our summer palace." Nishima smiled. "I believe I deserve a reward for my work. Cha. Does anyone wish to join me?"

Cha was brewed again. Secretly, Lady Nishima wished to cast the fortune of their new Spiritual Advisor, but would never suggest this, being unsure of his opinion of such frivolity. Yet she was curious to know what the coins would tell about this quiet monk who was now a member of their inner Household. She was curious, not least of all because she felt there had been some truth in what she had told the others. Some of the things she had said she had felt certain of in some inexplicable way.

Do I grow superstitious? she wondered, but Shonto interrupted this train of thought.

"Nishi-sum, it seems unfair that we have received the benefit of your Deep Insight, and yet your own future remains unknown to you. This cannot be correct." Shonto watched Komawara out of the corner of his eye but realized the young lord was too shy to take up the suggestion himself. Ah, well, Shonto thought, I have started this and now I will have to carry it through.

"I believe what Lord Shonto says is true, Lady Nishima," Shuyun said in his quiet tones. "It is only proper that you should know what the future holds for you. I would be honored to cast the coins for you, though I cannot claim to have your skill with them."

No one showed the surprise they felt at the monk's offer. Komawara immediately regretted his hesitation to make this proposal himself, for Nishima obviously was immensely flattered.

"I could never refuse such a kind offer, Brother Shuyun."

Collecting the coins in the canister, Lady Nishima passed it to Shuyun, but as she did so she was seized by a desire to fling them into the garden, as though what her future might hold was too frightening. But she did offer them and the monk shook the canister, producing what suddenly seemed an ominous rattle.

As deftly as Lady Nishima, Shuyun spread the coins across the table and as they came to rest Nishima could see that her fears had been groundless. They were only the coins of Kowan-sing, familiar, worn, in need of a polishing. What she had expected she did not know— something disturbing—coins she had never seen, bearing haunting images and an unwanted message. She closed her eyes and felt relief wash through her. It is the curse of my blood, the name that follows me like a banner. May it never become the rallying point for the war that so many desire. She shuddered involuntarily. Opening her eyes she tried to smile.

"Are you well, Lady?" Shuyun asked, his eyes searching her own.

"Well?" she said. "How can I be well. Look at this pattern. Is it not *The Mountain*, the symbol for calculated waiting and enlightenment." She laughed. "I have no patience whatsoever, it is my shame to admit. If I am to have enlightenment I would like it to arrive by sunset at the latest." She laughed again, a delightful laugh.

Shuyun smiled. "But Lady Nishima, I may be wrong, but I believe this is *The Crane*, symbol of the aesthetic, of beauty and art."

"Botahara has guided your hand, Brother." Shonto said.

The monk nodded. "Your reputation as an artist has reached even the Oracle, Lady Nishima. yet here *The Crane* stands erect, waiting. Patient, as you must be patient, even though you claim not to be. It is this waiting that makes a great artist. And look, your Prime Kowan is also the open fan. As you have said, this is the symbol for temptation, but it may also indicate that the artist cannot hide behind the painted fan. The artist must show herself. Part of her inner beauty must appear in her work. Of course temptation should not be ruled out, perhaps temptation that is related to the aesthetic or to beauty, I cannot say." He bowed toward her and again fell silent.

"I thank you, Brother Shuyun. It will be an honor to have your wisdom in the Shonto House."

After more mead, Lord Komawara offered to recite a poem he had just composed. All assented readily for poetry was common, even expected, on such occasions. Komawara had hesitated only because of Lady Nishima's reputation as a poetess.

> *"A crane waits, staring down at*
> *green water.*
> *Is it drawn to a reflection?*
> *Does it watch for movement*
> *In the still waters?"*

There was silence for a moment, as was the custom, so that the poem could be considered.

"You have been hiding your talent as a poet from us, Lord Komawara," Nishima said, and there was no doubting the sincerity of her words.

Komawara bowed. "Knowing of your skill, Lady Nishima, I thank you for your words, which are more than kind."

"Nishi-sum, you must have a poem for us," Shonto said, "You are never without inspiration."

"You embarrass me with your flattery, Uncle. Please allow me a moment to consider." She closed her eyes for only a few seconds before speaking.

> *"The crane stands,*
> *White in the green pond.*
> *Does it see the water's*
> *Stillness as illusion?*
> *But wait,*
> *Is it a crane or*
> *The reflection of a passing cloud?"*

"Ah, Lady Nishima, your fame is more than well deserved." Komawara said. "I am honored that you should use my simple verse as the beginnings of such masterful display."

Now Nishima bowed in thanks. "Your poem was not simple, Lord Komawara, and my verse merely tried to reflect its meaning, yeh? Look into its depths."

A final cup of cha was brewed and the conversation returned to a more relaxed tone. Seh was again a topic of discussion and Lord Komawara was given an opportunity to exhibit his knowledge.

"Brother Shuyun," Komawara addressed the monk, "I am not familiar with your name. Does it have significance in the teachings of Botahara?"

Shonto was glad the question had been asked, for he had been searching his memory of the Botahist texts trying to find it, assuming that, like most monks, Shuyun's name had originated there.

"It is adapted from the tongue of the mountain people, Lord Komawara, so it is not recognized in Wa. *Shuyung:* he who bears, or the bearer. It is a name for the humble carriers. A name which does not encourage pride."

Huh, Shonto thought, unlike the name Shonto or Fanisan or Komawara for that matter. Why does such a one consent to serve among the prideful? Of course, the lord thought, he did not consent, he was ordered by his superiors and obeyed without question. Brother Satake had done the same, once.

"Kowan-sing is also of the mountain tongue, is it not, Brother?" Nishima asked.

"It is from the archaic form, Lady Nishima, from a time when it is assumed the mountain dwellers lived in the plains and along the sea coast. Many place names remain from the ancient tongue; *yul-ho, yul-nan;* even Yankura derives from the same source, *Yan-khuro,* dwelling by the water. It was a beautiful tongue and only a few dialects remain among the mountain people to remind us of it."

A bell rang the hour of the tiger and it seemed a signal to everyone in the summerhouse, a reminder that each of them had much to do and that, despite the illusion of timelessness created in the garden, the day wore on.

Lord Komawara took his leave, needing to prepare for his journey with Lord Shonto, though he found the presence of Lady Nishima made it difficult to think of anything other than her lovely eyes and graceful movements.

Lady Nishima's ladies-in-waiting and her maid returned to accompany her through the gardens. She went in a rustle of silk, leaving only the scent of her perfume lingering in the summerhouse.

Shonto went to consult with Kamu on the preparations for the trip to Seh, leaving Shuyun unattended in the garden. For a few moments Shuyun sat listening to the sounds, appreciating the subtlety of the garden's design. This will be my home, the monk thought, or one of them. He looked around him. What wealth! How easy to forget the life of the spirit here. Yes, how easy.

Rising, Shuyun made his way slowly down from the summerhouse, planning to return to the apartment Kamu had had prepared for him. Everywhere he looked, the details of the garden seemed to call for his attention, slowing his progress.

As he bent down by a low wall to admire a climbing vine, Shuyun stopped as though he had seen a spirit. He cocked his head, listening to a sound that seemed almost to blend with the sounds of the breeze, but it was there, unmistakably, a sound he had heard far too often to not be absolutely sure. He felt his heart begin to race and quickly controlled it. What is this? he wondered. The sound of movement, the swish of soft material and the hiss of controlled breathing. He knew it like the sound of his own voice.

I must see, he thought, and began to examine his surroundings looking for observers. Shuyun realized he was taking a chance, but it could not be helped. What if he were seen?

He stepped back along the path a few paces and bent to examine the leaves of a chako bush. From this position he could see the windows of the main house. There was no movement, but it was difficult to be sure as they were all shaded.

He stepped carefully off the path behind a pine that hid him from view. Glancing around the garden again, afraid that Lord Shonto was having him observed, Shuyun reached up and tested the strength of the vines that climbed the walls. Hoping that, at least for that moment, he was not seen, Shuyun quickly clambered silently up the branches. He raised his head above the wall and his grip tightened on the vines. There, in a small enclosed garden, dressed in loose cotton robes, Lady Nishima moved through the measured dance of the Form—chi quan! As he watched, she reached the fifth closure and proceeded with confidence. It was almost beyond his ability to believe—*one of the uninitiated practicing the Form.* The key to the Secret Knowledge of the Botahist Orders.

He lowered himself to the ground, his heart pounding in a most un-Botahist-like manner, and continued down the path attempting to appear composed.

Brother Satake, the monk thought, the renowned Brother Satake. It could have been no one else. But why? Shonto's former advisor had been almost legendary, a man held in the highest regard by the most senior members of his Order. A man Shuyun had tried to emulate in his own learning.

The monk walked on, his head spinning. What shall I do? he thought, this is unimaginable! By the Nine Names of Botahara, *we have been betrayed!*

# Eight

**W**alls, Sister Morima thought, they are the "Significant Pattern" of our Empire, and the fact that no one notices them speaks of their complete acceptance by the entire culture. Here we draw the stylus and there is division—the Son of Heaven on that side and all of Wa on the other. We draw the stylus again and Lords of the First Rank make their position clear, they on one side and all of society on the other, and so on down to the paper screens of the poorest street vendor. Last of all we have the beggars and they can erect no walls at all.

Walls: they were everywhere and everywhere they went unnoticed—not that they weren't respected, that was not the case—they were simply not considered for what they were; the Significant Pattern.

But it had always been so. Even a thousand years before, the Lord Botahara had spoken of walls: "Between themselves and the weak the strong build walls, fearing that the weak will learn of their own strength. So it is that the poor are shut out into the wide world with all of its uncertainty but also with all of its purity and beauty. Whose palace garden compares to the wild perfection of the mountain meadows? So, thinking to shut out the poor and the weak, the strong succeed only in walling themselves in. Such is the nature of illusion."

Sister Morima walked stiffly up the graveled roadway that led along the base of the wall surrounding the Priory of the First Awakening—the Seat of her Order. Shielding her eyes, she looked up at the white stone rampart and wondered what the Enlightened One would think of a

religious order, based on his teachings, that hid itself
behind walls. The Significant Pattern, she thought again,
it was a Sister who had first spoken of the concept,
another Sister who had written the definitive work on
the idea.

I grow cynical, she thought. The Sisterhood needs the
walls to protect itself from those who have not yet developed their spirit sufficiently. She looked around her at
the pilgrims who crowded the roadway. Tired, covered
in dust, poor for the most part, some with the eyes that
looked beyond the world—yet all of them seemed to
exude a certain air of barely controlled passion, of deep
unrest. "May the Lord Botahara bring you peace," she
muttered under her breath.

Yes, it felt good to be returning. Her time among the
Brothers had left her feeling . . . tainted. She shuddered
involuntarily. I have much to tell you, Sister Saeja, she
thought, much that I don't understand.

She walked on, staring at the road before her feet,
listening to the sounds of the pilgrims walking, to their
mumbled prayers, the coughing of the desperately ill.
The morning air was fresh, still retaining a trace of the
night's chill, but the sun was warm. The autumn seemed
to have attained a point of balance; like a gull on a
current of wind, it seemed to hang in the air for an
impossibly long time. Each night you expected the balance to have been lost, but each morning the sun would
rise, as warm as the day before, and the smells of autumn
would return with the heat. It was as though time had
slowed—leaves floated down without hurry, flowers blossomed beyond their season. It was uncanny and very
beautiful.

The gate to the Priory of the First Awakening loomed
up as she rounded a corner and the usual horde of Seekers surrounded the Sisters of the Gate. Sister Morima
could see the desire on their faces, each of them hoping
to be allowed entry, to be housed for a few evenings, to
attend services or vespers, perhaps to hear a few words
from the Prioress, Sister Saeja, who, they all knew, was
coming close to her time of Completion.

Slowly Sister Morima moved through the throng, the pilgrims making way for her.

"Allow the honored Sister to pass."

"Make way, brother, a Sister comes."

"Intercede for us, Honored Sister, we have come all the way from Chou to hear a few words from the Prioress. All the way from Chou . . . Honored Sister?"

The Sisters of the Gate greeted her warmly, their eyes full of questions for they knew from where she returned. She passed through into the outer courtyard of the Priory, into the company of the privileged Seekers, those allowed through the main gate, their way eased by an introduction from a Sister in their home province, or by a donation to the worthy causes of the Sisterhood—or in some cases, simply because the pilgrim would not go away. The press of the crowd was gone here, the privileged few moving about in blissful silence.

Sister Morima prostrated herself on the cobbles in front of the statue of Botahara before she entered the second gate that led to the inner courtyard. Only robed Sisters and young Acolytes passed her here and the noise of the crowd outside was completely muffled by the high walls. She breathed a sigh of relief. *I do not bear my burden well,* she thought, *but soon I shall share it.* This did not gladden her as she hoped, for what she had to share was disturbing indeed.

The Acolytes who accompanied Sister Morima were anxious to be released, to bathe and to rest, but she said nothing and they continued obediently in her wake. *They must learn,* she thought, *our way never becomes easier, there is no reward of respite, not in this life.*

A senior Sister came toward her across the cobbles, obviously intending to meet her. The face was not familiar immediately, but then she realized—*Gatsa*, Sister Gatsa. So, the vultures gathered. The representatives of each faction would be here, then, waiting, plotting. A surge of fear passed through her. *No,* she told herself, *she knew the Sisters on duty at the gate, if Saeja-sum had arrived at the point of Completion they would have* warned her. But still the vultures circled, and this one was about to land.

"Go and assist with the pilgrims' meal," she said, turning to the Acolytes who attended her, and watched the disappointment and resentment flare in their eyes. Then it was gone.

"Immediately, Sister Morima, thank you for this opportunity." And they hurried off, burdens in hand.

Sister Morima nodded, satisfied; they understood, they would do well.

"Sister Morima, how pleased I am to see you. I did not know you were expected," and Sister Gatsa bowed to her.

Letting the lie pass, Sister Morima returned the bow and walked on, letting her fatigue show. Gatsa fell into step beside her. She was a tall woman, Sister Gatsa, somewhat regal in her bearing and in her speech, an odd manner to find in a humble servant of the Perfect Master. She was square jawed, but this harshness was relieved by a lovely mouth and eyes that seemed to dance with the pleasures of being alive—no staring into the great-beyond for this Sister. Her eyes were focused on the world around her, and they missed very little.

"I trust your journey has been productive?" Sister Gatsa said.

"Most pleasant. You honor me to enquire," Morima answered in her most formal tones. They turned inside an arch and continued down a wide portico.

"Then you actually *saw* the scrolls of the Enlightened One?" She turned and examined Sister Morima's face, awe apparent in her voice.

Sister Morima did not answer immediately and then looked away as she spoke. "I saw the Brothers' scrolls."

"And?"

"And what, Sister?" Morima asked.

"You saw the scrolls of the Lord Botahara and this is all you can say?" The tall Sister sounded annoyed.

Again Sister Morima hesitated, then released a long sigh. "It is not an experience words can convey, Sister." She paused and reached out to steady herself on a post.

Sister Gatsa regarded the large nun who looked as if she would burst into tears, but then Morima regained control. "You must excuse me, but I . . . I must meditate upon the experience. Perhaps then I will be able to explain my reaction."

Sister Gatsa took Morima's arm and continued along the walk. "I understand, Sister, it must be very moving to look upon the hand of Botahara. I do understand."

Nuns nodded to them as they walked, and, as the two passed, eyes followed. This is the Sister who was *chosen*, they thought. She has attended the ceremony of Divine Renewal. Whispers passed through the Priory like quiet breezes.

"She is back! Sister Kiko has seen her."

"And?"

"She is transformed, Sister! Morima-sum glows with inner knowledge. Yet she seems disturbed also."

"Who would not be—to look upon His words. Remember, too, that she has spent many days in the company of the Brothers. Would you not find this disturbing?"

"Your words are wisdom, Sister."

The two nuns came at last to the door Sister Morima sought. The door that would lead to her quarters. But Gatsa was not ready to release her yet, and Morima felt the tall nun's grip tighten on her arm.

"Much has happened in your absence, Sister Morima," Gatsa said, lowering her voice. "The Prioress has become weaker. I tell you this to prepare you, I know how close you are to her. There will be a Cloister before the year's end, I fear. We both know how large a part you will play in the Selection. The Empire changes, Sister, we must not be the victims of the change. The work of Botahara is all-important. You must feel that more than ever after what you have just seen. I know we have opposed each other in the past, Morima-sum, but I believe there may be a way to resolve our differences. This would be good for the Sisterhood and good for us also. Please consider my words. We can discuss this when you are rested." She let go of Morima's arm and stood facing her, eyes searching. "But don't wait too long, Sister." She bowed and swept off down the long portico, bearing herself, as always, like a Lady of the Emperor's Court.

A young Acolyte attendant met Morima as she mounted the stairs to her quarters.

"I have run your bath, honored Sister," the girl said bowing to her superior. "I am to tell you that the Prioress will see you when you are refreshed." She fell into step behind Sister Morima who nodded as she passed.

Yes, Morima thought, the Prioress will see me, but what am I to tell her? She rubbed her brow with a hand covered in dust. The question was one she had asked herself repeatedly since leaving the Brotherhood's Island Monastery. Still she had no answer. What do I know that is in any way certain? the nun asked herself again. Nothing, was the answer and she knew it, yet the feeling would not go away. There was something wrong in Jinjoh Monastery; all of her instincts told her so.

The bath the Acolyte had drawn was like a healing potion. Sister Morima sank into the steaming waters like a marine mammal returning to its element. She closed her eyes and allowed her shoulders and forehead to be massaged. To compose herself for the coming interview, she began to meditate. A calm began to flow through her body, the turmoil in her mind was pushed back and partially silenced.

Later, as she dressed, she pushed the screen aside and stood looking out from her small balcony across the plain. In the distance the Imperial Capital shimmered in the rising waves of heat. The palace of the Emperor wavered in the unstill air, white walls seeming to change their shape before the eye, one surface joining another then separating itself again. The harder she looked, the more difficult it became to be sure of the palace's true shape.

An endless line of Seekers moved along the road that meandered up the mountain to the Priory. Dust seemed to enclose them like a skein of silk—red-brown and drifting slowly to the north. The pilgrims, too, were caught in the rising waves of heat, their bodies distorted, billowing, insubstantial.

I am in the Priory of the First Awakening, Sister Morima told herself. I am a senior of the Botahist Order. Beyond the rice fields lies the Emperor's city. Its walls are white and quite solid. Down there are the Seekers—poor, hungry, and often quite foolish. That man among them in the blue rags is a cripple, and it is only the effect of the warm air that seems every so often to straighten his limbs.

Pulling the screen closed, she turned and went out to meet the head of her order.

The nun who was the Prioress' secretary smiled with real warmth when she saw Sister Morima. "How glad I am that you have returned, Sister," she said. "Our prayers have been with you."

"And my prayers have been with you, Sister Sutso. Your concern honors me." She bowed. "Tell me quickly, how is our beloved Prioress?"

The secretary lowered her gaze and shook her head. "She is an inspiration, Sister, but she is not well."

Morima reached out and touched her Sister's shoulder. "She can go only to a better life, Sutso-sum. Is she able to see me now?"

The secretary nodded her head. "But you mustn't tire her, Sister. She needs constant rest." She shook her head again sadly. "May Botahara smile upon her, she is so old and has served Him so well."

They walked down the hall that led to the apartment of the Prioress, both of them taking care to make as little noise as possible. Sister Sutso tapped lightly on the frame of the screen and then cracked it open ever so slightly. Her face lit up. "Ah, you are awake. Sister Morima is here to see you, Prioress. Shall I allow her entry?"

There was no sound from within, but Sister Sutso opened the screen and stepped aside, nodding to Morima.

Taking a deep breath and releasing it as she had been taught long ago, Sister Morima entered the room, feeling her tension flow out with the outgoing breath. She knelt

inside the door and bowed to the mat, hearing the Shoji
slide shut behind her.

"Morima-sum, it is always such a pleasure." Sister
Saeja said, her voice a whisper.

"I am honored that you receive me, Prioress."

"Yes, I know. Come closer, my child, I cannot see
you so far away."

Sister Morima moved forward on her knees to within
an arm's length of the old woman. Sister Saeja, the Prioress of the Botahist Sisterhood, sat propped on embroidered cotton cushions near an open screen that let onto
a balcony overlooking a view much like Sister Morima's
own. She was a tiny woman, wrinkled and thin, but she
had the kindest face Morima had ever seen. The ancient
eyes regarded her and the gentle face wrinkled into a
beatific smile.

"Ah, you are thin, Sister Morima. Has this been a
difficult task I have set you?"

"I am anything but thin, Prioress. And the task . . .
is done."

"The task is never done, child, not for those such as
you—those with special abilities, but we can talk of this
later." She reached out a thin hand and touched the
younger woman's arm, but then let her hand fall. "You
have already spoken with our good Sister Gatsa, I am
told." The old woman's eyes seemed alive with humor.
"I awake each morning and wonder if I awake on my
pyre, such is their haste. But there are tasks to be completed before I am truly done, Morima-sum. We both
know this. There will not be a Cloister as soon as they
would wish." She laughed a small laugh. Reaching out
again she took Morima's hand in her own. "Tell me of
your journey, my child, I sense that something troubles
you."

Old, yes, Morima thought, but the eyes still see. "The
journey itself was uneventful, Prioress—no storms no
pirates, only a calm sea and fair winds."

"Botahara protects you, child."

"The Brothers were no more arrogant than usual. For
ten days prior to the Ceremony of Divine Renewal I

fasted, as is the custom of the Brothers. The Ceremony of Purification took three days and was performed by their Supreme Master himself, the doddering Brother Nodaku. During this time, I was kept apart from the rest of the Monastery and was unable to observe any of their secret trainings or teaching.

"The Ceremony of Divine Renewal takes place at sunrise and is performed by seven senior Brothers. The Urn is removed from the altar by the Sacred Guards and set on a special stand. Unsealing it is a lengthy ordeal, as every precaution is taken to protect the scrolls from deterioration." Sister Morima fought hard to keep her hands from trembling. How do I tell her? she asked herself. She saw fatigue in the Prioress' eyes and felt the grip on her hand lessen. She seemed so frail.

"Are you well, Prioress?"

"Yes, go on," she whispered.

"The scrolls are removed from the Urn by the Supreme Master as the sun rises, and laid upon the stand. Outside, every person in the monastery chants thanksgiving." Sister Morima swallowed hard.

The Prioress had closed her eyes and Morima peered at the ancient nun, but again the whisper came, "Go on."

"The scrolls are then unrolled, one by one and examined with extreme care. I was allowed to watch though I could not touch them."

"Something was wrong?" Sister Saeja said, not opening her eyes.

"Yes!" Morima said hiding her face in her hands.

"Tell me, child."

"Prioress, in preparation for this event, I studied every known reference to, and every copy of our Lord's writing. I cannot explain what I saw there . . . They were very old scrolls, I'm sure but . . . I believe, *no,* I am *certain that those were not the scrolls written by our Lord Botahara in His own hand.*" She took a deep, uneven breath and looked at the face of her superior.

The old nun nodded almost imperceptibly. "Of course," she whispered and fell into a deep sleep.

# Nine

*The purpose of the move must not
be merely hidden within another
purpose.
It must be concealed entirely,
lost within the complexity of a
plan that is even more plausible
than the real one.*

Writings of the
Gii Master Soto

Shonto's fleet rounded the Point of Sublime Imperial Purpose and entered the Grand Canal, the ancient waterway which spanned the Empire from north to south. It was an impressive fleet that began the journey north, made up largely of flat bottomed river barges rowed by muscular oarsmen, but there were swifter craft also and not a few that had been armed for the journey.

It said much of the Empire under the rule of Akantsu II, that an Imperial Governor took measures to defend himself from robbers while traveling from the capital to his province. The truth was that Shonto could not have been more satisfied with the situation. It allowed him to arm himself openly, which meant he could protect himself more easily from those he saw as a real threat.

One of those Shonto felt threatened him stood on a guard tower watching the fleet through a narrow opening in the stone wall. Jaku Katta leaned on the worn sill and examined each ship as it passed, assessing Shonto's strength with professional deliberation. Nearby stood his youngest brother, the lieutenant Jaku Yasata, who waited obediently for the general to complete his surveillance. Occasionally Yasata cast a glance down the walkway toward the door where he had posted soldiers, but he did not really fear interruption here—the tower was an Imperial Guard stronghold and had been for centuries.

Jaku Yasata shifted his substantial weight almost imperceptibly back and forth from one foot to the other though his face betrayed no sign of his impatience. The youngest of the three Jaku brothers, Yasata had neither the martial skill of Katta nor the intellectual brilliance of Tadamoto. He was a soldier of no special merit other than his unquestioning loyalty to his elder brothers. This one trait, though, was enough to make him immeasurably valuable to both his brothers, which indicated the amount of trust they were willing to place in those around them.

Jaku Katta stared at length as each of the river craft passed and he was reassured by what he saw. It proved that his informants were performing their function and indicated, too, that Shonto went off to the north without suspecting the real dangers that lay in his path.

Jaku caught himself gloating and suppressed the emotion. The Emperor is right about one thing, Jaku thought, I must not become overconfident. It is a great weakness. But look how the great Shonto goes! Burdened down with the poorest travelers, luckless merchants, and near bankrupt peers. Everyone has sought his protection for their journey north and Shonto has refused no one. Jaku shook his head. He had expected more from a man of such renown. He felt a momentary flash of pity for Shonto Motoru, but then Jaku laughed. Soon, so soon. Everything goes as it should.

An image of Lady Nishima appeared in his mind—a very grateful Nishima—and this thought excited him.

"Less than five thousand troops," Yasata said peering over his brother's shoulder.

Jaku did not turn to answer him but nodded. "Yes, and half the sycophants in the Empire." He pointed through the opening in the stone wall. "Look at them all! Huddled together under the banner of the Imperial Governor—as though that would protect them." He dropped his hand to the window ledge and leaned forward as far as he dared.

Yasata peered over his shoulder. "I see no special preparations. He seems to go without suspicion."

"Shonto goes nowhere without suspicion, Yasata-sum. Do not be fooled. But this time his suspicions have been drawn from the true threat. He has special preparations, be sure of that, but for the wrong contingencies."

"The false-trap?" Yasata ventured hoping to learn some of his brother's plans.

"It is not *false,* it is *secondary*—but it is where Shonto's focus has been drawn. And when he falls, the great general will take others with him. Yasata-sum, but not the Jaku. The Jaku shall *rise.*" He turned and clapped his brother on the shoulder, surprising Yasata with his speed. "And that means you, Colonel Jaku. Yes! I make you a colonel. I must prepare you. I will have even greater need of your service in the future, you and Tadamoto-sum."

Yasata looked for words to thank the general, but Katta had already turned back to the window.

The general looked down on the canal as the last barge passed. A smile appeared on his face. No, Emperor, you are wrong, it is not I who am overconfident.

# Ten

*Our boat of gumwood and dark locust*
*Her paint scaling like serpent's skin,*
*Sets forth into the throng of craft*
*On the Grand Canal.*
*Uncounted travelers,*
*Uncounted desires*
*Borne over blue water.*
*Only the funeral barge*
*Covered in white petals*
*Appears to know its destination.*

> *"Grand Canal"*
> *From the later poems of*
> *Lady Nishima Fanisan Shonto*

The motion of the river barge, and the crying of the gulls seemed to lighten Lord Komawara's spirit. He had been too long in the Imperial capital for a country lord and now his spirit had need of the wider world. I belong in Seh, he thought, I am not made for this courtier's life of careful condescension. He took a deep breath of the fresh country air. The beginning of the journey, he thought, how the heart lifts at the beginning of a journey.

Along the riverbank entire villages of peasants gathered to show respect for the Imperial Governor's progress. They bowed low as the flotilla approached and did not move again until it was past. Komawara saw an old man push the head of a curious child down into the dirt and hold it there, teaching the young one proper respect.

The river bank was low here, only the slight swelling of a grass-covered levee between the water and the fields. Far ahead, around a bend in the canal, Komawara could see the first boats in the fleet and he began to count. Thirty to the barge he was on, and he had no idea how many more followed behind. It is not often that such a progress is seen, he thought, except when the Son of Heaven moves to his Summer Palace.

So many craft and who is aboard them? Soldiers, musicians, merchants, magicians, potters, swordmakers, scholars, smiths, fortune-tellers, swindlers, gamblers, Botahist Sisters, courtesans, priests. There is a representative of every part of our world, all gathered together aboard these ships. He thought a poem might be made of this, but the words would not come.

It had been a somewhat smaller flotilla that had brought him south. Of course, that had been before his attendance of the Emperor's party, before he had met Lord Shonto. Strange how karma worked. He had gone hoping to gain the Emperor's favor and had been ignored by the Highest One. Then, somehow, he had caught the attention of the man the Emperor felt was his greatest threat. Now here he was, returning to Seh in the entourage of the new governor.

He wondered, again, why Shonto had requested his presence. It seemed the new governor had time for many tasks. Most lords of Komawara's acquaintance would be completely overextended in an endeavor such as this, yet Shonto seemed to proceed as though nothing in his life had changed. He has an excellent and loyal staff, Komawara thought, not all lords could say this. I have the good fortune of the same blessing, I thank Botahara and my father's wisdom.

A member of the Komawara House Guard cleared his throat behind his young lord. Komawara looked over his shoulder.

"The sampan is here, lord."

He walked, on newly caulked planks, across the deck to the waiting boat. Crewman gathered amidships to raise the single sail, for a fair wind had come up aft of the beam and the oarsmen would get a rest. Two sailors lowered a ladder over the side and held it in place for him. Their muscled torsos glistened from the labor of rowing and Komawara had no doubt that they would take his weight with ease.

A small boat, manned by Shonto House Guards, lay alongside the barge and Komawara clambered down to it with characteristic agility. The Shonto Guards and the crewmen who bowed as he passed, knew him, though he was not aware of it—*the son of the swordsman,* they thought as he passed. Yet he appeared young to all of them, with that wiriness and length of limb one expected in a colt. But he is the son of the father, the guards thought. What a man to have had as swordmaster! And then there were the duels. Young Komawara was known for the duels he had won—several already—and it was said he feared no one.

Oblivious to all this, Komawara took his place in the boat feeling somewhat uncomfortable. The role of Shonto ally was disconcerting to him. His awe of Shonto Motoru was too great for him to see himself as in any way necessary to the Shonto purpose. Somehow it all seemed like a mistake that would soon be discovered. Perhaps this thought, which he realized was entirely without honor, was what made him apprehensive about meeting with Shonto.

Sculling up through the line of boats, the guards came skillfully alongside a large, ornate barge. Komawara stepped out onto the boarding platform and the guards there bowed to him with respect. It was strange the way the soldiers could do that, Komawara thought. A person of rank would receive a bow that was flawlessly polite, but a person of equal rank who was also a fighter would receive a bow that unquestionably conveyed more respect, yet Komawara could not say how it differed. He only knew that it was so.

Mounting the stairs to the main deck Komawara began to loosen the strings that held his scabbard in his sash, but as he reached the deck he met Shonto's steward Kamu, and the old man gestured to Komawara's sword.

"My lord asks that you wear your sword, Lord Komawara," he said bowing formally.

Komawara bowed equally in return. "I wear it always for his protection, Kamu-sum."

Kamu's face registered his approval. "Lord Shonto asks that you join him on the quarter deck, Sire."

Komawara nodded and followed the steward to the barge's stern where he could see Shonto sitting under a silk awning. The lord bent over a low table, brush in hand, and his secretary knelt in attendance to his right. The rattle of armor as guards bowed to Komawara caused Shonto to look up and his face creased into a smile of warmth.

"Lord Komawara, I am honored that you join me."

Bowing with formality, the two lords made the polite inquiries their strict etiquette required. Cha was served and the lords amused themselves by watching children on the barge behind as they threw scraps to the crying gulls. Only the occasional offering would land in the water, so quick of wing were the small, river birds.

The mid-morning sun was warm, casting a soft, autumn light over the lush countryside. Leaves drifted south in procession on flowing waters, as the flotilla made its way slowly north. A swift Imperial messenger swept by, the powerful oarsmen sending it shooting ahead with each stroke of their long, curved blades.

Shonto watched the messenger glide by. They report our progress to the Emperor, he thought, knowing that the farther from the capital he traveled, the closer he came to the Emperor's purpose.

"Will fourteen days see us in Seh, Lord Komawara?"

"If the winds remain fair, Sire. But we must expect at least some delay from the Butto-Hajiwara feud."

Shonto nodded. "Delay, yes," and he gestured to a guard who placed a tightly rolled scroll on the table before them. Shonto examined the seal carefully before breaking it and then spread the thick paper across the table. It was a detailed map of the area disputed by the warring families. All of the fortifications were drawn in, as well as the troop placements and the strengths of each garrison.

"If it is not an imposition, Lord Komawara, I would ask you to look at this map and verify its details to the best of your ability. Please, do not hurry."

Komawara bent over the map, examining each placement, each notation. He searched his memory and asked for the help of Botahara. Finally he raised his eyes from his task. "It seems to be correct in every detail, Lord Shonto."

Shonto nodded, "It was made up from the combined information of several spies." He rolled the map again and it was taken by a guard. "The words of spies should never stand without verification."

Lunch was served and this brought to Komawara's mind thoughts of Lady Nishima gracefully serving cha. The conversation strayed through an array of subjects before settling on the lords of Seh and how those of note would react to Shonto's arrival. It was a topic that Shonto and his advisors had discussed almost endlessly, but they knew that it was all speculation—nothing was sure.

Aware of the secretary who knelt beyond the awning, obviously waiting, Lord Komawara excused himself as soon as he could politely do so.

Shonto watched him go, watched the way the young lord carried himself. He will be tested severely within the year, Shonto thought, though he did not know where the thought came from.

From his sleeve pocket Shonto removed a small scroll that had come that morning, smuggled through the disputed area by a Shonto soldier disguised as a fish buyer. He unrolled it and again read the strong hand of his son. The words themselves were innocent enough. It was the message within, the message in one of the Shonto ciphers, that concerned the lord. There were two sentences that begged his attention again: "The Butto-Hajiwara feud is stable, the lines of battle have not changed in several months—I do not anticipate any problem there." and, "The barbarian problem is, as you expected, comparatively minor and the reports you received about large buildups on the border are certainly false."

Shonto read the characters again: ". . . the lines of battle have not changed in several months . . ." The feud was stable. So what do they wait for? Shonto wondered. Do they wait for the other to make a mistake or is it something else altogether? Do they wait for Shonto? And if so is it the Butto or the Hajiwara, or both, that I must fear? "I do not anticipate any problem there." Which, in cipher, meant BEWARE.

He misses very little, this son of mine, but he does not know the real danger or he would have written of it.

And the barbarians, that situation was not as it seemed either. Shonto had received no reports about a buildup of barbarian fighters along the border and he knew his son was aware of this. So Komawara had been right, Shonto had sensed it immediately; there was more to the raids in Seh than the northern lords were willing to see.

Shonto rolled the scroll and put it back in his sleeve. May Botahara smile down upon me for I sail toward the abyss. Yet had not Hakata said: "Only from the abyss can one turn and see the world as it truly is." Then soon I shall see.

From his son, Shonto's thoughts turned to Lady Nishima, alone in the capital. If it is my enemies' hope to distract me, they could not have chosen a more effective ploy, he reasoned. Lady Okara is the key to Nishima's safety—if she will agree to my plans. I must make no mistake in monitoring the situation in the capital. He thought of the distance to Seh. Fourteen days, though the Imperial messengers covered the distance in only seven.

Thus occupied, Shonto sat on the quarter deck of the Imperial Governor's barge and, to anyone watching, it would have seemed that he was enjoying the passing countryside and attending to the correspondence his position required.

It did not appear so to Shuyun, who emerged from a hatch on the foredeck and stood for a moment looking at his liege-lord. Shuyun was aware of the lord's concerns, both from his discussion with Brother Hutto, and from what he was able to learn from Tanaka and Shonto's steward, Kamu.

Shuyun had spent his short time in the Shonto household meeting as many of Shonto's staff as was possible. It was as his teachers had said—the Shonto had an unerring sense of a person's abilities. This seemed to be coupled with insight into where a person's talents could best be employed and an ability to inspire great loyalty.

If there was to be criticism of Shonto's staff, it would be that many of them were older, with the inherent weaknesses that age brought. Shuyun wondered if this was just the "prejudice of the young" his teachers had warned him against. He must consider this in his meditations.

To the degree that he had been able, Shuyun had talked and listened to Shonto's guards and soldiers and, more importantly he had watched them, gauging their attitudes by the thousand minute actions which spoke to his Botahist training. Everything he saw told him they had utter faith in their lord, but even so, all of them went to Seh with misgivings.

Shuyun turned his gaze from Lord Shonto to the canal bank. A tow path ran along the shore, though it was only used in the spring floods when the river craft could not make way against the strong currents. Several Botahist neophytes from a nearby monastery bowed low to the passing lord. In the fields behind, as far as the eye could see, peasants stopped their work and bent low until the progress passed. We minister to them also, Shuyun found himself thinking, but still the obeisance caused in him a feeling of discomfort. This is not the world of the spirit, he told himself, it is my task to dwell here while keeping the goal of the spirit at the center of my being.

Yet, as he said this, a vision of Lady Nishima, laughing in the summerhouse, came to him unbidden, and he could not easily push it from his mind.

# Eleven

*The cycle of the rise and fall of dynasties seems to be the reverse of the pattern which affects the flourishing of art. For at the end of a dynasty, art is invariably at its most vigorous, while it is at its crudest at the outset of a new political era.*
*One of the contributions of Lady Okara, and her few students, was the preservation of the Hanama aesthetic through the early days of the Yamaku.*

*From Study of Lady Okara*
*by Lady Nishima Fanisan Shonto*

Lady Nishima looked again into the mirror of polished bronze and felt nothing but dissatisfaction with the image she saw. "I am plain," she said in a whisper. "I am without talent. Lady Okara wastes her time with me. Oh, if only the Emperor had not forced me to take his patronage! Lady Okara would not be burdened with someone so undeserving of her attention, and I would be in Seh, away from the Emperor and his weakling sons. Close to my uncle, who may need my assistance." She worried about Lord Shonto, gone now three days. He is strong and wise, she told herself for the thousandth time, I can help him by avoiding any further traps the Emperor may lay.

The water clock in the courtyard rang the fifth hour and she knew it was time for her to leave. A boat waited. The guard captain himself had insisted upon accompanying her with a large escort, but she had refused, knowing this would only draw attention to her going to the Lady Okara—only draw attention to her shame, for that is what she felt. Shame that she was being forced on so great a painter, and only to fulfill the Emperor's hidden design. She felt anger and frustration boil up in her. And worse—she felt trapped.

Forcing an outward calm over her emotions, Nishima went out into the hall and down the wide stairs into the main courtyard. Rohku Saicha, Captain of the Shonto House Guard and the man charged with her safety, met her as she crossed the tiled enclosure.

"Your sampan awaits you, Lady Nishima," he said bowing. "I hope you have reconsidered. I do have orders from your father to . . ."

"I will take the responsibility, Captain Rohku, please be at your ease," she said, nodding but not stopping.

He fell into step beside her. "All well and good, my lady, but I'm not sure my lord would accept that if something were to happen."

"Shall I put it in writing, then?"

"It isn't that, Lady Nishima. I am concerned about your safety."

"And what do you foresee happening to me in the capital in broad daylight?"

He shrugged his shoulders. "I do not know, Lady Nishima."

"You have assigned guards, that will be adequate. The Shonto must not go about as though the wrath of the gods were about to fall upon them. Where is the dignity in that?"

"I understand your point, Lady Nishima . . ." he meant to say more but they had reached the stairs to the small dock the Shonto family used and she had given him her hand to assist her in boarding the sampan.

She looked back at him from her seat. "You have done all that is required, Saicha-sum," she said, chiding

him, "I will return by late afternoon or send a message
if I am detained. Do not be concerned." She motioned
to the boatmen and they pushed off—three sampans, two
as escort and Lady Nishima's personal craft.

Outside the gate, Nishima felt a pang of guilt at having
thwarted the captain's precautions. Uncle would be furious if he knew, she thought. Ah well, it was done.

Her thoughts turned again to Lady Okara. Despite her
guilt she felt excitement at the idea of seeing the great
painter's studio. She cannot know how much I admire
her, Nishima thought, and she is so modest, so unassum-
ing. How can she be so, when everyone agrees that she
is the most important painter in three generations? I
must try and learn this modesty myself, she thought. I
am too vain about my meager accomplishments. Already
she had forgotten her session in front of the bronze
mirror.

The escort took the sampans by a preselected route
that would be reasonably quick while not subjecting Lady
Nishima to the cruder areas of the city. Large residences
passed on either side, partially hidden by their walls. Few
of them were mysteries to Lady Nishima, though, for she
had been to social functions in many of the more important homes in the capital.

At last they came to the island on which Lady Okara
resided. It was one of the dozen islands on the edge of
the city where the homes overlooked the Lake of the
Lost Dragon and the rolling, green hills beyond. An
attendant of Lady Okara's met Nishima at the dock, a
man of middle age whose smile was as disarming as a
child's.

"Lady Nishima, it is a great honor that you choose to
visit. Lady Okara awaits you. Her home is nearby, but
a hundred paces—do you wish to ride?" He gestured to
an open chair and four bearers who bowed before it.

"It is a good morning for a walk," Nishima said and
waited for the attendant to show them the path.

They started along the narrow cobbled street that led
up the hill from the dock, the attendant and his bearers,
the empty chair, Lady Nishima and her escort.

"I have never been here before. Are there many homes on the island?" Nishima asked the attendant who walked beside her shading her from the sun with a parasol.

"Perhaps a hundred in all, Lady Nishima, though most are on the other side closer to the capital. Only those who choose a quiet existence live here on the lake, though as you can see, it is very pleasant."

Nishima looked around her and had to agree. The vine-maples had turned a bright crimson and the cherry trees lining the street were turning their own, darker reds. Fall flowers fell in drapes over the top of a low stone wall, and behind them the lake lay shimmering in the sunlight, white sails cast across the surface like petals in the wind.

They turned into a tree-lined lane and in a few paces crossed a small bridge over a gurgling stream. Beyond this stood a wooden gate set into a sun dappled stone wall.

Entering the courtyard Nishima saw a medium-size residence built in a charming country style she had always admired. From the upper terrace Lady Okara saw her guest arrive and she descended a wide stairway to greet her.

"Lady Nishima, I am honored that you are able to accept my invitation so soon." The two women bowed to each other.

"I . . . I wish it were only that, Lady Okara, but I come with some embarrassment. We both know why."

"We won't talk of that, Lady Nishima. Our families have had too much in common in the past for us to be concerned by such things. It is long past time that I took an interest in you. I had heard of your talent before, you should know. It is only a reflection on my terrible manners that I had not invited you here long ago."

"You are too kind, Lady Okara."

The great woman smiled warmly and gestured for Nishima to accompany her. "Tell me of your father, Lady Nishima. Did he set out as he'd hoped?"

The two women turned and walked back toward the

stairs. "He is gone three days now, Lady Okara. I received word from him this morning. They make excellent time and all goes well." Nishima paused. "If I am not being too presumptuous, Lady Okara, I would be pleased if you would call me Nishima-sum."

Lady Okara smiled. "You could never be too presumptuous with me, my dear, I have known Lord Shonto for over thirty years. I was also an acquaintance of your mother's—did you know that?"

Nishima shook her head in surprise.

"It was long ago, when we were younger than you are now. You look a great deal like her, you know, though you are more beautiful, I must say."

Lady Nishima went almost as red as the vine-maples. "That can't be, Lady Okara, I have seen the portraits of my mother in her youth and she was a great beauty."

"Nonetheless, you are more beautiful than she. Please call me Okara-sum; I too, would be honored."

The two ascended the stairs to the terrace where cha was served in steaming bowls.

"The view is breathtaking, Okara-sum, it must be very peaceful to live here." Nishima said as they sat taking their leisure in the warm autumn sunlight.

"It is, both beautiful and peaceful, but nothing is a fortress against the world, Nishima-sum. It is a good thing to remember.

"I worry about Motoru-sum and this appointment to Seh," Lady Okara said suddenly. She touched Lady Nishima's arm, "I don't mean to cause you anxiety. He is wise, your father, and far more clever than anyone realizes."

"You don't cause me anxiety, Okara-sum. It is true that he is wise, but he is also without fear, and that is what concerns me."

"He has always been that way. All the years I have known him. His father was no different. It is in the blood."

Yes, Nishima thought, it is in the blood and I do not share that. My blood is Fanisan. Inside her she felt her resolve suddenly strengthen and she thought, But my spirit is Shonto.

"Would you like to see my studio?" Lady Okara asked.

"Oh, yes. I would be honored." And they rose from their cha and walked down the terrace toward the studio doors.

A breeze had sprung up by the time Nishima left the home of Lady Okara and the lake had developed a short swell before her boat was into the system of canals of the Imperial Capital. Opening the curtains of the sampan, Nishima saw small whitecaps sweeping across the lake and suddenly the sailboats seemed to be hurrying on their way.

The experience of seeing Lady Okara's studio still excited and deflated her. What a wealth of talent! The decades of hard work showed themselves in the fine detail and control apparent in all of the paintings. It is as Shuyun said, Lady Nishima thought, a part of Lady Okara's inner beauty goes into each work. She does not hide herself in her art. Strange, for she obviously tried to seclude herself in life. But perhaps that was only to allow her time to work. Someone of her fame could be interrupted continuously if she were not careful.

The paintings Lady Nishima had seen appeared before her mind, all of them so perfect. One, an unfinished view of the lake from the terrace, struck Nishima particularly for its beauty. Yet when she said this to Lady Okara the painter had answered, "Oh, that. I started it years ago and was never happy with it. I don't think I'll finish it now." And she had gone on to something else.

Nishima was left feeling very humbled—she *dreamed* of starting a painting of such mastery and here Lady Okara abandoned such a work as though it were a mere trifle.

Lady Okara's life had immense appeal to Lady Nishima—the freedom, the removal from the social whirl and the responsibilities of one's House. It seemed the perfect life.

The artist had taken time to look at sketches Nishima had brought with her and had been most complimentary.

She is an old friend of my uncle's, Nishima thought, she could hardly say anything else. Yet a part of her wanted to believe Lady Okara's words and a few moments later she had convinced herself that Lady Okara was too honorable not to have told her the truth. An instant later she was sure this could not be—Lady Okara was simply being polite in her comments, as any person of breeding would do.

As she swung back and forth between her secret hopes and her lack of confidence, the boats rounded a corner into a larger waterway and were immediately confronted by a dozen craft waiting to pass through an Imperial Guard blockade. She heard her own guard on the escort boat in front of her begin to shout. "Make way for the Lady Nishima Fanisan Shonto! Make way! Make way!" How inconvenient, she thought, settling back into her cushions, and then her instincts told her to beware.

It was too late to turn back now—to avoid a blockade was forbidden, and her guards had announced her presence. Already, they had moved to the head of the line. She could hear the lieutenant of her escort talking to the Imperial Guard now. Her name was mentioned several times with the emphasis on *Shonto, Governor* Shonto. Yet they did not move.

Her sampan swayed as someone boarded it. The Shonto lieutenant bowed to her as the circumstances would allow. "The Guard wish to detain us, my lady, it is not clear why. They are claiming 'orders.' They wish to speak with you personally. I have told them it is out of the question, yet they insist and will not let us pass. I shall send a boat to the palace immediately, but it will take time. I apologize for this inconvenience, Lady Nishima."

She considered for a moment, controlling her fear. "Do they doubt that it is me here?" she asked.

"That does not seem to be the case, Lady Nishima."

"Huh. Tell them I will complain of their actions *directly* to the Emperor and see what effect that has."

The lieutenant bowed quickly and went forward again. Nishima pulled the curtains, leaving only a slit through which to watch. She could see the lieutenant draw himself up into a suitable posture of outrage as he approached the guards, but she could also see that they were not going to allow themselves to be intimidated. They argued back and forth for a moment, voices becoming louder on both sides. Without bowing, the Shonto guard turned and came back across his boat and stepped now onto hers.

"They refuse to let us pass," he said bowing, and she could see that he fought to control anger. "They are intolerably *insolent,*" he spat out suddenly. "Excuse me, Lady Nishima, pardon my outburst."

She said nothing, not seeming to notice his apology. The situation was becoming dangerous, and she could see the anger rising in the other Shonto guards. Do they seek to provoke us into violence? It could serve no purpose. She had never been put in a situation like this before and did not know how to deal with it. Rohku Saicha would be furious when he heard, she thought.

"Tell them I will speak with them," she said suddenly.

"Are you certain, my lady?" the lieutenant was obviously shocked by her decision.

"I am certain," she said forcing confidence into her voice. I am Shonto, she told herself, they dare not interfere with me.

The lieutenant crossed the boats to the Guard again, obviously feeling humiliated that they should be in such a situation. Nishima watched as he nodded to the Guard commander and explained his lady's decision. She could not quite hear the words, but suddenly the lieutenant went rigid for a split second and then reached for his sword. Imperial Guards jumped forward to protect their officer and Shonto Guards did the same. The lieutenant came to his senses before a melee erupted, though, and ordered his men back. He turned, again without bowing, and returned to Lady Nishima, his face scarlet with rage.

Lady Nishima's heart was pounding with fear.

"The officer in charge refuses to come to you, Lady

Nishima. He insists that you come to him. I'm sorry. I have demanded that he take us to his commander, but he refuses. This is intolerable, I have never witnessed such lack of respect. These are men without honor. I apologize, Lady Nishima, but I don't know what we should do. We cannot go back, other Guards block our way." He cast a glance behind him. "I am entirely at fault and dishonored." The man bowed his head in shame.

Nishima realized that Lord Shonto would agree with the man entirely, but she felt sympathy for him. It is not his fault, she said to herself, though his own code says that it is.

"Tell them I will come to them," she said.

"*My lady, it is out of the question!* These are not even soldiers of rank!"

"It doesn't matter. There is no choice but violence, and we are few while they are many." She turned to the crewmen. "Boatmen, move me forward."

Slowly, boats parted and Lady Nishima's sampan pushed through the crowd. Rivermen and their families stared at the spectacle. They are so close, she thought, never have I been so vulnerable. She was not afraid of the rivermen, who were hardworking and honest, but this was a perfect place to hide an assassin. She cursed herself for ignoring Rohku Saicha.

Finally she came up to the Imperial Guard's boat which blocked the canal. She could see the Emperor's soldiers now, dressed in their black armor. Their commander was only a Guard Captain, and a huge man he was. He leaned silently back on the boat's small cabin, his arms crossed before him casually. He chewed something as he waited, perhaps oona nut, she thought. It was terribly bad manners.

When her sampan was ten feet away, Lady Nishima pulled the curtain back fully and stared out coldly at the Imperial Guard Captain—the soldiers with him, she ignored entirely.

"I am Lady Nishima Fanisan Shonto, why am I being delayed?" she demanded.

"You are being delayed because I am an Imperial Guard and I choose to delay you," he answered without hesitation.

Again her escort reached for their swords, but she stopped them with a gesture.

"This is unpardonable insolence, Captain, I warn you. Give me your reason for this delay or let me pass immediately!"

"I must see your papers before I will consider whether you will go on or not," he said.

There was a buzz in the surrounding crowd now, they had never seen such a thing, not with the Shonto! Could it be that such a family was in disfavor with the Son of Heaven?

"*Papers*, Captain? Could it be that you believe the Shonto carry *papers*? Perhaps you think also that I sell *fish* from my sampan?" she said, gesturing to her elegant craft.

The crowd laughed and the Guard Captain stared them into an abrupt silence. "If you can produce no papers, then you will accompany me to our keep. I have my orders."

Lady Nishima went on to her next ploy without hesitation. "You," she said, addressing the captain's second in command, a tall, young sergeant. "Your captain has taken leave of his senses. He endangers your future if not your lives, for the Emperor is not tolerant of fools. This man is unfit to command. Relieve him of his position and you may yet save yourselves."

The captain turned to stare at the younger officer, but the man looked only straight ahead as though he had not heard Lady Nishima's words. But as the captain shifted his gaze back to Lady Nishima, the sergeant looked out of the corner of his eye at two guards directly behind the captain. They nodded almost imperceptibly and shifted their positions slightly. Other guards seemed also about to act. Lady Nishima's hopes rose.

An uproar exploded to the right, beyond the boats of the river people. Shonto Guards drew their swords and formed a protective barrier before their mistress. The crowd of onlookers parted as if by invisible command and more Imperial Guards rushed across the decks down the corridor they created. Lady Nishima's view was blocked, but suddenly a voice she recognized rang out over the din. The voice of Jaku Katta.

*The Emperor!* Nishima thought, unable to believe that this could have been done so boldly—in the capital in broad daylight with a hundred witnesses.

*"You!"* It was the voice of command and Nishima could feel even her own escort harken to it. *"Captain of the Guard. What is this you do?"*

*Anger!* Lady Nishima heard anger in the general's voice. Her hopes rose. Jaku Katta jumped from a barge and landed on the deck of the Imperial Guard boat. The Guard Captain bowed, a look of confusion on his face.

"I follow orders, General Jaku," he said defensively.

"You have orders to harass the Lady Nishima Fanisan?"

The guard's mouth worked, but no words came.

"I'm waiting, Captain."

"I was ordered to . . . " He did not finish. The back of Jaku's left hand smashed across his face. The guard reached for his sword, but Jaku's was out of its sheath before the captain's hand had found the hilt.

"Do you not bow to your commander, Captain?"

The man looked around him and realized he was the only one on the barge who had remained standing. Slowly he knelt, his hand to his bleeding mouth, his eyes riveted to Jaku's sword.

The general seemed to hesitate for a moment and then he sheathed his sword. "This man is your prisoner, Sergeant. Report yourselves when you return to your keep. All of you will face a Court of the Imperium's Military."

Giving a hand signal to one of his own elite guard to clear the area, Jaku Katta turned back to Lady Nishima's escort. He bowed to the Shonto lieutenant.

"I apologize for this incident, Lieutenant. It is unforgivable, I realize. I will inform the Emperor at the earliest opportunity. Would you ask if I may extend my apologies to Lady Nishima in person?"

The Shonto Guard bowed in return. "Certainly, General. But please, before I do, I must inform you that the insult inflicted upon the House of Shonto and the honor of my mistress by this barbarian in Imperial Guard livery, is beyond tolerance. I, too, feel that I have been dishonored by this man. I cannot accept this."

Nishima watched all of this through her partially drawn curtains. The words drifted to her only in part, but it was easy to guess what was being said. I am rescued yet I do not feel the danger has passed, she thought.

Jaku Katta shook his head in sympathy, one soldier to another. "I understand completely, Lieutenant, but is it not enough to know that his punishment will be . . . *extreme,* at the hands of the Court of the Military?"

The Shonto lieutenant seemed to weigh his words, but then asked, "Would you accept this insult, General?"

Jaku Katta considered this for only an instant, and then shook his head. "I would not." He turned to his second in command. "Clear a place on the quay and give the captain his sword. Be sure no one interferes." He turned back to the lieutenant. "Take two of your guard as witnesses." He bowed. "You choose the course of honor, Lieutenant. May the gods stand at your side."

The lieutenant bowed in return and relinquished his command to his second, a young captain with the face of a scholar. This young man went immediately to convey Jaku Katta's request to Lady Nishima.

"Is there to be a duel?" she asked as soon as the Shonto captain approached.

"It is unavoidable, Lady Nishima. I would have given the challenge myself if the lieutenant had not taken it up, as was his right."

"But the Imperial Guardsman is huge!" She raced through several arguments in her mind. Honor, she thought, this is about honor, not about fear. I must appeal to that. "Does not the lieutenant endanger the Shonto name more if he is to fail?"

"He will not fail, Lady, though I fear the cost may be great." He turned back to the quay where a crowd gathered to witness the conflict. The sight of the general reminded him of his duties. "General Katta has asked if he could convey his apologies to you in person, Lady Nishima."

"Of course, yes. Bring him to me." She could see the fight was about to begin, and there on the quay the difference in the size of the two men could truly be seen.

"General," Nishima said as Jaku approached. "Can you not stop this senseless fight? Will not the Imperial Guard be held responsible for his actions as it is?"

Jaku bowed low. "I tried to dissuade your lieutenant, Lady Nishima, but it is his right. He felt Shonto honor had been put in question. I am sorry."

Swords rang out in the silence that had settled. Lady Nishima hid her mouth behind an open fan, but in her eyes there was anguish. This is my fault, she thought. If I had listened to Rohku Saicha, this would never have happened. Or would it? Something still told her there was more to the situation than met the eye.

"Do you wish to move along the canal until this is completed? You can do nothing for your lieutenant here."

"Yes, please," she said. Anything to be beyond the sound of the swords.

Jaku signaled to her boatmen who obeyed him as though he were their commander. They rounded a corner and settled close to a stone quay.

Jaku broke the awkward silence first. "Please allow me to apologize for the actions of my guards, though I know they were unforgivable."

Lady Nishima interrupted him. "You need not apologize to me, General Katta. I remain indebted to you for your act of bravery in our garden. You saved my lord's life. This is a thing for which I can never repay you."

Jaku shrugged in modesty, then turned his tiger eyes on the young woman. "It was an honor to serve the Shonto, Lady Nishima, an honor which I would gladly repeat." He let the statement hang in the air and then turned his eyes away. "I have assured your esteemed uncle that you are in no danger while he is in Seh. Excuse my presumption, but I have been concerned about your safety since the . . . incident in Lord Shonto's garden."

"Your concern flatters me, General Jaku, but it is not the Shonto way to allow ourselves to be in another's debt."

"Debt? It is I who am in your debt, Lady Nishima, that you have not called me a presumptuous fool."

Lady Nishima nodded to Jaku for his kindness, but the ringing of swords, loud and frenzied drew her gaze away. There was silence then.

Jaku Katta cocked his head to one side concentrating on the distant sounds. "It is over, Lady Nishima. We may hope honor has been restored." He stood as an Imperial Guard came running up.

"The captain has fallen, General."

"And the Shonto lieutenant?"

"He lives, Sire, but his wounds are severe. We have taken the liberty of removing him to a doctor's care."

Lady Nishima hid her face in her hands for a second but then regained control.

The general nodded, dismissing the man. "I'm sorry, Lady Nishima, but he could not be dissuaded. I will see to his medical care myself and inform you of his condition."

"There was nothing you could do. Please do not feel the blame is yours. Pardon me, General, but I must continue, if I may."

Jaku bowed quickly. "'Of course, I did not mean to detain you." He stepped off the boat onto the quay. "Perhaps we will meet at the Emperor's celebration of his Ascension?"

You are bold, Nishima thought. "Perhaps."

He smiled and fixed her with a parting glance.

The cold eyes of the predator, Nishima thought, as the general turned away. But still she felt stirred by his presence. Had he not saved her uncle? Had he not rescued her from this impossible situation?

Her escort returned and the boatmen pushed off. A voice inside spoke, saying that despite all appearances, something was not right. What was it Jaku had said to the Imperial Guard captain when he appeared?—"You have orders to harass the Lady Nishima Fanisan?"

That is how he sees me, she realized suddenly, *Lady Nishima Fanisan—a daughter of the blood*. She felt the island of Lady Okara slipping away, and the life she desired gone with it. "I can never escape it," she said in a whisper, "though I would not choose it if offered a thousand times. My blood, I cannot change my blood."

As the dusk settled in the capital of Wa, the Lady Nishima rode toward her destination feeling, more than ever, that it had been chosen by forces beyond herself.

Not far away, Jaku Katta boarded his own sampan and signaled his boatmen to take him to the Imperial Palace. Once in the privacy of his craft, Jaku could not help smiling with satisfaction. She is not as unattainable as I had been led to believe, he thought. Oh, but she was no fool! Almost she had convinced the guards to mutiny against their captain! He shook his head in disbelief. If he had not appeared when he had . . . well, it was done now, and that fool of a captain would never tell what his orders had been. That had been a close moment, and the lieutenant was so small! Jaku had feared he would not be able to perform the deed. He should not have been concerned—Shonto men were trained to be the best and, except for Jaku's elite guard, they were.

The Emperor's general leaned forward as if to hurry his boat along. Battle had been engaged and now everything hung in the balance. Only time would tell if his plans were adequate. And the time would be short.

Only one doubt nagged at the Commander of the Imperial Guard. He knew it grew out of something that could almost be called superstition, but he could not reason this doubt away.

Jaku Katta could remember failing to accomplish something once in his life and the person who had brought about that failure had returned, and slipped through an assassination attempt already.

The famed kick boxer closed his eyes and rubbed his brow as if in sudden pain. It was not a memory that brought him comfort. Not one of the thousands of people who watched had seen what had occurred. But it had marked Jaku and he could not erase that mark.

A small Botahist monk had stood before him, utterly calm after deflecting a blow that had all the power of Jaku's huge frame behind it. Deflecting it, yet Jaku knew there had been no contact between them. He had felt the power though, the unheard of power. To turn a blow without touching the assailant. . . .

Jaku shook his head to free himself of his memory. He looked out to the banks of the canal and saw the people bow as he passed. Drawing a long breath, he forced a calm over himself. They no longer stood in the limited arena of the tournament ring. Here, the boy was hopelessly beyond his depth, there could be no doubt of that.

The boat rounded into the Canal of His Highest Wisdom, the widest canal in the capital, and there, at its end, the white palace of the Emperor seemed to glow in the failing light. It was Jaku's destination.

# Twelve

The Botahist Acolyte, Tesseko, knelt by the charcoal fire that burned amidships. The motion of the river junk was less noticeable there and her sensitive stomach appreciated that. A wind fanned the coals and smoke curled up to sting her eyes, but she did not seem to mind—it was a fair wind and it hurried them on their way to Seh.

She chanted the glory of the Perfect Master silently as she worked, knowing that this helped speed the time during the performance of menial tasks. (Glory, glory to His wisdom which leads me.)

She glanced up as she cooked and saw the people on the canal bank kneeling as the Imperial Governor's progress passed. She, herself, felt awe to be part of this procession. As she had thought herself immeasurably fortunate (Glory to the Seven Paths) when she was selected to accompany senior Sister Morima on this journey. Sister Morima, the woman who had looked upon the *Hand of Botahara* with her own eyes! Yes, she had felt fortunate.

Junior Acolyte Tesseko bent over the food she prepared, vegetables, steamed rice—the simple fare of the ascetic. Into this she mixed a secret blend of herbs, for Sister Morima had been taken ill, or so it seemed. Since they had set out from the Priory of the Divine Awakening, seven days past, Sister Morima had become more and more withdrawn. Her face had become pale and her skin waxy. This will set her to rights, Tesseko told herself.

She felt a certain disappointment at Sister Morima's

silence. She had hoped to learn more; after all, Tesseko was almost ready to become a senior Acolyte—and she was only eighteen—she had hoped the Sister would take her more into her confidence, there was so much Sister Morima could teach her. But she realized now that it was not to be so.

Tesseko did not even know the reason for this journey. Of course, she had not dared ask—the Sisterhood did many things in secret—it was the place of a junior Acolyte to serve. But still she could not help but wonder. She had begun to observe Sister Morima carefully, yet all she could learn was that there was a certain Botahist Brother, the Spiritual Advisor to the great Lord Shonto, that Sister Morima seemed to be very interested in. She watched him secretly, and Acolyte Tesseko was certain she wrote her observations down in a cypher. It was all very mysterious and exciting, she thought.

She tried to imagine why Sister Morima watched this young monk. Was he secretly a spy for the Sisterhood, living in the midst of the aristocracy and privy to the secrets of the Botahist Brothers? She did not know. All she knew was the young Brother was thought very gifted—she had heard much in her short time aboard— and he had greeted her with respect when they had met by accident, in the small town where the fleet had stopped two days previously. He seemed most kind. That was all she knew.

Perhaps she expected too much; the honored Sister was not herself, with this sudden illness taking hold of her as it had. Sister Morima had had fevers and delirium in the night, Acolyte Tesseko knew, for she had been forced to listen to the Botahist nun in the darkness of their shared cabin. It had frightened her to hear the Sister rant. And she had said such things! (Glory to His name, eternal glory.) Well, she did not want to think about the things Sister Morima had said. She shuddered involuntarily, for Acolyte Tesseko had seldom heard blasphemy before and certainly not from the mouth of a senior Sister.

She removed the food from the coals and served it

into porcelain bowls, which she set on a bamboo tray.
(Glory of His words, their perfection, glory.) Crossing
the deck she noticed a sailor watching her. Often, she
had been told she was pretty, though she could not imagine why anyone would think that—her black hair was
cropped short and her robe was shapeless and unflat-
tering. It is wrong to think of such things, she told herself. (Glory of His vision, highest glory of His vision.)

The steps to the cabin were steep and difficult, but the
training of the Sisterhood had given her suppleness and
strength beyond that of most inhabitants of Wa. Not
using even a hand for balance, she descended with ease.
She tapped on the screen to their cabin, but there was
no response. Sliding the shoji quietly, she entered the
darkened room. Sister Morima lay in a low bed, set
against one wall. Tesseko could hear her labored
breathing.

"Sister Morima?" Tesseko said as she crossed the
room. But there was no response. She set the tray on a
small, fixed table, and knelt beside the bed.

"Sister Morima?" she said again a bit louder, but still
there was only the sound of the Sister's breathing. She
felt the nun's brow and found it hot and clammy. Poor
Sister Morima, she thought. It was then that she noticed
that her superior was dressed in her outer robe, she could
see her shoulder protruding from beneath covers. Has
she been out of bed? Tesseko wondered. I should have
been here to assist her.

The young Acolyte moved away, deciding to let the
nun sleep, and was about to rise when something assailed
her nostrils. She turned her head to each side, testing
the air for the source of the odor. This cannot be, she
thought. It seemed to come from under the low table.
She bent down to look and could not believe the evidence of her eyes! There, pushed out of sight, was a
plate, and on it the remains of a meal of *flesh!* Bones
and pieces of disgusting fat. Acolyte Tesseko felt immediately ill. *May Botahara save her,* she thought, Sister
Morima has eaten of the *flesh of an animal!* She turned
and fled from the cabin.

\*   \*   \*

The boatmen guided the sampan with deft strokes, moving it quickly against the canal's current. Acolyte Tesseko sat in the prow watching the large junks and river barges as the sampan glided past them. It was another fine day in what seemed like an endless autumn. She breathed the spiced air in careful rhythm, as her instructors had taught her, forcing a calm over her body and mind. Acolyte Tesseko had been distraught, almost in a panic, since her discovery of the day before. Now she felt closer to being at peace. She was aware of the slight time-stretch that the Sisters spoke of, felt the chi-flow in her body. She wondered again if it was true that the Brothers had mastered their sense of subjective time?

This brought her back to the reason that she was aboard the sampan and shook the feeling of confidence she was trying to create, for the truth was, she was not sure that what she was about to do was correct. But were they not both followers of the Great Way? She could not believe that this young monk, Lord Shonto's Spiritual Advisor, was evil, as the Sisters said all Brothers were. Her instincts had told her immediately that he was good, a follower of the True Faith. Some of the Sisters believed that this strife between the Sisterhood and the Brotherhood went against the teaching of Botahara, for the struggle was centered on power, and the followers of Botahara renounced all claim to power as they renounced property and the desires of the flesh.

The desires of the flesh, well, she must not think of those. (Glory to the Seven Paths, glory.)

If what these Sisters believed was true, then it would be correct for her to speak with this Brother—whose name, she must remember, was Shuyun.

And besides, Tesseko realized, there was no one else she could discuss her problem with. Who else was there who understood the divine secrets of the human body? Sister Morima, in her few lucid moments, absolutely refused to be taken off the junk (they must get to Seh!) and there were no other Botahist Sisters in the flotilla. What I do is correct. In my soul I do not doubt.

They came abreast of the Imperial Governor's barge and Acolyte Tesseko was allowed to wait on the boarding platform while a guard went to find Shonto's steward.

It took only a moment for the guard to return, accompanied by a one-armed old man. He bowed to her formally.

"I am Kamu, Steward of Lord Shonto Motoru. Excuse our precautions, Sister, but is it true that you wish to see Lord Shonto's Spiritual Advisor?" He said this calmly, as though he were merely verifying information. He showed no surprise at the request.

"Please, Steward Kamu, it is most important."

He said nothing for a few seconds but then asked, "May I tell Shuyun-sum the reason that you wish to see him?" When he saw the pained expression on her face he raised his hand. "I will speak with him." He disappeared onto the deck and left Tesseko in the company of the Shonto Guards who, though stationed to watch her, seemed to be staring off at something in the distance, as was only polite.

A moment later Kamu reappeared. "Please, Sister, would you come with me?" He gave the guards a hand signal that the nun memorized. She would report it to her superiors. They recorded these things and, over a period of years could sometimes break a family's code altogether.

She crossed the deck in Kamu's wake and followed him to the bow. Out of a hatch emerged the monk she had spoken to in the town. He nodded to Kamu, who bowed respectfully.

"Acolyte Tesseko, I am honored that you visit me. Perhaps this is a sign of what will happen in the future between our faiths." He bowed politely and she returned his gesture.

"Perhaps, Brother Shuyun, though I must tell you that I am here on my own initiative, not on behalf of my Order."

Shuyun nodded and motioned to the bow area where they could speak in privacy. He leaned against the low rail and regarded the Acolyte. She was fine of form, he thought, and tall. Under the flat, conical hat, her eyes were guarded, she seemed to be suppressing agitation. She had not yet mastered the technique that would allow her to do this, for he could see tension there, in the tightening of the skin around the eyes and the redness of the tear ducts.

"Would you care for cha, Acolyte Tesseko?" he asked, following the etiquette of the situation.

"It is kind of you to offer, Brother, but I have other duties and can only speak with you briefly."

He sensed the urgency in her voice. "Perhaps it would be best if we did away with formality, and spoke openly, Acolyte Tesseko."

"I agree, that would be best." She took a breath in preparation but could not begin the speech she had rehearsed. Suddenly, she wondered if what she was doing was right.

"If it will make it easier, Acolyte Tesseko, I will swear by the Perfect Master that your words will not go beyond me."

She nodded. "I have come for advice, Brother, medical advice. I travel with a senior Sister who is very ill. I have not seen these symptoms before, Brother, I am most distressed."

"She would not consent to see me?"

"No, it is out of the question." She put a hand to the rail and turned to stare off across the canal.

"Can you describe these symptoms, Acolyte?"

"She is fevered, often at night. But in the day she seems distant, as though she were in the grip of fever, yet she is not. She eats, some days, in excess, while other days she cannot bear the sight of food. All of her behavior is uncharacteristic. I am not sure what should be done, Brother."

"It is unfortunate that she will not see me. Is there anything else you can tell me."

Tesseko looked off into the distance again, watching a swallow play with a feather. The tension around her eyes increased, and Shuyun wondered if she would be able to go on.

"There are other things . . . Brother. She speaks in her deliriums. She frightens me."

"Frightens you, Acolyte?"

"She says things that—it is only her illness—but these things endanger her spirit. They must. And Sister Morima is such an enlightened woman."

*Sister Morima!* Shuyun remembered her—the large nun in the Supreme Master's audience hall. ("Have you learned to stop the sand, Initiate?") Yes, he knew her, knew that she had been selected to witness the Ceremony of Divine Renewal.

"Tell me of these things, Acolyte, it may be important."

"I . . . I cannot repeat them, Brother, they are *blasphemous.*"

"Can you tell me something of their nature without repeating them, Acolyte?"

"She speaks of the Word of Lord Botahara, the actual written Word."

"I know that she attended the Ceremony of Divine Renewal, Acolyte Tesseko."

She nodded but continued to look away. "She says— she seems to say that the words of Botahara are not his words."

"She seems to say this? What do you mean."

"Over and over she repeats," the Acolyte half covered her mouth with her hand, " *'lies! all that we have learned is lies!'* " Tesseko closed her eyes tightly for a moment. "There is more. Sometimes in the darkness she yells: *'These are not the words of truth! These are not our Lord's words!'* I cannot say any more. I am most concerned, Brother."

"Yes," Shuyun said, and it was almost a whisper. She had started now, she would not stop until she had told all.

"When she eats, she gorges herself, entirely without discipline, and sometimes—I don't know where she gets it—she eats *flesh*, Brother!"

She covered her face completely now. Her shoulders shook, but there were no sobs. Shuyun let her cry, he had no experience in comforting women, and he was afraid anything he said would cause her embarrassment. The monk did not show the shock that he felt. *A Sister eating the flesh of animals!* It said so much. He felt a deep sense of revulsion.

Acolyte Tesseko regained her self-possession, though her hands still shook and she tried to hide them. "Pardon me, Brother, I do not deserve your respect after this display of weakness."

"Please, do not think of yourself this way. It must be difficult to see a Sister behaving in this manner. I am honored that you would choose to come to me with this. You must feel no shame.

"What you have described to me, Acolyte Tesseko, I have heard of before. I believe that Sister Morima suffers a crisis of the spirit. Her apparent illness is only a reflection of her inner sufferings. Why this is . . ?" he shrugged, "It seems to be connected with seeing the scrolls of Botahara. Perhaps she was not properly prepared for such an experience.

"You must not leave her, Acolyte, but word must be sent to your Order. They must know as soon as it can be arranged—a messenger tomorrow at the next stop. Do you have a cypher?"

Tesseko nodded.

"Good. Keep this as secret as possible. And you must stop her from eating flesh! Shame her if you must. Tell her everyone aboard speaks of it as scandal. It may well be the truth.

"Tell me what herbs you have given her." He saw how she hesitated. "It does not matter. I will tell you what I would treat her with and you may make a decision from that knowledge. In all likelihood what you have given her would be the same. Root of menta, steamed not boiled, mixed with tomal. Every fourth hour will be often enough. But it would be even better if you could convince her to meditate and to do chi exercises. How far north do you travel, Acolyte Tesseko?"

Again she hesitated, which he found strange. "We go to Seh, Brother."

"Then perhaps you should send a message ahead also. Your Sisters will know what to do, I would not fear. If you need to speak with me again, I will leave word with the guard to allow you through."

Tesseko bowed to him, formally. "I am indebted to you, Brother. I must return to Sister Morima now." She turned to go but stopped and smiled at him over her shoulder. "I thank you for your counsel, Brother Shuyun, it has been an honor meeting you."

He watched her go, a tall young woman in the yellow robe of the Botahist Sisters. He tried to make his mind address this new information but he could not.

*The Scrolls,* he thought. *The Scrolls of our Lord! The Sacred Scrolls.*

All of his years of training, and yet his mind refused to focus.

# Thirteen

*A moth in the dark,*
*Searching among the mulberry leaves,*
*And honor is so*
*Easily lost.*

*Jaku Tadamoto*

The Walk of Inner Peace was a long, covered hall, open
along one side, high in the Palace of the Emperor. It
looked east, over the vast gardens, toward the distant
hills, with their large temples and monasteries—white
walls stark against the dark green. Jaku Tadamoto strode
along the walk, his keen mind examining the latest information he had received. His brother Katta surprised even
him with his audacity. This report of the Imperial Guard
Captain who had interfered with Lady Nishima, it had
the signature of Jaku Katta brushed upon it. He shook
his head in disbelief.

*The Lady Nishima!* What was his brother thinking? It
could not be an alliance with the Shonto, that would be
unthinkable. The Shonto were too strong. Katta would
not take the chance of having allies to whom he would
be secondary. It was something else, something more.

It was this "something more" that frightened him. The
Jaku had risen beyond anyone's most secret hopes, did
that *fool* Katta wish to endanger this now? Tadamoto
increased his pace. In his sleeve he carried a written
report from Katta to the Emperor. It seemed to lay
there, heavy with purpose, waiting.

It was very early morning, too early for the great numbers of people who, each day, sought time to stroll the Walk of Inner Peace. Jaku Tadamoto was surprised, therefore, to see a solitary figure, half hidden by a column, near the far end of the walk. Golden robe, rich material (as all material worn in the palace was rich). A woman, he decided. A Lady of the Court, returning from an assignation? A courtesan who had pleased the Emperor? He walked on. But then, as he drew closer, his heart lifted. He recognized her—*Osha,* the Emperor's Sonsa dancer!

He approached so quietly that he startled her.

"Oh, Tadamoto-sum," she put her hand to her heart, "I was so far away."

He bowed to her. "I apologize for destroying your harmony, Osha-sum. I was surprised to find anyone here at this hour and was most inconsiderate of your presence."

She smiled at him, a lovely smile, though somehow full of cares. "Please, do not apologize. I am honored to have your company, it is so seldom that we speak." She held his eye for a second and then turned to the view over the grounds. She seemed to be inviting him to share this with her. Looking up and down the hall, Tadamoto moved to the low wall beside her.

Wisps of cloud still glowed faintly with the colors of the dawn.

"Is it not beautiful?" Osha asked.

"It is," he agreed.

"But so brief." She did not look at him. "Why is it that things of great beauty seem to come into this world for only an instant?"

Tadamoto shook his head. "To remain always a rarity, is that not part of their beauty?"

She turned to him then, seeming to search his eyes for the source of these words. "I can see why the Emperor values you so, Tadamoto-sum."

He nodded modestly, embarrassed by her flattery. Yet she had said this so strangely, with such an emphasis on "you."

She turned back to the scene which spread out below

them, the vibrant colors of autumn scattered among the greens and browns. She seemed sad somehow, and this pulled at Tadamoto's heart. He wanted to take her in his arms to comfort her, but he knew he dared not. A sound almost caused him to whirl around, but it was only a dove cooing softly.

"Does our Emperor seem . . . distant to you, Tadamoto-sum?" she asked suddenly. The moods of the Emperor were a highly sensitive subject, and Tadamoto was honored that she would trust him enough to ask.

"I have not found him so."

"Ah," she said, and nodded, "I have wondered."

She glanced back along the hall herself now, but still no one was there. "Tadamoto-sum, there is something I need to discuss with you. I would not ask you if I did not know how loyal you are to our Emperor."

"Of course."

"But we cannot talk here." She looked behind her again. "Could you meet with me? Do I ask too much?"

"You could not ask too much of me." he said.

"There is a place in the east wing. A Hanama shrine to Botahara. No one goes there now." She turned to him then, her eyes full of anguish. "Tonight, could you come tonight?"

He nodded, saying nothing.

"The hour of the owl," she whispered and suddenly brushed by him and was gone. He was left with the touch of her hand on his arm and the memory of silk brushing against him. His heart beat out his excitement.

Why did she wish to meet him? Was it truly something to do with the Emperor? Or did she wish only to meet with Jaku Tadamoto? He prayed that it was so—and that it was not so.

Her hands shaking with the danger of what she had just done, Osha slipped quietly into her own rooms. Cracking a screen on the far side of the room she said, "cha," to an unseen maid. To stop her hands from trembling, she clasped them to her breast.

What choice do I have? she asked herself, what choice?

She dropped her knees to a pillow. The Emperor was growing cold toward her. She put her hands to her face. It was all so sudden. Only three days ago he had seemed totally enamored of her. She shook her head. *"I don't understand!"* she whispered. Was it because the Empress would soon return from the Summer Palace? It could not be. He hated her openly, Osha knew. She had seen the way the Empress tried to keep her hold on him. She was a woman without dignity.

This will never happen to me, she told herself. But she was not convinced. Osha was aware of how far a mistress of the Emperor could fall when she earned his disfavor. *Earned!!* What had she done to earn his disfavor? Nothing, she said, he has simply grown tired of me, as he did of the others before me. I thought I would be different. I thought I could hold him. A sob escaped her, but she fought the tears.

A maid entered with cha, but Osha sent her away as soon as the hot liquid was poured. She wanted to be alone.

This is more than love-pain, she told herself. With whom would she dance when it became known that she was in disfavor with the Emperor? What troupe would risk offending the Son of Heaven by presenting him with someone he did not wish to see?

"I was a fool!" she said aloud, surprising herself with the outburst. She sipped slowly to calm her nerves.

She would need an ally, that was the decision she had come to. If she were to fall—and that had not happened yet—she would need a powerful supporter, someone the Emperor valued; as he valued Jaku Tadamoto. She knew this because the Emperor had spoken to her about this young man on more than one occasion. He had described Tadamoto in very flattering terms.

Osha had also considered the elder Jaku—Katta—but he would demand too much of her and then, no doubt, cast her aside. No, she was safer with Tadamoto; he was not as handsome as his older brother, but he was a man of honor and there was much to be said for that.

So, she was committed to this course, and the plan was simple. With the right ally she could dance again. She could keep her place as the preeminant Sonsa in the capital, and in time she could free herself of the need for others. She would live without a patron.

Setting her cha down, Osha went to change into her dance costume. She must dance now. Dance until every movement she made was flawless. Her world had changed. There would be no room now for mistakes.

The mats felt cool against his forehead as he bowed before the Most Revered Son of Heaven. Almost, he could have stayed there, eyes closed, feeling the cool grasses against his skin—it felt so safe. But he rose and faced the Emperor, and his green eyes did not waver.

"I understand that you are addressed now as 'Colonel'?" the Emperor said.

"This is true, Sire."

"Well, Colonel Jaku Tadamoto, I congratulate you. It is no more than you deserve."

"I am honored by your words, Sire."

The Emperor nodded. He sat upon the dais, his sword of office held across his lap. Tadamoto thought the Highest One looked as though the concerns of his Empire weighed upon him. Age seemed to show in the Emperor's face, and he kept pulling his sword half out of its sheath and then pushing it back, as though the sound gave him comfort.

"You have a report for us from your esteemed brother?"

"I have, Sire." Tadamoto removed the sealed scroll from his sleeve and placed it on the edge of the dais. The Emperor paid no attention to it.

"I have difficult decisions to make, Tadamoto-sum," the Emperor said suddenly.

"If I am not being presumptuous, Sire, I would be honored if I could assist in any small way."

"You are kind to offer, but these are decisions about my sons, Colonel."

"I understand, Emperor."

"Do you?" he asked, fixing Tadamoto with a searching gaze.

"I understand that these would be difficult decisions, Sire."

"I see," the Emperor said, pulling the sword half out of its sheath and pushing it back with a "click." He looked off, his eyes losing focus. "One of my sons must marry the Lady Nishima. You understand that, don't you Tadamoto-sum?"

"I do, Sire."

"The problem is many-faced. The Lady Nishima is the loyal protégée of Lord Shonto, a man who plots to gain control of the Throne, yeh?"

Tadamoto nodded agreement.

"And there are other problems with the Lady Nishima. Oh, she would be a perfect Empress, that is not in doubt. But she is strong and my sons are weak—it is the fault of my useless wife, she raised them to be fools and effetes." (*click*) "So, we have a problem. One must wed the Lady Nishima, and another," he paused, "another must become . . . an example. For the one who weds must be educated to his responsibilities. So, one will go to Seh to share in Lord Shonto's fate—do you understand what that means, Tadamoto-sum?"

"I do, Emperor."

"I appreciate how quickly you see things, Colonel." (*click*) "Who would accuse us of plotting the great lord's fall when our own son falls with him?" The Emperor was silent for a moment. "I wish it were otherwise, but my sons do not serve the Yamaku purpose well, and the one that is to wed must understand that he is not, not . . . *inexpendable*." (*click*)

"Katta-sum has been like a son to me." He pulled the sword half from its sheath, "yet he begins to disappoint me also. This interference with the Lady Nishima. . . ." The Son of Heaven shook his head sadly. "His appetite for ladies from the Great Houses is a terrible weakness,

Tadamoto-sum. Perhaps you should speak to him about this—you are wiser than he—Katta-sum listens to your counsel.

"Your brother has been of great value to us, Colonel, so we have indulged him—it is not always good to indulge a son, if your desire is that he will grow strong, yeh?"

The Emperor looked around the room as though something were missing, but before he discovered what it was he again became distracted and began to toy with his sword.

"It is a time of decisions, Tadamoto-sum, it is also a time of focus. The stars align for great occurrences—all of the seers agree. Houses may topple, Empires could be shaken. There can be no mistakes on our part, I hope your brother understands this. If there are mistakes, the whole Empire will be plunged into war. The Yamaku waited a thousand years for our Ascendancy. If it is endangered now. . . ." (*click*) The Emperor shrugged. "Speak to your brother, Tadamoto-sum; tell him how much his loyalty is valued."

Suddenly, the Emperor became present, as though he had just walked into the room. He smiled at Jaku Tadamoto. "We do not wish to burden you with our problems, Tadamoto-sum."

"I am honored that you would speak of these things to me, Sire, and certainly I will talk with my brother immediately."

The Emperor waved his hand as though this was understood, a small matter. "You have kept a watch on Osha-sum, Colonel?"

"As you have commanded, Sire." Tadamoto said too quickly. He was careful now to meet the Emperor's eyes.

The Emperor looked up to the heavens. "I have too many decisions. May the gods help me. She does not seem to understand my responsibilities, Tadamoto-sum. It is hard for someone in her position." He gripped his sword as though he would wring water from it. "Ah, well." He smiled at Tadamoto.

"We must speak again, Colonel, it helps to restore my

harmony." He nodded to Tadamoto who touched his head to the mat and backed from the room.

The Emperor watched the young man go. Will Osha have him? he wondered; it would be difficult after an Emperor. Ah, well, it hardly mattered. She served to keep the young Jaku loyal to his Emperor. He pulled his sword free of its sheath and hefted it, cutting across the air in front of him. Yes, he thought, Osha must be settled soon. She was delightful, it was true, but the Emperor had come to a decision—something he had told no one. He laughed to himself. I am not as old as everyone seems to think! They will soon see. He laughed again. Ah, how we will surprise them! He returned the sword of his office to its scabbard. I will have a new wife! *That* will give my scheming Empress and her useless sons pause to think.

He weighed the question again. Lady Nishima was Shonto—in spirit if not in blood. It would not be wise to have her too close to him, not wise at all. But her cousin, the Lady Kitsura Omawara! His blood *sang* at the thought. Well, he had made no decisions, but there were more paths open to him than those around him realized. Many more.

All that remained to be done was to rid himself of Shonto Motoru. And then the problem of the Fanisan daughter could be dealt with in any number of ways. Once Shonto was gone, there would be no one left in the realm strong enough to raise the great lords against the Throne. He could do what he pleased.

His mood of gaiety passed when he thought of his new governor. We cannot fail, he said for the thousandth time. We cannot.

But was Shonto not ever resourceful? He touched his palms to his forehead and felt the dampness on them. Everything goes as planned, he told himself, I must remain tranquil. I must wait. I must.

# Fourteen

The small stream which branched from the Grand Canal lay still in the gathering dusk. Willow trees hung over the bank dripping leaves into the dark waters. Hidden along the bank, Shonto guards waited for the boats they knew would come. A whistled signal went from sentry to sentry as their lord's sampan passed—the sound of a night bird calling in the dusk.

The flotilla had been left alongside the stone quay of the nearby town, the crews allowed a few hours ashore—"a break from their toils." The truth, though, was that the Imperial Governor wished to pay a visit to a very old man who had once been his gii Master.

Shuyun was surprised at this whim of Lord Shonto's. It was apparent to the young monk that more than just the currents of the canal swept Shonto toward Seh. Other forces, too, powerful forces, propelled the lord north—toward what, Shuyun did not know. Yet Shonto had somehow slipped aside, sloughing off the grip of the currents, to steal down this backwater on an endeavor that seemed merely sentimental.

The Lord of the Shonto sat beside his Spiritual Advisor in the sampan, saying nothing. Shuyun wondered about this Shonto predilection for loyalty. It had been loyalty that had allowed the first Yamaku Emperor to trap Shonto Motoru's father—and on that occasion the Shonto had almost been entered on the long scroll of names of Great Houses that were no more.

This trait of the Shonto, it is both a strength and a weakness, Shuyun thought, so it must be watched, and watched carefully.

The boats pushed out of the stream onto a small lake, released from shadow into the last of the day's light. The colors of evening spread in a wash across the western horizon, running from cloud to cloud. There wasn't a breeze to stir the surface of the lake and the sky seemed to lie on the water like a perfect print of the unfolding sunset.

On the far side of the lake, smoke curled out of the trees, and, as Shonto's sampan approached, a dock came into view, seeming to detach itself from the shadow of the bank. And then, behind it, the outline of a roof appeared. The boats of Shonto's guards lay drawn up on a narrow, sand beach, and the soldiers stood watch from the shadows of ancient trees.

As they approached the small wooden dock, a captain of Shonto's elite guard gave the "all clear" handsign from the wharfhead and the sampan slipped alongside. The guards knelt as Lord Shonto and his Spiritual Adviser emerged from their craft.

Raising his head, the captain nodded to his lord.

"Yes?" Shonto said.

"Excuse me, Sire," and he gestured toward the nearby point.

There, in the shallows under the branches of a tono tree, a tall bird stood silhoutted against the sunset in the waters.

"An autumn crane," Shonto whispered, his pleasure evident.

"A good omen, Sire," the guard said.

Yes, Shonto thought, and his mind went back to the coins of Kowan-sing—the crane had been the pattern cast for his daughter. Nishi-sum, the lord thought, you will be safe, I will not fail. He stayed for a moment, watching.

The crane stood, unmoving, and as the dark flowed out from among the trees and across the lake, it became easier to believe that the great bird was nothing more than a bent branch emerging from the waters. Just as Shonto was no longer sure of what he saw, the crane struck, coming up with a wiggling fish in its bill. It took two steps to the sand, disapearing into the shadows and then, an instant later, it emerged on the wing, sweeping across the water in slow powerful strokes. Where the wingtips touched, perfect rings appeared in the water's surface.

Shonto nodded to the captain and then turned toward the shore, Shuyun a step behind.

The lord had said very little on the short trip from the town, and he did not seem to want to break that silence now. Shuyun had expected to learn something more of the man they went to visit, but this did not happen. A favored teacher of the Shonto and a famous gii Master, that was all the information he had—except for the man's name, Myochin Ekun, and that Shuyun recognized from his own study of the board. The games of Myochin Ekun were among those chosen as exemplary, by the teaching Brothers. These were then examined by the Neophyte monks, who were taught to play gii so that they might learn to focus their young minds.

Myochin Ekun. Shuyun felt as if he was about to meet someone from the past, a legend in fact—Myochin Ekun: gii Master of gii Masters.

How is it that the Shonto drew such people to them? Shuyun wondered. The answer was almost too obvious—they were the Shonto. And now he had come to them, Initiate Brother Shuyun. This thought left him with nothing but questions.

Unlike the Lady Nishima, Shuyun thought, I cannot see the future. My history will be bound with that of the Shonto or I will be unknown. It does not matter, he reminded himself. One's karma is not dependent on one's service to the Shonto.

They approached the house in the trees. Shuyun could make it out now, a low building with a simple tile roof. There was no garden wall, though a sparse garden had been arranged around the porch.

An old man who does not take an interest in his garden, Shuyun thought, how odd.

Servants knelt beside the walkway to the house, most of them older. They smiled with great pleasure as Shonto

passed, and Shuyun was surprised by the lack of respect
this showed. But then, Shonto stopped before an old
woman who glowed like a proud mother.

"Kashiki-sum, you grow younger by the year." The
lord smiled, almost boyishly.

The woman laughed, the laugh of a girl, musical, light,
without cares. "It is the waters, Sire, we all approach
the Immortals here. But it is you who have remained
young." She broke into a large grin. "Young enough to
take another wife, I'm sure all would agree."

Everyone laughed, Shonto harder than the rest.

"I am waiting until I am older, Kashiki-sum, I must
slow down somewhat before a young woman will be able
to keep up with me." Shonto bowed to the woman and,
as he did so, gave a hand signal to a nearby guard. "I
have brought you something from the capital. Something
for each of you."

The staff bowed their thanks and Shonto went on.

Of course, he knows all of these servants, Shuyun realized, perhaps they helped raise him as a child.

There was only a single step to the porch and here
knelt the senior member of Myochin Ekun's staff.

"You honor us with your visit, Lord Shonto, Brother."

"The honor is ours, Leta. Where is your master?"

"He awaits you inside, Sire." The man rose, and taking a lantern from a hook, led them into the darkened
house. It was a small and comfortable home, open on
three sides where screens had been pushed back. The
servant held the lantern aloft to light three wide steps
that led to the next level. There, in the gloom, Shuyun
could just make out the form of a man, sitting, bent low
over a table.

"Master Myochin?" the servant said in a loud voice.

The form straightened, surprised by the sound.

"Your guests are here, Master."

He turned to them now, long white hair in confusion,
framing a face old with the whiteness of age, skin as
translucent as the wax of a candle. Shuyun was startled
by the man's eyes, porcelain white, pure, unmarred by
the dark circle of a pupil.

He is blind, Shuyun thought, he has been blind all of his days.

This apparition in a white robe smiled as benignly as a statue of Botahara.

"Motoru-sum?" came a soft voice.

"I am here, Eku-sum."

"Ah, what pleasure your voice brings. Come. Bring light for our guests, Leta. Come, Motoru-sum. You are not alone?"

"I am with my Spiritual Advisor, Brother Shuyun."

"I am honored. It is always a pleasure to have a pilgrim of the Seven Paths in my home. Do the young monks still play gii, Brother Shuyun?"

"They do, Master Myochin. And your games are chief among their lessons."

"After all these years?" His already apparent pleasure increased noticeably. "I do not deserve to be so honored. Still play my games? Imagine."

Servants brought lamps and mead for the gii Master and his guests. It was a most pleasant house, warm with the colors of rich woods. The scent of the nearby pines traveled freely through the open walls and an owl could be heard, calling softly over the lake.

Lord Shonto and his teacher talked briefly of Shonto's staff, the old man asking specifically after several people, Shonto's son and Lady Nishima first among them. To be polite to Shuyun, the conversation then turned to other things, the old man impressing the monk with his knowledge of the affairs of the Empire. It was hard to imagine how he received his information, the lake seemed so far removed from the rest of Wa. But the truth was, it was close to the canal and, as an Empress had once said, "if we could tax the rumors traveling the Grand Canal, we should not need to bother with the cargo."

"So you have taken this appointment to Seh, Motoru-sum?"

"I had little choice."

The old man nodded, a gesture Shuyun knew he could never have seen.

"I suppose that is true. Sometimes you must step into

the danger. You are too strong, Motoru-sum, he cannot abide that," the old man said in his soft voice. He seemed to pause for a moment, listening. "We must accept certain inevitabilities. You will never make peace with the Emperor as equals. Do not imagine it, Motoru-sum. That is the real trap for you, but it can never be. There is only one winner at the gii board. Do not have false hopes that Akantsu will come to his senses. He will not."

"I have thought the same thing." Shonto said.

The old man broke into a smile. "Of course you have. I did not waste my time training you!" He laughed.

As they spoke, Shuyun noticed that Lord Shonto's eyes were repeatedly drawn to the gii board set on the nearby table. Finally the lord could no longer contain his curiosity. "I see you cannot give it up entirely." He reached over and tapped the wooden table.

"Ah, well. It is the habit of a lifetime and I must do something to fill my days. Do you know, I have found a third solution to the Soto problem."

*"Really?"* Shonto's interest rose immediately.

"Yes, I was as surprised as you."

"I know the Kundima solution." Shonto said.

"Yes, my own teacher."

"And the Fujiki solution." Shuyun offered.

"Ah, Brother Shuyun, you do know the game."

"But a third . . ." Shonto said, again looking at the board.

"Perhaps you can find it," Myochin Ekun suggested. "Consider it while dinner is prepared."

The board was brought closer for Shuyun and Lord Shonto. The pieces were already arranged for the classic problem, contrived, more than three hundred years earlier, by the gii Master, Soto. Obviously the old man had been awaiting an opportunity to share his discovery.

Lord Shonto and his young advisor both stared at the board, but their companion had turned away, turned so that the small breeze, coming through the open screens, caressed his face.

"I could advance the *foot-soldier* in the fifth rank. This would put pressure on the keep." Shonto suggested.

"Huh." The old man considered this for a moment. "If I were defending, I would answer with the *swordmaster* to his own seventh file and you would be forced to retreat and cover. In the end this would cost you dearly in moves lost."

Shonto moved the two pieces accordingly, that he might examine the new position. "I understand." He said at last, and returned the pieces to their places.

"You must look deeper," the gii Master said in a whisper. "You will come to the disputed lands soon, will you not?" he asked suddenly.

"What? Oh, yes, yes, of course."

"A puzzling situation," the old man said, and Shuyun was not sure what he referred to. "The solution, if I may give you some indication, is entirely unconventional. It came to me like a revelation, something I'm sure you can appreciate, Brother."

"Any obvious attack has been explored a thousand times," Shonto said, thinking out loud.

"More, I would say, Motoru-sum."

Suddenly Shonto looked up. "If I do not attack, what will you do?"

"An important consideration." The gii Master sat with his blind eyes closed, turning his face slowly from side to side, enjoying the feel of the breeze. "I am much like any other Emperor; it is my purpose to win."

The two guests looked long at the board, hoping it would reveal its secret to them.

"We must attempt to draw you out of your keep, Master," Shuyun said, "but your position there is strong."

"That is true. I cannot be drawn out by a simple ruse."

Shonto moved a piece. "We could sacrifice a *dragonship*."

"I could refuse it."

Shonto considered this. "Huh," he said, and returned the piece to its position.

"A sacrifice is not effective unless your opponent has

no choice but to take it." Myochin quoted from Soto's treatise on gii.

"It is a dangerous error to rely on your opponent's stupidity," Shuyun added, quoting the same source.

The gii Master nodded agreement. "The Butto and the Hajiwara have reached an impasse, I understand," the old man said, changing the subject again.

"So it would appear, Eku-sum."

"Hmm. Good for them but not necessarily good for you."

"How so, Eku-sum?"

"You step into a situation without momentum, yet movement will be required. It is easier to redirect something that is in motion than to move something which is still. Is this not true?"

"So you have always said, and I must admit it has proven to be so."

Silence fell again and Shonto did not take his eyes from the gii board.

"Are you ready to give up now?" the old man asked suddenly, sounding somewhat annoyed.

Shonto laughed affectionately. "Give us a little more time, Eku-sum. Even you did not find the answer with only a few moments' contemplation."

"It is true, my lord. I grow less patient with others as I grow older. Ah, well." He paused, seeming to contemplate his statement. "I have said that you must look deeper, but remember, it is not enough to look deeper into the game, you must look within, also. It is always there that you will find the resources needed."

After a moment's more contemplation, Shuyun said, "I would move my *guard commander* back to the first rank."

The old man nodded again. He smiled. "An interesting thought."

"But you would open your flank to the wing of his greatest strength, Brother," Shonto said.

"Yes," the monk answered.

"What will you do when he attacks?"

"I do not know, Sire."

The old man laughed. "You see, Brother Shuyun, Lord Shonto has always played with his mind and never with his greater powers. He is a Master of the game, certainly, but this is his limitation. You, on the other hand, have been taught all of your life to draw upon other strengths. What makes Lord Shonto unique is that he recognizes his weakness. For this reason it has been arranged that you serve him. Did your teachers tell you that, Brother?" When Shuyun did not respond, the old man said, "I thought not.

"You see, Motoru-sum. Our young Brother has made a leap beyond logic. He knows that there is a solution—I have told him so. He knows that he must draw me from my keep—upon that we agree. Once he has come that far, he has let his instinct dictate the next move, an instinct that he trusts implicitly. His move, by the way, is correct, though the rest of the series is equally difficult. Ten moves to forced surrender." He rose slowly, but without assistance. "If you will excuse me, I must go out and feel the night for a moment, and then, if you will, we shall dine."

The gii Master, who had never in his life seen a gii board, walked out onto the porch, down the steps and into the garden. His white hair and robe could just be seen, fluttering in the breeze.

"Remarkable, yeh?" Shonto said, taking his eyes from the board.

Shuyun nodded. "I am honored that you would bring me to meet him, Lord Shonto."

Shonto shrugged. "My instincts, which I have never been able to apply to the gii board, told me that it was important that the two of you meet. It gives me pleasure to watch someone who is truly able to appreciate what he has accomplished. Did you know that he was the Champion of all of Wa six times!"

Shuyun shook his head.

What is remarkable, the young monk thought, is that he accomplished this without Botahist training. Shuyun pictured the gii board in his mind, the pieces arranged for the Soto problem, and began to explore the possibili-

ties of the first move he had made. He took the first step
into chi-ten, and felt his sense of time begin to stretch.
In his mind he moved the pieces through a hundred per-
mutations, all at what seemed a normal speed. He held
his focus and followed what came of it, move after move.
In a matter of minutes he had found the third solution
to the Soto problem. He opened his eyes to find Lord
Shonto staring at him.

"Show me," Shonto said simply.

He has had a Brother in his house before, Shuyun
reminded himself and let no sign of surprise show at
Shonto's request.

He controlled his time sense now, but still, he moved
the pieces through the solution too quickly. Shonto did
not grasp it for a moment, it had been done so fast, but
then his face lit up.

"Yes, yes! That is right, of course." He nodded, a
slight bow, to the monk. "It is sad that I could not have
been trained in your way when I was young."

"You cannot be a servant of the Perfect Master, Sire,
and a lord also," Shuyun said, but immediately he was
reminded of Lady Nishima, practicing chi quan in her
private garden. Did Lord Shonto know, he wondered?
Was it Brother Satake who had taught her? Shuyun could
not say.

Shonto shrugged, "It seems to be true."

Myochin Ekun returned to the room. "You will have
to take the problem of the third solution with you to
Seh, Motoru-sum. I was going to show you, but it will
give you something to do during the winter rains." He
chuckled. "Yes, that will keep you occupied. Ah, Leta,
where is our dinner?"

The meal was served, accompanied by hot rice wine
and spiced sauces. Warm robes were brought for the gii
Master and his guests, for the night grew cooler, yet no
one wanted to shut its beauty out.

Talk turned again to the Shonto household, as was
perhaps inevitable, and Shuyun was the willing audience
of the older men's favorite stories. Food and drink were
accompanied by much laughter.

"You were an impossible student, sometimes, Motoru-sum, I have not forgotten. I often envied Brother Satake's manner with you, I don't know what his secret was, but you listened to him without your attention wandering all over the wide world."

"He did have his way, didn't he?"

"Yes. Yes, he did. It has been so long, how is Satake-sum?"

Shonto paused before answering quietly. "Brother Satake is gone, Eku-sum."

The old man shook his head. "Of course, I . . . how could I forget?" He muttered something more, that Shuyun did not catch, and went back to his food. Lord Shonto gazed at the old man for a moment, sadness apparent in his face, then he, too, returned to his dinner. An attempt was made to resume the conversation, but it faltered and failed.

Shojis were set in place to create rooms for the night and beds were made, as was the custom, on the straw mats. Shuyun occupied the room in which the dinner had been eaten, but he did not sleep. He thought of the young Acolyte and the story she had told him. He thought of Sister Morima and the Sacred Scrolls.

It seemed odd to him that Myochin Ekun had forgotten the death of Brother Satake—a man who was still capable of finding a third solution to the Soto problem. It seemed very odd.

Outside the house, a large tulip tree surrendered to the increasing night breeze, and released its leaves to the wind. They fell in a slow rain, blowing into the house and scattering across the floor. Shuyun lay in this shower of leaves, entirely awake, until dawn slipped into the night sky. When he looked outside, the tulip tree was all but bare.

# Fifteen

There was no moon, though it would rise later, a waning disk floating in the morning sky. The quay and the cobbled square seemed to be made up of shades of gray, lines of black. Shapes that suggested things to the mind, things that moved and changed and flowed.

If Tanaka had not known the area, he would not have understood what it was he looked at. Across the square there was an inn, he knew it well, and to his left an Imperial customs house, its large doors darker rectangles in a dark wall. A line of ships rode quietly against the quay, tugging at their moorings—massive spice-traders and warships—single lights illuminating the quarter decks for the night watch.

Opposite the spice-traders, shops and the large Trading Houses stretched along the stone quay—the first building would belong to the Hashikara, and next to it, the Minikama, the Sadaku, and then the giant Sendai warehouses. None of these great families would allow their names to be attached to their trading concerns, but it did not matter, Tanaka knew them all, knew the vassal-merchants and which Houses each silently represented. Yankura was his city and little passed in it that he did not soon learn.

From the balcony of the inn, on which he waited, Tanaka could see all three roads entering the square, black mouths yawing, the glint of starlight on cobbles. Nothing moved there but a stray cat that searched along the wall of the inn, looking for a way to the food it no doubt smelled.

The old man who stood in the dark beside the merchant did not move. In fact, he hardly dared breathe, he was so frightened. It shocked him that he should react so. In his younger days he had served in the army of Lord Shonto Motoru's father. Once, the great lord had given him the Dagger of Bravery for his part in a battle against the Yamaku's allies. It was a memory he cherished, a story he had told his grandchildren a hundred times. But his days of being a warrior were long past, and tonight he felt fear as he could never remember feeling fear before. The apparent calmness of the vassal-merchant shamed him and made him determined to show none of what he felt. If only his stomach and bowels would cooperate! They churned and writhed like a dying serpent.

Neither man dared speak his thoughts, there in the shadow of the building which sheltered them. They remained as still as the shadows themselves. They listened.

Have I come on a fool's errand? Tanaka asked himself. Has this old man fallen into a fantasy that he can again play a part in the struggles of the Empire? He felt pity for the old man if that were so. It was hard to imagine, looking at the old man now, but he had been a full captain once, a good and competent man. Long ago, he had served on Tanaka's own guard. But tonight the merchant wondered if the retired captain was slipping into a sad state of senility. They had been standing in the dark for over three hours. The hour of the owl had just sounded. I believe I am wasting my time, Tanaka decided, and a certain relief accompanied that realization.

He was just about to put a hand on the old man's shoulder and take his leave when he heard, or thought he heard, a sound. But then there was nothing and Tanaka wondered if he was beginning to suffer the same fate as the old man. Again! A sound, so familiar, a sound he had heard since childhood. The sound of armor—leather creaking, the muffled jangle of metal rings. Tanaka pushed himself closer to the wall behind him.

Now he regretted coming without guard. If the captain had not insisted he would never have considered it, but the old warrior had been adamant. Tanaka pushed back and felt the wall, solid against his taut muscles. He tried

to wrap the shadow around him like a cloak. *Breathe,*
Tanaka ordered himself, *breathe.*

The sound came again, and suddenly there, by the
fountain in the middle of the square, there was a dark
form—a man. Tanaka could see him turning slowly,
searching the shadows with his eyes. How long had he
been there? The merchant fought panic. We cannot be
seen in this darkness, he told himself—*breathe!*

A second man came into view, silhouetted for an
instant against the reflection on the fountain's surface.
The captain did not lie, Tanaka thought, they are Imperial Guardsmen. If we are found now, we are lost.
*Breathe, breathe slowly.*

A third guard crossed the square almost silently, making his way toward the quay. He stopped before crossing
the last stretch of cobbles, but when he was sure there
was no activity along the waterfront he trotted directly
to an Imperial Warship. The ship's lone watchman did
not offer challenge but instead lowered the gangway.
Tanaka could hear the creak of the ropes and the dull
"thump" as planks hit stone. On deck the light was
extinguished.

Again there was a long silence. The merchant peered
into the shadows until he thought he saw guards hovering
everywhere. He felt completely trapped. There was nothing to do but remain still and pray to Botahara to hide
them.

The black rectangle of the customs house door began
to change shape suddenly, and Tanaka realized it had
opened without a sound. The hinges had been greased,
that was certain. More guards emerged—ten? twelve?
more?—Tanaka could not be sure. It was then that he
heard the breathing of someone below them. The scrape
of a sandal on wood. Stairs led from the square to the
balcony on Tanaka's right. He turned that way, staring
at the blackness.

If we cannot avoid discovery, he thought, I will smash
through a screen into the inn and hope to lose myself in
the confusion this act will cause. He braced himself and
listened for a foot on the stairs.

The guards from the customs house hurried across the square. They could not hide their noise completely now; there were too many of them. And they carried something, Tanaka realized, a box the size of a traveling trunk. It hung between poles and guards carried it. Imperial Guards carried it!—not bearers. Tanaka almost stepped forward, such was his surprise. They struggled with it, too, he could see that even in the dark. Eight men struggled with this burden!

He swallowed in a dry throat, it had not been just a story, then. The old man's nephew had indeed given him valuable information. The merchant wondered if the nephew could be among the guards below? Another reason that they should not be caught.

Tanaka glanced over at the dark form of his companion. The old man had shriveled into the wall, pulling his robe high to hide the lightness of his skin. The old warrior has not forgotten his Shonto training, Tanaka noted.

The stairs creaked! Or was it someone moving inside? Tanaka stared into the dark square of the stairwell until he could no longer discern anything at all. His muscles ached from the effort he made to be still.

Across the square, the guardsmen reached the Imperial Warship and began to load their burden. It went over the side quickly on tackle, but Tanaka could see nothing on the deck. There were more sounds, the sounds of men emerging from the ship's belly. Then they moved back across the square, fanning out, searching the periphery of the area.

There were sounds on the stairs—footsteps!—but then they seemed to hesitate. Tanaka looked wildly around— where would he hide? It was then that he saw the old man was gone! It hit him like a blast of cold wind—*I have been trapped*, the merchant thought.

Tanaka began to edge along the balcony toward the nearest shoji. It was his only hope. The footsteps approached now. He could hear breathing and the sounds of armor—an Imperial Guardsman, undoubtedly. A shape appeared in the opening, dark against the darkness. Tanaka tensed, ready to spring, wondering if it was too late to reach the shoji now. The guard set a foot onto the balcony.

He looks right at me, Tanaka thought. It was in that instant that the merchant saw them—on the balcony behind the guard—two figures, seeming to take form out of the shadow. One held a knife. The merchant stood frozen, watching.

But then the two figures seemed to melt into one and slump into the darkness of the floor. The guard stopped, Tanaka could see the glint of light on his chin strap, he turned slowly about and then, almost silently, descended the stairs.

I have not been seen, Tanaka thought. Thank the darkness, thank Botahara!

In another instant the guards were gone. The Imperial Warship slipped its lines and began to recede into the darkness. Tanaka told himself to breathe again. But still he dared not move. Out of the black pool of the floor a figure rose, small, catlike in its movements. It faced him on the dark balcony. It spoke.

"Do nothing rash," came the soft whisper. "He would have betrayed your presence." The figure motioned to the floor. "He will awaken soon. Then you must go."

Tanaka blinked, trying to focus. The figure evaporated, the merchant watched it happen, but his eyes would not believe it. He shook his head to clear it, but nothing changed. There was a sound now. In the darkness on the floor, something stirred. He heard a soft moan.

Tanaka went immediately to the sound. The old captain lay on the rough planks, his dagger by his head. The merchant put his fingers to the man's lips. "Make no sound. You are safe."

He propped the man's head up in his hand and listened, waiting for the old one's breathing to become regular. He felt the old man touch his arm and nod. Helping him to rise, Tanaka returned the captain's blade, and steered him toward the back stairs.

When they were around the side of the inn, the old man put his mouth close to Tanaka's ear. "What happened?"

"We were saved," Tanaka answered and said no more.

When they reached the alley, the man who had once been a warrior reached into his sleeve and removed a small leather bag and placed it in Tanaka's hand.

The merchant hefted it once, then leaned close to speak. "I will tell our lord." He lifted the bag again. "This will not be forgotten."

The two men parted, going silently through the streets of the Floating City. Tanaka felt more exhausted than he would have thought possible. His head spun with the significance of what he had just witnessed.

As soon as he had entered his own residence and assured his guard that he was, indeed, well, Tanaka pulled open the knot that closed the leather bag. Whatever was inside, had come from the trunk carried by the Imperial Guard. By the light of a single lamp he emptied the contents onto a table.

The merchant sank back on his heels. "May Botahara save us," he muttered. Before him, glinting in the lamp light, lay five square gold coins, unmarked but for a hole in the center of each. They bore no stamp of official coinage, yet, clearly, they were newly minted.

"My lord does not imagine his danger," Tanaka said to the room. "I must warn him."

As he reached for his brush and ink, the merchant recalled the figure in the dark—his savior. Tanaka smiled to himself. He had never known praying to Botahara to have such a direct effect, for unless his age had overtaken him entirely, what Tanaka had seen in the dark was an Initiate of the Botahist Order.

"Impossible," he whispered. "Impossible. The Botahist Brothers endanger their Order for no one!" He could fashion no explanation for what had occurred, though something told him it was not Tanaka the Brothers wished to save, nor even the Lord Shonto Motoru—no, he was sure, it was a young monk they were concerned with. A young monk who Tanaka had seen perform an impossible feat. Yes, he thought, Lord Shonto must be warned.

# Sixteen

*The smoke-flowers turn,*
*Deep purple.*
*And the dew lies upon them*
*Like cold tears.*

*It is said the Emperor*
*Is entertained by a young Sonsa.*
*Does she dance well*
*I wonder?*

*From "The Palace Book"*
*Lady Nikko*

A gong sounded—three times, a pause of two beats, and then a fourth deep ring. The sound echoed through the Palace of the Emperor, down long hallways and among the many courtyards. Then all was quiet again, all was still. In the cycle of the lengthening and shortening of the days, the hour of the owl never saw the light of the sun, and perhaps in balance, it never missed the moonlight. The autumn moon waned toward its last quarter, now, and its light seemed to take on the coldness and purity of the night air.

Jaku Tadamoto walked silently down an empty corridor, his sandaled feet making no sound on the marble floor. He wore the black uniform of the Imperial Guard, though without the insignia of a colonel on the breast, and he carried in his hand a bronze lantern.

It was not unusual for a colonel of the Imperial Guard to be walking the palace at night; security was, after all, their duty, but it was somewhat less common that a colonel would not display his rank. It indicated that he had other purposes, purposes of his own—perhaps a test of security—and did not want his rank seen. Perhaps, too, he went on an errand for his famous brother.

The truth was that Jaku Tadamoto wanted to reduce the chances of being recognized, yet he wanted the freedom to roam the palace that the black uniform would provide.

He walked on, confident that his knowledge would allow him to avoid the guards on their rounds. Coming to a junction in the halls, the young colonel stopped to light his lantern from a hanging lamp. Once sure that it had been lit and would not die, he closed the lantern so that no light could be seen. He removed a single iron key from his sleeve and, without hesitation, crossed to a large, hinged door.

The lock turned without sound and Jaku Tadamoto was immediately inside a darkened room. It was a cluttered place, he knew, one that he would not attempt to negotiate in the darkness. Opening the lantern for a brief second, Tadamoto examined his surroundings. He was in the Hall of Historical Truth, which in fact, was made up of twenty rooms of similar size. It was here that the scholars labored on their great work, the history and assessment of the Hanama Dynasty. Tadamoto knew much about this because the work fascinated him, and he came here often to speak with the historians.

Closing the lamp, he crossed the room, by memory, to the far shoji. The screens opened onto a balcony, lit only by light from the waning moon. Staying back in the shadows, Tadamoto went silently to the balcony's end parapet where he stopped to let his eyes adjust to the night. Far below, in a lantern-lit courtyard, the Palace Guard was changing. Tadamoto could hear the sound of muffled armor. Somehow this made him aware of the madness of what he did, yet the pounding of his heart was not from fear. The thought of Osha waiting for him caused a thrill to course through him.

We will not be found, he told himself, and wondered if his judgment was entirely clouded by his passion.

When his eyes had become accustomed to the darkness, Tadamoto leaned over the parapet, gauging the distance to the next balcony. Two arm's lengths, he decided—he did not even consider the distance to the stone courtyard—the darkness below him seemed endless. There are safer ways, Tadamoto told himself, but I might be seen, and that would not do. I must cross here—it is an easy jump, a child could do it. It is only the thought of height that makes it difficult.

He climbed up onto the parapet's wide top and balanced himself in the darkness. But still he hesitated. He bent his knees, flexing them for the leap, but then he straightened again. His palm, against the cool bronze of the lantern, was slippery with sweat.

Katta is the adventurer in our family, he told himself. So, he thought, perhaps I could have him come and carry me across to my assignation with the Emperor's mistress! He took a deep breath then, and jumped into the darkness. His foot landed squarely on the parapet of the next balcony and he let the momentum carry him farther. Landing on his feet on the tiled floor, he let out a low laugh and shook his head. It had been ridiculously easy, as he had known it would be.

"The mind must control the fears," he whispered to the night, and he turned to the nearest shoji. On an "inspection tour" earlier that day, he had left it unlatched and he found that it had not been discovered.

The east wing of the Imperial Palace had contained the private apartments of the Hanama before their fall, but now it was inhabited only by the royal ghosts. No one went there if it was not required of them.

Tadamoto did not let the fear of spirits overcome his very rational mind. He stepped into the room and pulled the screen closed behind him. Feeling his way, he crossed the wide floor before he dared let even a slight glow escape from his lamp. He breathed deeply to calm himself, but his lungs were assaulted by the mustiness of the unused rooms. The air seemed to smell of the past.

He opened a screen onto a large hallway, anxious to be moving, to leave the presence of the Hanama behind. His lamp picked out the wall paintings and the fine carvings in both stone and wood. The Hanama had exibited much more refined tastes than their successors. Their art had been simple and elegant, with a subtle use of color, yet the court painters of the Yamaku were not required to execute such cultivated work.

Tadamoto came to a wide flight of stone stairs which rose up into landings on the next three floors. He stopped to listen for a moment but all was silent, all was dark.

He went up, his thoughts turning now to the Sonsa dancer. How had she come to this place? Had she been seen? Was she not afraid? A vision of her filled his mind, a memory of her hand on his arm.

At the second landing he turned down the hall, his lantern casting a warm glow over the floor and walls. Finally, at the end of the hall, he came to a set of large doors, ornately carved, painted with gilt. Depicted in this relief, were the Door Wardens—the giants who guarded the sanctuary within from entry by the spirits of evil. The door on the right was slightly ajar. Tadamoto reached out and grasped the bronze handle and pulled it toward him. It started to move, but then came to a stop. He pulled harder; it gave but then stopped again.

"Who dares disturb the sleep of royalty?" a voice hissed from the dark.

Tadamoto let the door go and it closed with a bump.

A voice came to him again, a woman's voice. "Tadamoto-sum?"

He almost laughed with relief. "Yes. Osha-sum?"

The door swung open now, and in the light from his lamp Tadamoto could see the lovely Sonsa step back into the shrine.

"I . . . I was afraid you would not come," she said in a whisper.

"I would not miss an opportunity to see you," Tadamoto answered, and with that he opened the cover of his lantern. Osha wore an elegant kimono of the finest

silk, blue like the morning sky, with a pattern of clouds.
Her sash and inner robe were of gold. Around her, the
gold of the ornate Botahist shrine seemed to take up the
colors of her dress and reflect them, as though she were
part of this sacred place—a priestess, an Initiate of the
Way. She moved back across the floor, seeming to glide
in her steps, coming to a stop in the center of a septilateral set within a circle on the floor.

"It is said that the Brothers dance in patterns such as
this and that it is the secret of their power," she said
suddenly. And then she began to move—flowing,
effortless movement like the Brothers performed in their
defense, yet unlike this. Osha danced. She turned slowly
in the half light, her hands suggesting the movements of
resistance, yet they enticed, they called to Tadamoto's
senses as he had never felt before. In a final lithe motion,
Osha sank to her knees, eyes cast down, and she
remained thus for a long moment, unmoving.

At last she spoke in a forced calm. "I am no longer
the favorite of our Emperor, Tadamoto-sum."

The young colonel did not know what to answer. He
began a step toward her, but she looked up and something in her gaze stopped him.

"Is it justice that I will never dance again?" she asked.

"Why do you say this? You are the foremost Sonsa of
our time."

"It means nothing, if to have me dance is to risk the
displeasure of the Son of Heaven." She said this without
bitterness, a mere statement of the obvious.

"Displeasure? Our Emperor shows nothing but the
highest pleasure whenever you perform."

She sighed at this. "I fear that this will no longer be
so, Tadamoto-sum. And there is the *new favorite*—she
will not wish to see me, that is certain."

Yes, Tadamoto thought, that may be true. But the
Emperor seemed to express so much care for her, for
her happiness, would he not wish her to dance if that is
what created her happiness? "The Emperor is too
pleased by your . . . dancing to wish that you stop. And
if that were not true, which I'm sure it is, there are

places, other than the Imperial Palace where one may dance."

"If it were only the palace, I would not be concerned, but it is the capital we speak of, the capital and perhaps all the inner provinces. I would be exiled to the north or to the west. . . ." She shook her head. "After all my years of training, how could I accept this?" She looked down at the pattern around her. "It is not *right* that this should happen to me!"

Jaku Tadamoto sank to his knees before her. "It need not be as you say, Osha-sum. The Emperor is fair to those who are loyal, the Jaku know this." He reached out tentatively and took her hands. She returned his touch. "If I do not presume too much, when the time is right I would speak to the Son of Heaven on your behalf."

She looked up now and held his eyes. He felt her take both of his hands between hers and, with a pressure so slight he may have imagined it, she drew him toward her. She kissed his hand. "You are a man of honor, Jaku Tadamoto-sum. I was a young fool to allow myself to be ensnared by the Emperor and his promises."

She raised his hands and the warmth of her cheek against his fingers thrilled him. Jaku felt weak as his desire grew stronger. He bent down to her and their lips met in the most tentative kiss. Her breath was sweet, warm. Their lips brushed again, more certainly. He traced the curve of Osha's neck with a finger and she sighed and pushed her face into his chest. He held her there, close to him, certain that she could feel the pounding of his heart.

"Come with me," she said rising and drawing him to his feet. She swept the lantern up off the floor and turned, not releasing his hand, to lead him back into the small shrine. A hidden screen opened into a hall that ended in a flight of seven stairs. Osha led him up, hurrying now, and then through another screen into a dark room. In the lamplight Tadamoto could see the form of a large, low bed under a protective cotton cover; the room seemed to contain nothing else.

Osha turned now and kissed him, with longing, with promise. But then broke away, and, going to the far wall, unlatched a shoji, opening it wide to the night. And the moonlight fell upon her like a caress.

"The chamber of the Empress Jenna," she whispered, and laughed, a warm laugh. "What could be more fitting?"

"You are not as she," Tadamoto said.

"In my actions, no, I am much more circumspect. But in my soul?" Again she seemed to glide toward him. "In my soul, I am reborn the Yellow Empress Jenna." Taking his hands, she pulled him lightly toward the bed.

They removed the cotton cover and under it found rich quilts and pillows of the finest quality.

Kneeling on the bed, they kissed again, touching gently. With patience, Tadamoto unwound Osha's long sash and opened her silk robes. Her outer robe slipped from her shoulders and she was left with the thin, gold fabric of her inner kimono clinging to her skin. He kissed her breasts shyly, the beauty of her dancer's form stirring him. A shiver ran through Osha's body and she pushed him down into the quilts, falling lightly on top of him. She untied his sash and he felt her skin soft against his own.

They made love until the sky showed signs of morning, each bringing all of their skills to their tryst, each bringing a strong passion. If anyone passing below had heard, they would have been certain it was the moans, and sighs of the Hanama ghosts who were known to walk the halls still; ever restless, ever dissatisfied.

# Seventeen

The brush work was rather plain, but strong and clear. Nishima took it up from the table and looked at it again. The mulberry paper was of the best quality, almost heavy, and colored a pale, pale yellow. An arrangement of green autumn grain had been attached to the poem, a symbol of growth, while yellow was one of the traditional colors of fall.

> Autumn settles
> Among the fall grains,
> And they wait
> Only for a sign of spring.

Lady Nishima set the letter on the table again and turned back to the view of the garden beyond her balcony. She wondered if Jaku Katta had written the poem himself. The brush work was his, no doubt, but the poem? This revealed another side of him if it was, indeed, his composition. The verse was not terribly sophisticated, but it was not marred by the overornamentation that Lady Nishima believed was the major flaw in the court verse of that time. It did contain the obligatory reference to a classical poem; in this case to "The Wind From Chou-san."

> Her heart is as cold
> As the wind from Chou-san,
> Yet the fall grains appear
> In the fields.

He is bold, Nishima thought, and she was not entirely displeased. The contradiction that was Jaku Katta confused her thoroughly—the incident on the canal still seemed odd to her. And yet *it was possible* that such a thing could happen.

It was Jaku Katta who saved my uncle, she told herself again. And it can never be forgotten that he has the ear of the Emperor. Perhaps this would prove important to the Shonto in the future.

She took up her brush and wet her inkstone for the fourth time.

> *Cold is the wind*
> *That rattles my shoji,*
> *Yet I am told the fall grains*
> *Need little encouragement.*

She set the smoke-gray paper down beside the letter from Jaku Katta and examined the brush work critically. As modest as she was, the lady could not deny the great contrast between their hands. He is a soldier, after all, she thought, but still, she could find little to admire in Jaku's brush work once she had set it beside her own.

Lady Nishima read through her poem again and decided that it was exactly the tone she was looking for; discouraging, but not entirely so. She attached a small blossom of the twelve-petaled shinta flower to it—the symbol of the Shonto House. That would remind the general that the House of Fanisan was no more. She tapped a small gong to call a servant. The note must go off immediately, she had much to do to prepare for the Celebration of the Emperor's Acension.

The Lady Kitsura Omawara passed through the gate into the small garden attached to her father's rooms. The sound of water was a subdued burble and, beyond the high wall, a breeze seemed to breathe through the last leaves of the golden lime trees. The young aristocrat was dressed in a formal robe of pale plum, with the hems of her four under kimonos in the most carefully chosen colors, revealed properly at the sleeve and the neck.

She slipped her sandals off as she stepped onto the porch. A harsh cough came from behind a screen set on the porch and pain flashed across the young woman's face as though the cough had been her own.

"Father?" she said softly.

A long breath was drawn. "Kitsu-sum?"

She could almost see the smile of pleasure and, as though it were a mirror, her own face also creased in a warm smile. "Yes. It is a perfect evening, is it not, Father?"

"Perfect, yes." There was a pause as the lord caught his breath. Kitsura examined the design on the screen, a stand of bamboo beside a tranquil pond.

"Did you see the mist . . . in the garden . . . this morning?"

"Yes, Father, I did. But you should not have been up, breathing that cold air."

He laughed, almost silently, and to his daughter it sounded like a far off echo of his old laughter. "I cannot give up . . . the world just yet . . . Kitsu-sum." The clear, autumn air rattled in his lungs like dice in a cup and he fell to coughing terribly. The young lady cringed, closing her eyes as though this would block out the sound.

"Should I call Brother Tessa, Father?" she asked, referring to the Botahist monk who acted as the Omawara House physician. He was unable to answer her, but just as she rose to summon a servant, he spoke.

"No. I will stop in a . . . ." He coughed again, but then the fit ended and he lay gasping. His daughter waited, staring at the screen that allowed her father to maintain his dignity in the face of an illness that was certainly draining him of all life. If only he could be transported to the place I see on this screen, Kitsura thought. It looks so peaceful. May Botahara grant him favor for all that he has suffered in this life.

At last Lord Omawara lay quiet, and just when his daughter was sure he had fallen asleep, he spoke again.

"Will you . . . go to the palace . . . for the Cele . . . bration?"

"I will, Father. I intend to meet Nishima-sum and we shall attend the festivities together."

"Ah. Take her . . . my highest . . . respects."

"I will Father. She has often expressed a desire to visit you and asks always after your well-being."

"She is . . . kind." There was a long silence punctuated only by the lord's fight for air. "You must . . . assure her . . . that . . . my affection . . . is undying. . . . But to . . . see her . . . would be. . . ."

"I understand, Father. I will explain this to my cousin."

"What of . . . Motoru-sum? Has he . . . gone . . . to Seh?"

"I will speak to your staff who are not to worry you with such things."

The echo of laughter came from behind the screen.

"But, as you know so much already, yes, Lord Shonto left for Seh some ten days ago."

"I am . . . concerned."

"He is wise, Father. Lord Shonto Motoru should never be a cause for worry."

"There is more . . . than the eye . . . sees . . . Denji . . . Gorge, Seh." He fell into silence.

"Lord Shonto goes nowhere without the greatest care, Sire. Our concern would be better placed elsewhere."

"Wise . . . Kitsu-sum. . . . Your mother?"

"She is with you, Sire. This is her happiness. How could she be cause for concern?"

"She . . . does not rest. . . . Worries."

"But she is not happy otherwise, Father, you know that."

"She worries that . . ." he coughed again but weakly, "that you are unmarried."

"Father. I am hardly an old maid!" She laughed her infectious laugh. "There will be time yet."

"Yes . . . but Kitsu-sum . . . the Emperor has . . . three sons only."

"What a pity. If he had had a fourth, perhaps he would have a son worthy of consideration!"

The laughter echoed, ending in a wheeze. "I have . . . raised you with expectations . . . that are too high."

It was Kitsura's turn to laugh. "Why do you say that? Because I consider an Emperor's son beneath me? Well, to be honest, I would not let any of them marry my maid!"

"Ah. Then . . . the Princes . . . must have . . . cluttered rooms," the lord said.

Kitsura laughed. "I tire you, Father. I will have Brother Tessa lecturing me again."

"Yes. I am . . . tired."

"I must go, Father."

The curtain in the screen moved slightly, and a pale, withered hand pushed through the opening. Lady Kitsura reached out and took the cold fingers within her own. It was all she had seen of her father in over four years.

From the balcony, Lady Nishima could look down upon the celebration, a mass of swirling color, as the courtiers and other nobles moved through the three large rooms and out onto the open terrace.

The Emperor could be seen on his dais, surrounded by lords and ladies known for their discerning taste in the area of music. The Highest One involved himself in the judgment of a music competition.

Very close by, on the edge of the dais, sat Lady Kitsura Omawara. She had been invited to judge the music and was now the object of much of the Emperor's attention. Nishima could see her cousin struggling to remain polite, yet still keep her distance from the Son of Heaven. Nishima found the Emperor's behavior shocking, yet there was nothing she could do to help. Already the Empress had retired from the gathering, and the Emperor did not seem to notice. Somewhere in the halls, Nishima had seen the young Sonsa dancer who had been the object of the Emperor's affections so recently. Tonight, however, she was being entirely ignored and looked as one does in such circumstances. Lady Nishima stood at the rail thinking longingly of the quiet life of Lady Okara—if only. . . .

Young peers presented themselves before the distinguished judges and offered their very best compositions. The prizes for the winners would, no doubt, be lavish and the guests at that end of the large hall sat listening in complete silence. Strains of music drifted up to the Lady Nishima, but somehow this did not lift her spirits as it usually did.

In the next hall, the Hall of the Water's Voice, Chusa Seiki sat with a group of her most promising students and a few courtiers, composing a poem-series. A wine cup was set floating down the artificial stream and as it passed, each participant in turn would pick it up, drink, and recite a three line poem which echoed the verses before, incorporated a reference to a classical verse, and also added something original. Nishima had been asked to participate, but seeing that Prince Wakaro was one of the poets, she had politely declined. Besides, her mind was on other things and she did not feel that she would live up to her reputation. The subdued lamplight of the Hall of the Water's Voice did not draw her tonight, as it often did.

She was about to turn and rejoin the gathering when a man's voice came from behind her.

*"The wind that rattles*
*Your shoji*
*Seeks only the lamp's warmth.*
*Winter gives way to*
*Other seasons.*

"I thank you for the shinta flower, Lady Nishima."

"Not at all, General.

*"The wind through the shoji*
*Causes the lamp to flicker,*
*I fear that I shall be left*
*In darkness."*

She could feel his presence behind her, the Tiger in the darkness. Her breath quickened and she felt the nerves in her back come to life as though she expected to be touched at any second.

"I remember that we spoke of gratitude," he said.

Nishima almost turned toward him, but stopped. "Perhaps gratititude means different things in different circles, General Katta."

"Please excuse me, I did not mean to suggest what you seem to think. It was I who was grateful and who continue to be." He stopped as though to listen and then whispered. "I have information that may be of use to those who grow the shinta blossom."

Nishima nodded, staring down at the scene below.

"If I am not being too bold, Lady Nishima, please join me on the balcony for a moment." And she heard him retreat toward the open screens.

She stood there briefly, gathering her nerve, making sure that she was not watched, then she turned and went out into the light of the crescent moon. The night air was cool. Soft-edged clouds traveled across the sky, now covering the Bearer, now the sliver of the waxing moon.

No one else had ventured out onto the balcony, either because they were drawn to the entertainments inside, or because the air was too chill.

"This way, my lady." Jaku's voice came out of the darkness to the left and Lady Nishima could just make out the shape of a large man in the black of the Imperial Guard. She turned and followed.

At the end of the balcony a short set of steps led to a second balcony, though this one was small and secluded, no doubt attached to private rooms. Jaku knelt on grass mats here, his formal uniform spread out around him like a fan. Nishima could see his face in the moonlight, the strong features, the drooping mustache, the gleam of the gray eyes. She knelt across from him on the soft mats.

"I am honored that you place such trust in me, Lady Nishima.

*The shoji opens and*
*The light within*
*Warms even the night."*

"Did you say you had information that may benefit
my House, General?"

The Black Tiger nodded, surprised by her coolness. "I
do, my lady. Information of the most delicate nature."
He stood suddenly and went to the shoji, opening it and
looking carefully inside. Satisfied, he beckoned Nishima
to come with him. She hesitated but then rose and
entered the chamber. Jaku did not close the screen
entirely and they sat close to the opening, still lit by the
moon.

"I have information about plans that will affect your
uncle, Lady Nishima. I only wish that I had received the
information earlier." He paused as though waiting for a
response, but Nishima listened in silence.

"I do not know everything yet, but there is certainly
a plot against your uncle that has its origins very near
the Dragon Throne."

Still, Nishima said nothing.

"I take great risk telling you this. I hope that you will
see it as a token of my good faith." He said this with
difficulty, as though it was not usual for him to be in a
position of trying to please another.

Nishima produced a fan from her sleeve, but instead
of opening it she began to slowly tap the palm of her
hand. "As you have conveyed this, it is hardly news,
General Katta. Do you know more?"

The Black Tiger did not answer immediately and Lady
Nishima suppressed a smirk. Oh, my handsome soldier,
she thought, you expect so little of me. Should I throw
myself into your arms in gratitude?

"I have heard more, Lady Nishima, but I wish to be
certain of my reports. I would not want to give you false
information."

"I shall pass this on to my uncle, though he must be
almost in Seh by now.

*"A single warm night*
*Autumn lingers beyond the walls,*
*The fall grains*
*Bend in the breeze.*

"The shinta blossom is also endangered by the cold, Katta-sum. It is a matter of great concern to me, and I am grateful."

The warrior bent his head toward the mat, more than half a bow, and when he rose he was closer to her. He bent toward her, and she returned his kiss, though she was not sure why. Jaku reached for her then, but she easily eluded him and was on her feet and at the door before he realized what she had done. She stopped for an instant and spoke quietly in her lovely, warm voice. "We cannot take too much care, Katta-sum, you know that. But we must find a way to discuss the welfare of the shinta blossom further."

Slipping out the door and down the steps, Nishima found that she was nearly quivering with excitement and tension. Her head spun with questions. Was it possible that Jaku Katta could become loyal to the Shonto? What a coup that would be!

Lady Nishima returned to the entertainments and easily won a poetry contest. Many noted how lovely she looked that evening, how fully she laughed, and how engaging was her conversation. Among the ladies of the court this became the cause of much speculation.

Nishima ladled cha into a bowl for her cousin and then offered it, as etiquette required. It was, of course, refused, but then taken, after being offered the second time.

The two women sat in a small chamber in Lady Nishima's rooms. A charcoal burner glowed under the table, countering the slight breeze from the two screens that remained open to the garden. The moon was about to set and the stars were magnificent. A ground mist drifted in the garden, making dark islands of the trees and rocks.

"I don't know what I shall do!" Kitsura said. "It was

all so entirely unexpected. What could the Emperor possibly be thinking? He cannot believe that I would consider becoming a secondary wife!"

"Perhaps it is time for the Empress to retire to the quiet life of the nun," Nishima offered.

"Even so, I have no wish to be his principle wife either!" Kitsura seemed entirely desolate, her face contorted into a near grimace. "Oh, Nishi-sum, what am I to do?"

"It is indeed difficult. If one had known this would occur, it would have been possible to take steps to avoid any embarrassment. But now," she shook her head, "it has become a matter that, perhaps, no amount of delicacy may resolve." She looked concerned, yet her cousin could not help but notice that there was something about her—an air of heightened being, almost—and a smile seemed to be about to appear on Lady Nishima's face at any second, despite the seriousness of the conversation.

A servant, hearing the voices, knocked on the screen and delivered a message to her mistress—a letter on embossed rice paper of dusky mauve. Attached to the carefully folded message was a fan of autumn ginkyo leaves. Nishima put the letter into her sleeve pocket, but not before Kitsura had seen it, and the look of pleasure on Nishima's face.

"I see we have different problems, cousin," Lady Kitsura said dryly.

Nishima laughed, but kept her silence on the matter.

Later, alone in her rooms, Nishima examined the note. To her great surprise and disapointment, it was not from Jaku Katta! Amazed that she would have another suitor, one that she was unaware of, the lady turned up the lamp and unfolded the letter on the table. And it was from Tanaka! There was no mistaking his elegant hand. This was most irregular. To make matters even stranger, there were two unmarked gold coins attached carefully inside. She bent over the small script and began the laborious work of deciphering one of the Shonto codes.

When she had transposed a complete copy she sat up

straight, staring at the wall, her face suddenly pale. "May Botahara save us," she said aloud. "He is entirely mad."

Gold! Gold going secretly north. Tribute? Bribe? Payment? And who received it? Who was it the Emperor enriched in his effort to bring down the Shonto, for there was little doubt that this was the purpose. She pushed her hands to her eyes as though it would help her to see the meaning of this discovery, but her head seemed to spin. Picking up the coins, she rubbed them between her fingers as though she could divine their origin. Would Jaku be able to find out the destination of this fortune? But were there not Imperial Guards involved in its transport? She read the letter again. Yes. Did this mean that Jaku was party to it? In her heart she hoped this was not so. Oh, Father, what danger you journey toward.

# Eighteen

As a warrior, Lord Komawara did not like his position. He stared up at the high granite cliffs of Denji Gorge and counted the archers looking down on the ships below. We are vulnerable, he thought.

Ahead of his own barge, the first ships were entering the locks. It would take two days for all of the fleet to be locked through. The House of Butto had, after three days of delay, finally allowed the Imperial Governor and all those that accompanied him to pass through their lands. The depth of their suspicion had surprised even Lord Komawara, who had been expecting difficulty.

In the past four days the young lord had attended many councils with Shonto and his military advisors. Komawara's head spun with the mass of details, the thousand lines of speculation. The warriors who were Shonto's advisors ignored no possibility in their analysis. When Komawara thought of his own councils he was embarrassed at how inadequate they seemed in comparison.

The position of the Komawara has long been less complicated, he realized, but now that he was a Shonto ally, all would change. He must learn all he could from these meetings with the Shonto staff. These were men to be respected, and he felt honored to be among them.

Komawara left off counting the archers on the cliff top—there were many beyond many, that was certain. The barge that preceded his, and the three craft immediately behind it, were moving into the first lock now. Despite having been through locks on many occasions, Komawara was always amazed by the process, and his admiration for the ancient engineers who had built them never diminished. They had known so much then, he thought; today this would be considered an undertaking of immense difficulty and colossal scale.

They passed the giant bronze gates now, half as thick as Komawara's barge was wide. Butto soldiers were everywhere. Komawara tapped his breast with his hand, reassured by the feel of the armor hidden beneath his robe. The young lord was uncertain of the bargain that Shonto had struck with the Butto but, no matter what the details, they would not have satisfied him—he did not trust either of the feuding families, and that would never change.

The gates began to close, swinging slowly on giant hinges, their hidden mechanisms moving them inch by inch, as the lock-men allowed the water to flow through the wheels that powered the gates. So slow was their movement, that there was no sound as they came together.

Around his barge the water began to swirl and boil. The sun lit the white foam as it danced across the surface and, almost imperceptibly, the river barges began to rise. Three of Komawara's guards moved closer to him now, shielding him from the Butto archers as the ship rose toward them.

They will not care about me, Komawara thought, and then realized that, as a Shonto ally, his position in the world had taken on new significance. He chose to stay on deck. We are in the party of the Governor of Seh. We travel the Imperial Waterway, where all have the protection of the Son of Heaven. What these families do here is against the law of the Imperium and should not be countenanced. He planted his feet against the motion of the ship, crossed his arms, and stared at the bowmen on the walls.

The waters grew tranquil and the gates to the next lock began to open. The barges moved forward, towed by teams of oxen, and the process was repeated.

At last Komawara's barge passed under the narrow bridge that spanned the gap from the Butto lands to their

placements on the Hajiwara fief. The walls of the Denji
Gorge opened up around them as they slipped into the
Lake of the Seven Masters, named for the giant sculp-
tures of Botahara, carved into the cliff. Two of them
could be seen now—a Sitting Botahara, and the Perfect
Master in Meditation.

Komawara wondered what Brother Shuyun could tell
him about the massive figures, for their history was
clouded by rumor and time. The images were said to
have been carved in the two hundred years after the
passing of Botahara by a secretive sect that later fell
during the Inter-temple Wars. This was before the
Emperor, Chonso-sa, fought the Botahist Sects into submission and forbade them ever to bear arms again.

Strange, Komawara thought, followers of the Perfect
Master who warred across the Empire when their own
dogma forbade the taking of life except in the most
extreme cases of self-defense. No doubt, they justified it
somehow though the historians believed it was merely a
struggle for power, nothing more, even as this ill-considered feud was a struggle for supremecy.

Crewmen took up their positions now, and started the
boat forward with long sweeps of their oars. The seven
rih to the anchorage near the lake's northern end went
by quickly, though by the time Komawara's boat arrived
the sun had traveled far enough that they moored in the
shade of the western cliff.

An image of Botahara that was considered heretical
dominated the section of the cliff above the anchorage.
It depicted the Perfect Master in a state of conjugal bliss
with his young wife, though the faces of the figures had
been erased more than a thousand years before. What
remained had the oddest effect—two anonymous bodies
of cold stone entwined in the most intimate embrace, yet
where the faces should have been, showing signs of their
ecstasy, were two utterly blank sections of gray wall. It
was as though the act of love itself had been rendered
impersonal, an act of the body not participated in by the
mind. Somehow, it seemed to Lord Komawara this was
more obscene than any "erotic" drawings he had ever

seen. The act of love without humanity. He shook his head, yet he did not look away.

Not far from the barge bearing Lord Komawara of Seh, Initiate Brother Shuyun stood on the deck of a similar barge looking up at the same image. To him the stone relief represented something quite different. It spoke of a schism in the Botahist Brotherhood over basic doctrine. The sculpture had, before its erasure, depicted the Lord of all Wisdom, in the act of love, with the rays of Enlightenment shining out from his face—Botahara enjoying the pleasures of the flesh after his Enlightenment. This was heresy of the worst kind!

In this very valley, in ancient times, a sect who believed themselves followers of the Perfect Master, had practiced their doctrine of the Eightfold Path, believing that enjoyment of the flesh was the eighth way to Enlightenment.

The Botahist histories told how overzealous followers of the True Path had destroyed the Heretical Sect in a great siege. This act had brought the Brotherhood into open conflict with the Emperor, Chonso-sa, who didn't realize that it was not the Brotherhood, but a group of their followers, who had destroyed the sect of the Eightfold Path.

We have survived many times of hardship, Shuyun thought, yet Botahara had taught that the True Path was fraught with difficulties and deceptions.

All this, Shuyun had been taught; it was only now, after the words of Acolyte Tesseko, that it occurred to him that these teachings might not be inspired and divine truth. It was only now that he considered the possibility that there might be an element of self-interest in the purposes of his own Order.

Once given information, the mind that solved the Soto Problem could not easily be deflected. The Lord Botahara had sought the truth above all things, and for this He had known the displeasure of the religious leaders of His time. As a follower of the teachings of the Enlight-

ened One, Shuyun wondered if he could do less if that
was what the truth required of him.

He stared up at the figures above him, locked in an
embrace no Brother could know, and the thoughts this
image brought to his mind stirred him in a manner he
had always before resisted with all the discipline he had
been taught. But now these thoughts would not leave
him in peace.

Lord Shonto was not concerned with questions of history or doctrine as he regarded the stone lovers, it was
the Hajiwara soldiers who stood in the openings cut into
the granite relief that begged his attention. He clapped
his hands and a guard immediately knelt before him. "I
wish to speak to my Spiritual Advisor," the lord said.
The guard bowed and was gone.

Shonto could see soldiers in the livery of his House
being sculled ashore to the gravel bar behind which the
ships had anchored. It was one of the few places in the
gorge where men could actually land, the cliffs rose so
abruptly from the surface of the lake. Beyond the gravel
bar and the scrub brush that clung to it, the cliffs climbed
up, fifty times the height of a man, solid and unscalable,
yet Shonto still felt it prudent that the beach be in his
control and not a base for spies or Hajiwara treachery.
He would receive a report from the shore party as soon
as they had secured the area. He looked up again and
saw two Hajiwara men, in a dark granite window, pointing down at the beach. Yes, Shonto thought, they will
see everything we do . . . by daylight. That cannot be
helped. We will thank the gods for the darkness.

Shuyun mounted the steps to the quarter deck and the
guards bowed him through to Lord Shonto. He knelt
before his liege-lord, bowed his double bow, and waited.
Shonto regarded the young man kneeling before him.
"So, we have come through the first obstacle," he said,
ignoring all formality.

"It is as your advisors believed. The Butto, no matter
what their designs, would have to let us pass into Denji

Gorge—it is the only way they could be sure you would not escape."

"Then you do agree that this is, indeed, a trap, and we will not be allowed to pass unscathed."

"I do, Sire." Shuyun answered evenly.

Shonto turned and looked up at the stone figures. "Tell me of these windows that look out from the bodies of the faceless lovers."

The monk did not answer right away, but gazed up at the cliff face as though the answer would be written there. "Several of the images carved here were also fanes for the followers of the Eightfold Path. Behind the figures lie tunnels and chambers for both worship and for living. It was an effective way to defend themselves from their enemies. The windows we see are just that, openings to allow the entry of light and air. During festivals, the figures would be decorated with cloth of purple and gold which would be hung in place from the windows. Sometimes there were narrow ledges that could also be used for this purpose, though it has been so long it is doubtful that more than a trace of them remains."

"Huh." Lord Shonto rubbed his chin absentmindedly. "Where are the entrances?"

"Commonly there was only one." Shuyun pointed to the cliff top. "There are stairs down the face of the wall. They are narrow and enter a door equally narrow. High above the door is an opening large enough to pour boiling liquids from. It was an entrance easily defended."

Shonto considered this for a moment. "How did they draw their water?"

"A shaft was sunk below the level of the surface of the lake and then joined to the water. There has been much speculation about how this was done, but to this day it remains one of the secrets of the sect. To the best of my knowledge, they had no other source of water so it was crucial that this supply not be cut."

"They were thorough."

"It was a time of danger, Sire."

Shonto nodded. "It has not changed a great deal. Thank you for this information. I shall gather the council after dark. We would be pleased if you would join us, Brother Shuyun."

The Botahist Brother bowed and backed away, leaving the lord surrounded by his guards . . . alone.

# Nineteen

Lamps swung from bronze chains, moving almost imperceptibly as the ship rocked on the quiet waters. Shonto's nine senior generals sat in orderly rows before a dais in a chamber below decks. To the left of the dais sat Brother Shuyun, to the right, Kamu and Lord Komawara.

No one spoke as they waited; indeed, no one moved. They stared straight ahead at the silk cushion, armrest and sword-stand that had been placed on the dais. The sound of water lapping the ship's planking came in through an open port and the lamps flickered in a slight draught. All were left with their private thoughts, their search for solutions to their situation.

A screen to the right of the dais slid open without warning and two of Shonto's personal guards stepped into the room, knelt, and touched their heads to the floor. The members of the council did the same, remaining thus until their lord had entered and seated himself. A guard hurried to place Shonto's sword in its stand.

The generals raised themselves back to their waiting position, but Shonto did not speak. Instead he seemed to be lost in thought, unaware of the others around him. For an hour he remained so, and during this time none of his staff moved. No one cleared his throat or shifted to become more comfortable. The lamps continued to sway, the water lapped the hull.

At last, Shonto turned to his steward. "Report our situation at the Butto locks."

Kamu gave a brief bow. "All of your troops and staff

have locked through, Sire. The last of the barges bearing them come up the lake now. On the craft remaining, perhaps thirty boats, there is no one of importance to our purpose." Kamu paused to gather his thoughts. "The Butto still do not know if you have passed through their hands or not, though by now they must suspect you have. The large number of people in our fleet and the use of doubles have caused them great difficulty.

"Our information about the Butto has proven accurate—the father is old and no longer takes part in the ruling of his fief. Of the two sons, the younger is strong while the older is weak. There is no split in the Butto staff, though. All support the younger brother, which shows that there is wisdom among them. It is said, and I believe truthfully, that the older son is dissatisfied with his position. But it does not seem that he would be vulnerable to Hajiwara intrigue against his brother—he shares all of the Butto hatred for the Hajiwara House.

"The Butto give no indication of their true purpose in regard to you, Sire, but it is as you suspected—whatever their designs for the Shonto, their true hatred is for the Hajiwara, and, therefore, that is the key to their cooperation."

Shonto nodded and again silence settled in the room. "General Hojo Masakado, what has happened in your dealings with the Hajiwara?"

The general, a man of Shonto's age, though prematurely gray, bowed to his lord. "I have today requested that the Imperial Representative for the Province of Seh be allowed to pass into the upper section of the Grand Canal. The Hajiwara say they are willing to comply but, because of the special conditions which exist here at this time, they wish to confer personally with Lord Shonto. They insist that this meeting take place on their land, as is their right in this situation. I have told them that Lord Shonto is temporarily unwell and under the care of Brother Shuyun. The Hajiwara representative expressed concern and retired to report this to his lord. We have not yet received an answer from them.

"All evidence supports our information that this Hajiwara lord is not the man his father was, Sire. Though it is said he leads men well in battle, he constantly ignores his advisors and in the areas of state he is very weak.

"Reports from our spies say that every person passing through the Hajiwara locks is seen by two scholars who have met Lord Shonto in person. All craft are being searched in a most thorough manner—they do not seem sure that Lord Shonto has not secretly left his flotilla. This would seem to indicate that they have no spies close to our center."

Shonto shook his head. "So, they dare not make a mistake. To let the Lord of the Shonto escape while they fall upon innocent passengers on an Imperial waterway." He shook his head again. "This would be fatal. The Emperor would risk open war with the great Houses, and this he fears."

"It does seem to be so, Sire," General Hojo said. "The Emperor has chosen wisely. There would be few others in all of Wa foolish enough to move openly against the Shonto. Does not Hajiwara realize what this will mean? Can he not see that the Emperor will be forced to act against him?"

Shonto shrugged. "The Emperor can be a most convincing man when he wishes to be. I'm sure this Hajiwara has ignored the counsel of his advisors and listened to the wisdom of his own desires."

"Pardon me, Sire." Bowing low, another general addressed his lord. "I feel it may be dangerous to assume the Emperor, and no other, has contrived this situation."

Shonto stared at the man stonily. "Who, then?"

The general shook his head. "Anyone who is jealous of the Shonto."

"If I fall to the plot of another House, the Son of Heaven will have no choice but to destroy that House—it would be the only way he could disassociate himself from their action. He fears to be seen as the predator, falling upon those he hates. He knows this would lead to his downfall. The great Houses have never allowed such an Emperor to stay upon the Throne. History tells us that. So I ask you, who, other than a fool, would attack us knowing that the Son of Heaven, despite any secret agreements, would be forced to eliminate them?"

The general was unable to answer.

Shuyun bowed quickly. "A House that thinks they can eliminate the Shonto and, in the same action, turn the great Houses against the Emperor."

Surprise showed on Shonto's face as he turned to his Spiritual Advisor. He nodded, almost a slight bow. "Ah. This is truth, Brother, but neither the Hajiwara nor the Butto could rally the great Houses around them—they have not the strength. The Emperor would have them."

"I agree, Lord Shonto, but they may act as agents for another House, yeh? Their rewards would be great."

"Who would be so daring?"

"The Tora," offered General Hojo. "They feel they have as great a claim to the Throne as the Yamaku."

"The Senji, perhaps. The Minikama."

"The Sadaku," offered another.

"The Black Tiger," Kamu said, and his face twisted as though he had known a sudden premonition.

"Jaku Katta could never sit on the Dragon Throne." Shonto protested. "It is not possible, he has not the blood. . . ." Shonto stopped in mid-sentence and turned to a guard. "Prepare our fastest boat to return to the capital. Immediately! Call for my secretary. No. Bring me brush and paper."

Kamu bowed again. "Lord Shonto, such an action will only alert our enemies. 'While they do not suspect that we know their secret design, we are strong,' " he added, quoting the gii master, Soto.

"But Lady Nishima must know," Shonto protested. "If what you say is true, she is in grave danger. Jaku must not use her to seize the throne. In all probability he will fail, and Lady Nishima will pay for that failure." A daughter of the blood, Shonto thought, a great prize for the bold man. He cursed himself now for keeping his true thoughts concerning the incident in the garden from Lady Nishima. It was overly cautious of him.

"But Sire," Lord Komawara said, speaking for the first

time, "you must fall before Jaku could act and, for the
moment, that cannot happen."

"What Lord Komawara says is wisdom, Sire," Shuyun
said quietly. "Lady Nishima's safety can be assured most
effectively by Lord Shonto escaping from this situation."

Shonto nodded. "But if I fall, Jaku will raise my allies
against his own Emperor." The lord closed his eyes.
"Jaku, who it appears so recently saved my life—for
which my allies, not to mention my own daughter, are
no doubt grateful. I have underestimated him entirely."
Shonto banged his fist on his armrest. "Is this truly
possible?"

"It appears very possible, Sire," Kamu said evenly.
"And even if it is someone other than Jaku Katta who
moves the pieces, the game would seem to be the same."

"Then I bow to your counsel," Shonto said, nodding
to the assembled group. "I will send an encoded message
by the Imperial carriers, addressed to a friend. It will
reach Lady Nishima in less than three days. I will not
fall before then." He searched the faces before him.
"But now we must find a way to extract ourselves from
this situation." Shonto looked around the room as
though the walls were the cliffs of Denji Gorge. He
waited, but no one spoke.

Kamu's quote from the gii Master took Shonto back
to the house by the lake, back to the peace and the quiet
conversation.

"We must draw them from their keep," Shonto said,
quietly. "We must offer them a sacrifice."

"Sire?" Kamu leaned forward.

"It is obvious. Our forces are small, while their positions are strong. To draw them from their castles we
must offer them a sacrifice they cannot refuse."

"But what?" Kamu asked.

*"Each other,"* Shuyun said with finality.

Shonto smiled for the first time since entering the
room. "Of course." He gripped his armrest. "We shall
offer to deliver the Hajiwara to their mortal enemies,
the Butto. And we shall offer to deliver the Butto into
the hands of the Hajiwara. Each House may also believe

that they will gain an advantage over the Shonto, who are trapped and helpless at the bottom of Denji Gorge. Thus, they eliminate their rivals and capture the Shonto for those for whom they act as agents—if that is indeed their game.

"Two things become apparent. Our offers must be flawless and entirely believable. And we must find a way out of the gorge. Shuyun, how were the sects in these temples taken?"

"They were starved, Sire."

"An admirable tactic, but one we don't have time for."

"We must scale the figures to the windows, Lord Shonto," Shuyun said. "There is no other possibility."

"How do you propose this be done?"

Shuyun bowed quickly, and Shonto suspected he had entered a meditative trance, like the one he had seen at the home of Myochin Ekun. "I have taken the liberty of examining the figures on the cliff, without going close enough to arouse suspicion. The lower section, ten times the height of a man, is impassable, so we must find a way to raise a man above it. Once on the figures, there seem to be cracks and areas of broken stone. It is possible that they could be scaled to one of the lower openings. All must be done in stealth, the guards must be subdued without a sound. If it is accomplished as I have said, it would allow access to the plain inside the Hajiwara defenses." Shuyun bowed.

The generals exchanged glances and the senior member, Hojo Masakada, was silently selected as their spokesman. "Sire, it is a bold plan, and one which should receive consideration, but it has some weaknesses. The cliff must be scaled in the dark, which would be very nearly impossible. And if the climbers are detected, any other plans we have would be rendered useless—the Hajiwara will only be caught off guard once. The plan we select must not have so weak a link. And also, there is the matter of the cliff itself; who among us has the skill to climb such a face?"

"I would climb it, General," Shuyun said.

"Not alone, Brother." Lord Komawara said. "I would climb with you."

"Your courage is to be commended, Brother, Lord Komawara—and never to be doubted. But the danger of your failure is not confined to yourselves. All would fall with you."

Looking out at the faces before him, Shonto saw resistance, resistance to this new advisor. It will not do, the lord thought. They fear to look less skilled than this new one, this boy-man.

Shonto turned to his Spiritual Advisor. "Could you climb this cliff, Brother?"

The monk answered so quietly that all present leaned forward to hear his words. "I am Botahist trained," he said.

"Yes," Shonto said, nodding, "I have seen."

He turned back to his generals and spoke quickly. "We must draw the Hajiwara from their defenses and then they must find the Shonto army behind them. We need the cooperation of the Butto—this I'm sure we can achieve. But we must find a way out of Denji Gorge."

Shonto rose suddenly, a guard rushing to take up his sword. "I will hear your alternatives to Brother Shuyun's suggestion when I return."

The screen closed behind Lord Shonto and the room returned to perfect silence. The lamps swayed. Water lapped the hull.

# Twenty

The mansion of Butto Joda sat upon a hill looking west across the slopes that swept down to Denji Gorge. It was not coincidental that this situation also provided a perfect view of the lands of the Hajiwara. The fortifications surrounding the mansion were designed and built to be the strongest and most modern defenses possible, yet aesthetics had not been ignored entirely. The palisades and towers were of the finest local material and constructed in the sweeping style of the Mori period.

Kamu mounted the steps to the high tower, accompanied by Butto guards. Much negotiation had preceded this meeting with Butto Joda, the younger son of Lord Butto Taga, for Kamu had insisted that the meeting take place in privacy, away from the prying eyes of Joda's older brother.

A day had been lost in these arrangements, and Kamu knew he had no more time to lose. The bait must be offered and the Butto must take it without delay. Outwardly, Kamu maintained the serenity one would expect from a warrior who had seen many battles, yet this was a serenity that did not come from within. So much depended on this meeting—everything, in fact.

At the top of the stairway, guards flanked large painted screens depicting the Butto armies in victory over their rivals. The guards bowed low, showing respect to the representative of the great Lord Shonto Motoru, but also honoring the famous warrior, Tenge Kamu.

The screens slid aside, revealing Lord Butto Joda, sitting on a dais at the end of an audience chamber of modest proportion. Entering the room, Kamu knelt and bowed respectfully. The lord nodded, and Kamu was again surprised by his youthful appearance. Even Lord Komawara seemed older than this pup, yet Butto Joda was not to be taken lightly. For three years, he had directed the battles against the Hajiwara, and the Hajiwara House was headed by a man twice his age.

"It is an honor to receive you again so soon, Kamusum. I have looked forward to this private discussion with great anticipation. Tell me, has your lord's condition improved?"

"I thank you for your words, as does my lord's House. Lord Shonto recovers quickly and sends his regrets that he cannot meet with you in person. It was his wish that he could pay his respects to his old friend, your honored father. May I enquire after his well-being?"

"The Lord Butto will be most pleased to hear of your kind concern. He grows stronger and I hope he will soon take his place in our councils again—a place I hold by his wish, until his recovery." Polite enquiry followed polite enquiry until the host deemed it proper to discuss other matters. "Is there some issue that Lord Shonto has instructed you to convey to my father? If there is, I would be pleased to be the bearer of such information."

"You are most perceptive, Lord Butto, for indeed my lord wishes to ask the boon of advice in a matter which he deems most sensitive"

"Please, Kamu-sum, it would be our honor to comply, though it is difficult for me to imagine a lord as famed for wisdom as Lord Shonto requiring our humble counsel. Please go on."

"As I have said, it is a matter of great sensitivity, and Lord Shonto would not speak of it if it were not of present importance." Kamu stopped as if what he was about to say was terribly embarrassing to him. "The problem my lord wishes your opinion on has arisen in his dealings with your close neighbors, the House of Hajiwara."

"Ah," the youthful lord said as though he were surprised but understood.

"I am not sure how best to explain this, Lord Butto,

I don't wish my words to reflect badly upon a family you have, no doubt, been associated with for generations."

"I understand, Kamu-sum, but the Shonto are also our friends, please . . . speak as though you were in your own chambers."

Kamu bowed in thanks. "I am honored that you think of the Shonto as your friends, for so Lord Shonto regards the Butto." Kamu smiled warmly at the boy before him. Oh, he is bright, the warrior thought. No more than eighteen years old, and listen to the way he speaks! In ten years he will be a force to be reckoned with. "It has become apparent, in our short time here, that the Hajiwara have arrogated onto themselves powers that are the strict and exclusive domain of our revered Emperor. I hardly need to describe these to you, Lord Butto, for it is obvious that the Hajiwara control, for their own benefit, the traffic of the Imperial Waterway. As a representative of the Throne, Lord Shonto is most concerned by this situation."

The young lord nodded as Kamu spoke, a look of grave concern on his face. "For this very reason, and others also, my own House has been at odds with the Hajiwara for some length of time. In fact, I will tell you as one friend to another, this is only the most recent of a long history of such actions by the Hajiwara."

"Ah, Lord Butto, do you then share Lord Shonto's concern for this situation?"

"I hesitate to speak for my esteemed father, but I think I may say that this situation has been an insult to many Houses in this province that are loyal to the Son of Heaven, rather than to their own profit."

"What of the governor, then?"

Butta Joda laughed aloud. "Pardon my outburst, Kamu-sum. As you no doubt are aware, the Governor of Itsa Province is Lord Hajiwara's son-in-law, and loyal to the intentions of his wife's father." He said this with a trace of bitterness.

"I would not say this elsewhere, Lord Butto, but the Emperor has not paid close enough attention to your difficulties in Itsa."

The young lord nodded, but said nothing.

Kamu hesitated before speaking again. "It seems that a representative of the throne should deal with this problem, and soon." He watched Butto's expression carefully as he said this.

The youth did not hesitate. "How could this be done, Kamu-sum?"

Yes, the old warrior thought, he is interested, but is he brave enough? "It is the opinion of some members of Lord Shonto's council that the actions of the Hajiwara are outside of the laws of Wa and therefore subject to sanction. As the governor of the province, the Imperial representative has broken his oath of duty to allow his wife's family to disregard the edicts that govern the canal, it may be necessary for another to enforce those laws in his place."

"What you say is wise, Kamu-sum, but the governor is still, despite all, the representative of the Throne. To oppose him is to defy the Emperor."

"This is true, Lord Butto, but it is not necessary to oppose the governor. To do his proper duty for him, that is what I suggest. I would also suggest that another Imperial representative could take the initiative in this, thus making it clear to the Son of Heaven that this was not merely a jealousy between rival Houses."

"What you say would, no doubt, be of interest to my father, but before I approach him with your words, I cannot help but wonder where such a willing representative of the Throne could be found. The only person in Itsa with such a title is Lord Shonto, and is his fleet not trapped in the Denji Gorge by the very family we discuss?"

"Lord Shonto is an Imperial Governor; he may go where he pleases."

"Ah. Then I have misunderstood. I was under the impression that the Hajiwara . . . *hindered* Lord Shonto in his progress north."

Kamu touched his hand to his chin, considering these words carefully. "Hindered would seem a good description, Lord Butto, yes, but my lord is a most resourceful man and has found a way out of this predicament."

"This I am most happy to hear. Will he go on his way soon?"

"Not," Kamu said, "until he has dealt with this situation to his satisfaction."

"May I ask how Lord Shonto will accomplish this? I have lived beside Denji Gorge all of my life, and I confess I don't know how this could be done."

Kamu folded his hand in his lap. "It has been said that if one separates true lovers, they will find a way to surmount all difficulties that hold them apart. My lord is like this—there is no difficulty he cannot surmount."

The young man broke into a boyish smile. "The Butto are fortunate to have such a friend. My father is a loyal subject of the Emperor and willing to help his delegates in any way. Is there some specific task the Butto could perform that I may discuss with my father?"

"It is kind of you to enquire. There is something you could do which would be a great service to the Son of Heaven. . . ."

# Twenty-one

The chair Hojo Masakada rode in had once belonged to Chakao Isha, a famous general of the Dono Dynasty. Chakao Isha had been a forebear of the House of Hajiwara, so it was a great honor that they carried the emissary of Lord Shonto in such state.

Hojo Masakada thought it unfortunate that the Isha blood had been wed to, and finally found its end in, this House. He looked around at the green-liveried Hajiwara guards that accompanied him and could not tell that they were not farmers in costume.

They are a minor House in a small province, he told himself, and little different from any other in the same position. I must not forget that, at the moment, they have power over us.

The procession proceeded along a narrow road that led under long rows of peach trees. The sun cast the shadows of the almost bare, twisted branches onto the white gravel of the road, so that it appeared his bearers walked through a dark and tangled pattern.

Behind General Hojo came thirty Shonto guards in full armor and the blue livery of their House. It was a small retinue for such an occasion, but it had been calculated to appear so—an admission of the circumstances in which the Shonto found themselves.

Walls appeared at the end of the corridor of trees, the walls of a fortress, granite, like the walls that formed the famous gorge. As he drew closer, the general could see that it was a typical fortified dwelling of the country type, surrounded by a wide moat—though it appeared that this moat was not purely decorative. Unlike most other dwellings of its kind, this one was accessible only by drawbridge. It said much when a lord's home, only seven days' journey from the capital, had need of such defenses.

Hajiwara guards knelt in rows along either side of the wooden bridge as the procession passed, bowing carefully. The general wondered if the description he had read of Lord Hajiwara Harita would match the man he was about to meet. Shonto intelligence was seldom wrong, but when it came to men, Hojo liked to make his own assessments.

The Hajiwara steward received the Shonto emissary in the most formal manner. "General Hojo, my lord welcomes you to his house. His family is honored to receive you. Do you wish to refresh yourself before your audience?"

*Audience?* Hojo asked himself. Does this country lord think he sits on a throne? "I am honored that your lord receives me. The journey has been short, and I do not wish to detain your lord. If it is convenient, I would meet with him as soon as possible."

The steward bowed and the Shonto general was led up a wide flight of stone steps and through a gate. The garden they entered was of the middle Botahist period, sparsely planted, with large expanses of raked gravel broken by careful arrangements of stones—a type of garden once thought to be ideal for meditation. Behind a sculpted pine tree was a small summerhouse, and, as they rounded it, General Hojo could see, sitting inside, the large figure of the Hajiwara Lord. Hojo Masakada bowed to him and in return received a nod.

So it begins, the general thought, and entered the summerhouse.

The lord who sat before him had seen perhaps thirty-five summers, yet his face was lined like a much older man's. His hands, too, seemed to show more age—the large, tanned hands of a veteran campaigner. Yet, in contrast to this, he wore a robe of the latest and most elaborate fashion which, General Hojo thought, looked entirely out of place on the man's immense frame.

The lord welcomed him in a slow, deep tone, enquiring into the health of Lord Shonto. Cha was served and the two warriors discussed the unseasonal weather and the hunting in Itsa Province.

When the cha was gone, and the stories of hunting exhausted, Lord Hajiwara said, "I look forward to a meeting with Lord Shonto upon his recovery. I'm sure it is out of the question to move him while he is ill."

"My lord has instructed me to discuss this with you, Sire. He feels the need to continue on his way as soon as possible. He has a duty to the Emperor that cannot be ignored."

"Lord Shonto must not let duty endanger his health. It would be better for the people of Seh if their new governor would arrive with all of his strength. I'm sure the Son of Heaven would agree. Let us not speak of it any more."

The general almost smiled at this. Yes, my friend, he thought, you will have few surprises for us. "I am sure my liege-lord will be most grateful for your concern. He, too, has expressed concern for your own position, Lord Hajiwara."

The lord raised his eyebrows. "Pardon me, General—*my position?*"

"Your military situation, Sire. All of your efforts brought to a standstill, as they have been."

"Perhaps Lord Shonto is not truly aware of the situation, General, having only recently come to Itsa," the lord said, mustering all possible dignity.

Immediately, Hojo looked contrite. "I'm certain that is the case, Lord Hajiwara. It is never good to listen to the gossip around the Imperial Palace. I'm sure your position is not understood in the capital."

"They speak of my position in the capital?" The large man flushed now.

"Sire, I'm sorry to have mentioned it. You know the gossip that one hears from idle courtiers and Imperial functionaries," the general paused, "and ministers and generals."

The lord's eyes went wide. "What is it they say, General Hojo?"

"Pardon me, Sire, I do not believe what they say for a moment but . . . in the capital they say you are being mastered by a boy."

*"What!"* The lord wheeled on his guest, knocking the cups from the table. "Who dares say this? Who?"

The general began picking up the cha service hurriedly, all the while shaking his head. "Please Sire, pay no attention to this. These Imperial Guards know nothing of what happens in the provinces, truly."

The lord smashed his fist on the table. "Guardsmen! How dare they speak thus of me!"

Hojo observed every minute detail of the lord's reaction, just as Lord Shonto had instructed him. Hajiwara had responded to the mention of Imperial Guards just as Shonto had thought he would. Interesting.

"It is a despicable situation, Lord Hajiwara, and one my lord is equally offended by. So offended, in fact, that he has instructed me to relate a proposal that he believes would change your position entirely."

The lord sat upright, straightening his robe. "I do not need Lord Shonto's assistance." But then Hojo's words seemed to register. "What do you mean, *change my position?*"

"Well, if I have not been misinformed, have not the Butto established a fortress on your own fief, a fortress that has been there for several years? Has not your offensive been thwarted—for some time now, I believe. As a warrior, of course, I understand that these are only appearances, but others who are less well trained. . . ." The general gestured with an open hand. "Lord Shonto was only hoping to assist in a small way in your efforts against the arrogant Butto. Our passage through the Butto locks was hardly arranged with the honor due to an Imperial Governor! I see that it must be a constant insult to have to deal with this House headed by a boy."

"Huh! This will not continue. The Hajiwara will triumph!"

"I'm certain that is true, Sire. The information Lord

Shonto had thought to offer you would probably not change the final outcome." The general shrugged.

"But I do not wish to offend the great lord," Hajiwara said warmly, "if he has seen fit to send you with advice, then I would not think of ignoring it."

Hojo paused, thinking a long time before answering. "It is more than advice, Lord Hajiwara. Lord Shonto has intelligence that may prove of great benefit to you."

The lord assumed a posture of attentiveness. "Ah. The Shonto are known for their wisdom. I would be honored to hear Lord Shonto's words."

The general swept a drop of cha from the table absentmindedly. "If you were to know a time when Butto Joda was inspecting his defenses before the fortifications you have established on the Butto fief, would this be information you would deem useful?"

"*Indeed,* I believe it would. Do you know when this will happen?"

"We shall, Lord Hajiwara, we shall." The general regarded his companion closely.

"I see."

Neither man spoke, each hoping for the other to break the silence.

Finally, the Shonto general took the initiative. "Perhaps you should consider whether such information is of use to you, Sire," Hojo said, smiling and sitting back. He looked around him as though searching for his guard.

"This information, would it also include troop strengths and the number of Lord Butto's personal guard?"

"Of course."

"I see." The lord was deep in thought now.

General Hojo interrupted him, pressing, "This would be valuable knowledge, yeh?"

"It could be, General, it could be."

"Some would be willing to pay a great price for such information."

The lord seemed to shake himself out of his thoughts. "What you say is true, if the information were to prove correct."

"Of course, information from Lord Shonto would be above suspicion?"

"Certainly. But many things may happen between the time the information is received and the time it is to be acted upon."

"Ah. It would be best, then, if there could be mutual assurance in this matter, so that there will be no misunderstandings."

"How would this be arranged, General?"

"Half of our fleet would lock through upon receiving the information. The other half would lock through upon the fall of Butto Joda, providing he does not escape through a military error."

"I see." The lord rubbed his forehead. "For this to be truly effective, Lord Shonto must not leave the gorge until after the Butto Lord has fallen."

"It was assumed that this would be the case. His troops will stay with him, of course."

"Certainly."

"Except for those who accompany you against Butto Joda, those who will act as your personal guard."

The lord looked at Hojo in disbelief. "This cannot be, General! I have my own guard. I go nowhere without them."

General Hojo pressed his palms together, touching the fingers to his chin. "Despite your doubts, I think you should consider our proposal. It may prove very beneficial—your name will again be spoken with respect at court. The thorn will finally be drawn from your side. Speak of it with your advisors, with your kin. But do not wait too long, Lord, or the opportunity will be gone." He opened his hands to Lord Hajiwara, empty hands.

# Twenty-two

It was not an auspicious night, the night of the first-quarter moon. Dark, starless, clouded. A cold wind swept down Denji Gorge from the north, pushing the first sting of winter before it.

Shuyun ignored the chill of the wind, which tore at him as he clung to the rigging of the river junk. The ropes bit into his hands and feet, even through the strips of cotton he had wrapped so carefully around them.

The ship swayed in the darkness, buffeted by the winds that deflected off the high granite walls. Somewhere, near at hand, the cliffs lay hidden by darkness, and the ship sailed blindly toward them. Lookouts in the bow whispered anxiously among themselves, but their voices were carried off into the night. At least the Hajiwara soldiers would hear nothing over the voice of the Wind God.

The ship pitched, causing Shuyun to hug the rigging to him with all his strength. Below him, in the blackness, Lord Komawara waited, no doubt suffering the same discomfort, the same misgivings. Rain, Shuyun thought, will it rain? It was the only thing that would, with certainty, destroy their plans, leaving Lord Shonto trapped by the feuding houses. A blast of wind seemed to fall on them from directly above, shaking the ship as though it were but a floating leaf. And then it was gone, soaring over the wave tops.

Shuyun peered into the night, willing his eyes not to play tricks. Was that something there, off the starboard bow? The wind howled off the rock, like an evil spirit screaming into his ear. That sound . . . we must be close.

Yes! There! He reached down with his foot until he felt
Komawara's cold hand. The young lord understood—the
monk felt him move up another step.

Shuyun remembered the resistance this plan had pro-
voked among Shonto's generals and he wondered now if
he had been wrong to recommend it.

The wall of stone seemed to draw closer, though in
the dark it was difficult to judge—dark against dark.

Shuyun moved up the rope steps one by one, careful
not to lose his grip. The pitching of the ship was ampli-
fied more with each step. When he reached the top of
the mast, he knew it would be describing a long, quick
arc. The ship altered to port now, the sailors hoping to
ease alongside the wall—without becoming its victim.
The sculling oar pushed them on, rags silencing its inevitable creaking. Shuyun moved up again as he felt Lord
Komawara stop at his feet. He is strong, the monk
thought, but he is not Botahist trained. He did not scale
cliffs as a child to learn to control fear, to learn focus.

The walls were there now, solidly unmistakable, yet
the distance to them was still not clear. Shuyun began
searching for signs of the sculpture above him. His examination of the Lovers had revealed that there was a ledge,
or so it appeared, at the bottom of the stone relief. How
wide it was could not be seen, but it was there that they
must begin the climb. In the darkness below, Shuyun
could sense the presence of the sailors ready to carry out
their orders.

A gust of wind seemed to counter the motion of the
ship, and Shuyun used the few seconds of reduced
pitching to move up to the top of the mast. He was high
above the waters now, ten times the height of a man at
least, and the motion was terrible. Encircling the mast
with his arms, Shuyun held tightly to it; the wood was
cold against his face. All the while he tried to feel rain
in the force of the wind.

They were parallel to the cliff face now and the helms-
man, the best in Shonto's fleet, edged them closer. The
swell running in the lake was not large, but the winds

coming from all directions defied any attempt to compensate for their effects.

Shuyun tried to penetrate the darkness, looking for the ledge he knew must be there.

"The gunwhale of the ship almost scrapes the stone, Brother." Komawara's voice came to him—a whisper out of the darkness, out of the wind.

Yes, Shuyun thought, now is the time. And, as though his thoughts had been heard, the men below began to ease the lines they had set to the masthead. The spar, steadied by many guy lines, leaned toward the cliff face. It will work, Shuyun told himself, if we are not dashed against the rock.

He braced his foot on the mast and turned toward the cliff as best he could. He felt along the coil of rope over his head and shoulder to be sure that it would not snag as he jumped.

But still the cliff face seemed blank, featureless. The pitching of the boat threw the mast toward the rock and Shuyun braced himself for the impact—but it did not come, not this time.

There! A change in the blank stone, a shape that he could not be sure of—a curve, an area of gray. There was nothing else it could be. The sculpture was the only feature that broke the uniformity of the granite. The ledge should be directly below, Shuyun thought, and he prepared to leap, using every sense his teachers had trained, trusting them, for it was a leap of faith he would make, he had no doubt. He contolled his breathing, stretching his time sense, and felt the motion of the boat slow. The mast heaved toward the rock again and Shuyun focused all of his consciousness on its path.

There will be a split second when it stops, he thought. Then I must jump without hesitation or it will return and my jump will become a fall.

The huge spar seemed to attain an even greater speed, careening toward the granite wall, and then, just as quickly, it stopped. Shuyun leapt, crouching like a cat tossed by a child.

His feet and hands hit the shattered rock of the ledge

and he was thrown, shoulder first, into the cliff face. I am not injured, he told himself, and was up, feeling his way along the ledge in the direction the ship moved. He could hear nothing above the howl of the wind, the crash of the waves.

His hands groped before him, feeling the way. Thank Botahara, the ledge is wide, he thought as he went, and indeed it was, as wide as a man's shoulders, But it was broken and sloped and littered with moss and fallen stone. He scrambled on as quickly as he dared. Where was Komawara?

Suddenly his senses warned him, and he dropped flat to the stone as a body crashed into the rock above him. He made a desperate grab as the figure fell past and caught Komawara by his robe. The young lord lay half off the ledge now, dangling out over the dark waters, but he made no move to save himself.

*Dazed,* the monk thought. He felt himself slipping over the stone, Komawara's weight pulling him toward the edge. His hand scrabbled along the back of the ledge for a hold to pull against. His fingers curled around the stem of some stunted brush and he heaved against the dead weight of the young warrior.

*Let it hold,* Shuyun prayed. Komawara stirred, trying to pull free, but then he came to his senses and his hand grasped the monk by the back of his neck. He made a feeble effort to pull himself up. The bark of the bush began to slough off, letting go of its own stem like the skin of a shedding snake. Shuyun gripped it tighter, trying to bend it back on itself. Slowly Komawara came up over the edge, using the monk as a ladder. And then he lay on top of him for a long moment, gasping for breath.

"Are you injured, Lord?"

"No . . . I don't know, I'm. . . ." Komawara shook his head. He moved his left arm. "I am unhurt, Brother." He pushed himself off the monk and into a sitting position against the wall, the sword strapped to his back digging into his muscles.

"We must continue," Komawara said.

Shuyun sat also, concerned, afraid that the young lord

was not telling the truth about his injuries. Knowing also that Komawara was right.

The wind screamed at them for a long moment and neither of them moved or tried to speak. When it abated, Shuyun stood, running his hands along the rock face. "We must determine our position," he whispered. Moving to his left, he continued, testing the ledge with his feet, running his hands along the stone wall. Komawara followed him as he went, though the lord did not rise to his feet, preferring to keep himself close to the rock.

After a moment of exploration, Shuyun felt the granite swelling out toward him, reducing the width of the ledge. It is the foot of Botahara's Bride, Shuyun realized. So it was still a good distance to the cracks he had seen in the stone that would, he hoped, offer them purchase on the sheer face.

Shuyun reached as far as he could around the smooth projection. Wide, it was wide. Here, on the rock itself, he began to get a sense of the true scale of the carvings. The foot was probably three times the height of a man, and all else was in proportion to that.

He knelt down then and leaning out precariously, he explored the narrowing ledge, testing the stone, brushing it clean of debris. It was then that the Wind God struck, attacking the poorly balanced monk without warning. Shuyun's supporting hand came off the ledge and he pitched forward, but then he felt a pull on his sash, and he was safe. A voice close to his ear said, "My debt is repaid, Brother." And Komawara let the monk go.

Pushing the coil of rope over his head, Shuyun passed it to his companion before tying the end around his waist. This time he felt the tautness of the rope Komawara held as he leaned out to run his hand along the ledge.

Narrow, it became very narrow—no wider than a man's hand was long. He came back onto the ledge, another gust of cold wind tearing at them.

"We must not hesitate, Brother. There is the smell of rain in this air."

Shuyun nodded to the darkness. "If I slip, you must not fall with me. Let me go if you must."

"I understand." Komawara answered.

On his feet again, Shuyun moved to the narrowing of the ledge. He paused for a moment to push himself farther into chi ten; a blast of wind struck the ledge, but Shuyun seemed to have so much time to counter it.

Komawara's voice came to him, as though from the bottom of a pit. "Are you ready, Brother?"

"Yes," Shuyun answered, and stepped out onto the narrow edge. Against his hands the rock was smooth, featureless. He felt with his feet, edging along the shelf, testing each step. He faced the rock, careful to keep his body out, balanced over his feet. The sound of the waves echoed up from below, reminding him of what lay beneath, wrapped in darkness.

Shuyun came to the widest point of the giant foot and the ledge disapeared. He stopped and balanced himself. Reaching up with his left hand, he searched the stone for any irregularity, any break in the granite. There was nothing. He could hear Komawara shifting impatiently. I must be bold, Shuyun thought. He stretched to the limit of his balance and found a tiny edge—half the width of his fingertip, but an edge. Bracing himself, he tested it. It held. He risked a little more weight on it.

Yes, Shuyun decided, it will do. He pulled some rope from Komawara so he would have no resistance to work against, and then swung out into space. His left foot scrabbled on the hard stone, desperately searching. It was only then that he realized he could not return—there was no way to pull himself back to the ledge!

I am in the hands of Botahara, he told himself, and let his right foot slide off the safety of the ledge. He hung there by one hand, trying to reach around the swelling in the stone with his foot.

"The ledge must go on," he told himself, and brought his right hand up to the tiny edge to which he clung. There was only room for two fingers, but that would do. He called chi into his hands and took his weight on the two-fingered hold. In a smooth easy motion, his left hand moved in an arc out to his side. Yes! There, a vertical crack that took his fingers to the first knuckle. He pulled himself left, searching with his foot until he found flat stone. In one quick motion he pulled himself onto it, his breathing still even, unlabored.

"Praise to my teachers," he whispered, as he began exploring the rock with his hands. Following the crack up, he found it formed a cleft in the rock. He ran the rope through this natural groove, and began to draw it in. When he had taken in all the slack, he signaled his companion with two light tugs.

It was impossible to tell Komawara how he had found his way around, but with the rope positioned as it was, Shuyun felt confident that he could hold the young lord in case of a fall.

Shuyun tried to guess Komawara's movements by what happened to the rope. It slackened slightly, and Shuyun pulled it taut, taking it around his waist, sure that his companion was out on the narrowing ledge now. More rope came free and he gathered it in. He will come to the end of the ledge in another step, Shuyun thought. The rope stopped. The monk kept a light but positive pressure on it, reading Komawara's progress as though the line were a nerve connecting them.

He cannot find the way, Shuyun realized. He waited, willing the lord to reach out, to push himself. But there was no change in the tension on the rope. If he stays too long he will grow tired, his focus will waver, and he will lose his nerve.

Another moment passed, and Shuyun decided he could wait no longer. Slowly, but with great strength, he began to take in the rope. It will pull him up and to his left, the monk thought. Will he understand?

The wind continued its shrill chorus, whipping dust up from the ledge and shaking the monk's robe like an untended sail. There was only the same resistance on the rope, no sign that Komawara moved on. Then there was a sharp tug, then another. Shuyun answered it. He braced himself, and felt the increase of weight as the rope bit into his muscles. There was another tug and Shuyun realized that the warrior had not found the hand-hold, but instead was using the rope—climbing it hand over hand. Shuyun wrapped the rough fibers of the line tighter around him and waited. A second later, Komawara swung smoothly onto the ledge. Even above the sound of the wind, Shuyun could hear his ragged breathing.

Fear, the monk realized, and its odor was carried to him on the air before it was swept off into the night.

"Can you continue, Lord?" Shuyun asked.

Komawara fought to control himself. "Yes . . . don't be concerned. We must go on." He rose to his knees and began to coil the rope.

Shuyun waited a moment and then, tugging at Komawara's sleeve, he led on. The ledge did not change for several paces, but then they found some loose blocks of stone that the elements, ice and wind and sun, had pried from the solid cliff. Shuyun rocked the first block and decided it would hold. The others were much the same, though several small pieces had fallen away and others of similar size were ready to go. The two men picked their way across the rubble, realizing that even the storm would not hide the sound of sliding rock.

Again they came to a place where the stone seemed to swell out from the face of the cliff, though not as dramatically this time. The hip of the Bride, Shuyun thought, and the image on the wall seemed almost to taunt him. Shuyun felt along the walls here, looking for the cracks that he had seen running up the length of the relief.

In the darkness on the lake the lights of Shonto's fleet could be seen bobbing and swaying in the waves. They seemed far off now, far off and very small. He is a great general, Shuyun told himself; everything that could be done to insure our success has been done. If only the others do not fail. The plan depended on so many different elements, so many different people.

Shuyun pushed these thoughts from his mind as he came to the point he had looked for. He explored the cracks as far up as he could reach. They were smoother inside than he would have expected, older and more worn, but they were wider than he had dared hope. He thrust his hand into one and found it as wide as his fist and quite deep.

Now, Shuyun thought, we will see if the long hours of discussion with Lord Komawara will have been worth the effort. Shuyun retied the knot around his chest and made sure that Komawara had untied his. Taking a moment to compose himself, Shuyun searched his inner self to be sure that he had, as his teachers said, tranquillity of purpose.

He began to climb, twisting his cotton-wrapped feet and hands into the crack, forcing himself up the fracture in the stone. The rope was the length of twenty-five men, as long as he dared carry without fear of tangling, and Komawara carried a similar length. If the window they climbed toward was higher than their estimate, they would be unable to drop the rope back to the waters. Shuyun climbed, emptying his mind of such doubts, filling it with the convolutions of the stone, with each measured movement.

The wind tried to grasp him, but he could not be pried loose. The skin on his knuckles tore and both his ankle bones seeped fluid from their contact with the stone. Shuyun felt as though he climbed up into the spirit world, and though he did not consider himself superstitious, he felt a presence, as though the long vanquished Brothers hovered about him, still clinging to the earthly plane.

*There, there is our enemy, they would say. He climbs across the hip of Botahara's Bride as though it were not sacrilege to do so! May he fall into eternal darkness!*

The rock canted in slightly as he crossed the cold stone hip and he stopped to rest a moment before going on. A lifetime of Botahist training came into play, chi flowed into his arms and legs and, even against the unpredictable winds, his balance remained perfect.

He reached the point where the bodies of the Lovers joined. No amount of training had prepared him to meet this sight on such close terms.

"Heresy," Shuyun whispered to himself.

The very rock seemed to be stained with this crime. And yet he clung to it for his life.

It was only then that he realized he had stopped climbing, and this lapse shocked him. In his mind he began a chant to Botahara, attempting to regain his focus. The life of my liege-lord depends on my success, he told himself, and the lives of all his retainers and family.

*"Lady Nishima."* The whisper came to his lips unbidden. He leaned his head against the cold stone. I am unworthy of the efforts of my teachers, he thought. He began his chant again and started up the crack that led over the hip of the figure of the Perfect Master. In his mind he measured the rope that he had used and guessed that Lord Komawara still held half of it. The crack suddenly became deeper and wider, and Shuyun found that he could sink his arm in to its full length. It continued to grow as he progressed upward and he pushed his shoulder into the crevice.

Wind seemed to funnel down this widened fissure—a cold hand pushing him down—and he fought against it. Finally, after a long struggle, his fingers found the top of the stone hip and he realized then that it was formed by a narrow ledge. He pulled himself up onto it, struggling against the rock which seemed to clutch at his clothes and snag the rope.

Peering into the darkness, Shuyun tried to follow the path of the ledge. The gray line of its edge seemed to rise up on a steep diagonal, but then it blended into the colors of the night and Shuyun was unsure of its direction. He searched his memory of the relief, but it made no sense to him. The back of Botahara? Could it be? What else could be rising at that angle? He had crossed the sculpture at its thinnest section, so it was possible. The window they hoped to enter was almost directly above him now, but perhaps this ledge offered unexpected possibilities.

Bracing his feet against the ledge, Shuyun wedged himself back into the crack and began to take in the rope. When he reached the end, he gave it two light tugs and waited to feel Lord Komawara begin his ascent.

The wind did not seem about to abate, but continued to scream and fly in every direction like a mad dragon.

Komawara was only a few feet below Shuyun before the monk heard the sounds of his approach. It had seemed to take Komawara an age to reach the ledge, but Shuyun had not once felt the weight of the warrior on the rope.

With some difficulty Komawara found his way past Shuyun's feet and levered himself onto the ledge. He fought to regain his breath and his muscles were trembling with the exertion.

"Where?" Komawara said, finally.

"You sit astride the back of the Faceless Lover," Shuyun whispered.

"But what is this ledge?"

"The arch of His back. A ledge used long ago to drape material for festivals."

"Does it lead to a window, then?"

"It is not likely, Sire, the ancient monks were too careful. The ledge would have been reached by ropes or ladders. There should be an opening below us, though farther to the left. It is a question of whether it will be easier and quicker to continue up as we are or to cross the ledge and lower ourselves to the opening which we shall have to find in the dark."

Komawara was silent, thinking. "Surely, Brother, this opening to our left will be closer to the water and therefore will make an easier ascent for Shonto's soldiers."

Shuyun realized that in this darkness it was impossible to know which route would be easier. There was something attractive about the ledge, it was there and substantial, and somehow not as intimidating as climbing up again into total darkness.

"I think we should explore this ledge, Lord Komawara. It is as you say; we shall be lower this way, and there is little doubt that our ropes will reach."

With that, the monk stepped over his companion and set out along the ledge. He moved on his hands and knees at first, but as the ledge narrowed he dropped to his belly. The surface beneath him continued to shrink and Shuyun was forced to hang his leg and arm over the side. He crawled on, his eyes closed against the dust whipped off the ledge by the wind. Twice he was forced

to climb past areas where the stone had cracked and
fallen away, but these only slowed his progress and tested
his skill.

The ledge ended abruptly in a small platform, confirm-
ing Shuyun's theory that the monks had gained access to
them by ladder or rope. Searching with his bleeding fingers, he found a crack that ran along the back of the
ledge, but nothing wide enough for him to use as purchase or into which he could jam a knot.

Komawara will have to make the traverse alone. I cannot save him if he falls, or I will be swept from the ledge
myself. Untying the rope from his chest, he pulled in the
slack and gave Komawara the signal they had agreed
upon—two tugs, a pause, and then one more. A second
later the rope went slack, Shuyun took it in carefully,
arranging it so he would not be tangled in it should
Komawara fail.

Twice the intake of rope stopped, as Komawara found
his way past the breaks in the ledge, and each time Shuyun controlled his urge to take the line around his waist.
But then the line came in again as it had before.

They hardly dared speak when Komawara arrived on
the platform, they were so unsure of the location of the
opening they sought.

Komawara put his mouth close to Shuyun's ear. "Is it
not directly below, Brother?" Even in the darkness Shuyun could tell that the lord rubbed his eyes, trying to
free them of the dust.

"I cannot be sure." Shuyun whispered back. "It should
be nearby, perhaps three heights below, but to the left."

Komawara leaned over the edge, feeling with his hand.
When he sat back he again whispered into the monk's
ear. "The rock seems sheer—without holds. How?"

Shuyun felt again into the crack along the wall. "Your
sword, Lord Komawara, it must be the anchor." He took
the young warrior's hand and showed him the opening.

"*We must think of something else!*—my *sword!* It was
my father's—I cannot leave it."

Shuyun put his hand on the other's arm. "We have
nothing else."

The wind whirled about them, buffeting them on their small ledge. Deliberately, Komawara began to undo the harness that held his weapon. In a moment he had the sword and scabbard off and handed them to Shuyun without a word. Using the tip of the sheathed weapon, Shuyun explored the crevice, probing until he found the deepest spot, and here he pushed the scabbard and sword in the length of a man's hand. He tied the rope carefully around the weapon, working the knot down as far as he could.

"It is best that I go first, Sire. Perhaps, without a weapon, I will have an advantage." Not waiting for a reply, Shuyun took the rope around his waist and slipped over the edge of the rock.

The wind seemed far greater on the exposed face of the cliff. He put his feet against the stone and leaned back, but the wind seemed to rock him, pushing him first one way then another. Letting the rope slip slowly across the cotton wrappings on his hands, Shuyun swung himself downward, placing each foot with care.

The window must be nearby, Shuyun thought. He tried to peel aside the layers of darkness, but his eyes told him nothing. A smell came to him on the wind—salt, sweat, and oil. He turned his head, searching for the source of the scent. There! He smelled it again. Moving to the left, Shuyun tried to trace the odor. Yes, he thought, it comes from over here. He moved a step farther, but his foot began to slip and then stopped. As he moved off to the side of his point of attachment, like a pendulum he would tend to swing back toward the center. He forced himself over two more steps, but could go no farther. Was that a line there in the darkness—a hint of light?

Suddenly a voice drifted to him, though it might have been a trick of the wind. Lower, the monk thought, and let some rope slide through his hands. Again! He could almost make out the words now. He lowered himself farther, trying to grip the granite with his feet, forcing himself to the left.

"There is much movement on the plain tonight." The voice seemed almost at Shuyun's elbow!

"It is to do with Lord Shonto. Perhaps he will help our lord rid this land of those cattle thieves."

"Huh! It will be a warm winter when the Shonto and the Hajiwara become allies."

"Well, it has been a warm autumn, until today. Perhaps that is a sign. Please excuse me, I have duties to attend to."

Shuyun could almost hear them bowing in the dark. He realized that he must go lower, but first he must return to the center of his pendulum.

It would not be possible to move across as far as the opening without chancing a slip which could alert the Hajiwara guard to his presence. There was only one sure way to reach the window.

Shuyun moved to his right, away from the opening, pushing himself as far as he could. And then he waited for the Wind God to favor him. He chanted silently and prepared himself as if to spar. What is good for the Shonto will be good for my Order, he told himself. Yet he felt apprehension—not fear, but an anxiety that he would be forced to do battle in earnest. May I be forced to hurt no one, he prayed. The Brotherhood has fought battles before, Shuyun told himself, and though they were to insure the safety of the followers of Botahara, this is no different. Lord Shonto supports the Botahist religion against the wishes of the Emperor and therefore he deserves our complete loyalty.

Shuyun had no way of knowing where the guard would stand, or if he was in the opening at all. It seemed likely that the weather would force him back into the rock as far as duty would allow.

He braced himself, feeling the wind backing. When it favored him entirely, Shuyun ran across the face of the rock, becoming a human pendulum. He judged his distance to the window by his steps, steps which seemed unbelievably slow to his altered time sense. The stone seemed rough against his foot, rough and cold. His momentum grew until it carried him far into the arc.

The door should be here, the monk thought, and there in the dark rock a line appeared. He grasped the line—a hard edge of stone, and pulled himself into the opening. He hit the stone floor and carreened across it into the other side of the window. The sound of a sword coming out of its scabbard brought him to his knees. He could see the guard silhouetted against a dull glow that came from somewhere inside. Reaching out, Shuyun grasped the soldier by his armor, and, in one smooth motion, pulled the man toward him. The soldier fell forward, the blow he had aimed going wild, and then he was in the air. A scream seemed to come out of the wind, and the man was gone. There was only the noise of the waves below. May Botahara have mercy on him, Shuyun prayed, and on me.

Shuyun crept back into the light of the tunnel. It opened into a large room with a high, round ceiling that had the signs of a typical guard station—the remains of a meal, weapons neatly arranged, a single lamp on the table. There was no one there. Shuyun went to the door carved into the back wall and found an unlighted stairway that led upward. He heard no sound but the rushing of the wind as it funneled through the rock.

*The rope!* He had lost his grip on the rope! It was gone, lost in the darkness where Lord Komawara awaited his signal!

Shuyun ran back to the window. The wind made his eyes run with tears and he tried to shield them with his hand. In the darkness he could see nothing. Komawara must have my signal or it will be impossible for him to make a decision, Shuyun realized. He will not know if I have fallen or been taken.

Returning to the chamber, Shuyun looked for something, anything, that would help him reach the rope. A long spear with a barbed tip leaned against the wall. He took it up and felt its weight. Yes, he thought. A noise came from the stairway and Shuyun crouched, listening, ready to strike. It is only the wind taunting me, he thought.

Crossing to the window, he leaned out, blinded by the

force of the wind. He realized he had no time to spare, not knowing when the guard might be changed. When the wind veered toward him and he judged the rope would blow nearer, Shuyun reached out blindly with the spear. Something soft seemed to roll under the shaft as he pulled it along the rock, but it did not catch on the barb. Again the wind offered him a chance, but this time he did not feel the rope at all. If it catches on a projection, I am lost, the monk thought. Forcing a calm over himself he waited, dividing his attention between the direction of the wind and the stairway.

The fifth time the Wind God favored him, he felt the rope snag on the tip. Slowly and with great effort, Shuyun brought the rope toward him, never easing the pressure of the spear against the wall. Suddenly it was in his hand and he grasped it as though it were his line to life. Shuyun was about to signal Komawara but stopped. He laid the spear across the opening and tied the line to it. Back in the room he found a strong dagger in a sheath, and he tied it to the rope. He signaled his companion to take in, and then waited, keeping the bitter end in his hand.

When Komawara finally descended, Shuyun braced himself against the stone and pulled the lord across the cliff to the safety of the tunnel.

Feeling his feet on a solid stone floor, the young man clapped the monk on the back in a most disrespectful manner. "I shall tell Lord Shonto of your bravery, Brother. Never would I have climbed here alone. *And my sword* . . ." he bowed deeply. "I thank you." He glowed with the elation of one who has risked great danger and survived.

"There will be time later for discussion, Sire, but you must guard the door while I make the sign."

Komawara's face changed at the monk's words. He nodded, and drawing his weapon he went to the stairs.

Shuyun took the shield from the lamp and went to the door. May the watchmen be alert, he thought. Careful not to allow the wind to kill the flame, Shuyun gave the signal and waited. The lights on the lead ship died altogether as though the wind had had its way.

Now, Shuyun thought, we must lower the rope and hold this room at all costs. He returned to the chamber.

"They have seen," he told Lord Komawara.

It was in the hands of Lord Shonto's boatmen and soldiers now. The sound of the wind and the waves beating against the rock did not change. It is not done yet, Shuyun thought. He waited by the window, ready to pull up the rope ladder. The wind moaned all around him, and it was almost a moan of pleasure.

# Twenty-three

Dressed in full armor, with helmet and face-mask, Lord Hajiwara crossed the small yard of the keep accompanied by six Shonto officers and an equal number of his own guard. The rattle of armor could be heard everywhere in the dim light, as fifty Shonto soldiers prepared to escort Lord Hajiwara into battle.

The sound and smell of horses permeated the cool air and a shrill wind whistled among the towers, causing the many banners to flutter and crack.

The Shonto general, Hojo Masakado, almost ran to keep up with the giant stride of Lord Hajiwara.

"There must be no time wasted, General Hojo. None at all."

"My men await you, Sire."

They came to a stone stairway which they mounted two abreast. At the top, a platform looked out across the plain, yet in the storm and the darkness, nothing could be seen. Dust, collected by the dry autumn, filled the air and stung the eyes.

"Damn this wind!" Hajiwara said.

"It shall be the perfect mask, Sire," General Hojo said quietly.

"Yes, but it will also be the perfect screen." He stared out into the darkness, into the cloud of dust. "So, Butto Joda, you think to hide behind the skirt of the night." He banged a gloved fist against the stone parapet and then turned to his aides who dropped to their knees.

"All is ready, Sire," a senior officer reported.

"Then we must not hesitate," Hajiwara said, and strode across the platform to another set of stairs.

General Hojo jumped to his side. "This is not the way, Sire! My men await us here." He pointed back to the courtyard. A Hajiwara guard stepped between his lord and the general and swords were drawn all around. Hajiwara guards seemed to materialize out of the shadows and the Shonto men found themselves surrounded.

Drawing himself up, the general stared at the Hajiwara lord. "This is treachery," Hojo almost hissed. "Lord Shonto is not a man to trifle with. I strongly advise you to reconsider." The Shonto officers formed themselves into a tight knot around their commander.

Hajiwara stopped at the head of the stairway. "*Treachery*, General Hojo?" His voice sounded unreal through the metal of his face-mask. "These are strong words. I do this to assure myself that there will be no treachery. If the information your lord has provided proves to be true, then you shall be freed and your lord sped on his way. You may be sure of this. I take only the precautions any man would take—any man who was not the fool I seem to have been taken for. Be at your ease, General. You shall be treated with all due respect. Please see that your men cooperate." The lord gave a quick nod and disappeared down the stairway.

The Captain of the Hajiwara guard stepped forward and nodded, pointing with his sword to the stairs the men had ascended. Not exposing their backs, the Shonto soldiers passed down to the courtyard where their fellow soldiers waited.

So, General Hojo thought as he assessed the situation around him, Hajiwara is not the fool we had taken him for. Why, then, is he out chasing phantoms in the storm, while I am here, at the heart of the fortress that controls the locks to Denji Gorge?

Butto Joda dismounted and his horse was led away by an armed aide. The sounds of horses, stamping in agitation, mingled with the wail of the storm.

The Dragon Wind, the young lord thought, but who will it assist tonight? He sat upon his camp stool and a guard handed him a war fan bearing the Butto seal. Senior officers knelt waiting in the dim light of torches.

From this position on the hilltop the young lord could see the many fires of the two armies that faced each other on the broad plain. Far off, the lights of the Imperial Guard Keep, now occupied by the Hajiwara, were just visible, and to their left, the long black line of Denji Gorge bordered the entire plain.

If only we can trust the Shonto, the lord thought. They have lied to one or the other of us, there is no doubt of that. I pray to Botahara it is as I believe and removal of the Hajiwara is their true goal. He touched his forehead in the sign of obeisance to Botahara.

A senior general came forward and knelt before his young lord. "An army moves over the plain, Sire, though it is difficult to know how large a force it is. Our spies tell us that, even in this storm, it is clear the Hajiwara soldiers make preparations."

The young lord nodded, deep in thought. In his armor, laced in black and Butto purple, Joda looked even smaller and younger than usual, yet his generals showed no sign of lack of confidence in their lord. All waited, ready to carry out his orders without question.

"And what of the Butto, have we made our preparations?"

"The armies await your commands, Sire," the general said. "And the *goat* has been staked in the field. We wait only for the *leopard*."

Butto Joda nodded. "Our soldiers must be patient yet. The *leopard* comes to us. The Hajiwara will attack first, they must. And we will pull back in disarray, drawing them farther into Butto lands. A single battle stands between us and the victory we have so long prayed for. Bring me good news to take to your lord, my father. Let it be said that, in his lifetime, the Butto finally had retribution for generations of compromised honor."

The wind curled and howled around them, making speech impossible, but then it seemed to rise and throw itself at the sky. "It is a sign!" Butto Joda said. "The Dragon Wind comes to aid the Butto, have no doubt!"

The young lord reached up and tightened the cord on his helmet, and all of his retainers did the same.

Horses pawed the ground and snorted as the dragon howled around them. Their manes streamed in the wind, dancing in the torchlight. And then soldiers pushed the torches into the sand and the darkness was complete.

The hundredth Shonto soldier scrambled over the ledge, clawing his way up the cargo nets that had been made into a giant rope ladder. He nodded to Shuyun, observing some formality even in such circumstances.

Can they not come more quickly? Shuyun wondered, though he knew there really was nothing that could be done about it. Holding a boat next to the cliff was an almost impossible task in this storm. Two soldiers had been lost already—swept under by the weight of their armor when the boat lurched.

Leaving the soldiers to tend to their arriving companions, Shuyun entered the chamber of stone, and signaled Lord Komawara. They crossed to the stairway. It was time to see what lay ahead. The monk had a rough idea of what to expect in such a temple, for all Botahist fanes had certain things in common. But he also realized the sect that had dwelt here so long ago would no doubt have had their own needs.

The walls of the stairway had once been painted with elaborate figures, many in the act of love. They were difficult to discern now, for the centuries had not been kind to them. Ancient written characters left Botahara's word carved into the rock, but painted over them in many places were the blasphemies of heretics and nonbelievers.

The stairs seemed to twist up into the rock of the cliff so that soon the little light that came from below was gone. Komawara chanced a slight opening of his bronze lantern, but this showed no change—the stairs continued their long spiral. The two climbed on, making as little noise as they could, which slowed their progress painfully. Around the next corner a dull glow seemed to

come from above and the warrior and the monk slowed
their pace even more.

The stairs ended at a door in the rock and it was from
here that the light came. Komawara drew his sword, but
Shuyun stepped past him to approach the opening. Stopping to listen, he pushed chi through his body and slowed
his time sense; when he moved again, Lord Komawara
was unable to believe the speed of his motion.

The door opened into a corridor wide enough for four
men abreast. The sound of the storm was less here, but
the air still rushed and funneled through the doors and
tunnels.

This will be the level of the three windows, Shuyun
thought. I am in the hall that connects them. He stepped
farther into the corridor, looking toward the source of
the light. An eerie wail came from behind and Shuyun
whirled toward it . . . but there was nothing there except
the wind.

The voice of the dead Brothers is still in the wind, the
monk thought, and he turned back to the light. It seemed
to come from a door on the right. An inner chamber,
Shuyun thought, and signaled Komawara to wait while
he investigated. The lord took up a position in the doorway where he could watch the hall at the monk's back.

Shuyun moved forward, seeming to flow like a Sonsa.
His bare feet made no sound on the cold stone.

As he came close to the door, there was a noise from
the hallway's end—footsteps and the rattle of armor. A
light illuminated the opening and Shuyun could see
stairs. He stepped back, ready to run, but realized there
was no time. A soldier appeared, lamp in hand, his eyes
fixed to the floor in front of him. He was three steps
into the corridor before he looked up and saw the monk
crouched in the half-light.

The soldier's eyes went wide and he stopped. *"Spirit-
walker!"* he whispered and turned and fled.

Alerted by the noise, a second soldier appeared in the
door to the right. He, too, recoiled in shock at the sight
of the monk and Shuyun used the second of surprise to
drive a soft-fist into the bridge of the man's nose. There

was a "crack" like the sound of a breaking board and the guard fell to the stone in a heap. Shuyun jumped into the room and with a sweeping motion of his left hand deflected the blow of a second guard. Stepping aside, the monk found the center of resistance in his opponent and easily propelled the man across the hall into the solid granite wall. He fell and did not move.

Komawara was beside the monk now, sword in hand. "Did one escape, Brother?"

Shuyun nodded as he knelt to tie the guards.

"Then we are discovered! He will sound the alarm." The young lord's face twisted in what seemed like pain. "We have failed."

"I don't think we have, Sire. The guard is sure he saw a Spirit-walker—a ghost of the dead Brothers who once dwelt here. No doubt he is frightening his companions with his tale even now. I think no one will venture down here while this storm lasts. But we must be sure this level is secure so that no one escapes with the truth."

The lord nodded and was off to the other doors without hesitation, moving with the assurity and grace of a falcon about to strike.

Shonto slid his brush carefully across his inkstone and went back to the paper he worked on. *No man knows the weaknesses of his own child,* the lord wrote. *And no man knows the strength of the tree by the shape of the seed.*

It was an exercise Shonto had done a thousand times— ever since he was a child, in fact. He formed each character with the utmost care, focusing all of his attention on every stroke of the brush. *To exist beyond the world, beyond the emotions, in the purity of the act itself, that is tranquillity of purpose.* He inked his brush again and stopped to examine his effort. Was that the slightest sign of a shake? Had his attention wandered?

He set his brush to paper again, recopying the line that dissatisfied him. There was no reason for the brush work not to be perfect. The plan would work or it would not, and if it did, the fleet would be in the locks before

dawn. Then, and only then, would Shonto have things
to deal with. Until that time, thinking of what might or
might not be happening was of no use.

*Speak carelessly and your orders will be followed in the
same spirit.* The brush moved on the paper without
sound, and the lord bent over his work in total
concentration.

A horse galloped up the hill, rising with such speed it
seemed as though it were borne by the wind itself. Lord
Hajiwara listened to the sound as though he would tell
the news by the haste of the rider. It was the hour of
the dove, he guessed as he gazed up. The sky was broken
and ragged, clouds sailing like a fleet before the wind.
The quarter-moon glowed from behind a cloud on the
western horizon and in the east there would soon be the
beginnings of dawn. Around him, on the shoulders of
the hill, Hajiwara could see the signs of battle—fallen
soldiers and horses—though the color of their livery was
not visible.

*"Who wins the battle by night?"* Hajiwara said to himself, posing the question from an old adage. *"Those who
see the day break."*

The wind had not fallen and its howl mixed with the
sound of the battle that was still raging. It was a strange,
unsettling storm and none the less so for being dry. No
rain had fallen and now the clouds broke up and scattered as though they had accomplished their purpose.

The horse slowed at the outer ring of guards and then
raced on to the hilltop. Reining in his mount, the rider
appeared in the torchlight, a lieutenant attached to the
lord's staff. He dismounted as a guard hurried to take
the bridle, and then went directly to Lord Hajiwara. He
bowed without any sign of haste, and then pulled open
his face-mask. His mouth was surrounded by a black ring
where dust had stuck to sweat.

"Lieutenant?" the general at Lord Hajiwara's right
prompted.

"Sire, I come to report that we have taken Lord Butto
Joda."

Lord Hajiwara nodded and opened his face-mask. His staff knelt around him, bowing as the lord offered his thanks to the gods.

"Where is the vanquished lord?" Hajiwara asked. "You say you have 'taken him'?"

"Sire, he was captured unharmed and has been brought safely through the lines, though not without pursuit. I came ahead to allow you time to prepare."

The lord nodded and then he and his staff sat without discussion or sign of impatience. They noted the beauty and tranquillity of the moon in contrast to the sounds of battle. They reflected upon the state of their own spirits at that instant. The Hajiwara had waited generations for this; they intended now to make the moment perfect.

Horses galloped, a resonance like a heart pounding out of control. Twenty men slowed for the guards and then pushed on. In the half light the Hajiwara green was visible and, as the riders grew closer, purple on one horseman no bigger than a child. They reined in and untied the child from the saddle. He was forced to his knees before Lord Hajiwara, arms tied behind his back.

"Do you not bow, Lord Butto Joda?" Hajiwara asked quietly.

The figure in black and purple made no move but remained still and, somehow, dignified. Hajiwara gave a signal to his general who nodded to a guard who stepped forward and removed the young lord's face-mask and helmet. He pushed the boy's face down to the ground and then stepped back.

"Look up, young lord, see what your family's pride has brought you."

Slowly, ever so slowly, the boy rose until the flickering light of the torches illuminated his child's face. Hajiwara was on his feet, his sword half out. He glared at those around him like a crazed man who has discovered that everyone is a traitor. And all of the faces went pale with the realization.

*"Get him out of my sight!"* Hajiwara screamed.

"Sire, we did not know. . . . We thought . . ." The

lieutenant fell silent and then rose and dragged the false Joda off into the night.

The hammer of horses' hooves came from behind. The Hajiwara staff closed around their lord as the riders approached, but then relaxed as they saw the green lacing.

The senior officer of the group, an old captain, dropped to his knees before his superiors.

"Captain?" the general asked.

"Sire, there is an army on the plain at our rear."

This time Lord Hajiwara did draw his sword as he rose. "An army! This is not possible! How could the Butto penetrate our lines?"

"They do not seem to be the Butto, Sire."

"Not the Butto! What colors?—what colors do they show?"

"Blue, Sire."

Spinning, Hajiwara sliced through the pole of a torch, sending it rolling down the slope. "Shonto! It cannot be!"

"They are on foot, Sire. Yet they still come quickly. If you are to escape, you must go now."

Hajiwara's senior general took charge, ordering horses, setting guards off with the Hajiwara banners in a different direction. Torches were pushed into the dirt. The lord set out east, hoping to skirt the Shonto army and to gather reinforcements from the Hajiwara perimeter.

The sounds of battle did not diminish and no one noticed as the moon disappeared behind the hills. In the eastern sky, morning stained the clouds with its pale dye.

An arrow sparked off the stone above General Hojo's head, causing him to crouch as he leapt. The first Hajiwara guard went down to a single stroke and the second fell back, parrying madly, before he slipped from the walkway to his end.

Hojo Masakada moved quickly toward the tower now, not allowing himself to run. A dozen elite Shonto Guards followed behind him. It had all been easier than he had hoped. His assessment of the Hajiwara men had been correct—no match for the Shonto trained. But then the men Hajiwara had left in the keep were the weakest of his soldiers. He must have truly believed the Shonto Guards would sit meekly and wait for his return. The general almost laughed.

The main gate was open now, and Shonto soldiers poured in from the plain. He would bow low to Brother Shuyun and Lord Komawara when he saw them. He had not truly believed they would succeed.

In the darkness he saw figures pull back into the tower door. Let them hide there awhile, he thought. It does not matter. The bridge was open to them now. Only the locks remained. He hefted his sword; it was good to find that he was still a warrior. It was very good.

On the hillside, a mist hung in the branches of the northern pines. A hawk's call echoed across the slopes and mixed with the creaking of leather saddles. A flight of wood-crows went excitedly from tree to tree, watching the activities of man, eyeing the carnage. A line of riders passed under the hill, banners waving, but they were of no interest to the crows for they posed no threat and were strong and very much alive.

At the head of this column of soldiers, Lord Hajiwara entered the keep. It was early morning. His wrists were raw where the cords cut into them, but he ignored the pain. There was no sign of a Hajiwara soldier within the walls, though the evidence of battle was everywhere. High above the tower the Shonto banner, white shinta blossom on a blue field, fluttered in the falling wind. Hajiwara looked at it for only a second and then turned his gaze to the cobbles.

Two Shonto Guards pulled the lord from his saddle, not roughly but with little sign of respect. They moved him to the center of the courtyard and made him kneel. A noise on the stairs alerted him and he looked up. Lord Shonto descended, deep in conversation with General Hojo. He was followed by a monk, an old man with only one arm, and a young lord not wearing the Shonto blue.

Shonto did not even wear armor, though he carried his own sword.

At the bottom of the stairs Shonto stopped to complete his orders to the general, and then, finally, he turned to Hajiwara. He regarded the lord carefully, but without apparent emotion, as though the nobleman were a horse he might purchase. A stool was brought and Shonto sat, holding his sheathed sword across his knees.

" 'An act of treachery: a victim of the same.' Is that not the saying, Lord Hajiwara?" Shonto asked. The lord said nothing.

"It is close enough, though you say nothing. Yet you must speak, Lord Hajiwara, and it is treachery you must speak of, yeh?"

"The treachery I am aware of was not of my making," the kneeling lord spat out.

Shonto smiled openly. "Look around you, Lord Hajiwara—no, look! Do you think I have taken your stronghold and captured you this easily by being a fool? It seems that the mists cloud your sight, if that is what you believe. Yeh?" The kneeling lord maintained his silence and Shonto continued to regard him.

"So, Lord Hajiwara, let me tell you something of the message I am about to send to the capital. I intend to say in this letter, that you and your son-in-law, the Imperial Governor of Itsa, have conspired with a certain . . . officer in the Imperial Guard to end the life of Lord Shonto Motoru in such a way as to make it appear that the Dragon Throne has condoned, if not directed, this plot. This would have had the effect, had it been successful, of turning the Great Houses against the Throne, creating a situation that could have proved very advantageous to the officer I have mentioned." Shonto regarded Lord Hajiwara. "Even if I am not to use the name of this Imperial Officer, I think the Son of Heaven will quickly guess the name for himself. Do you still prefer to remain silent?" He waited for a long moment, but the lord said nothing.

"Lord Hajiwara, you disappoint me. You do not think the Emperor would have been involved in such a clumsy attempt do you? Was it not the *tiger*, the *tiger that speaks*, who came to you?"

Hajiwara glowered at the stones in front of him.

"Kamu," Shonto said addressing the aged steward.

"Sire?"

"In your dealings with Lord Butto, did you agree to pass Lord Hajiwara into Butto hands?"

"That is correct, Sire."

"Ah. Perhaps we were hasty. Lord Hajiwara, excuse me if I explain something that is already clear to you. The Butto army rages across your fief as we speak. You are captive without hope. Below us, my fleet passes through locks that are controlled by Shonto guards. Your son-in-law, the governor, has resigned his position and gone into hiding. Nothing remains to you: not family, not allies, not troops, not land, not even honor. Do you wish to suffer the humiliation of being the captive of a child whose name is Butto?"

Lord Hajiwara did not look up, but he shook his head slowly and with what seemed like great effort.

"Then it is perhaps wise that you speak to me of treachery. If you do so, and your words are deemed worthwhile, you will be given a sword. It shall be said that you died in battle, honorably. This is your choice, Lord Hajiwara, but you must make it now."

The kneeling lord closed his eyes, his body rigid with anger. "Do you give your word that I shall have the sword?"

"On the honor of my family. Bring Lord Hajiwara his weapon," Shonto said, then nodded to the man on the stones before him, an order to begin.

"It is as you said. Jaku Katta approached us through his youngest brother. It was he who arranged that the Hajiwara take this keep and he encouraged our just war with the enemy of our family. Jaku promised us that, in return for our services, he would, in time, give us the Butto and their fief. But this was all done in the name of the Emperor, not in the name of Jaku Katta, as you suggest. The service the Black Tiger wished performed, was the . . . interception of Lord Shonto at the locks."

The lord fell silent, seeming to contemplate the stone in front of him.

"'Interception,' Lord Hajiwara? Please explain?"

The kneeling lord met Shonto's eyes, but he paused before speaking. "He wanted you dead, Lord Shonto."

"Huh. Brother Shuyun?"

"I believe he is telling the truth, Sire."

"You have earned your sword, Lord Hajiwara," Shonto said. He rose and walked away.

# Twenty-four

They had entered the province of Seh before dawn and few but the night-watch had seen the border markers pass. Late morning still found the air cool, though the sailors did not complain for it filled the sails and gave them rest from their toil.

On the bow of the river barge Shuyun watched the passing landscape, wondering at the change of it. They had left the canal and locks for a quicker passage and were in a true river now, a river that wandered across the countryside and among the hills like the tail of a sleeping dragon. The shores broke down into long gravel banks which then rose again in great steps of gray-white stone.

Stands of pine and cedar scented the breeze. And then the boat rounded a bend to find a whole hillside atremble with ginkyo, leaves turning to copper-gold in the late autumn sun.

Shuyun had never known a place that felt so pure and alive. The very air seemed light and newly created, a sharp contrast to the capital where the air tasted as though it had been too long in too many lungs. Here the air caressed him.

As the day passed, Shuyun began to sense the pattern of Seh, began to discern a deeper design. Seh was a land frozen in the midst of great motion, as though Botahara himself had stopped all movement. And this stillness was balanced by the sense that motion could begin again at any instant.

Hills rolled and folded, and ran their crests off into the far distance, their sun greens turning finally to silhouettes of blue. Field and pasture, irregular in shape, appeared among the forests and pushed their way up hillsides and along valleys to end abruptly at walls of fall-turning trees.

Here and there, as random as only the earth could be, great fractured blocks of stone pushed through, as though the ruins of some mammoth fortress lay hidden beneath the land. The gray-white stone was layered in thick bands and broken into blocks of enormous proportion as though it were the stone work of a giant race, its mortar worn away through the ages of wind and rain. Moonstone, this was called, and it seemed ancient despite the freshness of the land.

Along the river's course, cliffs of great scale would suddenly rise up and echo the voices of the water back and forth until men would hear words and even their own names spoken among the tumult.

Shuyun rode the prow of the boat as it plunged down into a steep gorge and he felt as though his heart had been opened and his spirit exposed to beauties so great that he ached with the power of them. Never before had he risked his life; he did not know that many a man who had fought the Hajiwara and scaled the rope ladders into the ancient fane above Denji Gorge felt much as he did now. But unlike Shuyun, most had felt the shock of powerful emotions before. The young monk was alone in his experience, with nothing to compare.

They were swept into the white foam roar of the gorge and boatmen fought their steering oars to stop the barge from making a fatal broach. The tiny, pure white tinga gulls screeched their high notes and knifed into the whirlpools and crests as though they had made a pact with a river god to allow them passage.

The rushing of the water became deafening and the speed of its flow truly frightening when, with a sudden final drop, the boat shot out onto a lake as clear as air and as tranquil as an enlightened soul.

Seh, Shuyun thought. I have been swept up and carried by the great river into the far reaches of the north, borne on waves of cloud, and tossed out onto the still surface of a great mirror. Seh, where my liege-lord has come to wage a war that he can never name, for it is not the barbarians we have come to challenge. Seh, where I become the Imperial Governor's Advisor and bring honor to my teachers or shame to my Order.

The monk looked down into the waters and it was as if he looked into the infinite depths of the sky. Illusion he thought, it is the purpose of my life to dispel illusion.

There in the depths of the sky he saw clouds sailing east in great billowing fleets.

"I am the Gatherer of Clouds," he heard himself whisper. Clouds that change and grow and become dragons and sprawling lands and shape themselves into birds and mice and women of great beauty. I will gather them all.

An hour passed during which Shuyun had pushed himself deep into meditation. Footsteps sounded on the deck behind him. General Hojo, Shuyun thought without turning, he has strong chi for one untrained. Pulling himself up out of his meditation, the monk turned and bowed.

"General."

"I hope I do not interfere with your contemplation, Brother Shuyun."

"I spend too much time in contemplation and not enough studying the wisdom of my lord's advisors."

Hojo gave a slight bow. "I am honored, Brother, but it was I who argued against scaling the walls of Denji Gorge. Fortunately I was not listened to."

Shuyun felt embarrassed by the officer's words. "General, you were listened to and your council was wise. No one knew if Lord Komawara and I would succeed, and if we had failed?—as you said, this would have had disastrous consequences. There was great risk, but Botahara smiled upon us."

The general gave a slight bow again and then looked out at the shore, ready to change the subject. "I have read that you can only experience something for the first time once. Yet each time I come to Seh, it is for the first time."

"All that I had read and been told did not prepare me. . . ." Shuyun trailed off, at a loss for words.

The two men stood, watching the passing land for a long time without speaking. Finally Hojo broke the silence.

"It must be disconcerting for our lord to come to Seh knowing that his famous ancestor's name is so much a part of the history."

"This is true," Shuyun said. "The first Shonto Motoru: is his shrine not close to here?"

Hojo nodded without looking away from the scene. "Yes," he said quietly, "quite close, but difficult to reach from the river." He paused. "So a Shonto lord comes again—even bearing the sword his ancestor gave to his Emperor. If I were a man of Seh, this would affect me."

Hojo shook his head. "Of course, the situation is not at all the same. That was the time of the barbarians' great power. And this Emperor . . ." he held up his open palms, "he is not the poet Emperor Jirri was."

Shuyun smiled at the joke.

They fell silent again and Hojo's remark caused Shuyun to remember his reading of the history of the Shonto family. Many poems had been written of the great barbarian war. Lord Shonto had been celebrated in songs and poems and plays. Many besides Emperor Jirri had set their brush to paper, many of the great poets of the Empire.

*Broken stone.*
*As far as all horizons*
*Walls lie in terrifying ruin.*
*Everywhere one looks*
*The eye is pained.*
*Each report bears worse news,*
*The smoke of burning villages*
*Charcoaled across bitter winds.*

*Seh*
*In all her beauty*
*Is in flames.*

*Drums roll*
*Like the pounding of hearts,*
*Pipes call retreats that cost*
*Uncounted sons.*

*When a battle takes a lifetime*
*War is endless.*

*Hunger's forays*
*Leave as many in the field*
*As any battle,*
*Women, children*
*Fall to their silent enemy.*

*It is a whisper*
*From foot soldier*
*To horseman.*
*Shonto has come*
*Riding at the Emperor's side,*
*Shonto*
*And soldiers begin to sharpen swords*
*Despair had long left untended.*

Shuyun looked up at a hillside that spread itself in crimson and yellow across the western horizon. Seh, he thought, in all her beauty. . . .

And Shonto has come.

# Twenty-five

A bronze bell rang in the darkness, echoing across the water and returning again from the far shore of the slowly moving river. Brother Sotura could see the light-boat itself now. "Yul-sho," he whispered. The Floating City should appear by midday.

Releasing the rail he began a series of intricate finger exercises, the movements hidden in the long sleeve of his robe. His focus, however, was elsewhere: larger issues concerned him.

He had known the Supreme Master for twenty-two years, had been the senior monk's closest advisor for perhaps half that time, and never had he seen the Order's most senior Brother despondent—until now. It was the Supreme Master's misfortune to bear the great responsibility of his position at a most difficult time in history.

The plague had devastated the Empire of Wa and though the Brotherhood had finally found a cure, uncounted lives had been lost. Yet all of the senior Brothers were aware that if they had found the cure earlier, the Interim War would never have occurred. This weighed most heavily on the Supreme Master. Had the Hanama Imperial family not died of plague the Yamaku would never have seized the throne, and there would still be a Botahist Brother advising the Son of Heaven and the Order would have retained its place of power in the Empire.

A tiny spark of light grew until it became the bow lantern of a river scow being rowed out toward the sea; current behind them, wind against them. Sotura watched the boat pass, until even the sound of oars disappeared into the darkness.

The Supreme Master, Sotura realized, bore a harsh burden. But even more than the situation in the Empire, which Sotura was sure patience and time would change, it was the missing scrolls that destroyed the Supreme Master's tranquillity . . . and Brother Sotura shared responsibility for that loss.

The situation was so delicate that the Brotherhood had been forced to react to this blasphemy with the utmost secrecy. The scrolls of the Perfect Master contained much that was unknown outside the Botahist Orders; much that Sotura himself knew nothing of. Information that the Supreme Master was certain would endanger the Botahist Brotherhood's place in the empire if not its existence.

And yet they heard nothing! No demands for gold, not even a rumor that the scrolls were gone. Nothing.

Perhaps this inability to understand the thieves' motives was the most unsettling part. Where did one start to search for the scrolls when one did not even begin to know why they had been stolen? If it were for profit, that would be one thing. Stolen to blackmail the Brothers, that would be another. He would at least know where to start looking. But as it was. . . .

Perhaps his meeting with Brother Hutto would suggest a place to begin.

Meeting Brother Hutto would no doubt be a risk, but he could see no alternative. At least three days would be taken up arranging such a meeting. Three invaluable days.

The monk shifted his weight from one foot to the other and felt the unfamiliar robe move with him. After a lifetime in the garb of a Botahist monk he would never adjust to another form of dress. Yet the disguise seemed to be working. He was just another Seeker returning from a pilgrimage, even associating with the other religious fanatics on board, though he found their company oddly depressing. All the same, Brother Sotura, the chi quan Master of Jinjoh Monastery, had not been recognized.

If he could just get through this meeting with Brother Hutto. It was a problem. The Honorable Brother was watched too closely—the price he paid for being Primate in Yankura. Not that there was a better place for him—that was not the case. A man of Brother Hutto's talents was a necessity in a place like Yankura—but it was difficult to be there and not attract the attention of . . . certain people. Sotura could not afford to become an object of their curiosity, this was certain.

The ship came abreast of the light-boat and seemed to hover there, making almost no progress against the current. Sotura shook his head. Perhaps it would have been better to take passage on a faster boat—but he had deemed this one less likely to attract the attention of the Imperial Guards.

Luckily it was a dry autumn. If the rains had started, the old barge would never have made headway against the current. Patience, he reminded himself, Botahara rewards the patient. He continued his finger exercises, coming to the first closure and beginning the isolation series.

It had been a long time since Sotura had visited Wa and he wished now that it was daylight so he could see the country in its autumn beauty. All of his years on the island of Jinjoh Monastery had left him with the most romantic view of the Empire of Wa. He shook his head. He could not help it—the countryside seemed unimaginably beautiful to him.

He turned his gaze to the shoreline and his imagination swept the darkness aside as though it were a wind gathering up a black mist. A village spread its bone-bleached walls across the side of a hill like the skeleton of some mammoth beast that had fallen in the middle of a giant stride. Above the village, a small copse of pine and sweet linden stood in silhouette, dark against the starlit sky. Rice paddies fell in irregular terraces, their dikes tracing a blue-green web down the dark hillside.

The harvest would all be in now and the time of the

peasant celebrations was near. Sotura thought it unfortunate that he had missed the River Festival. He had always had an affection for this celebration, despite its pagan origins.

This thought seemed to break a spell and the darkness returned, pushing the shore into the distance despite all powers of the imagination.

The River Festival had been his destination on his last journey to Wa, eight years earlier. That, too, had been a journey with a political purpose, though he had not been forced to bear the indignity of a disguise.

The young initiate monk, Shuyun, had been his charge; there to compete in the Emperor's kick boxing tournament. On that journey Sotura had come as a teacher—to remind the people of Wa of the power of the Botahist monks. He had come as a teacher but had learned more than he taught.

Shuyun had been the perfect instrument for the lesson the Brotherhood needed to teach. In an Empire that was still unstable from the years of plague and the Interim Wars, respect for the Botahist monks was restored—again they could travel the roadways of the Empire without interference, though the same could be said of no others, except the heavily armed.

The second lesson they had hoped to teach had not been so successful. Shuyun had humiliated the Emperor's favorite, the arrogant Jaku Katta, but this only served to make the Emperor more wary of the Brotherhood, when the monks had hoped the Son of Heaven would see the value of taking a monk into his service.

So much for lessons taught.

The lesson Sotura had learned was more difficult to describe, for he had not been directly involved. In truth, he learned it only with the assistance of Jaku Katta. In the midst of the fight Sotura had seen Jaku lose all focus and, for an instant, entirely let down his guard. What Sotura had read in the kick boxer's reaction was *awe!* And yet nothing had occurred that Sotura had noted, and Sotura missed very little.

It was a strange and incomplete lesson. The chi quan

instructor had watched Shuyun carefully after that. Had even sparred with him on more than one occasion, and though Shuyun was skilled far beyond his years, Sotura could detect nothing that would cause a kick boxer of Jaku's skill to stop in awe.

Perhaps Jaku had reinforced the Emperor's fear of the Botahist Brotherhood, it was impossible to say. The entire incident had been a sad miscalculation and a serious one.

The problem with the present Emperor was that the Brotherhood knew so little of him. No monk was allowed near the Son of Heaven and so he remained a mystery which no amount of analysis seemed to unravel.

Of course, he was a highly unpredictable man, the Emperor, but even so, Brother Sotura was surprised at how unsuccessful the Brotherhood was at anticipating the Emperor's plans. It was most unsettling—sometimes Sotura found himself wondering if his Order had somehow earned the anger of heaven, such was their lack of good fortune—but, of course, this could not be.

The chi quan instructor finished his finger exercises and began a stillness meditation. Several hours later daylight found him standing on the prow of the ship; a strange figurehead dressed in a ragged robe that the wind could not leave alone.

The Jade Temple was the most ancient of the buildings that stood in the old section of the Floating City. Over the seven hundred years the temple had stood, its position on a rocky island had saved it from the not infrequent flooding that Yankura experienced. Botahara, it was said, protected it from fire.

Inside the walls that surrounded the temple grounds clustered other buildings constructed in the style of the early Botahist period, all arranged around courtyards and gardens of meditation. The Jade Temple was the destination of many of the pilgrims who traveled the roads and waterways of Wa, so beyond the walls of the temple there were large buildings to house the many Seekers who arrived without bedding or coins, all having taken a vow of poverty.

Brother Sotura lay on a wooden bench in the darkness in one of these dormitories, ignoring the cold that seemed to seep into his body like spring-water. Around him he could hear the sounds that men made in their sleep—not all of them healthy sounds—and the noises of men too troubled to find the peace of unconsciousness. Voices whispered in the darkness, and beyond the thin shutters Sotura could hear that familiar mumbling of someone in the garden intoning a long Bahitra; a prayer for forgiveness.

For the hundredth time an old man coughed harshly and then sighed in despair or relief—it was impossible to tell which.

Brother Sotura lay on his side pretending to be asleep, avoiding the constant trap of conversation—seeking the truth of Botahara did not seem to do away with many men's loneliness and they looked always for their own kind.

A temple bell sounded the hour of the owl and the sound was answered a dozen times throughout the crowded city. Waiting a moment, Brother Sotura rose noiselessly. It was a skill of the Botahist monks to be able to move without sound and now Sotura brought his training into play, stepping among the sleeping pilgrims with care. At the end of the dormitory he slid a screen aside.

A sliver of moon cast shadows at the foot of buildings and trees and shimmered off the surface of a small pond. Avoiding a path of gravel, Brother Sotura crossed an opening between buildings and stepped onto a low stone wall.

At the end he found the higher wall of the temple itself. Here the monk stopped and examined his surroundings, searching the shadows for any sign of movement, stretching his mind, searching for presence, for a sense of chi that would mark someone hiding in the dark.

Finally satisfied that no one watched, Brother Sotura stepped down onto a cobbled walkway and took three steps to a door half-hidden by a Tenti bush. In the darkness he ran his hands over the metal sheathed wood looking for a handle. When he found it, he pulled toward him and the door moved silently—but then came to an abrupt halt.

A deep voice whispered from the darkness beyond the door. "What is it you wish?"

"I have come to consult with your Master about the Master's words." Brother Sotura answered quietly. He heard the sound of a chain being released and then the door swung out toward him.

"Please enter," came the deep voice again and Sotura stepped through the opening into the inner grounds of the ancient temple.

The door closed silently behind him. "Please, Brother, follow me." And with a quick bow the dark form of a Botahist monk turned and stepped into the shadows of a nearby wall. Sotura was quick to follow and before they had gone twenty steps the monk opened a lamp slightly and Sotura could see a hint of the man's appearance.

"Brother Shinsha?"

The monk turned to him and Sotura sensed more than saw the smile.

"Brother Shinsha, and honored to be your servant, though excuse me for not speaking your name." The voice was as deep and resonant as the darkness itself.

"The night hears all things," Sotura muttered and saw the lamp jiggle as his guide chuckled silently.

They mounted a stone staircase that led to a covered veranda at the rear of a residence. Inside the walls, the sounds of the busiest city in the Empire could not be heard and Brother Sotura found this oddly comforting. His guide slid a screen open and stepped into a wide hallway. A few paces farther, they again mounted stairs which took them up four levels to another long hall. Two Brothers standing guard outside carved double doors bowed with deference to the older monk and the unkempt Seeker. Without knocking, Brother Shinsha pulled the doors open. Bowing to the chi quan Master as though he were an honored stranger, Brother Shinsha stepped aside.

Sotura entered the room and there, in its center, sat Brother Hutto, Primate of Wa, hunched over his famous double-sized writing table, scroll in hand.

"Ah, Brother Sotura." The old monk said, looking at the other monk's dress. "You should not be such a follower of fashion, Brother, it will endanger your spirit."

The Primate did not smile at his own joke—a habit that Sotura had once found disconcerting. That was before he had realized Brother Hutto enjoyed watching people decide whether it was appropriate to laugh. It was also a display of Brother Hutto's considerable intelligence and, once understood, not a small part of his charm.

"I shall heed your kind advice in this matter, Brother, though that is not what I have come to hear."

Hutto nodded and stroked his chin. He seemed to be staring into Brother Sotura who showed no signs of discomfort at this examination.

The Primate was a tiny man with a face that could appear either very old or surprisingly young depending on his mood. He had large features, like a peasant, yet his eyes were small and almost inky dark.

Brother Hutto stopped stroking his chin. "Words have never satisfied you, Brother Sotura. Please sit with me." He gestured to another cushion and as he did so he pushed the writing table away. One of the monks who had been guarding the door entered with a cha service on a lacquered stand. Setting this between the two men, he checked the fire in the iron kettle before leaving.

"You have word from our Supreme Master?" Brother Hutto asked. He had a way of stressing long vowels, stretching them out almost musically as though they had slipped out of a chant and into his conversation.

"He sends you his deepest regards but did not include a written message for fear that it would be discovered. I have many things to discuss with you, though, in his name."

"And what is it the Supreme Master thinks I am not telling him?"

"I am not aware of anything, Brother Hutto," the chi quan Master said evenly.

"Ah. Then you have come only for the pleasure of the Jade Temple's bells?"

"No, Brother," Sotura said, and then hesitated before going on. "I have come to discuss the sacred scrolls of Botahara."

Brother Hutto made a sign to Botahara. "Then speak quietly. My hearing is not yet old."

The chi quan instructor looked down, rubbing his fingertips in a circle on the grass mats. "We received your report. The Supreme Master praised your forethought at having the Shonto merchant watched. Yet what was observed in the dark has raised many questions." Sotura let the statement hang in the air, waiting to see what the other would do with it.

After a prolonged silence, Brother Hutto spoke. "I assume you are asking if I know more?"

"Not at all, Brother; the Supreme Master is interested in your opinion of this matter."

The Primate adjusted the flame on a lamp. "And I am interested in Brother Nodaku's own thoughts. If what was being so secretly spirited away were the scrolls that you—that we both seek, then I would think the Supreme Master might tell me. Where else would the scrolls be taken by sea except to Jinjoh Monastery?" Brother Hutto fixed his dark liquid gaze on the larger monk.

"The whereabouts of the scrolls is still a mystery, though it pains me to say this."

"Huh. I almost wish you had told me it had all been done behind the sleeve and the scrolls were back where they belong." Brother Hutto paused to serve cha. "I fear I must disappoint you. I do not know what it was the Imperial Guards were transporting. A box the size of a small traveling trunk. It was apparently very heavy. I say apparently. Could it have been the treasure we seek?" He shook his head sadly and offered his guest a bowl of cha. "I do not believe so. To think that they are gone. . . !" he exclaimed and then recovered his control immediately.

Somewhere below them, deep voices began a long melodic chant and the two monks made signs to Botahara. A gong sounded four times, then echoed through a long pause—sounded thrice more and was still. Into the stillness a single voice poured like liquid into an empty bowl. It was a beautiful, clear voice and the melody was lyrical, haunting. Slowly the other voices returned, soft and powerful.

Sotura took a long breath and offered a silent prayer.

"Forgive me, Brother, but I have little time." At a nod from the Primate, Sotura continued. "The Initiate who witnessed this incident—did he not hear anything the vassal-merchant said?"

The monk shook his head. "Tanaka and the old guard watched in silence and, I am told, fear. They did not speak. I know nothing that was not included in my letter to the Supreme Master."

"I hesitate to speculate, but it does seem obvious that what was being done so secretly was of great importance to someone of consequence. The presence of Shonto's vassal-merchant suggests that this occurrence was also of interest to the Great Lord. Perhaps it is dangerous to carry the thought too far?"

"I have observed the merchant Tanaka for many years and have learned much that surprised me. Perhaps it is most telling to say that, in private, Lord Shonto will share a table with his merchant and calls him *sum*. This man is one of Shonto's most valued advisors, not just in the area of trade. To risk himself on a dark night, with only an old man for a guard? Whatever was in the trunk was of great concern to the Shonto House.

"But who arranged for this trunk to be moved? Jaku Katta? The Emperor? Or perhaps one of the younger Jaku brothers? And where was it sent?" The old monk shook his head.

"It is most curious that Tanaka was interested in this affair, most curious. So where could this valuable trunk be going that it would be of interest to the Lord of the

Shonto? The obvious possibility is that it went where the
lord himself has gone." Brother Hutto closed his eyes
and sipped his cha and his face became the face of a
delighted youth. "As to the contents of the trunk. Gold.
Silver. Jade. A payment to Shonto's enemies . . ." He
opened his dark eyes: "Or those who would become his
enemies. All possibilities you have discussed with the
Supreme Master, I am sure."

"It is good to hear your words, Brother Hutto. We
are so isolated in the monastery that we have grown
concerned that we have not explored all possibilities. But
I am still concerned that it was the treasure we seek
that was being moved, or perhaps even delivered to our
enemies."

"It seems that you assume the Son of Heaven is the
thief?"

"He is the obvious choice and he has in his service
Katta, a cunning man who has his own reasons to hate
the Brotherhood." Sotura tasted his cha, breathing in its
rich perfume.

Brother Hutto laughed bitterly, surprising his companion. "Is it not ironic that we speculate in the dark like
men who have lost their faith?" He turned his dark eyes
on his ragged companion. "Look at you. Do you not
laugh when you see yourself? A Botahist Master reduced
to running around in costume like a courtier at a party."
He laughed again and leaned forward, whispering, "I
feel panic in you, Brother. Though you hide it well, still
I feel it. And it is not just you, it is in all of us who
know. Soon it will be felt by others in our ranks—an
unknown, unnamed panic—and then the speculation will
begin. Do you realize what that will mean?" The old
man took a deep breath and let it out slowly. "And I,
too, panic. Please, excuse me."

"Brother Hutto, this is the reason we must find the
scrolls. Nothing is more important, nothing."

The two men fell silent, sipping their cha. A breeze
slipped in through a half open shoji and with it the scent
of fallen leaves. Brother Sotura turned his attention to
the screens painted the length of the two-span hall. They

showed the Perfect Master giving the Sermon of Silence in which he told his disciples that he would speak to them of their desires and then he said nothing, rising finally at nightfall to go to his prayers. Yes, Sotura thought, we wear our desire on our faces even as His disciples did.

"Brother Hutto, I cannot stay long and there are things I must ask you. What of the Emperor and Shonto?"

"Yes. I neglect my duty." He paused to refill their cha bowls. "It is no secret, the Emperor's fear of the Shonto. Yet suddenly the Emperor treats Shonto as an old friend and charges him with the safety of the Empire. It is very strange. Some see it as a sign that the Emperor is maturing and losing his fear of the strong. Others are deeply suspicious. I would put Shonto himself in this latter group. The Emperor has gone to much trouble to separate the family—Shonto's son to their fief, Lady Nishima in the capital and Shonto himself in the north fighting a war, and who knows what can happen in a war? Even a general can fall to a stray arrow. How much gold is needed to hire a skilled bowman?

"If the Emperor plots against Shonto, then I suspect that Jaku Katta has contrived something more subtle—he is a consummate swordsman and would never finish a man clumsily. Shonto, of course, realizes the possibilities of his situation; so we watch as though it is a game of gii. The great families wonder who will be next if indeed the Emperor plots Shonto's fall—many would then question the wisdom of allowing the Yamaku to stay on the throne. But with Shonto gone, who would be strong enough to create an alliance that could defeat the Yamaku? It is a problem."

"No doubt the Emperor has his Imperial Guards close around him—a questionable tactic. There are rumors—and this I have not told the Supreme Master—that Katta may be in disfavor. They are only rumors, but if they are true . . . by Botahara! Jaku will not fall without a struggle. He will remain a fighter to his last breath." The Primate sipped his cha, excitement apparent in his voice.

"I have also discovered that the Lady Nishima has been an object of Jaku's attention."

Sotura snorted. "His appetite is too large!"

"Unquestionably, though his charm is legendary. But is it not strange?—the Commander of the Imperial Guard and Shonto's daughter? The Lady Nishima is a threat to the Yamaku, and you may be certain the Son of Heaven's sleep is troubled by this knowledge."

"Why does he not marry a son to Shonto's daughter and avoid this stupid feud?"

"They are weak young men, Sotura-sum. They did not have the benefit of a Brother Satake to teach them. The daughter Fanisan would overwhelm any of Akantsu's sons, that is certain."

"So Jaku Katta pursues the Lady Nishima. But she is no fool. Perhaps she turns the Emperor against his own creation?"

The Primate's face became suddenly youthful. "Ah, Brother Sotura," he said without a trace of a smile, "what a delightfully suspicious nature you have."

The chi quan Master laughed. "I, too, have had excellent teachers. Have you received word from my young protégé?"

"Initiate Brother Shuyun is probably in Seh with his liege-lord, or at least well on his way. There is a good chance that the Butto-Hajiwara feud is a trap for Shonto, but, if so, those who have laid the trap will get the measure of their opponent. Shonto is too much the gii Master to step into such a situation with his eyes closed.

"The young Brother is all that you have said, Sotura-sum, I met him." The monk nodded to the chi quan Master, a bow of acknowledgment. "Even the Sisters seem impressed, for they follow him to Seh, though I confess I am not sure why." The Primate examined the face of his guest now, looking for an answer.

They had entered into a game of trading, a game they both knew well, and information was the coinage.

"Karma manifests itself strangely, Brother Hutto. A Sister, one Morima, was present in our Monastery several years ago. Through lack of knowledge, Shuyun was indiscreet and this Sister learned something of his true abilities. The Sisterhood has taken an interest in him ever since."

"Huh. Most unusual, Brother, the boy is gifted, yes, but that does not warrant this degree of interest."

"I agree, Hutto-sum. The Supreme Master also concurs. It is his contention that the Sisters think Shuyun was not a Brother in his past life."

"Ah. So this is their secret desire! We do well to learn this, Sotura-sum. But still it is a mystery what the Sisters hope to gain by following your student."

"You are keeping Shuyun and the Sisters under observation?"

"As I can, from the other end of the Empire."

Brother Sotura pulled at his whiskers. "Perhaps we need to do more."

"Excuse me, Brother, I don't understand."

Sotura cleared his throat. "The Supreme Master wishes us to redouble our efforts to find the scrolls."

"This would be more easily done if I knew what efforts to double, Brother," the Primate said dryly.

"The Way is difficult, Brother."

"So I have read."

"I am to go north to Seh, Hutto-sum. It is clear from our meditations that many things seem to center around Lord Shonto and our young Brother. There is a focus on these two, as though suddenly all meridians connected in this one place. The Brotherhood cannot ignore this."

Brother Hutto sipped cha that had gone cold in its bowl. He considered a long time before speaking again. "It would be better if Shonto lived and the Emperor fell, would it not, Brother?"

"Hutto-sum, these are dangerous words."

"With the Yamaku on the Dragon Throne, we will always be in danger."

Sotura changed the subject. "What of the barbarians, does your intelligence extend to them also?"

"Among the barbarians I have no one, but the Brothers in Seh cross into the wastes as they can and they are concerned, as no doubt we would be if we lived under

threat of constant attack. There are rumors again that
the Golden Khan has come—at least the fifth time in my
short life this has been said. Seh, sadly, is far away. I
will be interested in your assessment of the situation."

"And the Emperor, what of him?"

"It seems likely that he will ask Lord Omawara for
the hand of Lady Kitsura." Brother Hutto enjoyed the
look of shock on his companion's face.

"Truly?"

Brother Hutto nodded once.

"So, the Empress feels a need to retire to a life of
spiritual contemplation. I did not imagine this, not at all.
More Imperial progeny. Now we shall see a House
divided!" Brother Sotura fell silent, contemplating this new
information.

"The Supreme Master will be most interested in this.
The Lady Kitsura Omawara!" Brother Sotura shook his
head. "What of the Sisters? Does their internal struggle
continue?"

"It does, Brother, but we must not be deceived. It is
not the Prioress, Sister Saeja, who is occupied with this
problem—it is the faction that opposes her. The old nun
keeps an eye turned outward. Events in the Empire do
not escape her, even a talented young Brother is worthy
of her attention."

"So there is no indication of who will win the struggle
when she is gone?"

Brother Hutto shrugged. "Perhaps you should consult
a fortune teller. I would not even begin to guess."

"Then no one can know, Brother."

"Shall I order more cha, Sotura-sum?"

"I am honored that you ask, but it grows late. I must
return to my brethren. If you could include your thoughts
about these matters in your next report to the Supreme
Master, I'm sure his harmony would be enhanced."

"I would deem it an honor if I could assist our Brother
in this way," the Primate said, bowing to his guest.
"There is something else, Brother," Hutto said as the
chi quan instructor stood.

Sotura stopped, almost crouching. "Yes."

"Another Brother, senior Master Den-Go, has disappeared."

Brother Sotura straightened. "I have forgotten, Brother; how many is this?"

"Twenty-two."

Sotura expelled a long controlled breath, and put his hand to his brow as though there were sudden pain. "In all our history I know of nothing as strange as these disappearances."

"There is one other thing, Brother." The Primate paused, watching Sotura's face. "I have not yet confirmed this, but I have received a reliable report from Monarta . . . it is said the Udumbara has blossomed on the slopes above the Perfect Master's shrine."

The chi quan Master sank back to his knees. "This cannot be true. It isn't possible."

Neither man spoke for several long minutes.

"Who could it be?" Sotura whispered finally. "Even among our most Enlightened Brothers there is no one who has progressed so far. No . . . it is not possible."

Hutto nodded. "Perhaps you are right." But the old monk looked like a man whose soul was overcome by doubt.

Brother Sotura felt his heart racing while some calm part of his mind noted that this had not happened since he had been trained in the ways of the Brotherhood.

"An Enlightened Master," Sotura heard himself whisper. It could not be.

# Twenty-six

*The west wind blows*
*And the grasses bow to my passing,*
*Perfect golden grasses*
*What do they know of my thoughts?*
*Or of the heart*
*They have torn asunder.*

*The Empress Shigei*

As daylight approached, Lady Nishima was barely able to hide her impatience. In the privacy of her rooms, she paced up and down the matted floor, regretting that Kitsura had gone. Not that she would necessarily have shared the information she had received from Tanaka, but still, it would have been comforting to have company.

Beginning a simple series of exercises taught to her by Brother Satake, Nishima attempted to subvert the thoughts that distracted her and pulled at her consciousness. With a great effort of will, she fell into the almost trancelike state the exercise required and began to feel the strange sensation of time slowing. It was only for an instant, a feeling so fleeting that it might have been imagined. But Nishima knew it was not. She opened her eyes and let out a long sigh. If only Brother Satake had been able to teach her more.

A light tap on the shoji reminded her of the things she had pushed from her mind, and it all came rushing back—the Emperor, Katta-sum, the message from Tanaka. The screen slid aside at a word from Nishima and a maid-servant entered carrying a folded letter on a small silver tray. Lady Nishima controlled an urge to leap to her feet and snatch the letter. Instead, she sat staring at an arrangement of flowers set into an alcove in the wall.

"Please excuse me, my lady. I did not mean to interrupt your meditations."

"You have acted correctly, Hara."

The maid knelt and set the tray carefully on the writing table. "Would you care for your morning meal, Lady Nishima?"

"Not now, Hara, I will call."

Nishima reached forward for the letter but stopped when she realized that her maid had not moved to leave.

"Hara?"

The maid nodded and drew in a sharp breath. "Excuse my boldness, Lady Nishima. . . ." she began and then stammered to a halt.

"What is it, Hara?" Nishima asked, keeping impatience from her voice.

"I fear I have conducted myself in a manner unworthy of your trust, my lady," the young woman said in a near whisper.

Now what is this? Nishima wondered. An indiscretion, no doubt. That handsome assistant to Kamu I would wager, but why tell me? "The Shonto value the truth, Hara. Please go on."

"During my retreat to the priory at Kano I met a senior Sister, a highly respected member of the Order, Lady Nishima." The young woman glanced up at the eyes that studied her and then back to the floor. A blush of crimson spread across her cheek. "I spoke with her several times. I . . . I was flattered by her attention. . . . She seemed very impressed that I served the Shonto House and, my lady, she praised you very highly. I did not mark it at the time, but she was very curious about the Shonto and as she was a Sister of such high standing . . ." her voice became suddenly thick, "I was perhaps less discreet than I would otherwise have been." The woman took a deep breath and it escaped from her in a half sob. She did not raise her eyes.

"I see." Lady Nishima folded her hands in her lap. "I must know how indiscreet, Hara. It is important that you leave out nothing."

The maid nodded quickly, obviously frightened, which in turn made Nishima fear the worst.

"She asked about our lord, about his character and his habits. She wanted to know if he was a good master or if he beat his servants."

"And what did you tell her?"

"My lady, I have nothing but praise for Lord Shonto."

"I see. Go on."

"The honored Sister asked about our lord's friends, though of course this is no secret and certainly many people know who frequents the Shonto house." She paused as if to gather her thoughts. "She asked me if I knew when Lord Shonto had left for Seh, which again was no secret. She asked who among Lord Shonto's staff were loyal followers of the true path. Also, she asked many questions about our new Spiritual Advisor, but of course he was here such a short time I could tell her little."

"Did you tell her of Brother Shuyun's display when he shattered the table?"

The maid nodded her head silently, knowing by her lady's tone that it was as she had feared—she had been played for a fool.

"Continue."

"She asked also about Brother Satake though I could tell her nothing, for I did not know him."

Lady Nishima put her hand to her face as though she would hide how pale she had become.

"She had great praise for Brother Satake, as does everyone." She fell silent again, searching for words or for courage. "Something else she asked, though I did not understand what she meant. This seemed important to her, though I do not understand why. She asked if you danced secretly, my lady." The maid looked up, curiosity as well as fear in her eyes.

Lady Nishima dropped her hand back into her lap, fighting now for control. How could they ever know? she wondered, and felt her breath begin to come in short gasps. Closing her eyes, Nishima forced herself to breathe normally. How could anyone know?—she was so careful. The Sisters? Nishima had no contact with them—no contact with them at all! Opening her eyes, Nishima forced herself to focus.

"Did this Sister . . . did she explain what she meant by this, Hara?" Lady Nishima asked evenly.

" 'Danced secretly,' were her words, Lady Nishima. Is that not strange?"

Nishima shrugged with an ease she did not feel. "Was there more?"

"The Sister also asked about Jaku Katta-sum; if he came here often and if I had heard the story of the Bla . . . of Jaku Katta-sum saving Lord Shonto. Of course I had, it was common knowledge throughout the capital. I told her that Lord Shonto had honored the general with a gift from his private garden." The maid kept her eyes cast down. "That is all, Lady Nishima."

"Are you certain, Hara?"

The maid closed her eyes, hesitating and then nodded.

"Hara?"

"Please, my lady . . ." A tear appeared at the corner of each eye.

"You must tell me," Nishima said softly.

"Yes, my lady. The senior Sister wanted to know if you had . . . lovers." She whispered the word, her eyes still closed and her face distorted by the effort to hold back her tears.

"I see."

"She seemed to suggest that it would not be uncommon . . . that it would be . . . as Lord Shonto was not your blood father, that . . ."

Nishima felt the sting of her hand striking the maid's face before she realized what she had done. The young woman lay stretched out on the floor like a pile of scattered clothes. She did not move.

Nishima froze, horrified. She looked at her hand which

she held away from her as though it were something dangerous, something not part of her.

Oh, Satake-sum, you taught me too well and too little. She slid across the grass mats to the unconscious maid and felt for a heartbeat. Yes, it was there, thank Botahara! Rising to her feet, Nishima slid the shoji aside and was relieved to find the hall empty. Rohku Saicha should be told of this, she thought. But what of these questions? Dancing secretly! How would she explain that?

Nishima closed the screen quietly. Why were the Sisters suddenly interested in her? I am Shonto, she thought, that is reason enough. But still, the Sisters? She shook her head. What will I tell Captain Rohku? She leaned her forehead against the shoji's wooden frame. Behind her the maid stirred and moaned softly.

Nishima crossed the room and took the young woman's head in her lap.

"Hara?" she said quietly.

"Lady Nishima?" the maid mumbled. "What. . . ?"

"Shh. You are unhurt. Be still now."

"But what happened?" The woman tried to sit up, but Nishima held her gently.

"I don't know, Hara. Be still. Don't struggle."

"But I was struck, my lady. I . . . it felt as though I were struck. May Botahara protect me. What happened?" She began to weep softly.

"Shh, my child. I don't know, it . . . it was terrible." Nishima fought her own tears. "Take long breaths, like this. Do as I do." Nishima led her through a simple breathing exercise, all the while stroking the young woman's brow.

"There, now, is that not better?"

The maid nodded. "Thank you, my lady. The gods are angry with me. I don't know what I shall do!"

"There are ways to appease the gods. Of course there are." Nishima thought for a second. "You must burn incense at the Seven Shrines and take a vow of silence for one year. You will be forgiven, but you must observe these things and not falter."

Hara nodded. "Thank you, my lady. I am not worthy of your attention."

"Shh. Tomorrow you will begin your vow of silence. The gods will forgive you, Hara."

"I pity the enemies of our lord, my lady."

Nishima nodded. "Yes," she said in a whisper. "Yes."

After a few moments the maid was able to stand without help, and when Nishima was sure she could manage, the woman left quietly. "Not a word of this," Nishima said as the maid left and she received a bow in answer.

When she was alone again, Nishima sat with her fingers pressed to her eyes. I struck someone! I struck her in anger. She shook her head in disbelief. What a terrible, terrible thing. It was this situation, Nishima told herself, it must be. Caught in the city while her uncle went off to the north without knowledge of things that put him in great danger. And this madness for an Imperial Guardsman! She buried her face in her hands. It was all more than she could bear.

Closing her eyes, Nishima began a long prayer for forgiveness, and felt somewhat better. I am Shonto, she told herself, and forced a calmness over her fears and confusion. My lord's life may depend on my ability to make clear decisions. Tranquillity of purpose, she heard Brother Satake say. Tranquillity of purpose.

We will survive, Nishima told herself, only if our course of action comes from the very center of a pure and tranquil spirit. She composed herself then and again practiced a breathing exercise to bring a stillness to her spirit. When she was done, she opened her eyes and looked around as though she had been transported to a new place and she was seeing it for the first time.

Daylight could be seen filtering through the screens and Nishima was glad. She leaned forward and blew out the lamp. It was then that she remembered the letter. She took it up—a tiny branch of slip-maple attached to a letter of deep purple mulberry paper.

It was folded in the most conventional manner, and not particularly elegantly. This cannot be from Lady

Okara, Nishima thought, it is not possible. Spreading out the paper she took a second to recognize the hand. Katta-sum! He had taken his time, she thought, but then, considering his literary abilities, she was not surprised.

Moving to the outside screen, Lady Nishima opened it a crack and the cold air of morning seemed to flood in like water into a lock.

*A whisper in the darkness,*
*The breeze speaks*
*In the voice of the poetess.*
*This cannot be the wind*
*From Chou-San?*

*There is much to say, my lady.*

Nishima read the poem through again. It was much better than she would have expected. Was it possible Jaku did not intend the double meaning of his final line? No, it was too obvious, certainly it was intentional.

The reference to Seh unsettled Nishima. Oh, Uncle, she thought, will the gods strike your enemies as Hara thought they had tonight?

She smoothed the paper on the small table, recalling the kiss she had allowed Jaku. The memory was almost as thrilling as she had found the kiss itself.

Nishima pushed the screen closed. This is foolish, she told herself. I have much to do. Decisions to make! When will I receive an answer from Lady Okara? It is only sunrise, Nishima told herself, I am too impatient.

Taking up a resin stick, she began to rub her inkstone rhythmically. I must answer Katta-sum, she thought, it will fill the time. But I must not rush the answer back to him, it is important that he not be overconfident. From an envelope she chose a piece of pale green paper, the color of fall grains, and a reminder of spring.

She wet her brush and began:

*The wind whispers its secrets*
*To so many,*
*It is difficult to tell*
*From where it blows.*

*Perhaps it is loyalty we should speak of.*

There, she thought, blowing gently on the fresh ink. She held the paper up to the light and examined the writing. It was not the work of Brother Satake, but he would have approved. Certainly it would have the desired effect on the impetuous Katta—I am from a different station in life, my handsome general, mark this well.

She laid the poem carefully on the table and began to fold the fine paper, her long fingers seeming to have knowledge independent of her mind. It was done in a second, but she knew it would take Jaku Katta a few minutes to find the key to unfolding it.

She set the letter aside to allow herself time to consider what should accompany it. Perhaps a leaf of laughing poplar? She would see.

Nishima rang a small gong on her writing desk and a maid appeared almost without sound. I wish to see Lady Kento and I will have my smaller meal."

Lady Kento, Nishima's senior lady-in-waiting, arrived almost immediately. Senior in this case was a relative term, Kento was only three years older than her young mistress. Nishima had an obvious partiality to Lady Kento which caused a certain amount of jealousy among the other ladies-in-waiting. But it couldn't be helped; Kento was simply more joyous than the others as well as being brighter. It was true that others surpassed her in many ways, Lady Jusha was a superb yara player, and the young Lady Shishika was never wrong in her advice on matters of ceremony and propriety, but they were not really close to their mistress. Their souls were not akin to hers.

The tiny Lady Kento knelt and bowed, her attractive

round face beaming even though it was composed in the most serious manner.

"Will you join me for cha, Kento-sum?"

"I would be honored," she answered as though it wasn't an established morning ritual.

"Kento-sum, before we go on to other matters, I must tell you of something I have learned. I have found that Hara has been gossiping, not in a harmful way, but this is not acceptable."

"I will speak to her at once, my lady."

"It is not necessary. I have already spoken with her. But I want her sent to the country. She could be given a position that is not sensitive. I don't imagine that she would do this again, but I will not take the chance. Hara has taken a vow of silence for a year. For someone with her weakness that will be punishment enough."

"I will see this done as you wish."

Nishima nodded. A servant brought cha and a light meal for one and then was dismissed before she could kneel nearby, ready to serve.

"Kento-sum, I need your assistance in a delicate matter."

"I am your servant, my lady."

"I must leave the capital very soon, perhaps even tomorrow. Of course, I have been honored by the Emperor with an Imperial Patronage so it would be impossible for me to leave without gravely insulting the Son of Heaven. Nonetheless, I must go. It will be up to you to preserve the appearance that I am still in residence here. It will not be easy and naturally I don't expect such a charade to go far without being uncovered. But I must have five days. Ten, if Botahara will allow it. Is this clear?"

"It is, Lady Nishima." Lady Kento offered her mistress a steaming cloth and then ladled cha into bowls.

Lady Nishima wiped her hands and face, realizing suddenly that she had not yet slept and still wore the formal robes she had worn to the palace. *I become more like my lord each day—caught up in the world around me,* not sleeping, forgetting meals. It is the way of our House.

"There is more, Kento-sum. I have written to Lady Okara. This ruse can hardly be accomplished without her cooperation, though I am asking more of her than I should ever presume to ask." She sighed. "I have no choice. I must go to Seh, I cannot tell you why. You must trust me. Lady Okara will certainly think her friendship has been misplaced, but it should appear that the Lady Nishima still visits the great painter. I will understand if she refuses to become involved, but if she will not help me then your task will be more difficult, if not impossible."

"Perhaps the lady's friendship with your esteemed father will be of help in this matter."

"Oh, yes. I presume on that, too. It will be hard for her not to say yes, though it will not be what her heart desires."

"Excuse me, my lady, but it is as Brother Satake always said: Each name brings its own obligations."

A fleeting smile crossed Nishima's face. "You know me too well, Kento-sum. And I consider it very unfair of you to quote my mentor." Nishima smiled again and turned her attention to her food but gave up the pretense of eating in a few seconds.

"Is the preparation not to your liking, my lady?"

"No, Kento-sum, it is good, really," she said, but pushed the tray away from her all the same. "There will be another problem." Lady Nishima blushed ever so slightly. "I have been corresponding with the Imperial Guardsman, Jaku Katta. It is important that all of his letters are answered. He is hardly a scholar, Kento-sum, so you need not worry about the quality of the poetry, but it must be obscure, and not too discouraging. The Black Tiger may yet have a place in our lord's plans. Can Shishika-sum copy my hand?"

"I'm sure she can approximate it, Lady Nishima, though your hand is very distinctive."

"No matter, if she can come close, it will be adequate. I will copy out all of the poems we have exchanged so you can refer to them and Shishika-sum can examine my hand."

"Have you discussed these arrangements with Rohku Saicha, Lady Nishima?"

Nishima shook her head. "No. I need time to consider how best to approach him."

"He has been in an uproar since the incident with the Imperial Guards, my lady. The men at every gate have orders to detain you if you attempt to leave without his express permission."

"He has given orders to detain me?" Outrage was not masked in Nishima's voice.

"Excuse me, my lady. I should have told you sooner, but I did not wish to precipitate difficulties unnecessarily." The woman bowed low.

"It is not your fault, Kento-sum. The captain has much to atone for which affects his decisions. And, as you say, there was the incident on the canal." Nishima fell silent, lost in thought, and her companion waited with no sign of impatience.

"That is all for now, Kento-sum. We will discuss arrangements for my departure after I have talked to Rohku Saicha. You may send him to me now. Oh, and Kento-sum, please have a maid bring me some small sprigs of laughing poplar."

"Certainly, Lady Nishima. The weeping birch still retains its leaves, if that would be appropriate."

Nishima laughed. Of course, Kento had seen the carefully folded letter on the table. "Perhaps not in this case."

"As you say." The small woman bowed and slipped out of the room. Almost immediately a maid came in to clear the morning meal away.

Nishima was left on her own. She suppressed an urge to open the letter she had written to Jaku and instead took Jaku's own letter from her sleeve. In doing so, she caused the coins Tanaka had given her to ring against each other.

"Uncle," Nishima whispered to the empty room, "do

not be too bold yet. There are things even you do not suspect."

Nishima pushed open the screen to her garden and walked out onto the veranda. A ground mist still wrapped itself around the bushes and boulders even though the sun was quickly burning off the thin cloud layer. Nishima leaned against a post and unfolded the letter from Jaku Katta. She found that reading it gave her a lightness of spirit that she could not suppress. This is foolish, she told herself. Jaku is certainly beyond redemption—a womanizer and an opportunist.

Yet despite these thoughts the lightness she felt did not disappear.

A tap on the screen caused Lady Nishima to bury Jaku's letter in her sleeve. The face of Lady Kento appeared in the opening. "Rohku Saicha, my lady."

"I will speak with him out here."

Almost immediately, there was a bustle of servants as mats and cushions were laid out on the low veranda. Lady Nishima seated herself and nodded to a servant.

Rohku Saicha entered the room from the hall, wearing the light armor of a guard on duty. This was a statement for Nishima and she did not fail to notice it. Crossing to the veranda, he knelt and bowed in the most rigid and military manner, setting his helmet carefully beside him.

He is determined, Lady Nishima thought. This will be difficult. The stocky frame of the Captain of the Guards betrayed his resolution. He would not easily allow his young mistress to have her way again—not after what had happened with the Imperial Guards on the canal.

"Saicha-sum," Nishima said warmly, "it is a pleasure to have your company."

"It is I who am honored, Lady Nishima." Rohku answered formally. "You wished to speak with me?"

"Yes. How is your son, Saicha-sum? Does he prosper?"

"He has journeyed to Seh in Lord Shonto's guard." Rohku kept his eyes cast down, as though he were not on less formal terms with Lady Nishima.

"I shall worry less knowing this," Nishima said. She

was about to go on in this vein when she realized that
Rohku Saicha sat before her as unmoving as a stone
Botahara. He would not be swayed by anything but an
irrefutable argument.

"Saicha-sum, I have received information from Tanaka
that is of crucial import to Lord Shonto."

"What information, my lady?"

Nishima struggled within herself, was about to tell him,
and then shook her head. "It is information of such a
delicate nature that if I were to tell you it would then
be dangerous to our lord for you to remain in the capital.
It is better that you do not know."

Rohku nodded his head. "Then it is unsafe for you to
remain here?"

"That is true."

"Yet you are the student of Lady Okara who has
received an Imperial Patronage to educate you. To leave
is to insult the Emperor. This is a difficult situation."

"Saicha-sum, I cannot stay. The information I have is
too significant; it is only a matter of time until it is discovered that I possess this knowledge. If the Emperor
were to find out what I know, he would assume that my
father had the same information and this would mean
open war between the Yamaku and the Shonto. You
must believe that."

"Lady Nishima, I would never doubt your words. It is
your response to this information that I question, as is
my duty. I believe you will now suggest that you must
go to Seh, taking this information to your father."

"It . . . it is the only course possible, Saicha-sum."

"While I, who am to guard you, will be forced to
choose between my duties in the capital and my sworn
duty to protect you. Either choice will mean that I have
broken my vow to my liege-lord."

"But when I explain, Lord Shonto will understand. He
does not value obedience to the point of stupidity. Our
lord understands that situations change and, to survive,
we must change also."

"Lady Nishima, what you ask is impossible. I cannot
allow it. You will not only offend the Son of Heaven by

your absence, but you will put yourself at risk, risk that
I have sworn to protect you from. And there is more.
Before your father left for the north, he told me that it
was possible that he would send for you. He did not say
why, but he did tell me that I was not to let you leave
until I received an order from him. Perhaps our lord
anticipated this information you have received, Lady Nishima, in which case it would be unwise to act before
Lord Shonto orders us to."

"Captain Rohku, let me assure you that my father
could not have anticipated this information. Of this I
entertain no doubts. If, as you say, Lord Shonto plans
that I shall join him in Seh, then it is only a matter of
timing. I shall go now with information that may save
his life."

"Lady Nishima there are other ways to send information secretly, even across the Empire."

"Other ways, yes, but for other information. This will
travel only in my head. I will accept nothing else." Nishima reached out as though she would touch the soldier
but instead she gripped the rail of the banister. "Saicha-
sum, you endanger your lord's life with this obstinacy.
You know that there is a plot against Lord Shonto. I
have crucial information about this. You are letting what
you think of as your recent oversight cloud your eyes.
But our lord trusts no one more than you or you would
not be sitting before me. He values you for your judgment. Do not lose faith in it. What I say must have the
feel of truth to it, I know it must."

The guard still avoided her gaze. "I cannot, my lady,
I. . . . Too many things argue against this. What of the
Emperor. . . ?"

"He need not know, Saicha-sum, but if it is discovered
that I am gone, the Son of Heaven will be forced to act
as though I left with his blessing. He will choose to save
face, Saicha-sum—what else can he do?"

Rohku Saicha looked at his young mistress. "For such
an insult, he could turn his back on the Shonto."

"Saicha-sum!" Nishima said in exasperation. "He is

our lord's mortal enemy! He plots against our House and you are worried that he will scorn us?"

"Lady Nishima, you need not lecture me. What you say is the whispered truth, but the spoken truth is that the Emperor honors our lord and trusts him with the security of our Empire. One cannot insult an Emperor who honors your family and, indeed, honors you with his patronage."

"Now it is you who lecture me, Saicha-sum. You must understand that the risk of the Emperor's displeasure in this matter is of no consequence compared to the risk of me remaining in the capital and of Lord Shonto not receiving this information."

"Lady Nishima," the Captain threw up his hands. "This is easily decided. We will ask Lord Shonto."

"But Saicha-sum, how can that be done? The reason I must travel to Seh cannot be trusted to a letter. It is not possible. Only the Imperial Messengers would be fast enough, and that is out of the question!"

"I have my orders from our liege-lord," he said, the emphasis on "our." "I will not break them, nor will I willingly insult the Emperor, thereby giving him reason to act against my lord's House. I am sorry, Lady Nishima, but without word from Lord Shonto you must stay in the capital. If you do not struggle against my precautions, I believe you will be safe here."

Nishima reached into her sleeve pocket and felt the coins she had received from Tanaka. It is no good, she thought. If I show these to Rohku, he cannot stay in the capital either. It can only be a last resort.

"Is this your final word then, Captain?"

"It is, Lady Nishima. I apologize for opposing your will in this matter, but I feel it is my duty to do so."

"Then you will excuse me, Captain, I have other things to attend to."

Rohku Saicha bowed and was about to rise but stopped. "There is one other matter, Lady Nishima. I am aware that you have received correspondence from the general, Jaku Katta. I must tell you that the general is an object of interest to Shonto security."

"Oh, really, Captain?" Nishima said innocently. "An advisor to our much revered Emperor is an object of our suspicion? Aren't you concerned that the Benevolent Son of Heaven will be offended by such an attitude?"

"Lady Nishima, there is nothing to be gained in fighting me," Rohku said seriously.

Lady Nishima raised her eyebrows. "Huh," she said, in imitation of her father. "It was only recently that General Katta was honored by my father for saving my father's life, just as the Emperor honors my father for his bravery in meeting the barbarian threat. It can hardly be indiscreet for me to correspond with a friend of Shonto—a friend who has the ear of the Emperor." Nishima had drawn herself up to full sitting height. "Captain."

Rohku Saicha seemed to struggle with himself for a split second, but then he bowed and began to rise.

"I don't remember giving you permission to rise in my presence."

The guard's mouth almost fell open, but he recovered instantly and dropped again to his knees. Bowing low, he backed across the veranda and through the inner room without rising.

Nishima fixed her eyes on her garden though in fact she saw nothing. The inner shoji closed with the slightest noise—Rohku Saicha was gone.

There, Nishima thought, I have acted like a spoiled child. She pushed her fingertips to her temples and closed her eyes. If I had not forced my way out of here without proper guard and ended up in that embarrassing situation on the canal, Saicha-sum would not be reacting as he is. I have taken advantage of his affection for me and now he has hardened himself to resist me, no matter what. He punishes himself for his perceived failures this way, earning coldness from me for doing what he sees as his duty. Yes, he hurts himself. I have known him many years and now I see him becoming a martyr to his duties. Poor Saicha-sum. Does he not know that he lets what happened in Lord Shonto's garden control him? This would be a great danger—he would be reacting only to his sense of failure rather than to the situations he encounters. This is something that could be easily exploited. I could exploit it.

Nishima stood and reached a pair of sandals on a high shelf, slipping them on as she stepped into the garden. I will not let Rohku Saicha stop me from traveling to Seh. If he cannot be made to change his mind by tomorrow evening, then I shall find a way to leave without his cooperation. If I leave with Saicha-sum's assistance, there is a good chance that Lord Shonto will accept this decision as necessary once he sees the letter from Tanaka. If I am forced to deceive Rohku so that I may leave, it will be the end of our good captain. Lord Shonto would never forgive him for stupidity. I hope he will see reason.

Lady Nishima stopped and took a deep breath of the morning air. It still went cold into the lung, but already the sun was having its effect; the sky cleared and the light fell warm into her small garden. It was a morning to gladden the heart and Lady Nishima found herself turning gracefully in the steps of a courtier's dance. Ah, see, she thought, I do dance secretly, and she laughed. Clapping her hands twice, she took a last look at her garden and then turned as a servant knelt on the edge of her veranda.

"Prepare my bath, and please have Lady Shishika lay out robes for me to choose from."

When the servant was gone, she again found herself dancing. We are in terrible danger, she told herself, how can I be light of heart at a time like this. She did not admit to herself that it was the poem in her sleeve that made her so. But when she swept her arm in a graceful circle and heard the jingle of coins, she stopped. Shaking her head as though she had just heard a lie, Nishima turned and went to her bath.

The wind came up out of the east and even a hundred miles inland, in the capital, it was called the "sea wind." When it heralded a storm, the big gulls that sailed the river as far as Yankura drifted into the capital like refugees driven before an advancing army. Nishima could hear their throaty calls even now.

The wind hissed through the plum trees outside her rooms sending a draft between the shojis, yet the sunlight still filtered through the screens oblivious to the changing weather. Fingers of steam rising from the bath wove among the shafts of sunlight as though they were strands of silk on a loom.

Nishima slipped out of the cold air into her bath. The water was deliciously hot and Nishima let herself sink down into it as though it were sleep itself, for the night had been long and without rest.

She closed her eyes and the patterns of color formed by courtiers' robes swam in her imagination. The celebration of the Emperor's ascension had been full of surprises. Poor Kitsura, she thought, I'm sure she never dreamed that such a thing could happen. The Emperor desires her, there is no doubt of that; and we know what Botahara said of desire.

She ran her hands up from her stomach over her breasts and then crossed them at her neck, pushing her breasts flat with her arms. So the handsome general courted her. Or was it her name that fascinated him? She felt nothing but confusion when she considered this question. It seemed that her usual womanly senses had deserted her in this matter.

"If the mind is too full of facts there is no room for knowledge," Satake had told her, yet she could not cast out the facts.

A knock on the shoji brought Nishima out of her reverie. "Yes?"

"I have your robes, my lady," came Kento's soft voice.

"But where is Lady Shishika?"

"Pardon me, Lady Nishima, but I have taken the liberty of replacing her so that we may speak. Rohku is having your rooms watched and I will appear less suspicious if I come to help you dress."

"There is no end to foolishness!" Nishima said, bitterly. "Enter."

Nishima's favorite swept in, a number of inner robes

of the sheerest silk folded over her arm. Stopping far
enough away that Nishima could see without moving,
Kento displayed each robe in turn.

"No, too dark—there is enough darkness. No Kento-
sum, lighter still. Pure white is what I want. Bring me a
robe made of the snow itself."

The lady-in-waiting bowed and hurried out in a swish
of silk. Nishima closed her eyes, and ran her fingertips
over her thighs, falling back into thoughts of the poem
she had received that morning. The hot bath seemed to
hold her, easing her tensions. She knew she was
exhausted, yet she could not sleep.

Kento returned, seeming to Nishima to bring the world
with her in her concern for her lady's dress.

"Ah, yes. Now that is closer. Yes, that one. And the
other, a shade darker. Perfect. Leave them, I will dress
and come out to you."

Maids hurried in bringing towels for their mistress, but
Nishima sent them out and dried herself with the narrow
lengths of rough cotton, rubbing briskly as though the
roughness would bring her mind back to matters at hand.
From a shelf she took an ornate lacquered box of tur-
quoise and azure which bore a pattern of white warisha
blossoms—the symbol of the ancient House of Fanisan.

The jewelry box, and much that it contained, had
belonged to Nishima's mother and the young woman
treasured it for more than its perfectly wrought contents.
She twisted the handle in the special way and the lid
popped open without a sound. Just the sight of what lay
within gave her deep pleasure. Her long fingers caressed
a set of silver bracelets and then a smooth jade pendant
and a string of black pearls.

Lifting out a small tray, Nishima uncovered Tanaka's
letter and her own decoding of it. Beneath these lay the
coins. She examined them again carefully, looking for
signs of their origin. They had been struck with great
skill even though they appeared very plain. She turned
them over on her palm, each coin about the size of her
thumbnail and unmarked but for perfectly round holes
in their centers. As Tanaka had written, they could well

have come from the Imperial Mint, but there was nothing specific about them that would prove this true.

Taking a length of mauve silk ribbon, Nishima strung the coins along it, the metal catching the sunlight and seeming to gain depth as only true gold could. Wrapping this around her naked waist, she felt the cold metal warm to the soft skin of her stomach. Nishima slipped the robes over this, being certain that no signs of the coins could be seen. Once dressed she knew that the many folds of her sash would conceal secrets far greater than this.

Nishima slid open the shoji and stepped into the next room where her lady-in-waiting had several wooden wardrobes open and an array of kimonos displayed according to color and formality.

"A letter has arrived from Lady Okara, my lady."

"Ah. Let me see it." Nishima said quickly.

A tiny branch of sweet smelling lintel herb, a vine often found growing on old stone walls, was attached to a fine cloth paper of pearl gray.

Lintel herb, Nishima thought, used to purify water. She dropped to her knees on a cushion, forgetting entirely about the kimonos spread about her. The letter was folded in the manner called "Gateway" though it scarcely resembled this, but Nishima noted it duly. Such things were invariably part of the message or added an additional level to it. For a second she was disappointed by the simplicity of the hand and then she smiled. It was absolutely correct for Lady Okara and on closer inspection she realized that "simple" was not an adequate description. "Pure" would perhaps be a better word.

> I have read your letter through now several times, Nishima-sum. And though I do not know your reasons for this proposed journey I do trust you. I can't help feeling that this situation you find yourself in is my fault and I feel great resentment over being used in this way. Not toward you, my dear, but to others. There is only one solution to our problem; I will travel to Seh with you. In this way you will not incur the displeasure of the Son

*of Heaven, for the Emperor said nothing of us
staying in the capital to pursue your studies. I
have not seen the great canal in many years and
I cannot imaging a more suitable place for us to
consider the essence of our artistic endeavors.*

*The white blossoms
Of the lintel vine
Are scattered by the winds.
They flow north on strong currents
Like the crests
Of a thousand small waves.
How will we open the gates
Now that the arches crumble?*

Nishima read the letter again and then refolded it as
it had come. Suddenly she felt an overwhelming need
for sleep—she could, now. Rohku Saicha would have no
argument against this!

May Botahara bless Okara-sum, Nishima thought, I
am going to Seh.

# Twenty-seven

The Emperor realized he was pacing and felt his anger return again. He crossed to the dais and looked down on the pile of scrolls and letters scattered across the mats. All of this, he thought, and no news to gladden the heart. Without warning, he kicked a silk cushion across the room. Its collision with the shoji brought a horde of guards and attendants rushing in from all sides.

"Yes?" the Emperor said loudly. "Did I call any of you? Get out! You!—bring me my cushion. Now get out."

He slumped down on his newly returned cushion and regarded the yards of paper spread around him. "May the gods take Jaku Katta. I *need* that young fool!" Reaching for the letter he had received from Lord Shonto, the Son of Heaven read it again carefully, looking for any sign that Shonto lied—that the lord pointed a finger at Jaku only to take away the Emperor's valued servant.

*Sire:*

*By now the Emperor knows of my difficulties at Denji Gorge but I have taken the liberty of writing, briefly, my impressions of what occurred there.*

*The northern locks of Denji Gorge have, for some years now, come under the control of the Hajiwara and during this time the Hajiwara House has used this control to increase their fortunes at the expense of the Imperial Treasury. The*

Hajiwara financial records I have sent to Your
Majesty will show that this is true.

The Hajiwara have accomplished this theft by
controlling the Imperial Keep above the northern
locks with the unspoken approval of the Imperial
Governor, the Lord Hajiwara's kinsman.

As I refused to pay a tithe to the Hajiwara, I
was held in the Gorge for several days and pre-
vented from fulfilling my duties to my Emperor.
This situation was intolerable and an affront to
your Majesty, so I arranged to take the locks from
the Hajiwara forces and return them to the control
of Imperial Authorities. Unfortunately, in this
struggle Lord Hajiwara and his family died. This
I regret for I will miss the pleasure of seeing the
Hajiwara before an Imperial Court.

It seems that an Imperial Messenger, one Jaku
Yasata was sent to Itsa some months ago, no
doubt to deal with this situation, but such was the
arrogance of the Hajiwara that Lieutenant Jaku
was ignored—in fact the situation grew worse after
his visit, as all Imperial Representatives were disallowed entry to the lock areas and were deprived
access to the lock records.

I believe, Sire, that I have acted as the situation
dictated and to restore respect for my Emperor.
In this matter I was aided greatly by Lord Butto
of Itsa whose bravery and loyalty were readily put
at the service of the Throne.

> I remain Your Majesty's servant,
> Shonto Motoru

The Emperor realized that his palms were damp and
he wiped them unceremoniously on his robe. Shonto
must believe it was the Emperor who arranged this stupid
escapade. All of the effort and cost that had gone into
sending Shonto to the north and now this! If the lord
had held any doubt that Seh was a trap, that doubt was
gone now.

I am in danger, the Emperor thought. Shonto and his one-armed advisor and that accursed monk plot even now—I can feel it. Katta, you fool! You have placed me in danger when every effort had been made to hide the hand that held the knife. Fool! Stupid fool! Now what would he do? Be calm. His father had always remained calm and it had won him a throne. Akantsu stared down at the pile of reports as though they were responsible for his loss of tranquillity.

He tossed the letter back onto the pile.

There was a similar letter from Lord Butto or, more correctly, from his youngest son though under the old lord's signature. What a fiasco! And this visit by Yasata. The Emperor massaged the temples of his throbbing head. Jaku had long recommended that this stupid feud be allowed to continue as it weakened those involved which, he argued, could never be to the Emperor's disadvantage—but it now appeared that he might have had other reasons for his recommendations. What could he have been thinking?

Picking up a long scroll, the Emperor began to read the report prepared for him by his own agents—as if they could be trusted! He read each word looking for hidden meanings, seeing the hand of a traitor everywhere.

> *The brief war that has taken place in Itsa is a continuation of the feud between the two chief Houses of this province with one significant difference. In these last battles Lord Shonto Motoru has sided with the Butto, no doubt planning all of the actions with his own formidable staff.*
>
> *Lord Shonto's reasons for involving himself in this affair seem to be self-interest only—he was being prevented from continuing his journey north—though it is almost certainly true that the Hajiwara plotted against him, no doubt as agents for another party.*
>
> *The Governor of Itsa is presently traveling to the capital to lodge official complaints with the Imperial Government and no doubt to plead his*

*innocence to any charges that he has misappropri-
ated funds destined for the Imperial Treasury—a
blatant lie.*

*There is as yet no evidence of who the Hajiwara
served in this matter and we are endeavoring with
all haste to discover this while it may still be possible to do so.*

*There is one other note that should be recorded.
Shonto found a way to move an army out of
Denji Gorge without the assistance of the Butto.
This was formerly believed to be impossible. We
have not yet determined how this was done.*

The Emperor found his heart was beating too quickly,
and he put his hand to his chest to try to calm himself.
This escape from Denji Gorge was what unsettled him.
How had Shonto managed that? The Emperor knew the
gorge from personal experience, knew its high barren
walls. It must be a trick, he thought, the army must
somehow have come across the land. It isn't possible for
a single man to escape from Denji Gorge, let alone an
army. But the Emperor knew that this was the lie and
that the truth was Shonto had escaped from an impossible situation. This knowledge did not bring Akantsu II
comfort.

The Emperor began rolling the scroll, keeping the
paper tight. So much hangs in the balance, he thought,
and now this? Who hid behind the screen of this feud
and whispered the orders to Hajiwara? And who would
be so stupid as to believe that fool Hajiwara could out-
maneuver the Lord of the Shonto? Could it be, as Shonto
implied, that Jaku Katta had arranged this entire
escapade?

Katta, the Emperor thought, you have been like a son
to me, and now, like a son, do you grow impatient for
the father to pass on?

A quiet knock on the shoji interrupted the Emperor's
thoughts. A screen slid aside and an attendant knelt in
the opening.

"Yes?"

"Sire, Colonel Jaku Tadamoto awaits your pleasure."

"Ah." The Emperor gestured to his reports. "Have this arranged and then I will see the colonel."

Two servants rushed in and began rolling scrolls and picking up papers. "Leave them with us," the Emperor ordered, "and give me my sword."

Doors at the end of the audience hall opened, revealing Jaku Katta's younger brother, a tall, slightly built, handsome man who looked to be the scholar he in fact was. He knelt outside the doors, his head bowed to the mat.

"You may approach, Colonel."

Jaku Tadamoto came forward on his knees, stopping a respectful distance from the dais.

"It gives me pleasure to see you, Colonel."

"I am honored that you feel so, Sire."

A half-smile crossed the Emperor's face at Tadamoto's words, but then it hardened into the look of a man with many things weighing upon him. "Tadamoto-sum, events in our Empire have made me aware again that the throne draws to it traitors of all kinds. There are so few we can trust, so few whose loyalty is not a mask for private ambitions."

"It grieves me that this is so, Sire."

Nodding his head sadly, the Emperor rubbed his hand along the scabbard of his sword as though it were a talisman. "But you, Tadamoto-sum, you, I think, are different. Is that not so?

"I am the Emperor's servant." Tadamoto said simply.

"Ah, I hope that is true, Tadamoto-Sum, I hope that is true." The Emperor paused, staring directly at the young officer. "Have you heard of these events at the gorge in Itsa?"

"I have, Sire."

"And?"

Tadamoto cleared his throat. "Excuse me for saying so, Sire, but I have long advocated putting an end to that feud and reestablishing Imperial Law on the Grand Canal."

"So you have. Tell me again your reasons for this."

"Sire, it is the lesson of history. Those Emperors who have offered stability have had the fewest internal problems to deal with. The canal has been unsafe ever since the Interim War, yet this canal is our link with half of the Empire. All of the provinces reached by the canal feel they are being ignored by the capital, they grow resentful, and soon there are problems resulting from this. I have never supported the policy of allowing the Empire to remain unstable, there is no evidence in our histories to support this idea."

The Emperor nodded. So, and it was Jaku Katta who recommended that I not allow the Great Houses to return to complete peace. Have I listened to the wrong brother all along?

"What you say has the sound of truth, Tadamoto-sum. But tell me what you think of this situation in Itsa."

"Sire, it is clear from the reports that Shonto used the Butto to push his way through the Hajiwara armies, though it is not yet known how this was done. The situation in Itsa was so contrary to the laws of the Imperium that Shonto was willing to take the situation into his own hands without fear of Imperial reprisal. No one in the Empire will feel that Shonto has acted without honor and respect for his Emperor. He has at once done the Emperor a favor while at the same time making it clear how inadequately the government has tended to certain of its duties. The Hajiwara were no match for the Shonto and I would not be surprised to learn that Lord Hajiwara thought he had come to an agreement with Lord Shonto that was to his advantage . . . only to learn that the Shonto never make agreements that do not favor them.

The Emperor caressed his sword again, with a certain compulsion. "I see. So what is to be done now?"

Tadamoto nodded, a quick bow, almost a reflex. "I believe, Sire, that you should seize the initiative in this situation. The Throne should restore order on the canals and the roads of the Empire. It will be costly to begin with, but once law is established then it shall become less so—and I fear the costs of not doing this will be much greater. There is much support for what the Lord

Shonto has done in Itsa—he is the hero of the Empire for the moment—but there would be equal support for this action if it were undertaken by the Imperial Government.

"But would we not simply appear to be finishing the work of Lord Shonto, scurrying about after him like servants?"

"Sire, I believe it is only a question of making enough noise. Form an Imperial Triumvirate to deal with the problem of the roads and canals. Send out Imperial Functionaries and large forces of guards with power to do your bidding. Have edicts read in the capitals of all the provinces and then parade the robbers and embezzlers through the streets. It will soon be forgotten that it was Lord Shonto who took the first steps."

"Ah, Tadamoto-sum, I value your counsel. Others give advice only to further their own aims but you . . . there is indeed an echo of Hakata in your words."

The young colonel bowed his head to the mat. "I am more than honored by your words, Sire."

The Emperor nodded. "I do not think my praise is misplaced. We shall see.

"There is another matter, Tadamoto-sum." The Emperor lowered his voice. "A matter we have spoken of previously. Your brother, in his zeal to ensure our safety, has surrounded us with many who report to him personally. I understand this is for reasons of security, but it is more than is necessary as I have said to you before. Have you managed to discover who these people are?"

Tadamoto nodded once, not meeting the Emperor's eyes. "I have, Sire."

"And you have made a list?"

Again Tadamoto nodded.

The Emperor smiled. "Leave it with us, Tadamoto-sum. I will speak with your brother. Taking such precautions is more than is necessary, even for one as conscientious as Katta-sum.

"What of the followers of Tomsoma?" the Emperor asked, his voice suddenly cool. He went on before Tadamoto could begin to answer. "This attempt to cause more tension between them and the Silent Brothers was foolish. The Brothers are treacherous, but they are not fools. Has that priest . . . what was his name?"

"Ashigaru, Sire."

"Has he surfaced?"

Tadamoto shook his head. "He has not, Sire. I don't think the Emperor need be concerned. The magic cults have begun to realize that there is no hope of converting the Imperial Family. They are resentful, Sire, no doubt, but so far they are silently so."

The Emperor shook his head. "They have been of little use and demanded much." He turned his gaze on the young officer then, and there seemed to be great affection there.

"And did you ever discuss the Lady Nishima with your brother, Tadamoto-sum."

"I did, Sire."

"Ah."

"He felt it was a service to his Emperor to observe the Lady Nishima, Sire."

"Of course. And does he continue to see the lady?"

"He has not met with her, to the best of my knowledge, Sire."

"Perhaps he has reconsidered the nature of his duties. That would be wisdom. There is a duty I would ask you to perform, Tadamoto-sum." The Emperor did not wait for Tadamoto to answer. "Osha is unhappy with her situation, as you could understand—perhaps it would cheer her if you would escort her to the Ceremony of the Gray Horses."

"I would, gladly, Sire. May I say that I am touched by your concern for those of humble station."

The Emperor nodded modestly. "We shall speak again soon, Tadamoto-sum. Very soon. There are other matters in which we would value your counsel. We shall see."

Tadamoto bowed low and backed from the room. Alone, the Emperor reached for the list Tadamoto had left, but he did not read it immediately. "The Shonto never make agreements that do not favor them," he whispered. "Never."

The two men circled each other slowly, each matching the other step for step. They wore the black split pants and white jackets of traditional Shishama fighters, and one, the designated aggressor, wore a red band of silk wrapped above cold gray eyes. A sword flicked right and down in the beginnings of "swallow flight," but the other countered quickly and the swords went back to the guard position. The aggressor, Jaku Katta, slowed his circling, then stopped, planting his bare feet firmly on the stone floor. His sword went high to the "falcon dive" position, causing the other to step back and parry. Swords flashed in the sunlight, too quick for the eye to follow and then in the clash of metal Jaku's blade found the other's sword arm just above the elbow and it was over. The man bowed deeply, his hand moving to massage his arm.

Jaku Katta bowed also. "I hope I have not caused you harm?"

"The stroke was most controlled, General. It has been an honor just to stand against you. I thank you."

"The honor was mine, Captain." The two men handed their blunt practice blades to waiting attendants. "Again, perhaps?"

"Certainly, General." The man bowed again and Jaku nodded turning to a waiting guard. "Yes?"

The guard knelt quickly. "General Katta, your reply from the office of the Emperor." The guard offered a folded letter to his general.

Jaku took it and continued toward the nearby door that led to his private quarters. The exercise had felt good; it never failed to restore his confidence and now he basked in that warm afterglow poets called "the sun within." Slowly he unfolded the letter and as he stepped up onto his veranda he began to read. Two steps farther, on he almost stumbled and then stopped. He read the letter again:

*General Jaku Katta, Commander, Imperial Guards:*

*Your request for an audience with the most revered Son of Heaven has been denied. His Majesty trusts he will have the honor of your presence at the Celebration of the Gray Horses.*

*Lord Bakai Jima,*
*Secretary.*
*For His Imperial Majesty,*
*Akantsu II*

Jaku almost sank to his knees but reached out and gripped a post. The letter had taken him like the stroke of a sword—suddenly it was over. One could not take back the mistake, the misplaced foot, the weak parry.

Ever since he had received the report from Itsa early that morning he had known a sense of foreboding. If he could see the Son of Heaven, explain to him—Jaku had no doubt of his influence over his Emperor—then he could redeem himself. But now this. He would not have a chance to give his carefully prepared speech; a speech that could be his salvation.

The explanation he had prepared was clear and simple; just the way Akantsu preferred things to be. Jaku Katta knew it would be foolish to deny his involvement in the attempt on Shonto at Denji Gorge, there were too many ways the Emperor could have found out otherwise. No, Jaku's plan was simply to take responsibility and claim there were reasons of security that had necessitated his secrecy.

The failure was something else altogether. Shonto had not only escaped the trap, but he had embarrassed the Throne by removing those parasites, the Hajiwara, from the Empire's main artery—parasites that were there with tacit Imperial approval. And this due to counsel from Jaku himself. The Black Tiger shook his head and proceeded to his bath.

Servants scrubbed him thoroughly before he lowered himself into the steaming water. And now what? He had never received a denial of a request for an audience before. Never. The significance of this action shook him. He felt like a man who had fallen off a ship in the night and now watched it sail away into the darkness. It couldn't be happening. Yet it was. It had, in fact, already happened.

Somehow, Jaku felt a sense of injustice as though his plans, no matter what they may be or who they might involve, deserved to succeed for no other reason than that they were his.

Was it not he who had contrived the entire plan to rid the Emperor of the constant shadow of Lord Shonto? Had he not performed a thousand deeds for his Emperor, many at great personal risk? Things could not be as they seemed. Jaku would go to the Imperial apartments and demand to see the Emperor on a matter of security. All of the men who surrounded the Emperor were Jaku's men, they would let him through without question. It could be done. He would yet take back the mistake.

Jaku shifted in the water, laying his head back and closing his eyes. Yes that was what he would do. Once he was before the Emperor, he would hold sway. Whoever conspired against him, and he had no doubt that someone did, could not know the key to Akantsu II as Jaku did. The Emperor was, at heart, a soldier and he respected only those whose spirit was as his. And Jaku was the essence of the fighter, the raw matter distilled down until it was as pure as the spirit of the wind. Jaku was the warrior of all warriors and the Emperor knew it.

Jaku's thoughts shifted inexplicably to Lady Nishima, to the poem he had received from her only an hour before. Her reticence was only an act, he knew. Jaku had seen it before in other well born young women. But her eyes told him the truth, and the truth was she was smitten with him. There was no question of it; this was one campaign Jaku had won. It had not even been difficult. Jaku laughed bitterly.

Everything had fit into his design until Shonto had

reached Itsa. What had really happened there? Jaku
stretched his muscular arms above him, letting the water
splash back onto his face. The plan had been without
flaw—but then Hajiwara was a fool, there was no doubt
of that. Jaku laughed again. All was not lost. He would
recover as a fighter did, turning his enemies' thrust to
his own advantage. He was still strong. The Lady Nishima would come into his plans soon enough and the
Emperor, the Emperor who refused his audience, would
understand that Jaku Katta was something more than he
had ever realized.

Jaku rose and stepped, dripping, from his bath. Servants entered with towels to dry him.

"Bring my duty armor and helmet," he ordered an
attendant. It was time to see this reticent Emperor. Time
for a bold stroke. Jaku dressed slowly, enjoying the feel
of his light armor, admiring the artistry of its maker.

"General Jaku," the attendant began. "General, there
are servants and guards outside awaiting your orders."

"What?" Jaku picked up his helmet and started for
the door.

The man bobbed in a quick succession of bows as he
rushed along beside his master. "They do not understand, General. They have been sent. You must see for
yourself."

Jaku preceded the attendant to the door and as it
opened he was greeted by a gathering of faces, all of
which he recognized. The servants of the Emperor. Jaku
stood without speaking, the eyes of this desperate gathering turned to him, the faces registering a depth of fear
that unsettled him so that he found himself taking a step,
unbidden, back into the protection of his rooms.

The Ceremony of the Gray Horses was performed in
the central courtyard of the Island Palace, a place well
known for its view of the setting sun. Garlands of autumn
flowers graced the columns of the nearby porticoes and
autumn leaves and petals had been scattered on the
ponds and streams. The many trees in their autumn colors needed no artistic assistance, and it was from their

autumn palette that other colors were drawn, including the robes of the courtiers and officials gathered for this ancient ceremony.

Directly across from the gate of the inner spirit the dais and Throne of the Emperor had been situated, and there the most revered Son of Heaven sat with the members of the Imperial family arrayed about him, including a sullen Empress. The Major Chancellor and the Ministers of both the Right and the Left sat in their appointed places, while to each side of these the ranks descended from the First to the Third, the lowest rank allowed to attend such an important ceremony. Even so, the numbers reached to several thousand men and women, all dressed with an acute awareness of the appropriate colors and degree of formality so that the overall effect was without a single point of disharmony in the entire composition.

Seated among those of the Third Rank of the Left, Jaku Katta assumed the attitude of the other courtiers—respectful anticipation—but he watched the Emperor's every move, searching for a sign of his intentions. Yet he saw nothing, and there among the many, Jaku did not draw a nod from his Emperor.

It is as though I have ceased to exist, Jaku thought, as though I am already dead. He caught the eye of a young woman who smiled demurely and then hid her face with a fan, yet this hardly registered in his mind at all. What shall I do? Jaku asked himself. Everything I have planned falls around me.

The subdued excitement of the crowd was almost tangible and seemed to flow like chi along all the meridian of the whole. A love of ceremony that was almost an obsession had long been a prominent feature of Waian court life. All waited for the signal from the Emperor.

Being semi-divine, the Emperor was expected to intercede for the people of Wa with his ancestors and the gods. Even the advent of Botahara a thousand years earlier had affected these rites in only the smallest ways—a thin veneer of Botahist doctrine layered over the rites of the ancient pantheism.

The story of the Gray Horses originated at the time
of the establishment of the Seven Kingdoms which later
became the central provinces of the Empire of Wa. It
was said that Po Wu, the father of the gods, gave the
Gray Horses to his sons, the Seven Princes, who then
drove the barbarians out of the lands of Cho-Wa and
planted the seeds of civilization.

The gray steeds were imbued with magical powers by
Po Wu and could not be injured or die in battle. From
their running hooves came a thunder which shook the
earth and split the hills, scattering their enemies before
them like gulls before a storm.

The Gray Horses of the ceremony were said to be
descendants of Po Wu's steeds, bred generation after
generation and carefully guarded by the Emperor's staff.

At a nod from the Emperor, the ceremony began with
the beating of drums like the sound of thunder and then
the airy voice of a thirteen pipe flute. From the Gate of
the Inner Spirit the clatter of unshod hooves striking
stone seemed to blend with the rhythm of the music and
then the horses appeared—seven pale gray mounts,
groomed until they glinted in the sunlight.

The riders were the best in the province; two Imperial
Guards, the sons of three lords, a Minor Counselor and
a hunt master—all dressed in Imperial crimson and
seated on saddles of gold and deep green. The horses
were arrayed in headdresses of gold and black and the
contrast of these strong colors with the pale tones of the
audience had an almost startling effect.

The riders moved their horses through carefully coordinated exercises of great intricacy, and all with commands so subtle that none could see them. A story grew
out of these exercises, the story of the Seven Princes and
their magical horses. Dancers joined in dressed as foot
soldiers and barbarians, yet there was never a confusion
nor loss of focus to the movement.

After sweeping the barbarians from the field, the seven
equestrians wheeled and paraded slowly before the Emperor, and as the living descendant of Po Wu he
rewarded them for their valor with generous gifts.

The riders all bowed their thanks and led their horses from the courtyard to the buzzing of the courtiers' praise. A silence settled over the audience then as they waited for the Emperor and the Imperial Family to rise and depart—but instead a Senior Assistant to the Minister of the Left struck a small gong to gain everyone's attention. Moving with a grace surprising for his age the assistant took up a position in front of the dais, bowed twice, and removed a scroll from his sleeve. His voice was soft, yet it carried well to all of his audience.

"On behalf of the Minister of the Left, I have been charged to read these, the words of the most revered Son of Heaven.

"Today we have witnessed not only an ancient ceremony of lasting significance but also a metaphor which is descriptive of our own time. The northern border of Wa is again pressed by the barbarians and we have, as is our duty, turned our eyes there. Yet this is not the only place where the spirit of the primitive peoples has been manifested. Within the borders of our own provinces those who are barbarians in spirit make many of our roads and waterways unsafe and, to our lasting disappointment, the lords of the provinces have been unable to curtail this activity. It is our pledge that we will not allow barbarism to threaten our Empire, either from within or without.

"Therefore, it is the will of the Throne that this situation shall end. To accomplish this, forces of Imperial Guards and Functionaries of the judiciary shall be sent throughout the Empire for the purpose of making all our routes of travel and commerce safe for even the most humble citizen of our Empire.

"Due to recent circumstances on the Grand Canal we realize that this, the cord that binds our great Empire together, is in peril and therefore will be our first concern. To deal with this situation we have chosen to send the Commander of the Imperial Guard, General Jaku Katta, as representative of the Throne and Sole Arbiter on the Grand Canal. He will be charged with returning the waterway to its former state of peace and efficiency.

"Others will be sent out with the same orders to effect the same changes on all the arteries of our Empire.

"By order of Akantsu II, Emperor, And the Great Council of the Empire."

The bureaucrat bowed as he finished his reading and the assembled guests bowed in turn to the Emperor and his family. A sound went through the crowd, an indescribable sound that everyone recognized as the sound of mass approval. The Emperor smiled as he rose and stepped into his waiting sedan chair.

Among those bowing as the Emperor made his exit was one general in Imperial Guard uniform who did not share this sense of approval. Jaku Katta sat waiting for those of higher rank to leave, accepting congratulations and good wishes with what appeared to be a stoic nod but was, in fact, perfectly contained fury.

What had been done to Shonto at Jaku's urging had now been done to Jaku. The Black Tiger took long slow breaths and tried to calm his mind, but his anger seemed to dart everywhere, now aimed at the Son of Heaven, now aimed at Lord Shonto, now at the foolish courtiers who congratulated him while having no notion of what was happening. He was like a bow drawn near its breaking point with an arrow notched and ready—and he looked everywhere in his mind for the appropriate target.

The members of the First and Second Ranks had risen and made their way leisurely from the square. Jaku rose with the people remaining, those of the Third Rank, and began to make his way through the crowd. Around him people laughed and commented on the beauty of the ceremony and the perfection of the equestrians, but Jaku walked under a cloud as dark as his black uniform. It was all he could do not to push these fools out of his way, but he held himself in check—it was important to know when to release an arrow.

Coming finally to the edge of the square, he mounted a set of steps that few others would use and there he broke free of the crowds and the foolish prattle. On the top step he turned to survey the square out of habit; he was, after all, in charge of security in the palace. And there among the throng that passed the foot of his steps he saw his brother, Tadamoto, walking in the company of Osha, the Emperor's Sonsa—and they were laughing. Jaku could almost hear them. They laughed a shared laugh and their faces glowed as only lovers could.

My own blood, Jaku thought.

# Twenty-eight

*Whispers behind the sleeve,*
*Words cooler than winter rain*
*Touch me where I stand,*
*Here, in the Governor's shadow.*
*No one has named me a traitor*
*To my province.*

*It is gratifying to know that*
*My sword retains its respect.*

   *Komawara Samyamu*

The afternoon sun broke through the storm clouds here and there, sending long shafts of light down to the earth; shafts that moved as the clouds moved, in swift, erratic formations.

The crests of waves tumbled into foam which was blown into white streaks across the dark waters. Crests mounted again, rushed on, and dashed themselves against the base of the stone wall.

Standing at the parapet, Lord Shonto looked down at the chaos below. Five days had passed since his arrival in Seh and Shonto had only that morning been able to free himself from the formal demands made upon a new governor. He had been frustrated by all the ceremony and was more than ready to begin the work that had brought him to Seh: the military work. He began with what was close at hand and launched an inspection of the capital's fortifications followed by an assessment of the state of the garrison.

The new governor walked along the wall with a stride that caused his companions to rush in a most undignified manner if they were not to be left behind. They weren't used to such exertions; governors were expected to travel by canal or sedan chair perhaps, on rare occasion, by horseback. But this!—a walking tour was unheard of.

The men rushing along in the governor's wake were a disparate group, many in long formal robes which the wind attacked with a certain glee. They naturally arrayed themselves by rank: the Major Chancellor Lord Gitoyo, and his son, a Middle Captain of the Third Rank followed the governor; the Minister of War, Lord Akima, a very old man who kept pace without sign of discomfort; two Ministers of the Second Rank wearing their formal blue robes and sweating profusely; General Hojo and Lord Komawara were next and then a Lieutenant Colonel of the garrison. A dozen attendants of varying rank followed by an appropriate number of guards completed the retinue.

A certain General Toshaki's military rank placed him officially in the Third Rank, but as a member of one of Seh's most important houses he walked beside Lord Shonto though deferring to him as was appropriate.

"As I said earlier, Lord Shonto," Toshaki said, not using the new governor's official title, "we do everything necessary to keep the city strong and the defenses in good repair." General Toshaki said this between deep gasps as he trotted along beside Shonto. It was the last set of stairs that had reduced him to this state and Shonto's pace was not allowing him to recover. The inspection had caught the men of Seh off guard though Shonto's own staff were not in the least surprised. They had learned the futility of trying to predict the action of their lord—it was better to keep abreast of all one's duties and let inspections come as they would.

Shonto said nothing in response to the general's statement which unsettled the soldier more than he would have expected. Stopping again, Shonto looked over the edge, down at the booming waves. The wall was indeed in good repair, that was clear even to his critical eye, but here and there at its base a dark shelf of rock extended out into the waves. Lack of rainfall that autumn had lowered the water level and exposed rock that was normally many feet under water. It caused Shonto concern. This shelf compromised the integrity of the defenses quite considerably, and worse than that, General Toshaki did not seem to realize it.

"Sire, you can see that Rhojo-ma is secure—her walls unbreachable. Perhaps we could . . ."

"There are no walls that cannot be breached, General," Shonto said as he stopped again and stared over the side.

"Of course you are right, Sire. On the land that is true, but here with a natural moat of three miles . . ."

"General Hojo." Shonto stopped and addressed his senior military advisor.

"Sire?"

Shonto nodded toward an exposed outcropping of smooth granite.

Hojo leaned out over the stone parapet. "I agree, Sire, this is a danger. A staging area is just what's needed to attempt these walls."

"Could you breach them, General?"

"From what I have seen I would say yes—if I could be sure of the element of surprise. The guards have too much confidence in the defenses and this is not good."

"General Toshaki?"

The tall soldier pulled himself even more erect. His words came out in a clipped mockery of politeness. "Sire; the general's observations are astute, but there are other factors to consider. A fleet large enough to attack Rhojo-ma could hardly be constructed in secret. There would always be some warning of such an attack. Any small scale excursion against the city, even if it was successful in passing beyond our first wall, would be isolated by our secondary walls. We would soon force them back into the waves, you can be sure. These rocks will be under water after only a few days of rain, and that rain will not be long in coming. The autumn storms are as reliable as the patience of Botahara, Sire."

Shonto and General Hojo glanced at each other but said nothing. Turning away from the parapet, Shonto continued on his tour.

It was a strange company of professional soldiers, bureaucrats, and peers of the realm who could be seen atop the outer walls, flapping in the wind like rag-guards in a peasant's garden. But it was not just the wind that controlled their movements: this new governor, this outsider, held sway over their futures in the hierarchy of Seh. It was a fact widely resented, and it showed.

But the situation was not that simple for the men of Seh; this new governor was no lackey of the Emperor's sent north to fulfill some political obligation. This was the Lord of the Shonto, a soldier of considerable fame, a man who was respected for more than just his ancient name. A name that history had woven into the very fabric of Seh. It was this complexity of situation that Shonto knew he must exploit if he was to succeed in the north.

The procession came to a large lookout station, a stone platform high in the fortifications. Here the new governor stopped, much to the relief of those following him. Stools were brought from a guard house for the persons of rank and they seated themselves in a semicircle around Shonto.

"Lord Akima," Shonto said, not waiting for anyone to catch his breath. "Tomorrow I will send members of my staff to outlying areas to begin inspections of our defenses. I am particularly interested in the border areas and our inner line of defense. Please detail senior officers from the garrison to accompany them. The details of this can be arranged with General Hojo.

"I will need to establish a primary base closer to the border and to the areas the barbarians have been threatening. This can be decided after I have assessed the present situation. Major Chancellor, I trust that if I leave the administration of Seh largely to you and your capable staff, you will not have cause for complaint?"

The Major Chancellor's surprise was quite well contained. He was a man selected by the former governor of Seh who had purged the remains of the corrupt administration that had typified Seh for the last hundred years. Shonto expected much from this man. All reports indicated that he was competent and just: even Komawara spoke highly of him.

"Lord Governor, I will do all within my power to see that the government of Seh is run efficiently and justly, as a bearer of the name Shonto would prefer it. I am honored by your trust."

Shonto nodded in return to the man's deep bow. The men surrounding the new governor were, in nature, typical northerners and Shonto couldn't help but like them despite their ill-concealed feelings of resentment toward him. They were a quiet, practical group showing little tendency toward extravagance. The hunting costume was their typical mode of dress and this was accepted at all but the most formal occasions: a marked contrast with the Imperial capital. The men who sat before Lord Shonto were tanned like men who worked the fields and they were not ashamed of it. From his other visits Shonto knew that a northern lord's saddle would be of good leather, worn by constant use, and that this wear was a mark of pride not of poverty—the horse was what mattered and the horses of Seh were the best in the Empire.

"General Toshaki, if you would take General Hojo on a tour of the barracks, I would be free to pursue other matters." Shonto rose to his feet suddenly and the others quickly followed suit. "I will request your presence when needed," Shonto said, addressing the entire company. "Lord Akima, Lord Komawara, if you would accompany me." Shonto turned and left the others scurrying to bow properly as he set off again along the wall. Guards preceding them discreetly cleared all nonmilitary and nonranking peoples off the walkway.

"Lord Akima," Shonto said, slowing his pace somewhat, "It appears that Rhojo-ma has benefited from careful attention, but I am told that the outlying fortifications have not received the same care."

The older man nodded, shaking his thick gray hair. "This is true, Lord Shonto. What allotments there have been for defense have largely been spent on the Governor's Palace and those areas immediately surrounding it. The Hanama Governors were, as you know, interested in filling their own coffers and extending the interest of their families. The governors appointed since the Hanama have been less opportunistic personally but instead have enriched the Emperor. There has been little concern for the security of Seh."

"An unfortunate situation and one over which I may have little control. The Son of Heaven demands his taxes. I understand you are of the opinion that the barbarians are no threat to your province?"

"Sire, the tribes are diminished, there is no doubt of this. There has been little rainfall in the desert these past years and it is said that the plague spread even across the sands. These raids . . . they are almost ineffectual. There have been virtually no losses from them. The barbarians have become timid, fearing to meet even our smallest armed parties. In this matter the Emperor has been poorly counseled, and I'm afraid, Lord Governor, that you will find your long journey futile. The barbarian threat exists only in the minds of a few Imperial Advisors whose knowledge of the situation is perhaps not as thorough as one would expect."

Shonto stopped at a major corner in the fortress and looked carefully along the two walls visible from that point. So, Shonto thought, in Seh the Emperor is not above criticism—how refreshing. "Do you not find the behavior of the barbarians strange—out of character for such renowned warriors?"

Lord Akima glanced at Komawara in obvious exasperation. "There are those who express this belief, Lord Governor, but I for one do not understand it. These raids are referred to as 'mysterious' by a small number of people, but the barbarians have been raiding throughout Seh for as long as we have recorded our history— what, then, is strange about that? The tribes have been drastically reduced in size and the warriors who remain are few in number and little able to afford losses. That is the explanation of the 'mystery,' nothing more."

"Huh. I appreciate your knowledge in this matter. Lord Komawara, do you share our companion's opinions?"

Komawara betrayed his anger as he had in the Emperor's garden, his face was flushed and his jaw tight, but his voice was controlled, even pleasant. "This is the common wisdom, Sire, and worth consideration but I believe there are reasons to look into the raids more closely, especially since it would cost so little to do so. Although it is often said that the tribes are reduced in number, it seems to me that it is merely a statement of hope. I can find no evidence for such a belief as no one ventures beyond our borders to make a proper assessment of the numbers of barbarians living in the wastes. The only thing we are certain of is a change in the behavior of the barbarians and though the explanation given by Lord Akima is perhaps true, it is only speculation and as such should not be given more weight than other explanations."

He learns quickly, Shonto thought, the argument was well presented, though perhaps not appreciated by Lord Akima.

"Excuse me for saying so, Lord Governor," Akima said, "but I have observed the barbarian tribes for many years and I cannot subscribe to this belief that the barbarians have suddenly begun to act in a mysterious manner. It can only appear sudden to one who has not been able to observe them over many decades. If it is not fear that causes the barbarians to run from the men of Seh, then perhaps Lord Komawara could tell me what it is?"

Shonto shifted his gaze to Komawara who shrugged and shook his head.

"I do not know, Lord Akima, that is what concerns me."

"And there is the weakness of the argument," the old aristocrat said with finality. "It explains nothing—if you will excuse me for saying so."

Surprising Lord Akima by turning behind a guard station and descending a little known set of stairs, Shonto let a silence accompany them to the foot of the steps where he stopped and addressed both of his companions. "Long ago, in conversation with one of the Shonto, Hakata observed that most people preferred an ill con-

sidered answer to an intelligent question. I have come to
Seh to seek truths, and in this endeavor I am prepared to
ask difficult questions and then to live without immediate
answers if that is what is required. I hope all advisors to
the Shonto are willing to do the same."

A hand signal to his guards set them off down a narrow
street, the three lords not far behind.

Let him not suggest again that age is synonymous with
wisdom, Shonto thought. "I will meet Lord Taiki after
midday. I thank you for arranging this, Lord Akima, it
was most kind of you."

"It is an honor to serve, even in such small capacities,"
the older man said, a coolness in his voice.

"Do you still feel the Lord Taiki will not support an
increase in armed effort?"

"I feel that Lord Taiki believes, as so many of us do,
Sire, there is no real threat and increased military actions
drain resources which could better be used elsewhere."

The seed of the resentment, Shonto thought; in paying
for their own defense the men of Seh pay for the defense
of the Empire. And they are entirely right; this is not just.

"It is clear to the Shonto, if not to the Emperor's
counselors, that the cost of protecting Wa should be born
by the Imperial Government. It is my intention to use
what little influence I may have at court to see that this
problem receives the attention it deserves. It is unfortunate that the situation at court is such that I cannot guarantee results. But I can tell you, Lord Akima, that the
matter will receive more careful consideration than it has
had in the past."

"You are to be honored for recognizing the justness
of our cause, Lord Governor, but I fear the Son of
Heaven is more concerned with the health of his treasury
than with the health of the people of Seh. Of course he
has sent a warrior to govern us, but it is a case of the
correct action in the wrong circumstance, if you will
excuse a candid observation. I must say, Lord Shonto,
that the Lords of Seh realize you have arrived with a
significant force of your own, well armed and trained.
You are the first governor in memory to have done so."

They came to the narrow canal that quartered the island city of Rhojo-ma and mounted a high arching stone bridge. Stopping on its crest, Shonto stood looking along the canal and its bordering walkways. Several bridges could be seen in the distance arching delicately over the waterway like colorless rainbows. The capital of Seh was a beautiful city, and though it had been built in the time of Seh's great power it was well maintained and, one might even say, loved by its inhabitants. Shonto was particularly fond of the roofs covered in tile of celestial blue. Faded as they were, he was sure they were more beautiful then when new.

A hand signal to a Shonto guard sent him scurrying off along the canal bank. "We will return to the palace by sampan," Shonto said, "we have walked enough for one day."

Little was said on the ride to the Governor's Palace, each occupied with his own thoughts. Shonto remembered Rhojo-ma from a previous visit and could see that the city itself was virtually unchanged—but for one thing. The throngs of people he remembered so clearly crowding the streets and waterways could no longer be seen. Rhojo-ma reminded him of a city on a day of spiritual rest—unnaturally quiet, avenues almost deserted or populated by such small numbers that the street seemed broader than they really were. Announcing the hour of the crane, the ringing of a temple bell seemed to echo endlessly among the buildings as though searching everywhere for someone to appreciate its aural splendor.

Sadly, the healing Brothers came to Seh last, Shonto realized, and this is the result: the plague reaped its largest harvest here among the people of the north.

The sampan bearing the three lords rounded a curve in the canal and entered a gate in the high wall which surrounded the Imperial Governor's residence.

The palace of the governor of Seh was situated on the southern side of the city on a low hill. A simplified Mori period style had been adopted for the buildings, and with their sweeping blue tile roofs and high stone walls they gave the impression of solidity combined with a simple beauty. Enclosed within the compound were the official buildings of the government of Seh, and among them the Palace of Justice was noticeable for its classical beauty. The Governor's Palace itself was no larger than Shonto's ancestral home, but for Seh, where ostentation was traditionally disfavored, the palace verged on the extravagant. Shonto's staff found the surrounding gardens crude by the standards they were used to, and not just because the climate was harsher, but Lord Shonto found something about their lack of sophistication attractive and often walked in the governor's private garden.

Disembarking from their boat, Shonto bid Komawara and Akima farewell and retired to his own apartments. He planned to meet Lord Taiki Kiyorama later that day and wanted time to prepare himself mentally.

The province of Seh was dominated by three major Houses: the Taiki, the large Ranan family, and the very ancient House of Toshaki of which the Senior General of the provincial armies, Lord Toshaki Shinga was the head of a lesser branch. There were numerous Houses of the Second and Third Ranks, the Komawara among them, but it was the three major Houses that held sway in matters of import in the province and Shonto knew that it was among them that he must find allies.

Most of the minor Houses owed allegiance to one or other of the major families and followed their policies virtually without question. Only a few of the lesser Houses had managed to retain the degree of independence that the Komawara exhibited, and the Komawara's situation was a prime example of the cost of this independence—without the support of a major House they became poorer each year.

Of the three important lords, the head of the Toshaki seemed to feel there would be an advantage to aligning himself with the present dynasty while Lord Ranan was widely known to despise the Yamaku and resent the governors sent by the Imperial family. This was not surprising; the Ranan had been favored by the Hanama and for a century had acted as the family's right hand in the north, for which they had been richly rewarded.

Only the lord of the Taiki seemed unsure of his position. It was known that he had little love for the Ranan and little respect for the Toshaki. The rumors were that he believed the barbarian threat was imaginary, which would seem to place him with the majority of northerners. Despite this belief, he held the Emperor's new governor in high regard, which is to say that he had respect for the Shonto, and this Shonto in particular. Shonto was not sure how Lord Taiki felt about the new dynasty, and it worried him somewhat. This was the man Shonto hoped to win to his side, and he realized that things in the north would be much more difficult without Taiki support.

Traditional methods of forming alliances would not be applicable in a province that was so insular, especially when it was clear that Shonto's stay there would be brief. A marriage between the Shonto and the Taiki was not feasible, not only because of their difference in position, but Lord Taiki's only son and heir had just recently celebrated his fourth birthday. Of course, such an arrangement was not unheard of, but Shonto would never subject Lady Nishima to such an indignity: he adored her far too much for the good of his family, he realized.

When Shonto took leave of Komawara and Lord Akima, the two men stood on the dock saying nothing, yet neither made a move to leave, as though there was something to be said but neither could grasp it.

Finally Lord Akima ended the silence. "Perhaps, Lord Komawara, if you stand close enough, you will one day be mistaken for a governor yourself." He bowed and walked down the quay to the place where his guards waited with his sampan.

Komawara felt like a man caught thieving: there was no denial possible—it *was* what he secretly hoped for, so secretly that he barely admitted it to himself. Yet old Akima had seen it easily. Seh, the young lord told himself, the welfare of my province is my true concern.

Akima, Komawara thought, is an old man, well past his prime, unable to see even the most obvious things: like the change in the pattern of barbarian raids. Yet was it not true that virtually all the lords of Seh agreed with Akima in this matter? Was the old man right? Was the lure of Governor's Palace really what attracted him?

Komawara stepped into his sampan and seated himself without even a nod to his guard or boatmen, so lost in thought was he. The old lord's remark had stung him more than he would ever have expected.

"I find this an interesting habit, Lord Shonto, perhaps one that is native only to my own province." Lord Taiki said. "I cannot understand how anyone can take a position on an entire dynasty. Certainly I can weigh the accomplishments of a past dynasty and decide if, on balance, they were good or bad. But this desire to take a position on an Imperial Family that has existed only eight years and has placed only two Emperors upon the Throne— I can only judge one Emperor at a time, myself. The Yamaku may well produce a second Jenni the Serene, but I have no way of knowing."

Lord Shonto and Lord Taiki walked in the garden of the Governor's Palace. They were followed by General Hojo and Shuyun, while Lord Taiki's young son Jima ran around them in circles, imitating the motions of a man on a horse and occasionally charging Shuyun with a shout and then veering off after he had run the monk through with an imaginary sword.

A path of raked gravel led them through the trees of late autumn, almost bare of leaves; those few that were left were the most beautifully colored. Wind cedars that had been shaped into living sculptures were placed where they would create the most striking effect, here among large gray rocks that suggested a cliff, and there beside a small carp pond. The palace walls blocked most of the wind, so the sunlight seemed to have more warmth than would have been expected.

"The present Emperor has allowed the thoroughfares of our Empire to fall into the hands of bandits. He has forced all trade beyond the Empire to take place through only one port, a port that is not close to Seh. This means that we must bring our ships into Yankura, instead of into our own province, pay exorbitant taxes and ware-

housing costs, then we must ship our goods a thousand
ri on a canal that is infested with criminals." Lord Taiki
gestured with his hands as if to say, "And you ask me
my opinion of this dynasty?"

Shonto shook his head. He was sympathetic to the
problem, and he would even state, in the right circumstances, that he felt this was unjust, but there was little
he could do about it.

Lord Taiki had turned out to be an immensely likable
man, not that "likability" was a quality that Shonto felt
was terribly important, but all the same this northern
lord radiated common sense and fairness and concern for
others in a way that one almost never saw in the aristocrats of Wa.

"Lord Taiki, your logic is undeniable, and I must say
that I wish others would cease this prejudging of entire
Imperial lines—leave that to history and the historians—
we need to be concerned with today. If the barbarians
are truly diminished and represent no threat, I for one
would be relieved. But these persistent raids have caused
concern at court. If the barbarians are no threat, then
why do we not stop the raids? That is the question continually asked."

"Certainly, Lord Shonto, you know the reason. A
handful of barbarians in a large desert are very hard to
find. We cannot fortify our entire border, it is not possible. And besides, these raids are little more than an
annoyance; we of Seh are used to them. People often
drown in the canals of the capital; you do not fill them
all in with sand. It is true that occasionally the barbarians
kill people of my province, but very few of them lately,
and there is little we can do. You do not send an army
to fight gnats; you learn to defend yourself and live with
the occasional bite, that is all."

Shonto smiled. "I understand what you say, Lord
Taiki, it is only that I would like more evidence that the
barbarians are so small a threat. Because you have only
seen one tiger in a forest, it may not be wise to assume
that there is only one. I will not write to my Emperor
that the tribes are diminished until I can clearly see that

it is the truth. I agree that these few raids would seem to indicate that the tribes are small, but perhaps it indicates other things though I confess I do not know what. I would only stress that we do not truly know what the desert is hiding from us."

Lord Taiki stopped suddenly. "Jima-sum? What are you playing at?"

The young child knelt at the edge of the gravel, staring fixedly into the base of a wisteria vine that climbed the nearby wall.

"Jima-sum?" the lord said and started forward.

Shonto gripped his arm suddenly. "Do not move."

Hojo reached out and took the lord's other arm. "Lord Shonto is right. No one must move."

There, within reach of the child, the head of a sand-viper seemed to hover above the bush. It stood erect, ready to strike. The three men held their breath for an instant.

"Let me go," Lord Taiki said. "I must draw its anger to me."

"Lord Taiki, if you move, it will strike your son and then you. It is that fast." Shuyun said.

"Shuyun, can you save him?" Lord Shonto asked.

Shuyun did not speak for a second and when he did his voice seemed to come from farther away. "I cannot reach the boy before the viper, Lord Shonto." The monk paused and Shonto could hear his breathing change rhythm. "I may be able to save his life, though at a cost."

"What cost, Brother?" Taiki asked.

"He will suffer the fate of Kamu."

Lord Taiki let out a long, ragged breath. "Is there no other way, Brother?"

"I cannot stop it. You know what will happen when he is bitten."

The lord went silent and then Shonto felt the muscles relax somewhat in the arm he still held.

"Jima-sum, do not be afraid, my son. You must do everything Brother Shuyun tells you to do. Do you hear me? Everything."

Shuyun began to slowly shift his weight and turn his body.

"Lord Shonto, please take your hand, slowly, from your sword hilt. Very slowly.

"Jima-sum, you must close your eyes and then extend the hand closest to me toward the snake," Shuyun said quietly and Shonto felt the father's arm, which he still held, go tense again.

The child hesitated. He shifted as though he would bolt, and the snake swayed toward his face but stopped as the child froze.

"Jima-sum! You must do as Shuyun-sum has said. You must be brave. Close your eyes, now."

Tears welled out of closed eyes, but the boy raised a small clenched hand toward the snake—a hand that trembled.

The viper struck. Lord Shonto felt the sword leave his scabbard though Shuyun was as much of a blur as the snake. Everything then seemed to occur simultaneously: the snake seemed to disappear toward the child; Jima screamed and pulled back his hand, but his hand was no longer there. Shonto saw the snake's body writhing on the ground, the head, jaws twitching, beside it. Shuyun has swung the sword twice, Shonto found himself thinking: twice and Shonto had not been able to focus on either movement. Shonto's sword lay on the ground and he realized that Shuyun was holding an unconscious child and staunching the flow of blood from the stub of his wrist.

Lord Taiki was moving now toward his son.

"Does he live?"

"Yes, Lord, and I will not let him die. We must carry him into the palace. Lord Hojo, could you please find a servant to bring my trunk?"

Shonto sat reading by the light of a lamp. He read the letter twice and then refolded it carefully and placed it on his small writing table. It was from Lord Taiki.

Shonto touched his fingertips together at his chin as though he were praying, but those who knew him well would recognize this action as one of his several poses of thought.

The snake in the garden did not find its way there unaided, that was certain, and the snake's intended victim was not a small boy, who would now live his life without the benefit of two hands. Shonto shook his head. The letter had been infused, understandably, with an air of deep sadness. And Shonto found some passages quite unsettling.

*As you might expect it was all rather confusing for a small child: he does not realize that it was your Spiritual Advisor who took his hand, but believes instead that it was the viper.*

*His mother is understandably distraught and there is little that I can say that will comfort her. The snake was not meant to find a small boy playing in the garden, so it is possible that the loss of my son's hand has served to save another's life. Who can say?*

*It is certain, however, that Jima-sum would not be alive if not for the actions of your advisor, Brother Shuyun. Even for one who has made many hard decisions I can say that never have I been forced to make a choice more difficult than the one I made in your garden.*

*But my son lives, and for this I am forever in your debt.*

*I have considered the things we discussed and presented your arguments to my own staff. There is no denying what you say: the evidence we have does not prove conclusively that the barbarians are diminished. Perhaps there is a viper hiding in the desert—I do not know—but I believe we must find out.*

Yes, Shonto thought, we must.

# Twenty-nine

*Having campaigned for seven years*
*And defeated the armies*
*Of the rebel general of Chou,*
*I was then spoken of at Court*
*As a threat to my Emperor.*
*Behind the sleeve I was said to be*
*Vain and ambitious*
*With my gaze fixed on the Throne.*

*So it is that I have come*
*To the house by the lake,*
*The House of Seven Willows,*
*And ask as a reward*
*For the years of my service*
*Only to rise each morning*
*To the sight of snow-covered Mount Jaika*
*Reflected in calm water.*

> *The House of Seven Willows,*
> *by Lord Daigi Sanyamu*

It was a three-decked Imperial barge ornately carved with dragons and cranes and painted crimson and gold. The Emperor's pennant was displayed high on the stern, and on carved staffs to either side of it the black pennant of the Commander of the Imperial Guard and the deep blue pennant bearing the Choka Hawk granted to the Jaku family waved in the gentle wind of the boat's passing.

Oarsmen pulled and the barge swept through the capi-

tal at first light, scattering all other craft before it. Along
the quays people of all classes bowed low, wondering
which Imperial Prince or Major Counselor hurried by to
do the Emperor's bidding. Many of those watching
offered a prayer to Botahara asking long life for the
esteemed occupant of the barge, whoever it might be.

On the upper deck, inside the house, the two brothers
Jaku—Tadamoto and Katta—sat on silk cushions and
drank hot plum wine which the elder brother ladled from
a heated cauldron. Servants set trays on stands beside
the small table that sat between the two brothers. Once
the trays were settled Jaku waved the servants out, for
this was the traditional meal of farewell and the occasion
required that there be no servants.

The meal itself consisted of the simplest foods, but
each course represented the participant's hopes for the
journey.

Tadamoto raised his wine bowl. "May you encounter
the finest of companions on your journey, brother."

Jaku raised his bowl in return. "You honor me with
your concern, Tadomoto-sum. May your companions be
many and light of heart, as I'm sure they will be." They
both drank, raised their glasses to each other again, and
then set them back on the table.

"The Emperor does you great honor, brother, to send
you off in one of the Imperial Family's own barges,"
Tadamoto said in his scholar's voice. As he spoke, he
began to serve the first course, a broth soup made with
a rare spicy mushroom.

Jaku nodded. "It is one of your many strengths, Tado-
sum, this understanding of honor." Katta sipped his wine
and tiny beads of the liquid clung to the ends of his
luxurious mustache. "If our father were still alive, he
would be proud to see what you've become. A respected
scholar, a confidant of the Emperor, a man desired by
the most beautiful women, and still one who honors his
elders and retains an unusual loyalty to his family. He
would be more than proud of you, my younger brother."

Tadamoto bowed slightly, as though modestly
acknowledging praise. "I thank you for your words,

brother, you are too generous, especially for one of your talents and position." He placed a bowl of soup before his brother. "May you carry the warmth of your family's home with you throughout your journey."

Jaku bowed slightly in aknowledgment. "And may the warmth of our home surround you in my absence."

Tadamoto bowed slightly in return and they fell silent for a moment as they ate. A fish hawker could be heard passing by, calling out the day's wares.

"I have not forgotten, Katta-sum, that it was your efforts that raised the Jaku from obscurity into the Emperor's favor." Tadamoto met his brother's gaze. "Just as it is your loyal service that has gained you your present appointment. Our Emperor is very wise and has long been aware of your labors. It is this wisdom that has allowed him to understand, as few others do, how well your efforts serve his purpose." Tadamoto glanced out the slightly open shoji as though suddenly taken by the passing scene.

"The common person who bows before you can little understand how tireless your efforts have been, Katta-sum. They do not understand what it means to reach above oneself, to exercise one's grasp." He began to raise the porcelain spoon to his lips, then stopped. "The common people are bound by superstition and fear and feel that it is the will of the gods that they occupy their place on this plane. These people do not even dream of moving up in the world, of knowing a life of refinement, or of courting a lady of high birth; but by and large they are not dissatisfied and thank the gods for what they have." Tadamoto raised a spoonful of the hot liquid to his mouth and drank it down slowly, taking time to savor its spices. "Not everyone constantly desires more, Katta-sum. Many feel they have been blessed to simply be alive—to be allowed to serve their Emperor would be a dream beyond imagining. And as the Emperor's boat passes, they bow readily and without resentment."

"It is a difference between you and me, Tadamoto-sum. Bowing is not an exercise I enjoy."

"That, brother, is obvious."

"But you see, unlike the common man, I do not fear the anger of the gods nor do I feel that my hands will not be strong enough. I simply reach out; it is my nature to do so and as a result the Jaku have risen with me." Jaku finished his soup and began to serve the next course, noodles covered with a pungent sauce made of marsh root.

"It is as you say, Katta-sum, you have brought the family honor. This cannot be denied. But now what will you bring us? Is it not enough to have become the Emperor's right hand? Is it not enough to have risen to the Third Rank and to have every reason to believe you will be raised to the Second, to one day perhaps be titled? I do not understand you, Katta-sum—how is it that the same blood flows in our veins?"

Jaku stopped in his preparations and placed his large hands on his thighs. He appeared to be completely calm as though he discussed the weather or the charms of the country in springtime. "It is a question I have often asked myself. I, for instance, would put loyalty to my House above desire for a woman, especially if desire for that woman were to endanger my House." He returned to his preparations and then set a bowl of noodles and steaming sauce before his brother.

Tadamoto did not seem to notice the food. "Ah. So this correspondence that you carry on so secretly does not endanger our House? I am glad to know this. You are aware of what the Emperor thinks of this matter?"

"This correspondence should do anything but endanger the Jaku. The lady in question is, after all, a woman free to make her own choices not bound to a husband . . . or lover. As for the Emperor's concern; I, for one, do not understand it. I cannot even imagine how such a trivial matter came to the attention of the Son of Heaven."

Tadamoto lit incense from the flame of a small lamp and placed it in a silver burner. "May Botahara bless your journey, brother," Tadamoto said quietly and they both raised their wine bowls again as they began their next course.

"I was also surprised," Tadamoto said, as though there

had been no interruption, "when the Emperor mentioned this correspondence to me. Perhaps it was the unfortunate incident with the Lady Nishima on the canal that piqued the Emperor's curiosity. Who can say? No matter, I have assured the Emperor that, to the best of my knowledge, you do not continue to see the lady. I hope, as always, that I have spoken the truth."

"It concerns me little whether, in this matter, you told the truth, brother," Jaku said, leveling his gaze at his kinsman.

Tadamoto looked down at his wine. "It does concern the Emperor, however."

"Ah, yes, the Emperor. In your reading of history, brother, has it come to your attention that dynasties do not just rise, they have also been known to fall?"

Tadamoto shook his head as though overcome by great sadness. "It has not escaped my notice, General, nor has it escaped my notice that in all of our history there have been only six dynasties while the same period has seen the fall of ten thousand ambitious advisors. It is a point that I feel is worthy of careful consideration, just as I think you should consider the meaning of your present appointment. The Emperor does not need to act as a teacher to his advisors and would only do so when such an advisor was dear to him."

Jaku banged his fist on the table but then stopped the rush of anger and calmed himself. His face became almost serene. "I am not a child in need of instruction, brother. The Emperor owes much of his security to the Jaku and I have not forgotten this."

"Perhaps not, Katta-sum, but Denji Gorge has not been forgotten either."

Jaku now shook his head sadly, as though he had just heard a terrible lie from a favored son. "I am loyal to my family and their interests, brother. Has that been forgotten?"

"It is something we have in common, Katta-sum. I, too, am concerned with the interests of our family. I would not want to see the Jaku's position undermined by ill-considered ambition."

"Was it ill-considered ambition that secured us our present position, brother? Was it fear of our own shadows that brought the Jaku to the Emperor's attention? It is interesting to me that suddenly you have taken it upon yourself to arbitrate in this matter, deciding what is and what is not in the interests of our family. It must be a terrible burden to bear at your age. Of course, the Emperor must be delighted to see such a man making these decisions—a man with no personal ambition." Katta held his hand over his wine bowl as though warming himself—a hand that showed no sign of the tremor of anger. "I have forgotten to congratulate you, Colonel Jaku. I understand that you will act as Commander of the Imperial Guard while I am away from the capital. Your lack of ambition seems to have worked admirably for you."

Tadamoto stared down at his hands. "Perhaps this journey you undertake will allow you time to reflect on these matters we have discussed, Katta-sum. I believe that was the Emperor's true purpose in assigning you this task. Few rulers would overlook the implications of a situation such as Denji Gorge. You are being treated with great kindness, brother, though I know you do not see it. If I may give you some advice: don't underestimate our Emperor, Katta-sum. It is a grave and dangerous error; dangerous not just for yourself."

Katta said nothing but only stared at his younger brother with a look of undisguised contempt. The steady rhythm of the oarsmen stopped and the boat glided on smoothly.

"We have come to the edge of the city, brother," Jaku said coldly, "from here I go on alone."

Tadamoto nodded, but his gaze fell on the serving table where the final course of sweet rice cakes waited; the course that was offered for luck on the journey. He bowed deeply and rose to his feet, not meeting his brother's eyes. "It saddens me, Katta-sum, but perhaps you will reconsider in time. I am truly your loyal brother, more loyal than you realize. I would not see you . . ." Tadamoto stopped in mid-sentence as Katta rose and turned away, leaving the deckhouse by the rear shoji.

Jaku Tadamoto stood for a moment staring at the screen, struggling with an urge to go after his brother. This is not the companion of my childhood, Tadamoto reminded himself, nor is this one of the child's moods. This is a grown man who makes difficult decisions and lives by them. He will not listen to me. Only time can teach such a man . . . if he has that much time. Turning on his heel, Tadamoto left the cabin for the boat waiting to return him to the Island Palace.

From the upper deck Jaku Katta watched his brother go, watched his sampan disappear into the mist and the traffic on the canal. He gripped the railing that was wet with condensation and watched his breath come out in a fine mist. The cold of late autumn was in the air and a breeze from the far off ocean pulled at his uniform.

Jaku shook his head. The sight of his brother with the Emperor's Sonsa still haunted him. None of my lieutenants would have succumbed to such a ploy, he told himself. Jaku felt an unusual sadness come over him. My own brother, he thought, my own blood. He wiped his hand along the rail, sending a shower of water raining down onto the lower deck. Did not Hakata say that betrayal was the greatest unhappiness of honorable men? He dried his hand on his robe. Jaku Katta, the general thought, is not happy.

Turning from the rail, he returned to his cabin and, sitting down, ladled himself a bowl of hot wine. From the sleeve pocket of his outer jacket he took a sheet of pale green paper. It was the poem he had received a few days earlier from the lady in question, Lady Nishima Fanisan Shonto.

*The wind whispers its secrets*
*To so many,*
*It is difficult to tell*
*From where the wind blows.*

　*Perhaps it is loyalty we should speak of.*

Jaku sipped his cha and read the poem again. He felt a thrill every time he looked at the elegant hand of the Lady Nishima. There was a part of him that would hardly believe such a woman could be his—yet he did not doubt that she was; or would have been if he had not been forced to leave the capital so suddenly. He had tried to see the lady before his departure, but she had been ill and unable to receive him. He cursed aloud. His plans were falling to pieces all around him and the Lady Nishima was central to his designs. Damn Tadamoto!

Jaku took another drink of his wine and calmed himself, breathing slowly. It was not over yet. The Black Tiger was still alive. There were still those at court who were indebted to him and there were even a few of his people, missed in the purge, who remained near the Emperor. It was far from over. That coward Tadamoto could do him little harm now, and Jaku's agents in the palace would be looking for a chance to undermine the younger brother's position with the Son of Heaven. The Emperor trusted no one, so it would not be difficult to arouse suspicions about the brilliant young colonel. Jaku smiled. It would be almost too easy.

# Thirty

*Our river boat*
*Pushes its bow into blue waters,*
*Dividing the rushing currents*
*Even as my spirit divides;*
*Half staying with you,*
*Half going north.*

*In the depths of the sky*
*The last geese are bound*
*For the hidden south.*
*I would send my spirit with them,*
*Stragglers all.*

The Lady Nishima swirled her brush in water, watching the black ink curl out from it in sweeping coils. I will call the series *Secret Journeys*, she thought as she read the poem again. Kitsura-sum and Lady Okara may see them after we arrive in Seh—a chronicle of our journey, and of my inner journey also. She set the brush carefully on a jade rest carved in the shape of a tiger, then rose from her cushion. Through the stern window she could just see the bow of the boat behind as it cut through the mist and the constant drizzle that seemed to travel with them.

*The mist over the canal*
*and the sound of rain*
*on wooden decks,*
*Traveling companions.*

Yes, Nishima thought, that will be part of *Secret Journeys* also.

She went back to her cushion and the charcoal fire that warmed her small cabin. Three days now they had been on the canal and she had not dared to show her face on deck. Lady Okara had gone out that morning and told Nishima that the mists would certainly hide her from the curious, but Nishima decided it would be better to wait. They were still too close to the capital for her to feel they had truly escaped. Kitsura shared this feeling, so the two young women spent their days below, often sharing meals and talking late into the night.

After lengthy discussion in the Omawara House, it had been decided that it would be best for Kitsura to travel north with Nishima before an official offer was made on behalf of the Emperor. No doubt Kitsura's flight would still be taken as an affront to the person of the Emperor, but it was believed the Omawara were prominent enough to survive such a thing. It was, after all, entirely the Emperor's fault for not conforming to the proper etiquette of the situation.

Of course it was uncommon for a family not to want their daughter to become an Empress, but Kitsura had confided to Nishima something her father had said: "This is a dangerous situation. If there is a new Empress there will be new heirs and that will raise the jealousy of the Princes and their supporters. If the Emperor were to fall or to pass on through illness, the new Empress and her children would be in grave danger."

So the Lady Kitsura Omawara set out secretly for the north in the company of her cousin and the famous painter, Lady Okara Haroshu.

A rumor was spread that a Lady Okara Tuamo traveled north with her two over-protected daughters. The name Tuamo was so common that a person bearing it could belong to any of a dozen families of moderate position. The few guards and servants who accompanied the women, though well enough appointed, wore no livery and could have been the staff of any well-to-do minor House. They would raise no suspicions.

Nishima rang a small gong and a servant appeared. "Please have my inkstone and brushes cleaned and ask my companions if they will join me for the evening meal." The servant took up the writing utensils, bowed, and left silently.

Is she afraid? Nishima wondered. Of course, no one on her staff knew all the reasons for this journey, but they understood that it was made in secret for they were, of necessity, party to the ruse. No doubt that had an effect on them. The Shonto have such loyal staff, Nishima thought, would I be like this if my karma had brought me into this world to a completely different station?

It was, she knew, idle speculation—duty was duty and the spirit that appeared in the world as Nishima Fanisan Shonto understood this concept only too well. It was duty that took her to Seh and duty that led her to carry the coins which she could feel lying against the soft skin of her waist. Despite her rather romantic view of this "Secret Journey" Nishima understood the danger she could be in. The coins she carried were like a terrible secret; one that she was sure had the potential to tear the Empire apart.

Rising again, she went to the small port which looked out the starboard side. Calypta trees lined the bank, standing in a litter of fallen leaves. Like tears, Nishima thought as she gazed at the scattered leaves, and the trees seemed bent under a weight of sadness. She felt this sense of melancholy herself as though it traveled through the medium of the mist.

The calypta gave way to a grassy shore and in the clearing stood a shrine to the plague-dead. She made a sign to Botahara. "May they attain perfection in their next lives," Nishima whispered.

Less than ten years since the plague had swept through Wa and already it seemed a distant memory, as though it had been a chapter of ancient history, yet it had taken a huge toll, including many people close to Nishima, even her true father. It is too terrible to remember, Nishima thought. We bury the memories so that they only surface in our most frightening dreams. A knock on the shoji brought her back to the present.

"Yes?"

"Lady Kitsura, my lady."

Nishima smiled, "Please show her in."

A rustle of silk and the scent of a fine perfume preceded the young aristocrat through the door.

"Ah, the artist has been at work." Kitsura said, glancing at the paper on Nishima's writing table.

"Notes to myself," Nishima said, the polite response when one did not wish to share one's writings with another.

Kitsura nodded; they had many understandings, and this was one—poetry was not shared until the author felt ready.

Lady Kitsura wore informal robes, though very beautifully dyed and embroidered, and matched in color by an artist's eye. Her long black hair hung down her back in a carefully tended cascade.

Nishima felt a flash of envy as she looked at her cousin. It is not surprising that even the Emperor desires her, Nishima thought. But there was something more there, a tightness around the eyes and the mouth. She worries, Nishima realized.

The two women drew cushions up to the heat, glad of each other's company.

"I am concerned about our companion, Kitsu-sum. Do you think the Lady Okara resents making this journey?"

Kitsura turned her lovely eyes to the fire and taking up the poker began to rearrange the coals efficiently. "She is troubled Nishi-sum. We have both seen this, though she tries to hide it. But I am not convinced that this is because she suddenly finds herself on the canal to Seh. It seems to me, though I am not sure why I think this, that it is something else that haunts the Lady Okara. My sense is that for Oka-sum, this is not a journey to Seh but a journey inward. . . . I believe she comes willingly though perhaps not happily."

"A secret journey," Nishima almost whispered.

A knock on the shoji was answered by Kitsura. "Cha,"

she said to her cousin and a servant entered bearing a cha service on a simple bamboo tray. "Look how completely we play the country peers," Kitsura laughed gesturing to the tray. "Am I overdressed for my part?"

"You are always overdressed for your part, cousin," Nishima said innocently.

Kitsura laughed. "Oh. A tongue as sharp as her brush."

"Now, Kitsu-sum, you know that I jest."

"Oh, yes, I do, and it is only fitting; I have always been jealous of your abundance of talent."

"You who have no need to be jealous of anyone's talent." Both women laughed. They had known each other all their lives and viewed even their differences with affection.

Kitsura ladled cha into a bowl and offered it to Nishima. "This first cup must be for you, cousin."

"Of course it must," Nishima said taking the cup that etiquette dictated she must first refuse.

Kitsura laughed her musical laughter. "So the mischievous Nishi-sum of my childhood seems to have returned."

"It is the pleasure of your company, cousin. How can I not be gay in your presence."

Tasting her cha, Kitsura smiled. "You know me too well, Nishi-sum. I am honored that you try to cheer me."

Nishima turned her cha bowl in her hands, suddenly serious. "You worry about your father, Kitsu-sum, but he has made his peace with Botahara. It is we who are in danger, we who are still trapped by the concerns of the flesh."

"What you say is wisdom, cousin."

"Easy wisdom, Kitsu-sum; it is not my father who is ill." Nishima said quietly.

The other woman nodded. "He often speaks of you— asks after you. I read him your poems and he praises them."

"The Lord Omawara is too kind, far too kind."

Kitsura nodded without thinking, her focus elsewhere. "Anyone else would have had his daughter marry the

Emperor, though her life would have been a misery. Perhaps his . . . nearness to completion allows him to see this life differently."

"I believe that is true, Kitsu-sum. Perhaps we can discuss this with Brother Shuyun when we arrive in Seh."

"Ah, yes, Brother Shuyun." Kitsura said, obviously ready to change the subject. "Tell me about him, cousin. Is the rumor true that he shattered an iroko table with only a gesture?"

"Kitsura-sum!" Nishima said in mock disappointment. "You listen to rumors? It is not true. I was not present when this occurred, but I know he did not accomplish such a thing with a gesture. Tanaka told me he shattered the table by pressing on it with his hand, though he was sitting at the time."

"Ah. I did not really believe that he could have done such a thing without some direct force. Only Botahara could have done that. But still, that was quite an amazing act even so; wouldn't you agree?"

"Oh, yes. Tanaka said that if he had not seen it with his own eyes he would never have believed it."

"I look forward to meeting our Brother. Is he so forceful in appearance?"

Nishima shrugged. "He is not large, by any means, and he is very soft spoken, yet he does seem to possess some . . . power. I cannot describe it—a quiet power, like a tiger possesses. You will see."

"Like a black tiger?" Kitsura asked with a wicked smile.

"You have been listening to rumors haven't you?" Nishima said, though she was not as displeased as she sounded.

"I'm not sure, cousin. Are these rumors that I hear?"

Nishima sipped her cha, turning the cup in her hands the way Lord Shonto did when he was thinking. "I do not know what the rumors say, Kitsu-sum. The general in question has expressed his interest and I have not been as discouraging perhaps as one in my station should be."

Kitsura shrugged. "One cannot go on discouraging all those whom one meets simply because they are not suitable husbands. After all, one is not always looking for a husband," she gestured to herself, "as you can see." she smiled. "He is certainly the most handsome man in the Empire, or at least the most handsome I have seen. But can he be trusted, do you think?"

Setting her cha down, it was Nishima's turn to take up the poker and move the coals. "I don't know Kitsura-sum. There was the incident in our garden. He is certainly very brave. I don't know." She thrust the poker into the fire and looked up. "I want to trust him. . . ."

"I understand, but he does seem too much the opportunist to me. I don't know how things stand, Nishi-sum, but I would be careful of how close I would allow such a man." She smiled engagingly. "I would allow him no closer than my own rooms on dark evenings . . . but not often."

Lady Nishima laughed softly. "He is, no doubt, the pawn of our Emperor, and our Emperor will be none too pleased with the Ladies Kitsura and Nishima when he finds that they have slipped away in the night like the heroines of an old romance." Nishima thrust the poker deep into the fire again. "How have our lives suddenly become so strange?"

Kitsura reached out her hand and touched her cousin's sleeve. "The word strange has no meaning in our lives. Our ancestors have lived in caves while they fought to regain their lands. Both of us have the blood of the old Emperors and know that Shatsima did not endure the wilds for seven years to ennoble her spirit but because she would never resign herself to the loss of her throne— and her uncle learned that it had been a mistake to allow the child to live, for a girl becomes a woman.

"What has history demanded of the Shonto? The sacrifice of a son in battle. A lifetime of exile. A hundred years of warfare.

"To flee to Seh in secret is nothing, it is child's play. And you, Nishima, are both Shonto and Fanisan. Who is this young upstart Jaku that he thinks to approach the heir of such history? If his intentions are what one would expect of an opportunist, it is Jaku I will be sorry for, not the Lady Nishima; he cannot know what he toys with.

"The Fanisan carved their fief out of the wilds, fighting both rival Houses and numberless barbarians. Have we forgotten this? Does Jaku Katta know that I carry a knife hidden in my robes and that I know how to use it? He is used to the ladies of the court, to the families that rise and fall at the whim of the Emperor. That is not the Omawara nor the Fanisan nor the Shonto. What we do now is not strange; what is strange is that we have not had to do such a thing until now."

Nishima sipped her cha. "I know what you say is more than true. Yet we do forget. Even Okara-sum's family has had its ordeals and the Shonto, of course, are the Shonto." The young woman straightened suddenly. "Excuse my weakness, Kitsu-sum, it is being shut up like this that begins to wear on me. Do you think that tomorrow we may dare to show ourselves?"

Glancing toward the stern windows, Kitsura nodded. "I don't think we need fear discovery in this fog, and it is possible that there is no one on any of these boats who would recognize us. We are already some distance from the capital. Fujima-sha was passed just after sunrise."

"We make excellent time," Nishima said. The conversation had lifted her spirits considerably. As the miles went by, she felt freer than she had in weeks. "I don't want to wait until tomorrow, I want to breathe fresh air now."

Clapping her hands together, Kitsura rose quickly to her feet. "I agree. I have been cloistered too long."

Sliding the shoji aside, the two young women mounted the steps to the deck, gathering their long robes about them, their sleeves swaying as they went.

Both sails and current moved the boats along and the Shonto guards who acted as rowers and crew lounged about the deck in small groups talking and laughing. The guards fell silent as the two women appeared so that the only sounds to be heard were the cries of the gulls and surge of the ship as it pushed north.

The mist moved among the trees on the shores, wafted among the groves by a light breeze. Many of the trees were barren of leaves while others appeared in fall hues muted by the fog.

"It is a scene for Okara-sum's brush," Nishima said quietly, as though the sound of her voice would break a spell and all of the beauty would disappear.

"It is a scene for the Lady Nishima's brush." Kitsura said equally softly.

"Perhaps. I like the swamp spears growing along the banks. They seem to have their own strongly developed sense of composition."

"Yes, that is true." Kitsura did not finish, for there was a creaking sound that carried to them and then a splash. They both froze. And then laughed at the other's reaction.

"We do not seem to exhibit quite the spirit of our indomitable ancestors," Kitsura said.

Nishima nodded, but she did not relax. "Should we go below, do you think?"

"Let's wait a moment. It is probably nothing. The canal is full of boats, we must remember, and there is nothing terribly suspicious about two ladies enjoying the scenery." Kitsura answered.

The creaking continued though it remained impossible to tell from which direction it came. Suddenly out of the mist the bow of a small boat appeared almost beside them. Nishima and Kitsura stepped back from the rail into the protection of the quarter deck.

"Guards!" Nishima whispered, and both ladies sank to their knees, afraid to cross the deck to the companionway.

"If they see us hiding, they will certainly be suspicious." Kitsura whispered in her cousin's ear.

"But it is us they look for. We must get below."

At a word from one "sailor," the nearest group of Shonto Guards moved themselves to the rail, hiding the two women. Scrambling quickly, Nishima and Kitsura almost pushed each other down the steps. Hearing the clatter, Lady Okara emerged from her cabin and was confronted by the frightened faces of her companions.

"What is it?"

"Imperial Guardsmen, Okara-sum."

The painter stepped aside. "Come quickly," she whispered and followed them into her cabin. Voices could be heard alongside, but the words were unclear.

"What do they say?" Lady Okara asked as Nishima dared a few steps toward the half-open port.

"A fleet of Imperial Guards has attached itself to our own." She leaned closer. "I cannot hear . . . Imperial Edicts concerning canals. Something else . . ." she turned to face her companions. "Botahara save us! They enquire after the young women aboard."

The creaking of the oars began again and the voices faded. None of the women spoke for a few seconds.

"We do nothing illegal," Lady Okara said finally. "We may go where we choose. The Emperor would not dare interfere with us."

Footsteps on the stairs echoed in the silence. A knock on the shoji and then a maid's face appeared in the opening. "Pardon my intrusion. Captain Tenda of our guard wishes to speak with Lady Nishima."

"By all means, send him in," Nishima said.

The screen slid wide and a Shonto Guard dressed like a common soldier knelt in the opening.

"Yes, Captain, please tell us what just occurred."

"Senior guard officers were passing up the line of our fleet, Lady Nishima. They questioned me as to the passengers of this craft. They saw Lady Kitsura and you, my lady, but I'm sure they did not recognize you. I explained that as you were dressed informally, you were embarrassed to be seen by officers of the Emperor's guard. Recent Imperial Edicts have been read and as a result Imperial Guards have been sent out across all the Empire with orders to make the roads and canals safe again. It seems that, at least temporarily, we will have the protection of Imperial forces. That is all I am able to report." He bowed and remained kneeling.

"Thank you, Captain. Your answer to their question

was most clever. I will be sure to report this to my father. Thank you." The captain bowed again and was gone.

"What unusual timing," Kitsura said. "Though, of course, the canals have deserved this attention for too long. Yet is it not strange that the Son of Heaven would chose this moment when we are secretly on the canal?"

Sinking down near the charcoal burner, Lady Okara rubbed her hands over its warmth. "The world beyond my own island is something I know little about, but is it not possible that this is mere coincidence?"

"I think you are right Oka-sum," Nishima said. "We grow too suspicious. Perhaps it is due to being shut up with little knowledge of what goes on around us. We must send men ahead to gather some news. Sailors love to gossip, so we might learn something of value. We will see."

This was agreed upon and the Lady Okara and her two "daughters" sat down to their evening meal, followed by music and the reading of poetry.

It was long after darkness had fallen. The Lady Nishima was alone in her cabin, embroidering a sash by lamplight, when a maid knocked on the screen.

"Pardon my intrusion, my lady. Captain Tenda says he must speak with you despite the hour. He is most adamant."

"I will see him," Nishima said setting her work aside.

The captain knelt in the door frame; the cabin was so small that he dared come no closer without being disrespectful.

"Captain?"

"Lady Nishima, please excuse my presumption. I felt this was a matter too important to wait until morning."

"Of course. Go on."

"An Imperial Guard boat came alongside a moment ago and a guard handed me this letter." He produced a folded sheet of mulberry paper of gray-blue with a stalk of fall grain attached to it. "He said it was for Lady Nishima, and though I protested that he had made a mistake he had his men row off. Shall we lower a boat and try to return it, my lady?"

Nishima felt as though her thoughts had suddenly been disassociated from her body. It was as though the mind floated freely in the air some distance away watching the entire scene. She was surprised to hear herself speak.

"I see no point in that. Leave the letter with me. Thank you."

The guard looked shocked. "Excuse me, my lady, but is there not something we should do?"

"Do you follow the teaching of the Perfect Master?"

"Certainly, my lady, but . . ."

"Then you might pray. Thank you, Captain." The guard bowed and closed the shoji.

Nishima watched herself bend forward and retrieve the letter, yet she did not feel its texture and could not tell if it was warm or cool. We are discovered, she told herself. We thought the Emperor could be deceived, but we were the fools. What will he do?

She unfolded the paper slowly as though her sense of time no longer related to reality. Was this the state Brother Satake had spoken of? She opened the letter to the light and from her station, floating above her body, she read:

*The wind from Chou-San*
*Bears us toward our destinations,*
*Yet it warms me to think*
*That I draw nearer to you.*

*Your presence is known only to me.*

"Katta-sum," Nishima whispered. The letter slipped from her fingers and fell to the cushion. She felt her senses return suddenly, joyously. She felt desire singing along all the nerves of her body and then just as suddenly she felt terrible, terrible fear. How could he have known? Every precaution possible had been taken. Botahara save her, she felt suddenly that he must know her very thoughts, her most secret desires.

# Thirty-one

It had been months since Shonto had sat a horse and despite his awareness of what was being done to his unsuspecting muscles, he was glad to be riding again—glad to be beyond the long reach of the city and the court of Rhojo-ma.

The governor's party crested a small rise which afforded the briefest glimpse of a stone tower—gray blocks covered in lintel vine . . . then gone. Soon, Shonto thought, then I will see if the reports I receive are true.

The new Governor of Seh was on a tour of inspection within a day's ride of the city. The expressed object of his concern was the inner line of Seh's defense; a broadly spread chain of towers and, in some areas, sections of wall, built a hundred years before. Built in a time when the barbarians were truly strong.

The outer precincts of the province had fallen to the tribes then, and during a long, relentless war, the inner defenses had been built. The Imperial Armies had stopped the barbarians there, though driving them back to the borders of the Empire had taken three long years. In the end, the barbarians had been broken and the remains of their invading armies had been swept into the wastes of the northern steppe, and then into the deep desert—disappearing as they always did; without a trace.

Shonto's own grandfather had been a very young general in that war, perhaps the only time that the Empire had been truly threatened . . . from outside its own borders, that is. To say that one's grandfather or great-grandfather "fought the barbarians in the time of their

great strength" was still a mark of pride in the families
of the inner provinces. In Seh everyone's grandfathers
and great-grandfathers had gone out to meet the barbarian armies, and too few had returned. It was a war
remembered differently in Seh, and Shonto did not forget that.

Nor did the men of Seh forget that it was a Shonto
who, with the young Emperor, had planned the desperate battles that finally halted the barbarian armies that
had overrun their land. Shonto's famous ancestor had
planted the banner of their House, the white shinta blossom, in the soil of Seh and it was a story still told by the
north's proud warriors; that Shonto's name had also been
Motoru.

"When I pass this place again, the barbarians will have
hidden themselves in the deepest reaches of the desert;
or my head will rest upon a barbarian pole. Shonto will
retreat no further." So he had said, and though he had
fallen in the final great battle, he had not retreated again.
When he did pass the Shonto banner, he had been carried in state.

And the Emperor Jirri had fallen to his knees when
told of Shonto's death.

*The blood of our enemy*
*Mixes here with the blood*
*Of our brothers, generals,*
*Foot soldiers.*

*Motoru,*
*An arrow, a flet of wood.*

*To save an Empire*
*And then to fall*
*Among the nameless.*

> *The Emperor, Jirri*

Shonto had known the poem since he was a child. As
a boy it had been eerie to find his name linked to such

deeds, to history. A man loved and mourned by an Emperor. Had that Motoru ridden this road? It was a disconcerting thought. Shonto shook his head and tried to force himself back to the present. But the link with the past would not let him go.

A guard carried the sword the Emperor had recently given Lord Shonto—his ancestor's gift to another Emperor—awaiting his need of it. Even now, if he signaled and held out his hand, the hilt of that sword would be laid in his palm. Despite his certainty that the Emperor plotted his downfall, Shonto had to admit that the gift, the gesture, was worthy of an Emperor.

There were a few in Seh who saw the return of a Shonto General now as cause for concern, perhaps an omen. After all, there were rumors of the coming of the Golden Khan; coming yet again. To the superstitious, the return of Shonto at this time was too significant to be coincidence—and their sleep was troubled.

Shonto's party started into a small wood and there was a marked difference in the temperature once out of the sunlight. Here there were ferns that still bore traces of the morning's frost. A reminder of the true season, a season that the sun's heat was not yet admitting. The horses snorted and blew and their breath appeared like the breath of dragons in the calm air.

Shonto glanced over his shoulder and saw his Spiritual Advisor riding close at hand. They prepared him well, Shonto thought; I am a field commander and therefore I ride. Obviously my advisors must ride, though not one in five hundred monks have sat upon a horse.

Shuyun rode well. It crossed Shonto's mind to wonder where they had found someone to teach him—the Brothers would never trust instruction to anyone from outside, it was not their way. Shuyun also showed a rather unspiritual grasp of warfare: the Brothers had missed nothing nor had they let their spiritual beliefs stand in the way of their training of this young protégé. Even the followers of the Enlightened One had become creatures of expediency. Despite the obvious benefit he was receiving from this preparation, Shonto found it somewhat disturbing.

He shook his head and turned his mind back to matters at hand. They passed a party of soldiers, the second since coming into sight of the woods. Shonto spurred his horse forward in time to hear a junior officer report that the clearing beyond the wood had been swept by troops. It appeared that security measures were elaborate, which Shonto thought strange considering how often he was assured that the barbarians were no threat and brigands almost unheard of.

Shonto signaled to Lord Komawara and the young man came up beside him.

"Sire?"

"Are outlaws so common in these woods that we need half the soldiers of Seh to protect us?"

Komawara cleared his throat. "I am as mystified as you, my lord. There seems to be no logic in this. I would ride to this place with three men. Truly, I feel I could come alone." Komawara contemplated for a moment. "Why. . . ? To impress a new governor? An officer over-zealous in his duty?" Komawara paused for a second as the realization struck him. "Or perhaps something has occurred nearby to cause concern though I have of heard no such thing."

"Huh. I wondered the same."

They rode on in silence. "Who would know of such an occurrence?"

Komawara said nothing for a few seconds. He mentally listed all the ranking men in their party and realized that they would have reported any such activity . . . unless they hid such information from Lord Shonto.

"Almost anyone who lives within the area, Sire, I'm certain."

Shonto nodded. "Please find out what is known," Shonto said. "Don't let anyone beyond your own staff know your purpose."

Komawara looked around to see who might listen. "I will try to be at the tower before the hour of the horse, Sire."

Shonto spurred his horse on, looking up at the tower appearing through the trees—a crumbling tower.

The men of Seh were more than disconcerted. They did not know where their loyalties should lie. Shonto—Shonto Motoru had come to Seh to fight beside them. The feelings this engendered in them were difficult to understand. More than one man found himself looking at the lord, wondering how much of the spirit had been reborn, how much of the legend had returned to them.

Yet this Shonto was also the minion of a despised Emperor who would not contribute a handful of ril to the defence of Seh yet insulted them by sending a famous general now, when only the occasional barbarian incursion was dared. It was an insult almost beyond bearing.

And now the Emperor's governor had found one of the many run-down fortifications, left to decay for lack of Imperial funds, or lack of vigilance. And Shonto Motoru walked among the sorry ruin of stone, and the northerners felt they had somehow failed in the sight of the man who had given his life beside their own ancestors to preserve the borders of Seh. The war raging inside these men was written on their faces, and Shonto wondered at it.

The fort had been created around one of Seh's natural outcroppings of stone that thrust up here and there, breaking up the landscape with their stark, unnaturally angular forms. This one was almost a natural castle in its own right and had needed little help from the Imperial Engineers.

Shonto walked along the remains of a rampart, stepping up onto blocks of stone long dislodged from their places. Whole sections of the wall had been carted away and no doubt formed the foundations of some local land owner's buildings. The new governor had an impulse to have the stone hunted down and the party who had taken it executed for theft from the Province of Seh, theft affecting the security of the Empire, but he realized it would be likely that the thief was either dead or very old. He shook his head and the men of Seh looked at each other, questions in their eyes, for the lord had said nothing since his arrival at the tower.

"Is this tower typical of the fortifications I will find in Seh, General Toshaki?" Shonto spoke quietly.

The general assigned to Shonto by Lord Akima hesitated for a moment and then said with some difficulty; "There are others that are better, Sire—closer to the border—but the state of repair you see here would not be thought uncommon."

Shonto stared out at the view of the fields and forest, the road winding among the hills. "General Hojo, if this is the state of the province's defenses, how difficult do you think it would be for a barbarian army to push through Seh?"

Shifting uncomfortably from foot to foot, the Shonto general cast a glance at the northerners around him. "When your numbers are small and the area to be protected large, fortifications become more important, Sire." He paused again but then seemed to brace himself before speaking. "A committed commander with an army of reasonable size, perhaps fifty thousand, could push the warriors of Seh, for all their skill, back into the capital in a very short time, Sire."

General Toshaki turned to his supporters with a look that said; *have I not told you?—do you see what we must put up with from these southerners!* But when he spoke, his voice was full of respect. "General Hojo is a commander of great repute, Lord Shonto, there can be no doubt, and I cannot dispute what he has said. But where is this barbarian army? I have lived here all my life and I still have not seen it."

Shonto did not answer, but stared off as though Toshaki had not spoken. He raised his hand and pointed to the east. "Who are those horsemen, General?"

Toshaki moved to the wall. "I don't know, Sire." He turned and nodded to his second in command. "We will find out immediately."

Far off, a small party of riders rounded a stand of pine and plunged into a low mist that still hung in a small draw, half disappearing as though they forded a stream.

Although they did not gallop, there was definitely haste in their bearing and their destination was obvious; they rode straight toward the tower.

Shonto stood watching as men from Toshaki's guard rode out to intercept the advancing horsemen. Squint as he might, Shonto was not able to make out even the color of their dress. Hojo looked over at his liege-lord and shook his head.

It could be seen, however, that one rider bore a standard with a figure on its crest, though what the figure was could not be guessed. Behind him Shonto heard men begin to whisper, but when he turned toward them they fell silent and did not meet his eye, which was unusual behavior for the men of Seh.

Toshaki's riders disappeared behind a rise and then appeared again, racing toward the party of eight whose numbers could be counted now. Twenty men of the capital's garrison wheeled up before the approaching riders who slowed, then stopped, then tried to push on and were stopped again.

"What is this?" Hojo muttered, but no one offered an explanation.

It was clear to Shonto that something was wrong. The men of the garrison reeled their horses back and forth and it appeared that threats were made. He could see arms gesturing, men standing up in their stirrups and pointing at the standard.

"Who commands our men?" Shonto asked.

General Hojo turned to Lord Toshaki.

"Lord Gitoyo Kinishi, Sire. The son of Lord Gitoyo . . ."

"Hojo!" Shonto barked. Suddenly, an all too familiar glint had appeared among the riders; swords were drawn! The Shonto general pushed past Lord Toshaki and the sound of men in armor, running, echoed among the stones.

Below, Shonto could see that no blades had crossed, but there was every indication that this would not last. What is it? Shonto wondered, and suddenly he felt truly the outsider. Truly the man cast into the unknown. And then Hojo and his men erupted out of the fallen gate, bent low over the necks of their mounts. The sound of their approach tipped the balance and the two groups separated, though no swords were sheathed.

"Well, General," Shonto said to Toshaki, "let us find out who has slipped through your net of guards."

Shonto turned and stepped off the stone onto the grass earthwork that backed the wall and descended toward the courtyard.

Horses jostled in the gate as Shonto found his way around yet more broken down stone. The men of the garrison pushed into the yard, their horses sweating from the run and agitated by the anger of their riders.

Outside the gate, Hojo sat his horse as though he marshaled the men inside. His face was set, cold as the broken stone that framed him.

Shonto felt his own anger rising but controlled it. *"To lose control because you do not feel in control is a most confused response, don't you think? I will certainly win now."* So Brother Satake had once teased him as they played gii. And, indeed, Shonto had lost the game—but he had learned the lesson.

The riders filed in behind the men of the garrison and Shonto recognized Komawara's livery, then Komawara himself appeared in the midst of his guard. Behind him rode the man bearing the standard. Shonto stopped without realizing it. It was the standard of no lord of Seh, for the man carried a pole *surmounted by a human head!*—the features slack, but twisted as though in rage or agony. The men in the courtyard cast their gaze down and none looked to their new governor.

Shonto continued to stare at the head of the barbarian warrior. Everyone waited.

"Lord Komawara," Shonto said quietly.

The young lord did not dismount nor, Shonto noted, did he take his hand from his sword hilt. "A holding nearby was raided two nights ago, Lord Shonto. One barbarian lost his horse when it broke its leg jumping a wall. He was surrounded and brought down." Komawara nodded toward the grisly pole. "We lost three men and four horses. No women or children were hurt."

Shonto noticed the "We . . ."—"We lost three men . . ."—men of Seh. It affected him somehow. Komawara obviously had no idea who the people were, they were simply northerners, people who fought the same battle.

Shonto looked around the circle of faces. Some looked away, others obviously fought to control their anger. Shonto thought of how recently he had sat in the Emperor's garden and watched the Sonsa dancers under a pale moon. But none of the men of Seh seemed particularly horrified by Komawara's prize.

I am far from the concerns of the courtiers, Shonto thought, very far.

The Imperial Governor looked from face to face. "Who knew nothing of this?" he asked.

Glances were cast from one man to the other. None spoke, as though the answers to all silent questions were known. Of this group, some turned to their governor and nodded.

"You may leave us," Shonto said.

Men, both on foot and on horse, turned and began to make their way toward the gate, leaving Shonto and his guard with half a dozen others. Komawara, too, had stayed, and Shonto noted that the young lord learned his role of Shonto ally quickly.

Looking at the men who remained in the courtyard, Shonto noted that there was little difference in demeanor between them and his own guard, though they stood accused of a crime approaching treason. They are northerners, the lord thought, and had to admire their calm.

"I trust no one has a satisfactory reason for keeping information that pertains to the security of Seh from the Imperial Governor?" Shonto let the question hang in the air. He looked from one man to the next, all met his gaze—he could detect no resentment.

"Let all senior officers step forward." Three men left their places, joined by another who dismounted his horse: Gitoyo Kinishi who had led the horsemen of Seh to intercept Lord Komawara.

Shonto stood before the four men. There was no question in his mind as to his course of action, though he wished it were otherwise. "You have your swords," Shonto said, his voice suddenly soft. "We will leave you to your preparations."

"May I speak on behalf of another, Lord Shonto?" A voice broke the silence. It was Komawara.

Shonto turned to his young ally and nodded.

"I do not think that Lord Gitoyo Kinishi understood what was taking place when he came out to intercept me, Sire."

Shonto stared at Komawara for a few seconds as if he needed to digest this information, then turned to the young man who stood his ground among the condemned. "It is not my habit to repeat myself, Lord Gitoyo. Did you know of the barbarian raid before meeting Lord Komawara?"

The young man opened his mouth to speak, but no words came. Finally he shook his head, "No, Sire," he managed, through a mouth without trace of moisture.

"Then why did you try to stop Lord Komawara?"

A soldier from Gitoyo's company stepped forward and gave his commander a draught from a water skin.

"I . . . I did not think it was necessary to bring the barbarian head into your presence, Sire." He hesitated again. "Obviously, some present must have known of the raid . . . bringing in the remains would be offensive to many. I was afraid such an act might influence your judgment, Lord Shonto."

Shonto eyed the young man for a moment as though he pondered what was said. "Yet you chose to stand among these others."

The young man nodded. "It was unlikely that I would be believed, after the altercation with Lord Komawara. I would have appeared a coward to claim ignorance, Sire."

Shonto shook his head and noticed two of the condemned officers did the same. He turned to his Spiritual Advisor who stood close by, watching as always. One of the Silent Ones, Shonto found himself thinking. "Shuyun-sum?"

"I believe he tells the truth, Sire."

Turning back to Gitoyo, Shonto said, "You risk being called a fool, young lord, but perhaps that concerns you less. Step away from these others. You are free to go."

Shonto turned away and walked back toward the lookout but then changed his mind and continued up the hill.

Shonto stood upon the hilltop and stared out toward the north. The position commanded a view in all directions. Fields and woods seemed to fold themselves to the rolling countryside. Even this far north a few autumn colors remained and in the fair sunlight they looked as though a painter of some skill had crossed the landscape, daubing his brush here and there in a brilliant design.

"Autumn refuses to let go, does it not?" Shonto said to Lord Komawara.

Komawara cleared his throat. "I remember only one year like this, Lord Shonto, in my youth."

Despite his mood, this brought a fleeting smile to Shonto's lips. He had watched another youth almost throw his life away only moments before, so the remark lost its humor immediately.

Shuyun came up the grass slope toward them. He had stayed in the courtyard to give the condemned the comfort of Botahara's blessing.

"I wonder how this will be seen in your province, Lord Komawara."

The young lord knew that Shonto did not refer to the weather. "It was certainly just, Sire; none can deny that. We live in a harsh world, here: pity is thought wasted on the foolish. These men knew who you were—they knew what would happen to them if they were found out. They did not show surprise at your sentence, Sire—only anger that they had underestimated you. Do not concern yourself with the reaction of the people of Seh. If anything, Lord Shonto, this act will increase people's respect for you."

"Huh."

Shuyun had come up and bowed, remaining silent

when he heard what was being said. Now he cleared his throat.

"If I may speak, Lord Shonto . . . Lord Botahara sits in judgment, Sire, returning all those who are not yet ready to the wheel. Botahara has no mercy, yet He is all merciful. The Perfect Master will judge them, Sire, not you. And my Lord has not been harsh. There is no death as cruel as the lives some will be given. Yet it must be so if they are ever to attain Perfection. Mercy does not always appear merciful."

"Thank you, Brother." Shonto turned to the east, toward the sea. "And what of Lord Toshaki?"

Komawara did not hesitate. "He certainly knew, Sire. That is beyond question."

"To say this in public would mean a duel, yeh?"

Komawara laughed. "We would be well rid of him, Sire."

"Perhaps."

"I would be more willing to . . . speak my suspicions aloud, Lord Shonto . . ." Komawara said.

"We will keep Lord Toshaki near us, Lord Komawara. It is certain that he has been placed as close to me as anyone outside my own staff can be. We should appreciate such manipulations. Lord Toshaki shall have access to more and more of my most sensitive decisions.

"How long would it take to restore these fortifications, Lord Komawara?"

"Anything is possible, Sire, if the resources are limitless. Under most circumstances I would estimate eight months, perhaps nine. It could be done in five if need was great."

"And the rest of the inner defenses?"

"Much the same, Lord Shonto, though in places they are at least functional—a few places."

Shonto turned now to the great expanse of the northern horizon. He could not even begin to see the border from this spot, but he could feel it—an imaginary line drawn across a section of a continent and disputed for as long as history had been recorded. We drove the tribes

into the desert, Shonto thought, it was their land once
. . . once.

"We could do much by spring, if the Lords of Seh
were committed to this."

"It would take until spring to gain enough support to
even begin such a project, Sire." Komawara said with
some bitterness.

"Huh. And we cannot prove that it is necessary, not
even to ourselves." Shonto gestured to the clouds that
swept low across the northern horizon. "It is all hidden
from us, Lord Komawara. We know nothing. Yet something does not seem right. You have felt that. And I have
questions that I cannot answer. We need a spy among the
barbarians. Is there none that gold would buy us?"

Komawara seemed surprised by Shonto's words. "I
had almost forgotten, Sire." The young lord reached into
a pouch at his waist and what he removed jingled like
the coins of Koan-sing, reminding Shonto again of his
daughter. May Botahara protect her, he found himself
thinking.

"These were found strung on a cord on the barbarian's
sash." He held out his hand and indeed it did hold coins,
but they were coins of *gold!*

Shonto's eyes betrayed his surprise. "He must have
been a chief of some stature!"

"I agree, but there was nothing else about him that
would indicate that this was so. His companions abandoned him without any attempt of rescue. Nor did he
seem to lead the raid. Only this gold would indicate he
was anything other than a typical barbarian warrior. Yet
this is a great deal of gold—a fortune to a barbarian.
I—I do not understand."

Shonto took a few coins from Komawara and examined them closely in the sunlight. "This is most curious.
They are very finely minted. I have seen the 'coins' the
barbarians use and they bear no resemblance to these.
Huh. Look at this." The lord turned one coin over in
his hand. It was like the others in that it was square and
had a uniform hole in its center, but this one bore the
design of a dragon. Not the Imperial Dragon with its

five claws and its distinctive mane, but a strange, large-headed, long-tailed beast—though a dragon nonetheless.

He handed it to Shuyun.

The monk examined it carefully and then rubbed it slowly between his fingers. "This design was etched into the metal after the coin was struck. You can feel the edges of the lines: they are raised." He handed it to Komawara, who also rubbed it between his fingers.

"I cannot tell, Shuyun-sum, but I do not doubt you."

"These coins," Shonto went on, "would they be found in Seh?"

"They are certainly not Imperial coinage and if they were struck in Seh, or anywhere else for that matter, I cannot think they would be so finely made."

"And the barbarians have no history of working gold?"

"They have no gold to work, Sire."

"Most odd." Shonto turned back to the view north. "Another question without an answer. Did pirates break their vessel upon the northern coast? The coins could come from across the sea." The lord shaded his eyes and searched the horizon. "Somehow I cannot think that it is that simple. Everything is complex, hidden." His voice trailed off.

Komawara hesitated and then spoke. "I do not think we could buy a barbarian spy, but I believe there is a way that we may go into the desert—at least some distance. . . ."

Shonto turned away from his examination of the horizon and it was as though he returned to the present from some far off time. "I would hear this."

Komawara gathered his thoughts. "None may travel beyond our border without fear of capture. Although the wastes are vast, all have need of water and the barbarians control the springs. In the past, the men of Seh chased the tribes deep into the desert and, in doing so, charted all the springs between here and the deep desert. Of the people of Wa only those with the power to heal are welcome among the barbarians." Komawara rushed on, "I do not suggest a Brother should go as a spy but, with the assistance of Shuyun-sum, I could pass into the wastes as a Brother of the Faith." He turned to the monk. "I realize your faith may not allow you to assist in such an endeavor, Brother. Please excuse my presumption."

Shonto spoke before Shuyun could reply. "But how far into the wastes could you go? I understand that even the Brothers are only welcome to cross the border; they do not travel freely."

Komawara looked slightly embarrassed at having made this suggestion without consulting Shuyun first. It showed terrible manners and he knew it. "It is true, Sire. The monks do not penetrate deep into the tribal lands, but it is possible that a monk discovered far north of Seh's border would not be treated too harshly. Brothers have been lost in the wastes before and the barbarians have returned them to Seh's border. I would like to try, Sire, even if I may not have Shuyun-sum's help."

Shonto turned back to the north again. "It is an idea worthy of consideration." He faced his companions again. "Shuyun, what do you say to this?"

If he was offended by the idea of someone impersonating a Botahist monk, he did not allow it to show. "It is not possible," he said quietly, "it is the healing power that the barbarians respect. They have superstitions connected to the Brotherhood, it is true, but it is our ability to heal that makes us welcome among the tribes. They would not treat an imposter well; especially an imposter who came seeking to know their strength. It is a brave plan, but I fear, Lord Komawara, you would be throwing your life away for no gain, excuse me for saying so."

Shonto considered this for a moment. "I believe Shuyun-sum is correct, Lord Komawara. This is a brave plan, but it would be seen too quickly that you do not have the power to heal. You would fail, certainly. Our need to know what transpires beyond our border is great, but we are not so desperate that we will throw lives away needlessly."

Silence followed. Shonto saw General Hojo walking

up the hill toward them. It is finished, Shonto thought, may Botahara have mercy on their souls.

Shuyun's quiet tones brought him back to the moment.

"I could go with Lord Komawara, Lord Governor. I can heal."

Shonto was stunned into silence for a second. "It is out of the question. You are a member of my personal staff. I would no more send you into the desert than I would send Lady Nishima. You have risked your life once already, for which I will always be grateful, but that was only at our greatest need; this can never happen again. I respect you for making such an offer, but it is not possible."

Shuyun and Komawara exchanged a look as Shonto turned back toward the north.

In the late afternoon light, the coins in Shonto's hands took on a richness of hue that did not seem real. He rubbed them between his fingers and felt the embossed dragon form.

"Power and mystery," he heard Nishima whisper.

# Thirty-two

Lord Agatua had never before been kept waiting in the Shonto house. Although he and Motoru-sum did not spend the hours together that they had years ago, there was still a lasting bond, a friendship strong enough that Shonto would choose him to deliver a message to Lady Nishima. He had no idea what the message contained or why it had to be delivered so circuitously, but Lord Agatua was the kind of friend who would never question those close to him: Motoru-sum felt the precautions were necessary so that must be true.

But he was kept waiting. Lady Nishima was ill, he had been informed, and when he had made a fuss the servants had rushed off to fine someone of authority. That had been some time ago. He was not a man who waited well.

A screen was pushed aside and Lady Kento whisked into the room. Agatua's face brightened perceptibly.

"Lady Kento, at last, a person of reason." He bowed and Lady Kento did the same.

"I apologize, Lord Agatua, it is unforgivable that you were kept waiting. Please, accept my apologies." She bowed again.

Lord Agatua shrugged. "These things occur, but it is past and forgotten. Please take me to Lady Nishima, I have a message of the utmost urgency."

Lady Kento bowed again quickly. "I will take it to her personally, Lord Agatua, be assured."

"Lady Kento, I have just finished explaining to a servant that I cannot allow that. The message is from Lord Shonto and he expressly instructed that I should deliver it into the hands of Lady Nishima and no other. I will not break trust with your liege-lord by doing other than he has asked. We have no way of knowing how important this message is. I will do nothing but deliver it into the lady's hand, let me assure you."

The small woman stood her ground. "It is not possible, Lord Agatua. My lady is very ill, and her physician will not allow her to be disturbed. I'm very sorry, but there is nothing I can do."

Lord Agatua almost exploded with frustration, but when he spoke his voice was even and reasonable. "Lady Kento, Lady Nishima's own life may be in danger—we do not know. It would be the greatest folly to allow the instructions of a physician to overrule the orders of your liege-lord. Please, take me to your mistress at once."

Lady Kento did not move. She shook her head again. "I apologize again, but what you ask is impossible."

Lord Agatua stepped past Kento and headed for the door that led to the inner house.

"Guards have been ordered to detain you if you go further, Lord Agatua." Kento said quietly.

He turned toward her. "This is madness!" But he knew, somehow, that the woman was in earnest. "When will I be able to see Lady Nishima?"

Kento shrugged. "It is impossible to say—perhaps three days?"

Shaking his head Lord Agatua turned to leave, but as he reached the door he stopped. "You will have no opportunities to make such serious errors as a street sweeper." He left.

Kento stood staring at the door. It had been only a few days and already it was difficult to maintain the ruse that Nishima was in the house. First General Katta had tried to see her, though that had been not so difficult, and now this. Kento worried about the message from Lord Shonto. Certainly, it must be important, but there was no way to intercept Lady Nishima now, at least not without bringing a great deal of attention to her. She would be in Seh before a message, sent by any conventional means, would catch her. There was nothing to be done—except, perhaps, begin preparation for her new position. She believed the brooms were kept near the kitchen.

# Thirty-three

Lady Nishima had never known a day so long. It had been only the previous evening that she had received the poem from Jaku Katta, and since then time had slowed as it never had when she practiced chi ten with Brother Satake.

Nothing—no word—and she could not bring herself to contact him: at least she retained that degree of dignity.

Watched from the deck of her river boat, the shore passed as it had throughout the first days of her journey, but now the eye of the poetess regarded it differently.

*Calypta leaves drift toward winter,*
*Borne on winds*
*In the reflected surface*
*Of the autumn sky.*
*Trees line ancient canal banks,*
*And weep for the passing procession*

*Branches as barren as my heart.*

*Why do you not speak my name?*

The Ladies Okara and Kitsura were resting and Nishima had come out on deck in the last light to be "alone with her thoughts." Alone with her desire, she admitted to herself.

Does he not want to see me as I wish to see him? It was the question that destroyed her tranquillity. I begin to feel like a fool, Nishima thought and resolved to return below to her cabin and her writing when a boat, sculled by two Imperial Guards, appeared under the bow. Nishima felt her pulse jump, but at the same time she felt more a fool to be standing at the rail as though awaiting word. It was too late to go below, so she turned her attention to the fading shoreline and feigned not to notice the boat and its occupants until it was before her.

"Excuse our presumption, Lady Nishima," the officer aboard said quietly, "we do not mean to disturb your contemplation," He seemed to have no doubt of whom he addressed. "If you will allow me, I bring you a letter from General Katta and will certainly return at your convenience if you wish to make a reply." He reached into his sleeve and removed a letter.

Nishima reached out automatically and took the letter. "I thank you," she said and walking a few feet toward the quarter deck, she leaned against the gunnel, took a deep calming breath, and opened the letter she had been awaiting for one interminable day.

Jaku's too large hand wandered down the page, but she found his failed attempt at elegance somewhat endearing.

*The wind, the wind, the wind*
*I wish to hear no more of it.*
*I am ruined for duty,*
*A single brush of your lips*
*Is all I can think of.*

> *My heart will not leave me in peace*
> *Until I speak to you.*

Nishima found she was reaching out to steady herself on the rail. She realized that no matter what her head told her, she was going to ignore it in this matter. In fact, the decision was already made. She walked back to the gangway where the Imperial Guard boat waited.

"Where is General Katta?"

"The general is aboard an Imperial barge near the head of the fleet, my lady."

"Will you take me to him?" she asked, her voice much smaller than she expected.

The officer did not know how to respond. He had not been told to expect this. "I—I can, my lady, I can, if that is what you wish."

"It is." Nishima turned to the Shonto guard who stood watch at the gangway. "Tell my companions I will return shortly." She descended the ladder to the guards' boat. This is the worst foolishness, she found herself thinking, though she allowed herself to be assisted aboard.

The fleet was long. Nishima did not count the boats—more boats than hours in the day, she was certain of that. Anticipation built within her. The kiss she had allowed Jaku came back to her now and it seemed like no kiss she had ever known: tender and full of promise.

This excitement was balanced by a fear. Fear that Jaku would not feel as she did, despite his words. Fear that he would not even be aboard his boat, and her impetuous act would lead to nothing but embarrassment. She was going, unannounced and without invitation, to the dwelling of a man she knew hardly at all.

Finally they came to the Imperial barge that was Jaku's transportation to Seh. Nishima found the size and richness of this craft strangely reassuring, though she did not know why.

Waiting in the boat while her presence was announced, fear almost ate away her desire, but then Jaku arrived; his silhouette was unmistakable as he appeared at the rail—black uniform against the dark sky. He descended the stair with a surefootedness that was uncanny—catlike, as an entire Empire had noted. At least he did not merely have me brought to him, Nishima found herself thinking and was surprised that she felt gratitude.

"Lady Nishima," Jaku said in his rich tones. "I am honored beyond my poor command of words to describe." Jaku extended his hand to her. "Allow me to assist you."

Nishima ignored all the expected formalities of the situation and did not apologize for intruding; she merely extended her hand and felt the strong grasp and the heat of Jaku's hand as it enclosed her own.

\*      \*      \*

The stern cabin of the Imperial barge was impressive: beams lacquered a deep red, large windows, now draped, looking out through the transom, celestial blue wall hangings, and cloud designs painted on the ceiling; all of this lit by hanging lanterns. The straw-matted floor had been covered with thick carpets from the land of the barbarians; a custom in Seh but only recently popular in the capital.

Jaku Katta and Lady Nishima sat facing each other on cushions spread upon the barbarian carpets. The rush of excitement at their meeting had given way to an awkward politeness.

"So often it seems futile," Jaku was saying. "I have long been counseling the Son of Heaven to make our roads and waterways safe. I don't know how often I have repeated this but there are so many counselors in the court, so many with the Emperor's ear. There is no end to the foolishness that passes for wisdom. But I have finally been heard: the lesson of history has won out. The Throne can only be secured by assuring peace in the Empire, and that must start with securing the roads and waterways."

Jaku paused for a second and caught the eye of Nishima. "And in doing this I will come to Seh . . . to a situation that is of . . ." he searched for the words, "military concern. If I may be of small service to Lord Shonto when I arrive, I would consider it an honor." Jaku lowered his voice and Nishima moved closer to hear. "I do not know what transpires in Seh, my lady, but I fear it is not the barbarians that will test your liege. Because of my duties on the canal, I cannot be there for several weeks, but I hurry. This situation is of great concern to me, Lady Nishima."

"But you have already done so much. If it weren't for you, I don't know what would have happened in our garden."

Jaku shrugged modestly. "Who can say?" He paused and then leaned toward her, his voice now barely a whisper. "I would not say this to anyone else, Nishima-sum, but I have begun to have doubts. I do not know what

my Emperor intends nor how often I have been the
instrument in the . . . Court's intrigues. I have been as
loyal as a son and now I am uncertain of my loyalties.
Not everyone is a man such as your father; renowned
for constancy."

Nishima found herself whispering also, sharing secrets
like a lover. "You have served more than the Emperor,
Katta-sum, even as you serve the Empire and its citizens
on the canal. You cannot bear responsibility for the
actions of your liege: duty does not require that. Loyalty
. . . is a matter of the heart."

Jaku reached out and caressed Nishima's cheek and a
visible shudder of pleasure trilled through her. "Your
words bring me comfort, Nishi-sum, they are Shonto-
wise." Jaku leaned forward and kissed Nishima; a lingering kiss of great tenderness. Nishima found herself pushing into his arms and returning his kiss with a need that
surprised her. Strong arms pulled her closer. Fingers
brushed her breast through the folds of her robes.

Jaku whispered in her ear. "I do not know all of the
details of what occurred in Denji Gorge. So many
arrangements were made after I had initiated contact
with the Hajiwara. If I had only known . . . thank the
gods that Lord Shonto is the general he is and that no
harm was done."

His mouth covered hers before she could respond.
And suddenly Nishima was alarmed. What was he saying? What of Denji Gorge?

Jaku lowered her slowly to the cushions. His hands
moved along her sash and Nishima felt the press of coins
strung around her waist.

"No," Nishima managed weakly as Jaku began to pull
at the knot. "No." More firmly this time, but Jaku did
not seem to hear. She tried to push him away a little.
"Katta-sum—what is this you. . . ?" He kissed her as
though this would stop her questions.

Nishima felt panic grip her. What of my uncle? What
is it that this man feels he must deny? Suddenly, Jaku's
words seemed false to her.

Hands began to unwind her sash. She pushed against

him, but he was so large he did not even seem aware. This must not happen. He is false. The coins—they were carried by Imperial Guards. How could their commander not know?

Grabbing the hand that unwound her sash, Nishima tried to hold it to her. She had allowed this to start. Had initiated it of her own volition. How was she to expect him to respond? But it could not be.

The trained strength of the kick boxer would not be denied, and Jaku began again to remove the length of brocade that held her robes and hid the silk ribbon around her waist. A hand touched the skin beneath her robes and Nishima felt a weakness wash through her. Warm fingers caressing her breast. He saved my uncle's life, Nishima found herself thinking, though why the thought surfaced amid the flood of pleasure she did not know.

Jaku's hand slid from her breast toward her waist, and Nishima's will returned in a rush.

"No!"

Jaku was flung back and found himself in an awkward heap at the base of a pillar.

Nishima stood before him, gathering her robes and sash into a semblance of order.

"Tell me what occurred at Denji Gorge," Nishima said evenly.

Jaku looked as confused as any cornered animal. "You are in league with the Brothers."

"I am in league with the Shonto, make no mistake. Has my uncle come to harm?"

"Lord Shonto . . ." He trailed off as though dazed. "Lord Shonto is, no doubt, in Seh, Nishima-sum, in Seh and unharmed. The Hajiwara tried to trap him in the gorge. I do not know what alliance planned this, though I would look to the court. I assure you Lady Nishima, I did nothing beyond establish contact with the Hajiwara, and that I did not do in person but left to my brother." Jaku moved to a more dignified position but did not rise.

"How is it you know the fighting skills of the Botahist monks?"

"I do not know what you mean, General," Nishima said. She had returned her clothing to order, but a flush remained on her face and neck. "If you have a boat that can return me to my own, I will impose upon you no further."

"Nishima-sum . . . I know you doubt me, but I am more of an ally than you realize. There is much I do not know that I may yet discover, to the benefit of the Shonto. I am a man of honor, and will only serve those who are the same."

Nishima crossed to the door of the cabin. "I must have time to think, Katta-sum," she said softly. "There is much going on below the surface, in the Empire and in my heart as well. I have treated you unfairly and for this I apologize; I cannot make decisions according to my desires. Lord Shonto saved my mother and myself—no, do not deny the Emperor's intentions, you know that it is true. I could be a threat to the throne, if that were my desire. Your Emperor will never forgive that.

"I have many duties, too many duties. Please, Katta-sum, do not cause me more confusion." She slid the screen aside herself but paused before leaving. "Come to Seh. We will speak there—in Seh."

# Thirty-four

The ponies were surefooted and strong, bred for hardiness and life on the northern steppe. As they picked their way down a narrow trail in failing light, hooves drumming up the long ravine, they inspired their riders with the utmost confidence.

Despite being wrapped in thick cloaks it was easily seen that these men wore the robes of Botahist monks—an Initiate and a Neophyte—out of place in this arid landscape.

The trail leveled and broadened somewhat as they found the bottom of the ravine. Scrub brush and the occasional stunted tree appeared here and there as though scattered down the draw by the relentless wind of the high steppe.

They rode on in silence until a large rock offered some shelter and here they dismounted. Komawara immediately began tending to the horses, the two mounts they rode and a third pony that acted as a pack animal carrying a burden that was largely water. Shuyun prepared a cold meal. It was a routine that they had fallen into in the six days they had been traveling north beyond the border of Seh and neither man seemed inclined to change it.

The northwest wind sounded like an endless breath from the lungs of a dying man, neither a moan nor a whistle but blending something of each. It was a voice that spoke of a long pain. The steppe was slowly being consumed by the desert, though no one knew why, but for a hundred years the men of Seh had been aware that the high steppe was disappearing. And the wind registered a desperate agony.

Whirling around their sheltering rock the wind picked up dust and spun it into the air, into the clothes, into the pores. Rubbing reddened eyes, Komawara came over to where Shuyun crouched.

"You must use the compress on your eyes again this night, Brother."

"I do not want to be blind in this place. It seems the worst possible course. We have no idea what may appear in the night."

"My teachers taught that in the darkness one uses one's hearing, one's sense of smell. Feel the vibration of movement—if you search the darkness with your eyes you will not focus on what is heard, what is sensed. We learned this lesson with cloth bound over our eyes. You can learn it with compresses over yours. You cannot continue with your eyes as they are. If we meet the tribal people, they will know. A Brother who is ill is not Botahist. I will prepare the compresses; let me worry about what hides in the darkness."

Komawara nodded and, as he did so, absently rubbed his recently tonsured scalp. A look from his companion and he withdrew his hand with an embarrassed smile. He was Shuyun's student in this endeavor: no longer a peer of the Empire of Wa but a Botahist Neophyte—not even that. Shuyun taught him some simple breathing exercises and meditations as well as the outward habits of the monks. To be truly believable, the monk felt Komawara should understand some of the basis of the Brothers' manner and had explained several principles of the training given to young monks.

At one point, as a demonstration of focus, Shuyun and Komawara had "pushed hands"—palm to palm trying to find resistance in Shuyun's movement, but whenever Komawara pushed, Shuyun's hands gave way though they never broke contact. It was, as Shuyun said, like pushing water or air, there was nothing to offer any purchase. Shuyun had twice put Komawara on his back and, the young lord realized, could have done it at any time but even so Komawara did not feel it was pride in his skill that led Shuyun to do this. The monk merely wanted Komawara to know what error he made by resisting.

After these sessions of pushing hands, Komawara had begun to question his martial training which was largely based on resistance. And so Komawara, a lord of the province of Seh, slowly and, at times, painfully, began to acquire some of the surface attributes, the mannerisms and posture, of a Botahist monk. He also began to develop a new respect for the Brothers and their level of skill and discipline. This respect was made even stronger by the knowledge that what Shuyun had revealed was not a thousandth part of his knowledge: there was that much the young Botahist was not revealing, and never would.

"I wish we could risk a fire," Komawara said.

Shuyun gave a small shrug. It was a gesture Komawara was getting used to: it meant that nothing could be of less importance to Shuyun, though he felt that it would be impolite to say so.

Komawara began to draw in the sand with his finger and a very rudimentary map appeared. He placed a small white stone on his cartography and said; "The spring should be only a few rih away." He tapped the earth. "We are here. This is believed to be an ancient river bed, though it is hard to imagine that water ever flowed here. If we follow it for another day, we should come to water—if the spring hasn't dried up. I don't know if we will meet barbarians there, but it is very likely. We must have water if it is at all possible."

Shuyun shrugged. "We can last many days on the water we have."

"*You* could last many days, Brother, but the horses and I have received poor training in survival without sustenance. We occasionally must eat food, also. Please excuse our weakness."

"For your weakness," Shuyun said, and passed the lord a flat bread stuffed with vegetables and a paste he did not recognize. The neophyte monk, Brother Koma, looked at this offering with unconcealed disgust, making his teacher smile.

"You are a typically ungrateful student, Brother. You will not progress until you become thankful for your chance on the wheel. It is possible that even you will make some progress toward perfection in this lifetime. This food will help sustain you so you may do that. Therefore, you should be thankful for it: flavor is not important."

"I did not realize that striving toward perfection was so intimately entwined with continual discomfort, Brother. Tonight I will attempt to find a rockier place to lay my bed."

Shuyun lay still in the darkness. The wind moved over him and seemed to cause the stars to blur and waver in a cold sky.

I am assisting a man who is impersonating a Botahist Brother, he thought. I could be ousted from the Botahist Order forever.

He went over the argument in his head again. He had been given the task of serving Lord Shonto, a man of vast importance in the Empire of Wa. A man who supported the Botahist faith in a time when the Emperor did not favor this faith nor those who practiced it. This alone made Shonto vastly important to the Botahist Brotherhood. The lord was also responsible for the defense of Seh and, for all practical purposes, the Empire: an Empire that even under its present Emperor was still the one and only home of the Botahist faith. And despite the attitudes of the Son of Heaven, the true faith was practiced by most of Wa's population. The tribal people of the high steppe and the desert were not followers of the Perfect Master—if anything, they could be a threat to the practice of the Botahist faith. Shuyun went over the words of the Supreme Master at their last meeting.

"You must not always think of your own salvation. There may be times when your liege-lord will ask things of you that seem incompatible with the tenets of the

Botahist faith. At such times you will have to make a decision that will favor the situation of the Brotherhood, for it is the Brotherhood and the Brotherhood alone that keeps the teachings of the Perfect Master alive."

So Shuyun had been told . . . and then he had met a young Botahist nun on the Grand Canal who cared for a respected Sister—a Sister who, it seemed, had lost her faith. A Sister who had seen the hand of Botahara and, miraculously had ceased to believe. A Sister who was convinced that what she had seen was false. The young monk no longer knew what to believe and what to disbelieve.

For the first time in his adult life Shuyun experienced unsettling dreams and awoke from his sleep with no feeling of renewal.

Komawara bent over the hoofprints, now touching them with his finger, then bending down till his face was almost in the sand and blowing into the depressions.

"A half-day ago, at most. Any longer and the wind would have hidden them completely. At least a dozen riders and perhaps eight animals of burden." He came back to his horse and took the reins from Shuyun. "There seems to be more and more evidence of barbarian . . . I do not know what else to call them but patrols." He shook his head. "Common wisdom says the barbarians move in their tribal groups: woman, children, animals, and all belongings. Groups of a hundred or more and never less than fifty or sixty. I am at a loss, Shuyun-sum. This is unexplainable."

Shuyun shaded his eyes and scanned the ridge of the dry river bed. "A young lord of Seh, Komawara, I believe, holds unpopular notions that the tribal people have changed their patterns in the last few years. You would do well to listen to his views if the opportunity ever presents itself. A senior member of my own faith believes there is something amiss in the historical pattern of attacks on the Empire—and the members of my order hold historical evidence in very high regard. What do you suggest we do?"

Komawara mounted his pony. "We can do nothing but press on. As of yet we know nothing."

Shuyun gestured and Komawara again took the lead, picking his way among a maze of house-sized boulders.

The day was cool, made cooler by the wind and a high thin film of cloud which filtered the sun and muted all shadows so that things at a distance were harder to distinguish.

A hundred yards farther along, Komawara again dismounted and bent his knee.

"This seems to be turning into a trail again, Brother. There should be a spring not far off, if our maps are not too ancient. Who will be there, however, our map does not show."

They moved on again, single file until the trail became unmistakable. Here, Komawara led them up an incline of solid rock and into a grotto formed by massive boulders. He took some care to hide the marks of their passing and, when he was satisfied, returned to Shuyun who watered the horses.

"I don't think we should approach this spring without making an attempt to observe any who are there before they have an opportunity to observe us." Shuyun nodded his agreement. They each took a drink from a water skin—Shuyun's much smaller than his companion's—and made a light meal.

The ponies were hobbled and the two men proceeded on foot. Komawara took a staff with him, regretting again that he had no sword. The blade had been a matter of contention, but finally Shuyun had convinced him that there could be no explanation for a Botahist neophyte to be carrying a sword, no explanation at all. Komawara had finally realized that Shuyun was right, but the sword was missed almost hourly.

They chose a path that seemed to run parallel to the trail they assumed led to the spring but soon were finding dead ends and forced corners that led them away from their goal. The trail appeared, unexpectedly, and they decided to cross it and try their luck on the other side.

After an hour of this maze they heard a noise that at first neither of them recognized, it was so unexpected.

"What is that?" Komawara asked.

"The wind. The wind blowing through leaves."

Komawara nodded. "It seems impossible but . . . I believe you're right."

They crawled up onto a shattered boulder and looked down into a long gully. The wind came down the gully and blew in their faces, a wind soft with moisture. Two stooped and aged trees bent down over a tiny pool of water as though they knelt to drink. The gully itself was a gradation of color from the stiff brown grasses of the high steppe to a deep green at the heart of the spring.

Shuyun reached out and touched his companion's sleeve and pointed. In the darkest part of the shadow at the base of the trees a man bent over the water filling a skin. He stood up so that his face came into the light, and if it had been Lord Shonto neither of the travelers would have been more surprised . . . the man was a Botahist monk.

Komawara turned to Shuyun. "What is this?" he hissed, and it was apparent that he believed he had been betrayed.

"I do not know, Lord Komawara, I have no explanation."

The Brother looked up at the two travelers and a smile spread across his face. He motioned to them to approach and gestured down at the spring.

"What do we do?" Komawara asked.

"He is a Brother of my faith, he will not lead us into danger, but I would suggest you say as little as possible, under the circumstances, Brother Koma."

Shuyun led the way, now, and they quickly picked up the trail and followed it into the grotto. Another surprise awaited them: tents and a rough corral containing ponies of the barbarians stood in the shade of the cliff.

The monk saw their reaction to this discovery and smiled and waved reassuringly. He did not speak until they were very close, as though he did not want others to hear. "It is indeed an honor to meet Brothers of the true path wandering here where so few travel." He made the double bow of his kind and Shuyun and Komawara did the same. "I am Brother Hitara," the monk added. "Welcome to Uhlat-la; the Spring of the Ancient Brothers." He gestured to the gnarled trees. "A fitting place for us to meet."

Shuyun bowed again. The monk who addressed him was young, perhaps only three years older than Shuyun, but his face was dark and creased from too much time in the sun and his body was thin and wiry from long rationing of water.

"The honor is indeed ours, Brother. I am Shuyun and this is Neophyte Koma, who has taken the vow of Barahama and apologizes for his inability to speak."

"There is no need to make apologies, Brother, the Way is difficult enough without need of making apologies for pursuing it." He gestured to the small pool. "The water is good, I have drunk it on several occasions."

Shuyun and Komawara went to the water where Brother Hitara offered them a half gourd for a cup. Shuyun drank sparingly and offered the cup to Komawara but then stopped the lord as he began to dip water from the pool. "Have care, Brother, too much water will destroy your focus and cause you other unpleasantness."

Komawara showed reasonable restraint, though not perhaps as much as Shuyun would have liked.

"It is a great honor and also a surprise to meet the Spiritual Advisor to the great Lord Shonto here in the wastes. I assume that you are no other?"

Shuyun was only slightly taken aback by the directness of the question. A Botahist monk wandering in the high steppe could perhaps be expected to have forgotten a few formalities. "You are well informed, Brother."

"Not at all, Brother Shuyun, you are merely unaware of your own reputation. The youngest Spiritual Advisor to a Great House—in our history. Winner of the Emperor's kick boxing tournament at the age of twelve. I have even heard of your destruction of what I have been told was a finely wrought table. Even more is said about your level of accomplishment, but I do not wish to test your conquest of pride by saying more. I will confess to stand somewhat in awe of you, Brother."

Shuyun shrugged. "I am equally impressed to find a Brother of the Faith wandering here. How is it you have come to the high steppe alone, Brother Hitara?"

Hitara opened a saddlebag and began to remove the makings of a meal. "I minister to those of other faiths. It should never be repeated, Brother, but I have made more than one convert, though I have not spoken a word to bring this about. I heal the sick. If I am asked questions, I answer. I meditate in the ancient places. It is a small part that I play, Brother Shuyun, but it gives me ample opportunity to meditate upon the word of our Master. I do not need more.

"Would you join me in a meal, Brothers?" Hitara said and offered a stick of dried fruit to Komawara who reached for it readily. The fruit was drawn back, however, before Komawara touched it. "I had forgotten your vow, Brother. Please excuse me, I have been alone for too long. Please forgive my lapse."

A sound ended all conversation. A sound masked and distorted by the huge boulders and the high rock cliffs of the old river bed. It was some time before it was apparent that this was the echo of a horse's hooves.

"It is the man who guards this encampment. The others will be gone for several days," Hitara said offering food to Shuyun. "I once saved this man's son. He remains grateful."

They waited in silence for several minutes until finally a warrior of the tribes appeared, leading his pony. He looked up and caught sight of the monks and immediately cast his eyes down and turned back the way he had come.

Komawara was tensed like a man before battle and twice, while they waited, Shuyun had noticed him reach down to touch a sword hilt that was not there. If Hitara had seen, he said nothing.

"What is this camp, Brother, and where do they ride to from this place?"

It was Hitara's turn to shrug. "I find it is better not

to ask." He began collecting up his belongings. You should take water before Padama-ja returns. He cannot be expected to turn a blind eye always."

"You go so soon, Brother? I had hoped you would be able to speak with us longer. We have so many unanswered questions."

The monk strapped his few belongings onto a small brown pony and swung himself into the saddle. "I fear the questions you want answered I have found it wise not to know the answers to, Brother. I also fear that your purpose will endanger my own, for if you are found here, in the future all Brothers will be suspect. I do not mean to interfere, your karma is your own, but this is not a good place for you, Brother Shuyun. Return to Seh." He hesitated before he went on, speaking quietly now. "Tell your lord that his worst fears are true. Tell him to beware of those who worship the desert dragon." His horse began to shy suddenly and he fought to control it. "I do not know what transpires here, nor is it my concern . . . but war brings no soul to perfection—of this I am sure—so I do my small part to discourage its veneration. The tribes prepare for battle—I am certain of this. Gold has appeared among them and a new Khan commands the loyalty of all but a few. Look not to meet the few, for they are scattered and do not wish to be found. Return to Seh. Here you can do nothing."

Komawara stepped forward. "But we have seen nothing with our own eyes. Your word is all we have. Return with us. If there is a warning to give, then it is from you it must come."

"My place is here." He bowed from the waist, turned his horse then stopped and turned back to them. "If you must have proof, warriors gather not far to the north. I do not go there. Three days toward the spike mountain where the Two Sisters rise at sunset.

"Until the Udumbara blossoms." Hitara bowed again. "Brother Shuyun. Lord of Seh." He wheeled his horse and disappeared among the giant rocks of the ancient river bed.

# Thirty-five

As a pilgrim and Seeker, Brother Sotura could afford only deck passage. As a Master of the Botahist Faith and chi quan instructor of Jinjoh Monastery there were other things he could not afford in his present situation: he could not afford to wear any sign of the position he held within his church, nor could he afford to use his name.

The fall winds continued to blow in from the sea and the river barge on which he took passage lumbered along the Grand Canal as the great waterway made its patient way toward the northern provinces. Some few days ahead of Sotura's own barge it was said that the Imperial Guard, led by General Jaku himself, was clearing the canal of pirates and those parasites who levied charges for safe conduct through sections of the waterway. There was a great deal of relief aboard the vessel, as far as Sotura could tell.

He sat leaning up against the side of a raised cargo hatch and watched the shore pass in the light mist and starlight. Although he was, according to the position he had attained in the order, beyond the reach of earthly things such as beauty, Sotura found the Empire of Wa to be irresistible—even more so as he grew older. He was not sure why, but there seemed to be little he could do about it. At one point he even found himself sighing as they passed calypta trees with the stars caught in the net of their branches. He closed his eyes tightly and tried to focus on other things.

The disappearing Brothers, for instance. Except for the missing scrolls, there had been no greater mystery in the long annals of the Botahist Faith. Sotura wondered again what, if anything, the connection might be and, as always, he could think of none.

He traveled now toward Seh because his order felt that there was a focus there—events were about to occur that could shake the entire Empire. And somehow at the center of all this was a young monk and former student of the chi quan instructor—Brother Shuyun. Sotura pressed his fingers to his eyes as though he was in pain, but it was merely a reaction to his own confusion.

The confusion was caused by this news from Brother Hutto. . . . The Udumbara had blossomed! It was not true, how could it be? Sotura had once journeyed to Monarta and visited the grove where Botahara had attained Enlightenment. It was an experience he would never forget. And he found that place, too, unimaginably beautiful. The Perfect Master had said the Udumbara would blossom again to herald the coming of a Teacher.

But the trees had not blossomed in a thousand years, though they lived on, almost unchanged, through the rise and fall of dynasties and through the wars and famines of the centuries. How could there be a new Perfect Master and the Brotherhood not know? He could not believe it: it was simply not possible.

He opened his eyes as the barge passed the mouth of a small stream crossed by the arc of a stone bridge built in the northern style. Starlight reflected in the water and mist clung to the shore softening all the lines, blending them into the flowing river.

All streams lead to the river, Sotura thought, and sighed without knowing it.

# Thirty-six

They rode after dark that evening, wanting to put as much distance between themselves and the spring as they could. They made their way east for several hours and then mixed their tracks with those on another trail. They rode over shelves of rock and doubled back down their own track. Always they set course by the constellation of the Two Sisters.

They passed more and more places where the dry grasses and scrub were broken by expanses of sand spreading like ulcers across the skin of the high steppe. Neither of them spoke of this, but it was apparent that the wandering tribes were losing their world to the encroaching desert and both Komawara and Shuyun knew what this meant for the province of Seh.

While it was still dark, they found shelter beneath a cliff and when morning came awoke to a view of the vast northern wastes. No grass—no sign of anything living. A few solitary rock sentinels thrust up from the growing dunes and in the near distance the sand gave way to a warren of eroded cliffs and toppled sentinels, all faded grays and reds that only a desert could produce.

The pack pony had gone lame in the night and Komawara cursed as no Botahist monk had ever done. He came and threw himself down on his saddle and Shuyun handed him a roll of flatbread filled with bean curd, vegetables cured to last, and cold rice. There was a sauce of delicate flavor over this that Komawara could not name. In light of his earlier reaction to such fare, he was not about to admit that he was developing a taste for the monk's food. Left to his own, Shuyun would not have bothered with even the time it took to prepare a meal such as this, but he made a concession for Komawara's sake. Obviously, the young lord had never produced a meal in his life.

"The gray is somewhat lame. It will be more than a day before she can bear weight again."

Shuyun shrugged. "We can carry more on our own mounts. We could even do with less."

"That is true, Brother, but we will not travel as quickly."

"Then we will travel slowly, it cannot be helped."

"Are you *never* impatient, Brother, do you . . ." Komawara caught himself.

"If impatience would help, Lord Komawara, I would become impatient."

"Excuse me, Shuyun-sum, I let my concern govern me."

"There is no need to apologize. We share a difficult venture, Lord Komawara." He smiled. "I will try to be a little impatient in the future."

The day was spent in camp. Shuyun meditated and neither ate nor drank. Komawara slept as he could and, when awake, paced. He tried all his skill with the lame mare and toward nightfall felt she could go some distance, providing she bore nothing. The other horses carried more of the burden and it slowed them noticeably.

In the night the wind carried voices to them, though Shuyun was more sure than Komawara that it was not the wind through the rock speaking in its own strange tongue. They hid themselves and were silent but were soon convinced the wind that brought the voices to them masked the sounds of their own passage.

They went on, more carefully now, and near sunrise they found a place to make camp that offered protection from the wind and afforded escape from more than one direction.

Komawara slept while Shuyun kept the first watch. The young monk had no strong desire to sleep: his dreams troubled him with questions he could not answer and feelings he did not recognize. Often he returned to his meeting with the young nun on the canal and the information he gained from her, information so momentous that he had trouble focusing his mind on its implications.

He realized also that he dreamed often of Lady Nishima and somehow the image of the Faceless Lovers carved into the wall of the gorge became confused with the images of his liege-lord's daughter. Often it was the face of Nishima he saw on the cliff, but the man she held close to her continually altered and changed. Sometimes her lover was unclear, as though viewed through water, and then Shuyun knew that it was he the lady embraced.

The monk was ashamed of the weakness of will that this indicated, but he also felt a quiet defiance which he did not recognize—the Botahist Initiate had begun to entertain the thought that he could have been lied to by his own Order and this thought began an erosion in his spirit much like the desert had begun in the high steppe.

They ate quickly and began to travel before sunset. The long ride of the previous night had done nothing to improve the condition of the gray, but the rest during the day had brought her back so that she could go on, though her pace was even slower.

"Does he not have a superior?" Komawara asked. They spoke of the monk they had met at the spring.

"All members of our Order have a superior, with the exception of the Supreme Master. I will enquire after Brother Hitara when we return. No brother could be here without permission of the Prefect of Seh, I'm certain."

Shuyun reigned in his horse suddenly. "There is something on the wind."

Komawara reached for the sword hilt that was not there and looked about him with apprehension. "I hear nothing."

Shuyun turned his head from side to side, his eyes closed. "Men. Ahead of us."

They turned their horses immediately, and as they did so three barbarians slid down the steep walls of the gully in a cloud of dust and rocks. They had swords drawn but

did not attack, as though it was sufficient to block the
monks' line of retreat. Komawara wheeled his horse and
found three others had appeared in that direction.

The men yelled to each other across the distance and
began to advance slowly.

Komawara cursed his luck for not bringing a sword
and pulled the staff from his saddle, letting the lead to
the pack animal go.

"They are brigands," Shuyun said. "They intend to
murder us for whatever we have. They do not imagine
that we would know their language. These we face will
rush us to allow those behind to cut us down." Saying
so, he dismounted his horse.

Komawara started to protest and then remembered
Shuyun in the fane and knew he had not been trained to
fight from horseback. The young lord dismounted also.

"They are about to come, Brother," Shuyun said, and
his voice sounded thick and far off. "When they do,
drive our horses at those behind. That will provide the
time we need to deal with these three."

A shout went up from the barbarians as they charged.
It was easy for Komawara to turn the horses, who pan-
icked at the charge. The lord turned in time to see Shuyun take stance before the first attacker. The barbarian
risked little and aimed a long, downward cut at his opponent, intending to take him at the join of neck and shoulder. Shuyun's hand was a blur as it went up and matched
the arc of the sword and then parried so that the blade
passed harmlessly to one side. Even as he did so, he
reached forward and took the brigand by his hair, pulling
him forward, face first, into his driving knee. The man
fell beside Shuyun who spun, and all in one endless
motion, threw the man's sword, hilt first, to Komawara.

Although he jumped to the monk's assistance, the
northerner was not quick enough. The next two attackers
went down as quickly as the first, their joint attack
turned against them and their sword strokes redirected so
that they staggered to avoid disemboweling each other.

Komawara spun into guard position as the three robbers, who had been dodging fleeing horses, came out of

the dust. The lord found himself blinking madly as the dust blew down on him, but his attackers seemed to be suffering at least as badly.

This time, one was not quicker or braver than the others and the three fell on the young lord together. This was not a haphazard attack, but a coordinated effort to bring him down. If it wasn't for the fact that they did not risk themselves, they might have taken him in their first rush. Fortunately the young lord had not gained his reputation as a swordsman without reason. He drew back and had them believing he was desperately retreating until one overreached, blocking another—this man fell to a lightening thrust of Komawara's point. And then the young lord returned to his retreat, pursued by two more careful opponents.

The larger of the two disengaged suddenly and his remaining companion fell to Komawara as he looked aside for a instant to see where his fellow went. The lord spun, prepared to give chase to a running man, but realized the other had turned aside, not out of cowardice, but to engage Shuyun.

Again the lord watched as the small monk deflected a sword stroke with his bare hand. This time Shuyun grabbed the blade in his hand and held it as though it bore no edge. Thrusting out with the flat of his free hand, he propelled the barbarian away from him with a force that Komawara did not believe possible. The brigand, who was larger than Shuyun by half, hit a rock and lay unmoving in the settling dust.

Surveying the field of battle and convinced that all opponents were, at least temporarily, not a threat, Komawara crossed to the monk and took the sword from his hand. And then forgetting his manners entirely, the lord lifted Shuyun's hand and examined it closely.

"How is it that you are unmarked?"

Shuyun did not answer immediately, and Komawara was surprised by the look in the monk's eyes. He achieves a meditative state in battle, the lord thought.

When Shuyun spoke, it appeared that he did so with difficulty. "You cannot let the edge press against the skin: I was scratched many times learning this. The hand must first match the speed and motion of the sword, but once the blade is grasped firmly along its sides it can be directed as you wish. It is a skill simple in principle, Brother.''

Komawara stood stunned for a moment by the monk's words. It is a journey on which one constantly sees the impossible, he thought, and found himself looking at the monk's hands again as though he would discover the trick.

One of the tribesmen Shuyun had felled rolled over and moaned.

Komawara went to him immediately and bound the man with his own sash. The lord found that he was trembling with anger as he tied the man and it took all of his effort not to attack the helpless man. They raid my country, Komawara found himself thinking, they have killed people close to me, members of my family, they will never leave us in peace. He wrenched the knot tight and then glanced up and found Shuyun staring at him and mastered his anger.

A dagger, a skinning knife, and a pouch were found in the man's tunic. He bore no other possessions.

"We had best bind them all though I do not know what we shall do with them, Brother.''

Shuyun went to the two men Komawara had dispatched and found them both dead and he wondered at the hatred he had just witnessed in the young lord. A brief entreaty for the tribesmen's souls and a prayer of forgiveness were all time would allow.

The first of the men Komawara had bound was conscious now, and looking from monk to lord with deep fear. Though the man's face was dark and lined from the sun, Shuyun realized that he was not old. A youth, the monk thought, no older than his two captors, perhaps younger.

"Look at this, Shuyun-sum." Komawara said and held out his hand. In the pouch the man carried, the lord had found gold coins identical to those that had been carried by the barbarian raiders in Seh—square, finely minted with the round hole in the center.

"They do not rob out of need, Brother," Komawara said, and there was disdain in his voice.

Shuyun nodded. "Their dialect is of the Haja-mal; the hunters of the western steppe. I do not know why, but they are far from their own lands."

"These are not the swords of hunters, Shuyun-sum. Nor do I see the spears or bows I would expect." He hefted the skinning knife. "Only this. I wonder what it is they hunt."

Shuyun turned to the tribesman and spoke to him gently in his own language. "Why do you attack us, tribesman?" the monk asked, "we meant you no harm."

The barbarian did not speak, but looked from one to the other until Komawara moved his sword to a position where it could be put to quick use. The man stared up at the lord's face and began to speak, though quietly, with neither anger nor resentment in his tone.

"He says that they follow the Gensi, their leader—one of the men who fell to your sword. The Gensi wished to attack us though they argued against this."

"Why?"

The monk repeated the question and listened patiently.

"He says he does not know, but it is clear that he does not tell the truth."

"What is his word for 'lie'?" Komawara asked.

"Malati."

The lord flicked the point of the barbarian sword against the tribesman's neck and repeated the word.

Again the man spoke, though this time his tone changed and he spoke quickly.

"He says the Gensi wanted our 'Botara denu'—I am not sure: perhaps 'gem of strength' is an approximation." Shuyun reached inside his robe and withdrew the jade pendant on its chain and showed it to the barbarian. The man's eyes went wide and he nodded as much as the sword pressed to his throat would allow. "He says they

argued that this endeavor would bring them . . . *bad luck*
is a poor translation, but there is no other.

"What would the Gensi do with this stone?" Shuyun
asked and listened as the man spoke again.

"Make favor with the Khan, who desires the power of
the gem," Shuyun translated. "These men are members
of a tribe that does not support the Khan and he claims
they hoped to be given gold for bringing the Khan the
Botara denu. This seems to be a half-truth, lord."

Komawara lowered his sword. "Let him lie to us,
Shuyun-sum. Lies will tell us the truth more quickly than
he can be convinced of the value of honesty. Ask him
where the coins came from."

Shuyun spoke again and the man answered readily.
"He says the gold came from trade with the Khan's men
for ponies, though this is another lie." Again Shuyun
questioned him. "He says that he has never raided into
Seh, and for once this appears to be a truth."

Without being questioned, the tribesman spoke again,
and Komawara saw the man was uneasy.

"What does he say, Brother?"

"The raiders are also given gold; this is a reward for
bravery and also to compensate them for taking no
women, which the Khan has forbidden."

"How strange!"

"He assures us that the gold he carries was for honest
trade and he bears no . . . grudge against the men of
Seh."

Komawara snorted, causing the barbarian to flinch.
His eye now flicked back and forth between Shuyun and
the lord's sword blade.

"So. Where did he get the gold if not from this Khan?"

"I believe he is a brigand, Lord Komawara. From
some luckless member of a rival tribe."

"Would you ask him who this Khan is and where he
gets his gold?"

Shuyun spoke again and both men watched the transformation of the man as he spoke: the tone of his voice
spoke of awe. "He believes the Khan is the son of a
desert god and says that he is stronger than twenty men.

He squeezes rocks with his hands to make gold for the worthy. The mighty fear him, even the Emperor of Wa pays him tribute and has offered him his daughters as wives. The Khan revealed the holy place where the bones of the dragon were buried. He calls this place 'Ama-Haji'—*the Soul of the Desert.* No one can stand against the Khan: all men are his servants, all woman his concubines."

"This man is obviously crazed," Komawara said.

"He does not appear to be crazed, Lord Komawara. He also believes everything he just told us. It is often the nature of faiths other than the True Path to affect men deeply, to draw them away from Botahara. Few will find the Way among so many false paths; the Way is difficult and offers no gold nor easy answers."

"Barbarians," Komawara said with some finality. "What will we do with these?" He gestured to the other tribesmen, who were showing signs of life.

Shuyun spoke to the tribesman again, and he answered earnestly and at great length. Shuyun listened and nodded, making no attempt to translate until the man was finished.

"This man says that the army of the Khan is camped not far from here, but he says that if we make him free he will not attempt to join the Khan but instead he will return to his tribe and give his word to do no harm to the men of Wa or any member of my faith. He says also that if we give him his life, he will be Tha-telor—in our debt or service. We may demand service or payment for his life. He offers us his gold. I believe he is telling the truth in this."

"Truth!" Komawara spat out. "They are entirely without honor, Brother. It is generous of him to offer us his gold when he is bound and helpless and the coins are already in my hand."

"It is the opinion of my order, Lord Komawara, that the tribes have a code, though it is not as yours or mine, but it is a code nonetheless and they are as bound by it as you are by your own."

"My code does not let me easily take an unarmed

man's life, but I do not doubt that this is what we should
do, for our safety and the safety of Seh. I know you
cannot be party to this, Brother, yet I am sure it is the
wisest course."

"These men are all kin, Sire. If we take one with us,
the others will not endanger his life. I believe we should
take this man. There is no doubt that we need a guide."

"Brother Shuyun! These others will run to their Khan.
This one has said that the Khan wants a pendant such
as yours. If there is even a small force nearby, any number of men could be dispatched to track us. Once they
know we are here, I have not enough skill to keep us
from being found. Excuse me for saying so, but I cannot
believe this is a wise course."

"These men are not in favor with the Khan, Lord
Komawara. To go to this leader with nothing in hand
but a story would be a dangerous undertaking. It is also
true that they, too, would be Tha-telor. I believe that
this binds them totally. If there is an army nearby, we
must be sure of it and we must know its extent. I believe
a guide would save us much valued time."

"Can you ask him how large this army is?"

Shuyun spoke again to the man who nodded eagerly.
He knew they debated his future and was anxious to
please them.

"He says the army is too large to count, but he has
seen it with his own eyes and it is more than half a day's
ride to encircle their encampment."

"He is a liar!—a crazed liar. There are not enough
barbarians in a hundred deserts to make an army of half
that number."

Shuyun questioned the man again.

"Though what he says is fantastic beyond belief, Lord
Komawara, he tells the truth. He and his tribesmen
observed the army at their encampment only five days
ago."

"Botahara save us, Brother, I pray this is not so."

"Kalam," Komawara said, using what he believed to
be the tribesman's name. In fact it was more of a title,

though a title was perhaps too official: Kalam meant "sand fox." Most of the hunting tribes would have someone among them who bore this name, for it was traditionally given to a young hunter who ranged far and showed great cunning in his hunt. This was the one who guided the two men from the Empire of Wa, a young hunter who was Tha-telor, though neither Waian was aware of what that meant.

The tribesman reined in his horse and Komawara pointed at what appeared to be haze in the south. The barbarian nodded vigorously and then catching Shuyun's attention began to speak rapidly in his own tongue.

"He says that is the dust of the Khan's army. They travel now toward Seh, Lord Komawara." Shuyun could see the look of anxiety on the northern lord's face.

"Who would begin a campaign just as the winter is upon us? The rains will start. There will be snow and some weeks at least of bitter cold. Nothing he says makes sense to me."

"Perhaps not, lord, if we assume he is wrong about the size of the army. If it is as the Kalam says, then an army of great size attacking a land that is poorly defended and unaware of the threat may expect a quick victory. Seh offers the fruits of a bountiful harvest. The winter rains will come, as you say, and the inner provinces will not send an army until late spring by which time the Khan will have had time to create defences, if indeed it is his intention to take Seh and hold it."

Shaking his head, Komawara scanned the southern horizon again. "It could also be a dust storm, Brother, nothing more." He pointed to the western horizon where a faint haze was apparent. "There is also dust there. Is that an army?—and if so why do they travel away from Seh?" He scanned the entire horizon then, but found no more dust storms to support his argument. "How far to the encampment?"

Shuyun spoke again to Kalam.

"We will be there before sunset, Lord Komawara."

Shaking his head again, the young lord of Seh gestured for the tribesman to lead on.

Much had changed in the day since the barbarian ambush. With great reluctance, Komawara had agreed to take Kalam as their guide and had released the others. They had replaced their lame pack animal with one of the barbarian's own mounts and set off for the encampment of, what Komawara believed, was a mythical army.

They bound Kalam by night and stood watch turn about, but there was no sign of his kinsmen falling on them in the dark. They made good time now; with Kalam guiding, they took no false turns nor met with any dead ends. All in all, the tribesman was proving to be an excellent guide and he had even worn away a little of Komawara's suspicion that morning by killing a viper and providing the lord with meat for a meal.

Shuyun looked over at the young lord, riding silently, lost in a whirlwind of thought and concern. He carried a sword now and no longer bothered to keep up his tonsure and neither he nor Shuyun spoke of this. If they were captured by a leader who was about to make war on the Empire, it would not matter that they were healers . . . especially if it was true that the Khan desired a Botahist pendant for his own.

This thought made Shuyun worry about the safety of Brother Hitara, though there was something about this wandering monk that made Shuyun wonder if his concern would be better focused elsewhere.

Perhaps two hours before sunset Kalam brought them to the base of a cliff. "The way changes, Lord Komawara," Shuyun said as he dismounted. "From here we must leave our horses and proceed on foot." He stared up at the cliffs that rose above them, and Komawara's gaze followed.

"We climb again?"

"Yes."

Komawara rolled his eyes as he left his saddle.

They followed Kalam as he found his way upward among the shattered ledges and broken boulders of the cliff face. It was strenuous but not steep or difficult. Shuyun could see relief on Komawara's face—glad that he did not have to repeat their ascent of the face in Denji Gorge, for this, by comparison, was only a scramble.

Finally, Kalam motioned for them to stop and proceeded to a vantage where he hid, searching with his eyes for what Shuyun could not tell. Then, he motioned them forward and signed that they should be silent. Coming up to the rocks that hid the tribesman, the monk looked out and there, below them, stood a sentry in the shadow of the cliff—a sentry dressed entirely in a soft light gray from his boots to his turbaned head.

As out of place as a garden in the desert, Shuyun thought, for the man was richly dressed. The detail of his clothing was clear at a distance and they could easily see the gold worked into the hilt of his sword and onto the horn he wore slung about his shoulder. He leaned on a long spear and surveyed the view before him with some concentration.

"This is not a man asleep at his post," Komawara whispered.

The tribesman nodded and held a hand to his lips. He led them up again through a narrow cleft, doubly careful to kick no rock free. Twice more, they came to vantages where they could see the guard, but he gave no indication that he was aware of their passing.

Farther on, they skirted a second sentry dressed identically to the first and again were struck by the man's appearance. Shuyun found himself looking at their dust-covered guide and then at the guard again. These sentries do not seem to be of the desert, he thought.

They began to make their way down. A rim appeared before them and it was here Kalam finally stopped. Shuyun thought he heard chanting echoing up through the rock—low, eerie, haunting—but it may have simply been the wind.

Lying flat on his belly, the tribesman eased himself up to the edge and looked over. He signaled his companions forward and they did as the hunter did, sliding forward on their stomachs.

They peered over the edge of the rift and found a grotto into which a shaft of failing sunlight fell. Torches set into the rock mixed their red light with the rays from the setting sun and illuminated a sight that neither Shuyun nor Komawara expected.

"Ama-Haji," Shuyun whispered and Kalam nodded his eyes wide with wonder.

"Look, Shuyun-sum," Komawara said softly, and pointed to a part of the cliff face slightly hidden by an overhang of stone. Here, set into a bank of reddish clay, lay an enormous skeleton—large-jawed head, a snaking spine longer than ten men, the bones of small legs.

"A dragon," Shuyun intoned. "It is the skeleton of an actual dragon! Botahara be praised. A true wonder! The beast of antiquity . . ." And he sounded for the first time like the youth he was; entirely swept away by what he witnessed. And from Komawara he heard a sound like a weak laugh and the lord rubbed his eyes.

Men in long gray robes were preparing a pyre before the skeleton, a pyre of stunted, twisted wood and they chanted the low chant Shuyun had thought he heard.

"Kalam?" Shuyun whispered.

The tribesman spoke only one word.

"What does he say, Brother?"

"Ritual sacrifice. The goat you can see."

Kalam moved away from the edge, pushing past Shuyun, and he made a warding sign. Gesturing to the setting sun, he turned and made his way back as they had come; his companions from the great Empire followed him as silently as they could.

They sat in the darkness talking. Komawara could hear the sounds of the barbarian language from where he lay trying to rest. He wondered what had suddenly made the tribesman so talkative. But he did not wonder long, the memory of the dragon skeleton, the dragon that was etched onto the gold coins he had seen, returned to him over and over. It was as though the Five Princes had ridden down out of the clouds, lightning flashing from the hooves of their gray mounts. Impossible! Myth no grown man believed. A dragon! And he had seen it with his own eyes!

*     *     *

Morning saw a continuation of the eerie veil of high, thin cloud. The wind shrilled on unabated. The day was cooler. Only Komawara had dismounted, as though he needed to get closer to the ground to be sure his eyes were not deceiving him.

They had ridden to the center of an abandoned encampment—an encampment so enormous that the young lord's mind would not seem to accept it.

"No . . . no. This cannot be. This cannot . . ." He looked around him like a man returned to his fief to find it razed to the ground—sick to his heart yet the mind still refusing to accept what he saw.

"Lord Komawara . . . Sire? We must return to Seh as quickly as possible. We dare not linger here. Lord Komawara?"


"How do you know he'll return?" It was the first time Komawara had spoken since they had left the barbarian encampment the previous day.

"He is Tha-telor." Shuyun said. "And he is frightened of the Khan."

"Frightened of he who squeezes rocks into gold?—he who is as strong as twenty men?"

"The Kalam is in awe of the Khan, there is no doubt. But the Khan is cruel. The Kalam has heard stories."

"Cruel? He is a barbarian chieftain. I hardly think he can shock another of his kind."

"Perhaps, but a simple hunter from the steppe is another matter."

"A simple hunter who tried to remove your head, excuse me for reminding you."

"I pushed a man from the mouth of a cavern into the waters of Denji Gorge because he was the soldier of an enemy of my liege-lord. I do not think you would call me a barbarian. I pray that man will reach perfection in his next life, but his karma is his own, as is mine." Shuyun paused and scanned the horizon. "Our barbarian guide did not act so differently, Lord Komawara; we are not, after all, his traditional allies. The Khan frightens him, perhaps only because he upsets the accustomed order of their tribal life."

"Huh."

They fell silent again, riding on as quickly as they dared without exhausting the ponies. A rider on the horizon brought them up short, but it was soon apparent that it was Kalam returning to them. Behind him the dust cloud from the Khan's army rose into the sky and swept away on the north wind.

"They can be seen from the next rise." Shuyun translated as the tribesman began to talk, spouting words in his excitement as though he could not catch his breath. "Few outriders can be seen, they must not fear discovery. This is not the whole army, he says, and they have turned to the east, now."

Again Komawara returned to the state of shock he had experienced in the encampment. "We must see for ourselves," he said finally.

They did not hurry to the rise but kept their pace, perhaps even slowed it. There was no rush. Only their eyes lacked the evidence, but Shuyun and Komawara knew in their hearts what they would see.

Even so, the sight stunned them and they were silent for some time. Moving across the sand in the center of an enormous dust cloud was a mass of humanity.

"Fifty thousand?" the lord said finally.

"Not quite that," Shuyun said, his voice taking on that strange quality that Komawara had noticed before, "perhaps forty thousand."

"Forty thousand armed men," Komawara said slowly. "and look how many are on horse! There has never been a barbarian army this large. Not in the days of my grandfather, not in the time of the Mori—never. . . . This dust cloud must blow all the way to Seh and the people will think it is merely a storm in the desert."

Shuyun spoke to Kalam and listened carefully to their reply. "It seems you may have been right, Lord Komawara. These are warriors of the high steppe who have their lands to the east near to the sea. Kalam believes they return to their tribes to winter. If this is true, the campaign will not begin until the spring."

Komawara hardly seemed to hear this. "In Seh we might raise forty thousand if we also count old men and boys. The plague stripped us of our people, of our fighters."

Shuyun spoke quietly to Kalam, nodding thoughtfully to the tribesman's response. "The Kalam says the scattered tribes have sent their sons from the breadth of the steppe and the desert. No one knew that there were so many. No one knew how many clans there were. This is but half the number he saw at the encampment, and from seeing that place I believe he is not wrong."

"How do they feed them? You cannot grow food in the sand."

Shuyun spoke to Kalam and the answer seemed to shake him. "He says that they drain everything but enough to survive from the tribes, and also much food and many weapons come from pirates whom the Khan pays in gold."

"Gold he squeezes from rocks. . . ."

"It is a mystery. We must return to Seh, Lord Komawara. We have seen all that we need to see."

"You are right, Brother. And you were right in another matter." The lord nodded to the barbarian tribesman. "We should release him now. He has given us true service."

"I'm afraid, my lord, that it is not as simple as that."

# Thirty-seven

The day was chill, the light from the sun filtering through high cloud that covered the sky like a layer of sheer silk. Despite the temperature, Shonto sat on a small covered porch overlooking the gardens of the Governor's Palace. He progressed slowly through his daily correspondence, most of it official, routine and of no great importance. A letter from Lord Taiki, however, required a second reading.

After describing how his son adapted to the loss of his hand, and praise for Shonto's steward Kamu, who had visited the child several times, the Lord went on to matters of greater interest:

> There is one thing that has come to my attention that seems most unusual, especially since our recent discussion. Coins such as those the barbarian raiders carried, have come to light in Seh. Only two days ago one of my nephews sold his prize stallion for a great deal of gold. The coinage was not Imperial nor was it stamped with a family symbol but was as you described: square, simply formed, with a round hole in the center. The purchaser was the youngest son of Lord Kintari, Lord Kintari Jabo. Lord Kintari's son is not known for his skills beyond the wine house, and it is surprising that he would have gold in such quantity to purchase one of the finest animals in Seh, if not all of Wa—for he paid dearly to become its master.

*This would be interesting enough as it stands, but more occurred: Lord Kintari Jabo's older brothers came to my nephew saying that a mistake had been made and they asked most humbly if the horse could be returned and the gold refunded. My nephew, being a man of strict principle, felt that the transaction was fair and in all ways honorable and politely declined. This did not please the brothers who then explained that the gold was of importance to their father as an heirloom and that their brother had been in error to use it in this matter. Would my nephew consider exchanging the coins for Imperial currency?—of course, the Kintari would think it only correct to pay him a generous portion of the purchase price for his inconvenience and his consideration in this matter. This then was done, except for a few coins that my nephew had already used which could not then be found.*

*These few coins have since come into my possession and I will bring them to the palace when we next meet. I am quite certain that they are identical to those described to me when I last had the pleasure of the governor's company. This matter begins to concern me as greatly as it does my governor.*

*Your servant,*

Shonto read the letter through a second time and then folded it and put it into his sleeve. He sat looking out over the garden for a moment. The obvious explanation for this was that the Kintari had been raided and the coins taken from them. If this was the case there was no mystery to the gold nor would it be difficult to discover if this was the truth.

Shonto clapped his hands and requested cha from the servant who appeared. Why, then, the lord wondered, were the sons of Lord Kintari so anxious to have these coins returned? If these were the same as the coins he had seen, then they would be new—hardly heirlooms.

Cha arrived and Shonto gladly accepted a cup, setting it on his writing table and turning it slowly, staring into the steam as though looking into the distance. Again he found himself wondering how Komawara and Shuyun fared, then shook his head. He should never have sent the monk to the desert . . . but what choice had there been? Shuyun was the only member of Shonto's staff who had any chance of surviving capture by the barbarians. The only one who could possibly return with the information they so desperately needed. Even so, the monk was too valuable an advisor to be used in this way.

What would the Brothers think if they knew that one of their own order wandered in the wastes with a Lord of Seh disguised as a Botahist monk? The Brotherhood were, Shonto was well sure, pragmatists to the center of their much vaunted spirits—they would swallow hard and then look away. As defenders of the faith of the Perfect Master, they had been involved in some questionable practices themselves.

There was noise in the hallway close by, and Shonto found himself very alert. He did not have his sword at hand, but he touched the hilt of a dagger in his robes. Two voices muted by the walls: a woman's and another that was certainly Kamu's. Shonto was on the verge of rising when the shoji slid aside and there stood his only daughter, Lady Nishima.

She knelt immediately, bowing deeply before entering the room. Kamu's face appeared in the opening and at a single gesture from his lord, disappeared. The shoji slid silently closed. Neither Shonto nor his daughter spoke for a few seconds.

"It seems, Uncle, that for once you have been caught without words."

"This is not true; I have so many words I do not know which to speak first."

They both laughed and then fell silent again.

"At this moment," Nishima said, "I wish I were seven years old."

"Oh?"

"For if were that delightful age I could throw myself into your arms again."

"At your present age that would be a most unseemly thing to do."

Nishima nodded. "That is true."

"Brother Satake, however, had different beliefs about the nature of time . . ."

He did not finish. Nishima flung her arms about him and crushed him to her.

Shonto managed to emerge from the folds of her silk sleeves and said with difficulty. "As a seven-year-old you would never have missed my correspondence."

Without looking, Nishima reached back and tipped the contents of his table—cha, inkstone and brushes—spreading them across the porch.

"Better," Shonto said and though Nishima laughed he felt a cold tear run down her cheek and onto his own.

At length, they parted and Shonto clapped his hands for a servant. "Cha."

The servant noticed the pile of correspondence and the lord saw the surprise register.

"Do not bother with it now."

The servant disappeared.

"Here only a moment and already creating disorder for the staff."

"They are fortunate my younger self is forever banished to the past." She gestured to the litter of ink and correspondence. "This, after all, is contained within a single room."

Cha arrived, which Nishima took charge of.

"Do you wish to hear the story now, or does your office require your attention?"

"Now would be convenient. I am most anxious to know how we will explain your presence here to our Emperor who expended great effort to ensure that you could not come to Seh without deeply insulting the throne."

"I would never dream of offending our Emperor, Uncle. The Son of Heaven generously arranged for me to study with an artist of great stature and I continue to do so. Lady Okara has accompanied me."

"I see," the lord said, and sounded annoyed. "That was my plan also . . . if I felt it was necessary for you to come to Seh."

Nishima looked down and sipped her cha. "I did not come without a good reason."

"I do not doubt you for an instant, Nishi-sum."

She smiled. "Kitsu-sum came also."

Shonto shook his head. "Naturally, one would hope she would not miss an outing to the country."

Nishima laughed. "She also has good reason."

Shonto nodded, half a bow of acknowledgment.

"But first my own. Only a few days after you had left, I received a letter from Tanaka. Your vassal-merchant had information that disturbed him and he acted accordingly. A former officer of the Shonto, now an old man, learned from his grandson, who is an Imperial Guard, that the guard was involved in the secret movement of very large quantities of gold. Gold coins being sent north by ship."

"Coins?"

Nishima nodded and reached into her sleeve. Removing a brocade purse, she emptied the contents into her hand and held them out to her uncle. "Shipped north secretly. The involvement of the Imperial Guard and the sheer quantity of gold. . . . It spoke only of Seh and our worst fears."

Shonto reached out and picked up one of the coins.

"I could trust this to no one else, Sire, nor did I feel I could remain in the capital with this knowledge. We have always known that he could not abide the Shonto strength and the name of my family."

"And who might that be?"

"Sire, only the Emperor, of course."

"And why not Jaku Katta?"

"It seems if Jaku plotted against you, he would hardly have saved your life so recently."

"True. If you believe that he saved my life."

"Father?"

Shonto rubbed the coin between his hands. "The Black Tiger saved his own life, I believe."

"The assassination was directed at Katta-sum?"

Shonto nodded and Nishima stared down at her hands. "Have you heard of our delay in Denji Gorge?"

"Not in detail, Sire."

"There is every indication that Jaku plotted with the Hajiwara to end my journey there, though we escaped, thank Botahara. Now it is said that Jaku is in disfavor with his Emperor." Nishima looked up in surprise. "You had not heard? He comes north, apparently 'bringing order' to the canal that he kept in disorder for so long. It is rumored that this is an exile. I expect him to arrive in Seh at any time. No doubt he will have sensitive information with which to prove his break with the Son of Heaven. A perfect Shonto ally at a time when the Shonto need allies. Huh. He must believe I am a fool."

"No, Sire, I believe he reserves that judgment for me."

"Nishima-sum?"

She took a deep draught of her cha. "I have been in correspondence with the general recently and I met with him, briefly, on the canal as we came north."

Shonto said nothing.

"I was not informed of the truth of the incident in my lord's garden. I do not make excuses, but I labored under a mistaken impression that Jaku Katta had saved your life."

Neither of them spoke for several minutes. Finally Shonto broke the silence. "It is my habit to share information only where it is absolutely necessary." He looked for a moment at his daughter, who sat before him with her eyes cast down. "Discretion is not a characteristic of our race."

"The mistake, Sire, was mine entirely. Fortunately it has not proven too momentous. Have I come to Seh on the errand of a fool? Do you already know of the coins?"

Shonto shook his head. "You have acted wisely in this. It is true I know of the coins, but the information you have learned from Tanaka is new and valuable." Again he rubbed the coins between his hands. "The coins are put on a ship and what then?" He made as though he threw the coin off the balcony but palmed it instead, as though he did a magic trick for a child. "They next appear on the corpse of a barbarian raider; though one coin has been embossed with the design of a strange dragon. Remember your fortune telling?" Shonto smiled. "Most unusual. Today I discover that a major family in the province of Seh has coins that are very likely identical." He took the letter from his sleeve and read to Nishima.

"My assumption was," he said, returning the letter to his sleeve, "that the barbarian's coins had been stolen from the Kintari in a raid. We will see. Why is this great fortune in gold being secretly shipped north? Guardsmen, you say, ship this gold? Does that point to the Son of Heaven or the Commander of the Imperial Guard? And why does this gold appear in the hands of the least-favored son of a major family of the Province of Seh?" He gestured to the sky with his hands. "And how is it that a barbarian raider possesses what appear to be the same coins? Most unusual. Do you know my own staff tried to hide the evidence of raids from me?" he asked suddenly, outraged.

"Several men paid for this with their lives." Shonto shook his head somewhat sadly. The anger disappeared. "But you have acted wisely. The Emperor will be very angry when he learns that he has been outwitted. He trusted too much to Lady Okara's reputation. He did not know that her time with you would make her long for her youth again—long for adventure." Shonto laughed and smiled at his daughter.

"Certainly that cannot be the case. I'm sure I have had no such effect."

"Oh, I'm sure you have. It is a family trait; I have that effect on people all the time."

Nishima laughed.

"You laugh? Only moments ago you yourself wished to be seven years old—hardly younger than you are now but a year or two."

Nishima clapped her hands together and laughed. "The Emperor will be less pleased when he discovers that Lady Kitsura Omawara has also left the capital, and in my company at that."

Shonto raised his eyebrows.

"The Son of Heaven suddenly began to pay a great deal of attention to poor Kitsu-sum."

"Nishima-sum, are you saying the Son of Heaven paid court to your cousin?"

"I would not use the word 'court.' I have seldom seen such a display of bad manners. He acted as though she were . . ." Nishima searched for words and then said with disdain, "a Fujitsura, or a Nojimi. Not an Omawara. It was unconscionable. Lord Omawara acted correctly in this matter, though this has placed my lord in a less than comfortable position."

Shonto seemed to brighten; a look closely akin to a smirk threatened to appear. "I am far from the capital, Nishi-sum, and little aware of the goings on of the court. Lord Omawara asked if Lady Kitsura could accompany my daughter to Seh; after all, he is very ill and may wish to spare his daughter pain. Lord Omawara is a friend of many years. I agreed, of course. Do you have any other surprises for me?"

"Not that appear to mind immediately, my lord."

"Oka-sum is well?"

"She seems to be, though she is quite . . . thoughtful."

"Poor Okara-sum, torn from her retreat after so many years. And look where she has come? To the eye of the storm." Shonto produced the coin again, staring at it as though it might reveal its origin. "All because of these."

"I hope she will not find reason to regret this journey."

"That is my wish for us all."

"It was not possible for you to know." Kitsura said soothingly.

Nishima shook her head. "How is it that someone in Seh would know of Jaku's alleged fall from favor before I knew in the capital?"

"It seems that Jaku's fall occurred simultaneously with our departure from the city. You would be a fortune teller indeed if you had known." They walked along a high wall in the last light of the day.

"It was understandable. I would have been no less tempted than you." Kitsura flashed her perfect smile. "And may have shown less resistance at the end."

Nishima tried to smile and failed. They stopped a moment to admire the view of a garden.

"Does your heart ache, cousin?"

"My dignity is injured, only." They walked a few steps further. "A little, Kitsu-sum, a little."

They moved on until they came to a view of the Imperial park and its curving canal, the sun settling into the mountains beyond.

"Perhaps you should speak of this with your Spiritual Advisor."

Nishima shook her head. "I think not."

"You have said yourself that he is wise beyond his years."

"I—I couldn't. I don't wish to."

Nishima turned and walked on and her companion followed.

"At least we are here, beyond the reach of the Emperor."

"There are many things to be glad of, Kitsura-sum. I will try to be more cheerful. Please excuse my mood."

A guard in Shonto blue hurried toward them. When he came closer, the two women could see the flying horse of the Imperial Governor of Seh over the man's heart.

"Excuse my intrusion, Lady Nishima. Lord Shonto requests your presence."

"This moment?"

"Yes, lady."

Nishima turned to Kitsura.

"Of course, please, do not apologize."

Nishima set off, followed by the guard. It was a short distance to the palace proper and not much farther to the hall where Lord Shonto awaited.

The hallway and door were manned by an unusually

high number of Shonto's elite bodyguard and Nishima noted this with some alarm. A screen was opened for her and as she knelt to enter she found herself across the room from what was certainly a barbarian warrior. Nishima stopped and then saw her father, Lord Komawara, General Hojo, Kamu, and Shuyun.

"Please. Enter. This palace is full of everyone's spies."

Nishima bowed quickly and moved into the room. A cushion was set for her and she took her place.

Shonto did not bother explaining why his daughter was present, though she had never attended important sessions of strategy or intelligence before. All present bowed to her.

"Nishima, this man is Kalam. He has come from the desert with Lord Komawara and Shuyun-sum."

Shuyun spoke to the man in his own language and the tribesman bowed as he had been shown. He hardly dared a glance at Lady Nishima but kept his eyes fixed to the mat in front of him. The man appeared suddenly disconcerted.

"Excuse us if we proceed. Certainly I will discuss this with you later."

Nishima gave a short bow of acknowledgment.

"How is it you agreed to these terms, Shuyun-sum."

"My understanding of the tribal dialect was at that time imperfect, Sire, I did not understand the full implications of Tha-telor. I believed that it meant he would buy his life and the lives of his kin with service of shorter duration. I did not realize that Tha-telor actually meant that we exchanged the lives and honor of his kin for his life and honor. He is bound to me for the length of his life. If I send him back into the desert, he will allow himself to die. The only honor that remains to him is in his service to me."

"Do you believe these claims, Brother?"

"Totally, Sire."

"Huh." Shonto shrugged. "I myself am less trusting."

"Excuse me for saying so, Lord Shonto," Komawara said, "but I believe Shuyun is correct in this matter. I did not trust Kalam myself but . . . I believe he would jump from the balcony if Shuyun ordered him to."

Shonto turned toward the balcony. "I wonder," he said. "It seems, Lord Komawara, that you once suggested to me that we should take a barbarian prisoner for the purpose of gaining information. Here is such a man."

"I thought we would have to resort to stronger means of persuasion, Sire. Kalam speaks readily, at least to his master."

"Most convenient. So you went on then with a guide toward this place of worship?"

Komawara took up the story. "Yes, to Ama-Haji. It is a grotto hidden at the base of the mountains . . . an ancient place, Lord Shonto, and difficult to describe. We slipped past several guards to the edge."

"These seem like very poor guards." Shonto offered.

"It seems that intruders are unexpected. Kalam's tribesmen seldom venture there and people from Seh, never."

"But for this Brother you have spoken of."

"Yes, Sire, and ourselves. Even so, they are little prepared for people venturing into their lands. In Ama-Haji we saw a sight that cannot be believed unless one sees it with one's own eyes." Komawara looked to Shuyun for an instant, who nodded imperceptibly.

"Embedded in a clay wall," Shuyun said softly, "we saw what is unquestionably the skeleton of a dragon."

There was silence in the room. Kamu was the first to speak. "How is it you are so certain? Did you see this at hand, Shuyun-sum? Did you touch it?"

"The skeleton was seen at a distance, Kamu-sum, yet I do not doubt what I saw. The situation was almost too natural to have been contrived. The position of the dragon was strange, somewhat twisted as one might lie having fallen in death, and there were parts of the skeleton missing, randomly as though from natural causes. It was also very large—larger than our ancient accounts would suggest. The proportion, too, was unusual; the head was not in proportion to the whole, and the body was thicker than one would have expected. These things convinced me that what I saw was real. If it had been contrived, I'm sure it would have been made more impressive, and more true to our idea of what a dragon should be. I believe that I have looked upon the remains of an actual dragon, as impossible as that seems."

Hojo shook his head. "I wish I had been with you, Lord Komawara, Brother. It is difficult for me to imagine such a thing."

"But such a thing," Nishima offered, "would be a powerful symbol to . . . those of less sophisticated culture. This is the same dragon embossed on the coins?"

"Undoubtedly," Komawara said. "It has strengthened the mystique of this Khan, I'm sure. Kalam is both awed and terrified by what we saw. I would imagine it affects others the same. I, too, was left with a feeling of awe. Ama-Haji is a place of power, regardless of one's sophistication."

"Perhaps we should hear the rest of the story and return to speculate upon this matter later." Lord Shonto said.

"Beyond Ama-Haji," Shuyun continued, "the Kalam took us down onto a plain where the army of the Khan had made their encampment. It was larger than we ever imagined. Large enough to have contained sixty to seventy thousand warriors. Perhaps more."

Hojo interrupted. "Encampments have been contrived to lie about the size of an army before, Shuyun-sum. We battle warriors, not encampments. How many warriors did you see?"

"We followed the tracks of a large force detached from that army—they seemed to be moving toward Seh, General Hojo. They altered their direction, though, and turned east toward the sea. This force contained forty thousand men, to my count, and we believe it was but a part of the larger whole."

Hojo cursed under his breath and Kamu clutched at the shoulder of his missing arm, his face contorted as though in sudden pain.

"This cannot be," the steward whispered, "cannot."

"If they have forces in such number," Shonto said, "and I do not doubt you, why do they hesitate? With such an army I could sweep through Seh in weeks. The north would be mine before the Empire awoke to the victory, and then the winter would guard me until spring. By that time I would be ready for armies from the south. Seh could be taken and held. This waiting makes no sense."

"They may not know the strength of Seh, Sire," Nishima offered. "The raiders who venture here see richness and concentrations of people beyond their experience. Perhaps they cannot tell how vulnerable we are. If they were to attack now and Seh were to hold for even a few short weeks, until the weather changes, then the element of surprise would be gone entirely. I am not a general, but it seems to me that the safe course would be to wait until spring. Surprise, they believe, will still be their ally, and if the campaign takes longer, the season will favor them."

General Hojo nodded, more than half a bow, to Lady Nishima, his face registering both surprise and an almost paternal pride.

Shonto eyed his military advisor. "General?"

"Lady Nishima's reasoning seems sound, Sire. Many battles have been lost that could have easily been won had the generals only known the exact moment to attack. We should also consider that there may be other reasons for the barbarians waiting—despite the importance of the information we have received from Shuyun-sum and Lord Komawara, there is still much we do not know."

Shonto nodded. "This is true. Shuyun-sum, can your servant cast a light on this matter?"

Shuyun spoke quietly to the Kalam who responded with what was obviously a question. Shuyun spoke again and then, nodding, the tribesman spoke at length. "The Kalam says the Dragon priests warned that an attack now would fail—that spring was the propitious time for certain victory—or so it is said. His Gensi, a term like hunt leader, believed that the Khan had heard that a great warrior chief came to Seh—this is not clear to me,

Sire—the Kalam uses a word that has no meaning in our own language. Perhaps 'ancient reborn' would be an approximation. It was said that this chief came with a formidable army. The Gensi believed this was the real reason that plans were altered." Shuyun gave a half bow. "This great warrior chief is clearly you, Lord Shonto."

"Huh." Shonto shook his head. "This does not explain why they hesitate. I will be here in the spring." Shonto looked around the room but no one offered an explanation.

Reaching behind him, Shonto took his sword off its stand. He composed himself and all present waited without sign of impatience. "Though there is much we do not know, there can be no question, now, that war will come to Seh as winter ends. In four months we will face a barbarian army. We have that time to gain the support necessary and, even here where the blow will be struck, there are many who will not believe what has been seen in the desert.

"I must gain the support of the Throne, though how we will do this when gold, that in all likelihood comes from the Imperial mint, appears in the hands of our enemy, I do not know. This barbarian has said that the Emperor of Wa pays tribute to the Khan—but for what purpose? It is my fear that in an attempt to bring down the Shonto, the Emperor has been sending gold into the desert. Is this Khan a creature of our revered Emperor?" Shonto paused. "It does not take an army of sixty thousand to bring down one family. This has every indication of plan that has gone horribly awry. This Khan has designs of his own, do not doubt it."

Shonto fell silent for a moment but attention did not waver from him. "I do not believe that Jaku has fallen from grace with his Emperor. This is too convenient. If Jaku can be made to see the true danger, then I'm sure we will win the Emperor's support."

"I agree entirely, Sire," Kamu offered. "Jaku is the key to our Emperor, but I cannot see how we will accomplish Jaku's enlightenment."

Shonto looked down at the sword in his hands. "We will find a way," he said quietly.

"Seh is now on a war footing. In four months we will be prepared for the battles that will come if we have to strip this city of its furnishings and sell them to the Emperor himself." Shonto looked at his daughter for a moment and his face softened. Almost immediately he turned his attention back to the others. "There may be some unavoidable delays in the submission of Seh's taxes to the Emperor this year." Both Kamu and Hojo smiled.

"Four months to prepare, to win the support that we require. The fate of an entire province depends on how well we perform this task. We must not fail. We cannot." Shonto fell silent for a moment.

Shuyun cleared his throat. "Sire? There is another explanation for this delaying of battle. It is undoubtedly true, as my Lord says, that an attack now would see the fall of Seh. But the fall of Seh would give the south warning and the entire winter to prepare." Shuyun looked up at those around him. "If one wishes to conquer Seh, one would attack now. If one has decided to conquer an Empire . . . one would wait."